(

Someone sneezed be~~l~~. didn't even notice until Dave started shrieking.

"Don't you know there's a terrible flu going around? How dare you show up here and infect everybody. Go home."

The temp on the other side of the cubicle wall burst into tears and began scrabbling for her purse. Henry leaned back in his computer chair and rubbed his temple with his thumb. "Relax David. If you were going to get it you would already have it by now. It's December. People get colds."

The temp gave him a worried glance as she shuffled by. He tried to give her an encouraging smile. "Besides," he said in a quieter tone, "we don't exactly have the staff to keep this place running right now. We need every temp we can get."

Dave squished hand sanitizer around in his puffy hands. "Screw that. I'm not taking that flu home to my family just to make sure Joe Smith makes his credit card payment on time."

Henry sighed and sat up again. He stood up and looked out over the almost– empty office. "What are you doing here then? Don't you have some vacation time saved up until this blows over?"

"Yeah, but good luck getting it approved–" David stopped as he heard Randall, the receptionist begin to raise his voice.

"Sorry ma'am, but he's not available, you'll have to come–"

A shrill, wheedling voice cut through the cubicle walls. "I will NOT come back. I shouldn't have been charged for–"

"Jesus, that's the third wacko today," said Dave.

"Must be a full moon or something," said Henry. There was a surprised shout from Randall and then a bang as his rolling chair hit the wall. Henry leapt up and ran toward the front with Dave. They were close enough to hear the sickening thunk of the woman's teeth as they closed around the receptionist's arm. Randall yelled again, this time it was shrill and panicked. Henry reached the woman and tried to pull her off, but she wouldn't let go. She tried to tear away the chunk of skin between her teeth and Henry saw Randall's eyes roll backward as if he were about to faint.

"Dave help me!" shouted Henry.

Dave grabbed the company's shiny, new glass award from the desk. "What are you doing?" asked Henry, "She's gonna take a hunk right out of him, you have to help me get her off."

Dave raised the glinting square of glass over his head, his paunchy stomach heaving as if he'd run a mile. He brought the glass down on the woman's head, flinching and turning his face as he did so. Henry felt the blow vibrate through the woman as he tried to pull her back.

"Jesus! What are you doing?" shouted Henry. The award fell onto the floor and the woman's jaw relaxed. Henry fell backward as the woman's bite released. Dave was already yelling into the phone for security. Henry checked Randall first, who was groaning and holding his arm. Seeing that he was still conscious, Henry turned back to the woman. Her head was lying in a growing pool of blood. The award's clear lettering was staining in the dark liquid. "Best Customer Service" stood out like a vicious joke against the frosted background. Henry shook himself and looked around.

"You better call an ambulance Dave," he said as he raced past the desk toward the first aid kit. He tripped on his way back, just as the elevator opened. The security guard caught him before he could hit the floor.

"You okay?" the guard asked. Henry straightened up.

"Yeah, I just…" He trailed off as he looked around for what he'd tripped on. There was nothing there.

"Someone from this floor called in an emergency?"

"Yeah," said Henry holding up the kit, "follow me."

Henry did his best to revive the woman while the security guard bandaged the receptionist and questioned Dave who was looking pasty and winded. Henry hoped he wouldn't have a heart attack before the ambulance arrived.

Henry tried to remember what he was supposed to do in an emergency, but all he could think of was to keep her warm. So he took off his suit jacket and covered her with it. Randall looked down at her with a scowl. "Crazy bitch," he muttered, holding a gauze pad tightly over his arm.

"What did you say to make her go off?" Henry asked.

"Nothing! She wanted to see Gary, but he's been out sick. I told her he wasn't here and she flew at me."

Henry stared at the unconscious woman. Her clothes were perfectly tailored and her hair freshly styled, except where Dave had hit her. Even her hands were manicured, not a nail was chipped. Definitely not the bar room brawl type. What had made her snap?

"Where the hell are the paramedics?" the security guard growled into his radio.

"On their way," crackled the reply. But it was almost an hour before they arrived.

The woman's breathing was no longer even by the time the elevator dinged again. Only one paramedic got off, rolling a stretcher.

"Where've you been?" asked the guard.

"We've been running all morning. Just call after call," sighed the paramedic, "I got here as fast as I could." She started to work on the woman. Henry helped move the woman onto the stretcher.

"Is she– is she going to be okay?" asked Dave, pushing his glasses farther up his sweaty nose.

The paramedic shook her head. "I'm not sure, she's had a pretty nasty blow."

Dave glanced around at them. "If I didn't do it, she would have killed Randall. You saw Henry– I had to stop her. Right Randall? I had no choice."

The paramedic turned toward the receptionist with a shrug, stripping off her bloody gloves and snapping on new ones. "I'm not the cops. I just patch 'em up." She told Randall it would be faster if someone drove him to the emergency room and Henry agreed to take him. She was still bandaging Randall's arm when her partner stepped off the elevator.

"C'mon Christine, we've got a line of calls backing up here," he pushed the stretcher toward the elevator with a frown. The paramedic stood up.

"Sorry, got to go, that will probably hold you until you get to the hospital." She reached the elevator and turned around, "I don't know what happened here, but if you're waiting for the police, I don't think they're coming today." She stepped into the elevator and the doors slid shut. Henry exchanged a worried glance with the security guard.

TWO

Traffic was so heavy that Henry had to park on the street almost half a mile from the hospital. "Jesus," swore the receptionist, looking at the line spilling out of the emergency room. "Did a bomb go off somewhere?" he asked as they drew closer.

Henry shook his head. "Something awful must have happened. But where are all the ambulances and firetrucks? Why aren't the police at least directing traffic?"

Some of the people in the waiting line had small lacerations and scratch marks, but many were cradling broken limbs or bleeding from bite marks like the receptionist. Some were sitting or lying on the concrete seemingly unconscious. Many were moaning or crying. A nurse knelt next to one of the people in line, taking his pulse. Her scrubs were creased and wrinkled and her eyes were dark circles in her pinched face. She didn't look at her patient but wrote down a number and moved to the next one. People called out to her, but she didn't acknowledge them. If this was the waiting line, what was the actual ER going to be like? A fist fight broke out in front of the glass doors over someone's place in line. It quickly escalated as people began shouting and a security guard stepped outside to help.

"Uh Henry, maybe I should just call my regular doctor," said Randall.

Henry nodded and they walked back to the car. Henry gradually pulled out of his parking space and into the slow-moving traffic. They came to an intersection and Henry winced as the car in front of him was T-boned by another car.

"At least we're near the hospital," Randall joked. Henry watched as both drivers got out of their cars. There was no room to pull around them. The man who had been hit walked around to the side of his car, bending to look at the damage. The woman who had struck him limped as if she'd been injured.

"Oh, she's been hurt, we should–" Henry began.

"Holy shit!" yelled Randall, "Did you see that?"

The woman had leapt at the other driver, swinging her purse at him as they both fell over. The woman straddled the bewildered man and began scratching at him with long, perfectly painted nails. The man tried to grab her arms to stop her and the woman leaned in and bit the man's nose. Randall opened the car door and got out, yelling for the woman to stop. He began running toward the woman. Henry sat still behind the wheel, dumbfounded. The man on the ground was screaming with the woman's red lips still wrapped around his nose. Henry began to open his door, but the woman sat up and looked straight at Randall. Strings of skin and blood and cartilage jiggled in her mouth. She spat out the nose and began to get up, tottering on her high heels and slipping into a limp with each step. The man on the ground was still screaming, the center of his face a red crater. "Oh shit!" Randall screamed, and scrambled back to the car, slamming the door behind him. Henry hit the lock button just as the woman smacked into the side of the windshield. She climbed slowly onto the hood, trying to use the wipers as handles and breaking them off in the process. Her mouth was still dripping with the man's blood and she left greasy, dark smears on the bottom of the glass. She scrambled up, her heels sliding on the metal with a screeching scrape that made Henry's teeth ache. He honked the horn to both to block out the noise of heel on metal and in hopes that a police car was nearby. It seemed only to make the woman more angry. She hovered over the glass, snarling.

"What do I do?" asked Henry.

"Back up," yelled Randall.

Henry looked behind him. "I can't, there's a huge line of cars."

The woman started hitting the windshield. Her teeth snapped together. Henry noticed they were straight and bright white except for the dark blood in the crack between each one. He honked again. The man from the accident had stopped screaming now and Henry could see him shaking on the cement. No one was coming to help him. Henry realized no one was going to come help them either.

"Well, do *something*."

"I could pull forward into the other lane, but I don't want to hurt her."

"She obviously doesn't feel the same way. I think she killed that other guy."

As if to emphasize Randall's point, the woman began slamming her head into the windshield. It cracked as she knocked herself unconscious and rolled off the hood and onto the shoulder of the road. Henry didn't waste any time. He pulled forward into oncoming traffic. The other cars were too busy rubbernecking at the accident to pay attention to him and they crawled toward him. He steered the car quickly into the side street and took off.

"What the hell *was* that?" Henry asked.

Randall shrugged. "Just crazy road rage. Drugs probably."

"But what about all those people at the hospital? They looked like they'd been in fights too. Or that woman who bit you this morning? Do you think they were exposed to some chemical or something?"

"I can't think of a chemical that would do that. Besides, why would it get released here? It's not like this is a major airport hub or anything. I don't think we're high on the priority list."

"Do me a favor and turn on the radio, maybe we can find some news." The traffic was lighter as they moved farther from the hospital. Henry headed for Randall's house. The receptionist clicked on the radio and scanned the channels. Bright, jarring holiday music jumbled in with static or dead silence. Randall scowled.

"They're all on those looping feeds for the holiday."

"Try AM then. There has to be somebody on."

"I'll just check online. There's no need to be medieval about it." Randall smirked and fiddled with his phone.

"I can't exactly look while I'm driving," said Henry, somewhat nettled. "Look, we're here, I'll just check at my house. Do you want some help getting inside? Or do you need me to call your doctor?"

Randall shook his head. "No, I'm okay. Do you think we should call the police about that guy in the road?"

"I think we should call the police about Dave hitting a crazy woman over the head with a chunk of glass. But they don't seem to be responding. I don't know what's going on, but it must be some pretty bad shit. When it clears up in a few days we can come forward and tell what we know. For now–" A giant crash came from a neighbor's house and Henry instinctively flinched. He glanced at Randall with concern. "For now, we should make sure we're safe and ready in case whatever is happening spreads."

Randall nodded. "Thanks for the ride," he said, opening the car door.

"Listen," Henry called after him, "You got a way to get out of here if you need to?"

The receptionist gave him a dismissive wave. "Yeah, I'm fine, my girlfriend's got a car. I'll see you after the holidays I guess." He walked into the house and Henry began reluctantly to back out of the drive.

I always hated that guy, he thought, *but I hope nothing happens to him.* He scanned the fuzzy AM band with one hand as he drove. He could take his pick of angry preachers predicting the end of days, but that was about it. He was profoundly depressed to realize that he wasn't sure whether they were the normal broadcasts or something special cooked up just for the current situation. He flipped back to FM and mostly ignored the constant stream of jingling bells and children's voices, waiting for the five-minute news snippet that came on at the beginning of each hour. But it never came. Not even the cheerful ski report looped from that morning. Just more music and canned commercials.

THREE

The parking lot of Henry's small apartment building was empty. *People are still at work. It's still early,* Henry thought. But where were the extra cars? The stay-at-home dad in 3C? Mrs. Krandall, the landlady? There were always one or two in the lot, even at odd times. Henry's chest cramped as he began to panic in earnest. *Shopping. Christmas shopping. That's all. Calm down,* Henry tried to take a deep breath as he pulled into his parking spot. He sat for a moment, trying to rationalize the events of the day and failing miserably. A choir began singing *Silent Night* on the radio. He reached for his keys just as a lump of porcelain hit his windshield. He jerked backward in surprise. It was a doll, it's shattered limbs rolling out of its velveteen dress and its curly wig flying away. The head, unbroken and hollow, rolled to a stop and looked at him through the window, its glass eyes glittering the reflection of the cracked windshield. There was a roar from above him echoed by a thin wail. Henry leaned cautiously forward as the choir sang about "Love's pure light."

A window a few floors up was a jagged wreck of sparkles. The thin wail came again and dragged itself into a shriek and then stopped. Henry twisted the key so hard it almost snapped and he leapt from the car. It was Mrs. Palmer, it had to be. He was pretty sure it was her window and the old lady was crazy about her dolls. Henry ran up the stairs until he got to her door. It hung open, the top hinge ripped out of the wall, the frame a splintered, raw white.

"Mrs. Palmer? It's Henry Broom, from upstairs," Henry stepped in and immediately felt the cold air from the broken window. "I heard some trouble and I came to see if you're alright." The hallway smelled like fresh snow and there was no answer. Henry suddenly realized how alone he was. There was a cane leaning against an end table in front of him. He grabbed it and realized it was too light to do anything. Still, it would have to do. He inched down the hallway. "Whoever is in here, just leave. I've already called the police and I'm armed," he bluffed, his voice too shaky to be convincing. The hallway opened into the living room. Henry gave it a quick glance. The little fake Christmas tree was tipped over in front of the television, its tiny lights still blinking their cheerful, plastic colors. Several of Mrs. Palmer's dolls were lying on the floor, limbs askew, their little, cold bodies slowly being lined with snow blown into the window. The others looked at him from their shelf, each glass eye reflecting the manic twinkle of the fallen tree. The curtains shifted and caught on Mrs. Palmer's easy chair as they blasted apart in the cold wind, but nobody was in the room. Henry turned toward the small kitchen. A ceramic crock pot lay on its side on the floor under the humming florescent light. The glass lid was shattered and floating in the brown puddle of steaming beans that had spilled from the pot. The refrigerator door hung open and it tilted slightly forward as if someone had tried to pull it over. Henry gingerly stepped around the beans and glass, trying not to slip. He tipped the refrigerator back and shut the door so that it wouldn't fall. He noticed a set of long silver scratches in the dark finish of the table as he passed back into the hallway, but Mrs. Palmer didn't have long fingernails.

Henry crept slowly toward the bathroom and bedroom. He pushed the bathroom door slowly open with the end of the cane and tensed. It was dark and windowless. He reached one hand in and groped for the light switch, wincing with every soft thud of his hand on the wall. It wasn't there. Henry held his breath and stepped in and reached up, finding a cord. The light turned on but the fan was louder than he'd expected. He jumped a little as the clear shower curtain rippled in the sudden breeze. There was no one there and the room was clean and undisturbed. He took a deep breath and headed for the bedroom.

Henry could hear low voices from behind the closed door. He couldn't make out what they were saying, but they were too even, too calm to be real. He nudged the door open a crack until he saw the bedside television tuned to a news station. It had fallen from the dresser and lay, flickering, on it's side. Henry opened the door further and inched his way inside. Mrs. Palmer's top dentures smiled up at him from the carpet. The porcelain teeth were tipped with pink and the floor around the denture was dark and wet. Henry shuddered.

The closet's flimsy door panel rattled and he jumped. He took a step toward it, raising the cane as if it were a heavy wooden bat. "Mrs. Palmer?" he whispered. There was no answer except the ongoing stream of calm reporting from the television. Henry glanced around him quickly and then looked back at the closet door. "Mrs. Palmer, it's Henry," he whispered a little louder, "I'm going to open the door now, please don't be frightened." The cane was still raised over his head. He let go with one hand and wiped the sweat that was rolling into his eyes. He gripped the cool ceramic door knob. *This is really stupid Henry,* he thought, *Just get out of here and call the police.* Henry glanced back down the hallway toward the living room. It was still empty. There was a sad wail from behind the closet door. Henry knew he wasn't leaving. He turned the knob, holding his breath at the same time. He slowly pulled the door open between himself and whatever lay behind it, tensed and ready to slam it shut again if he needed to. Henry took a deep breath and peered around the open door. With a yowl and a sharp hiss, Mrs. Palmer's siamese cat sprang at him. Startled, Henry brought the cane down without knowing what he was doing. The cat was faster than him and darted off down the hallway toward the living room. The closet was empty. Henry sagged against the door. He wondered whether he should search the rest of the building for Mrs. Palmer or just hole up in his own apartment until the police came. The reporter's voice broke through his thoughts as he caught his breath.

"– are saying that the hospitals are jammed with victims who have been brutally beaten and the police are answering calls as quickly as possible but there are just too many attacks to answer them all. Emergency services are stretched to the breaking point. We managed to talk to a physician this morning before the last wave of attacks."

Henry closed the closet door and walked over to the television set. He righted it as the camera focused on a haggard doctor in disheveled scrubs. He was slumped into an office chair and talking to an interviewer.

"Can you give us any information about what is going on?"

"We are seeing lots of injuries today, both from violent attacks and to a lesser extent, from household accidents."

"Why so many?"

The doctor shrugged. "I'm not a sociologist or law enforcement. Holiday pressure maybe? You might want to try the doctors in the psych ward instead. Although they've been awfully busy today too."

"But they must have something in common. People have been attacking each other. Not just their enemies, but perfect strangers and loved ones as well. And when questioned they don't respond. This has to be more than seasonal blues. Could a chemical cause this type of reaction? Have we been hit by a terrorist attack?"

The doctor rubbed his temples. "I don't know, I've never seen anything like it. None of the toxicology screens are showing any type of unusual drug or chemical in these people's systems– at least, none in common. The only thing that seems to be a common thread is that the ones who have had household accidents are all running a very low-grade fever. Our labs haven't come back yet on that, but it's December. People are inside a lot. They have colds, they're going to run a small fever. Look, whatever it is, it's not a terrorist plot, okay?"

"What makes you say that?"

The doctor scratched at his chin uncomfortably. "I don't want to cause a panic," he said directly to the interviewer.

"Don't worry, we'll edit it out," lied the reporter.

The doctor pulled a few pieces of paper from his desk. "This, whatever this is, has been coming for a few weeks." He held up one piece of paper. "This is an email from a colleague in India. His hospital has been overrun for a week now. Same results, low-grade fever coupled with clumsy accidents and the rest victims of brutal attacks. All he's been able to find are some early stages of a weak strep strain and a few instances of flu. Nothing more."

He waved another paper. "This one is from my brother who is on vacation in Venezuela. The police there are overwhelmed, they've told tourists to stay in their hotels for the time being. My brother got a piece of bad fish and went to the local hospital to see a doctor and he was turned away because they had too many patients."

The doctor unfolded the last sheet. "This one is a copy of the front page of a French paper. There was a minor fender bender on a busy street about three weeks ago. It turned into a riot, leaving over 200 people hospitalized and 40 dead. Whatever this is, it's everywhere."

"You were looking for these incidents. Why?"

The doctor leaned forward and slowly took off his cap, crumpling the cloth between his fingers. "Look, one of my old med school buddies brought his girlfriend in a few weeks ago after she cut herself on a piece of glass. I stitched her up and didn't think much more about it. Later that day, he called me and told me to keep an eye out for anything unusual, like a spike in accidents. That I should do blood work if I saw it. I asked him what I should be looking for and he just said, 'it's probably nothing, but you'll know it when you see it, I hope.' And then we were disconnected. But this guy was panicked. And he isn't someone I've ever known to lose his cool. So I started watching my patients and watching the news. That's the only reason we've done blood tests on any of these people." The doctor collapsed backward into his seat. "Look," he said squinting at the reporter, "I don't want to cause a panic, you can't air any of that. I don't know anything for sure yet. I just thought someone else should be watching out too."

The feed cut out and returned to the news room. "Jim," said the anchor, with an embarrassed smile, "I don't know if we ought to have run that– "

Jim interrupted with a spiel about the public's right to know and Henry shook himself. This was not a place he wanted to stay. What should he do? He thought about knocking on each door, but there were over thirty apartments in the building. The thought of what he might encounter behind each one made his flesh ache with adrenaline. He walked quickly and quietly out of Mrs. Palmer's apartment and up to his own. He was still holding the cane as he closed his door behind him. He picked up the phone and called the police. While he listened to the repeated hold message, Henry glanced out of his front window. His car was still the only one in the lot. It's windshield was a web of fractures. The shattered doll looked like a dead baby from that distance. Henry felt sick. He was finally transferred, but instead of getting an officer, he got the station's answering machine. He began with the woman at his office and ended with Mrs. Palmer's cat, hardly knowing what he said. Then he hung up. He flipped the television on and then ignored it, pacing his small kitchen. Finally, he grabbed a marker and some masking tape and headed carefully down the stairs to the building's front door.

He covered a large square of the door with masking tape, looking around every few seconds for Mrs. Palmer or whatever had been in the apartment with her. "BE CAREFUL," he wrote, "Police: Apartment 4A broken into, resident missing maybe injured. Everyone else: Stay inside. Call Henry. Don't get near anyone." His hand shook as he wrote it and the wet snow smeared against the tape, but it was legible. Henry didn't want to hang around to redo it.

He vaulted up the stairs and into his apartment, locking the door behind him. He looked at the door for a moment, thinking of Mrs. Palmer's, hanging like a snapped bone in its frame. He pushed the couch against the door and then collapsed into it. He was exhausted and hot. Henry guessed it was the stress. He pulled off his sweatshirt and turned the television on. He didn't bother changing the channel to the news. It was everywhere now, even the cable channels were broadcasting emergency bulletins. Henry fell asleep in the gray light of the television as the broadcast replayed the same shots of riots and hospitals filled to the brim and the reporters convinced themselves that it was the result of a terrorist plot.

He woke with a start when the phone rang. It was dark except for the blue light of the television, and Henry couldn't remember where he was for a few long moments. The phone stopped ringing and Henry at last stood up. He heard running footsteps on the stairs outside his apartment and began pulling the couch away from his door. He stopped as the footsteps outside the door stopped, expecting a knock. But there was no knock. Henry tried to look out the peephole, but the hallway light was too dim to make out who was standing in front of his apartment. He put his ear to the door, holding his breath. He could hear a sort of wheezy snuffling but nothing else.

"Hello," he called, "who is out there? Do you need help?"

Something hit the door with a bang and there was a scrabbling on the wood, as if it were a dog trying to come home. For a split second Henry assumed that's exactly what it was, but then the brass doorknob jiggled and half turned. Henry was glad he had locked it.

"Look," he yelled, "Just tell me if you're hurt and I'll let you in. I just want–"

He was cut off by a deep growl on the other side of the wood. Henry felt his skin tighten and pinch. He backed away from the door. The thing outside hit it with a hollow boom and the door shuddered. Henry pushed the couch back against the door. He tried the police again, but there was only the dead blatt of a busy signal. He paced the living room as the thing smashed into the door again and again. He looked out the window overlooking the parking lot. The landlady's car was parked halfway across the lot. Henry wondered if the thing outside his apartment had gotten to her. Or if it *was* her. After half an hour, the thing gave up and either fell asleep or wandered away. Henry wasn't going to open the door to find out.

His phone rang and Henry leapt for it, afraid the noise would bring the scrabbling thing back. "Hello?" he whispered.

"Henry, are you okay? It's Dave."

"Yeah, I'm holed up in my apartment but I'm okay. What is going on?"

"I don't think anybody knows. Some of the news stations are saying it's linked to the flu and others are saying it's something else. All I know is that it's worse in the city. I'm taking Elizabeth and Marnie to my brother's hunting lodge. There'll be no one there and it's fully stocked, if we bring a few things, we'll be able to hunker down for a while. I want you to come with us."

"What about that woman from this morning?"

"What about her?"

"Well, don't you have to wait for the police to say it's okay before you leave?"

"Henry, the police never showed up. I don't think they are going to. Besides, you saw, it was self-defense. If they want me they can come find me. Do you want to come or not?"

"Yeah. Okay. What do you need me to do?"

"Just get your clothes and whatever canned goods you've got and be ready to go. Oh, I don't suppose you have a gun do you?"

"No," said Henry, "do you?"

"No, but I guess we'll be okay as long as we avoid people anyway. Be ready and I'll honk the horn when I get to your apartment."

"You can't do that," said Henry quickly, "There's at least one of those– those people in here with me. They are attracted to noise I think."

"What do you suggest?"

"Have Elizabeth call me right before you get here. You turn off your lights and pull around to the back. There's a fire escape from the bedroom. I'll climb down that. Just try not to make any noise."

"Okay, we'll do our best, but if you aren't ready–"

"Relax Dave, I'll be ready. I want to get out of here as much as you do."

FOUR

Dave was a coward. Henry knew that. He wasn't just a coward in extreme situations, Henry couldn't blame him for being afraid of what was happening. But Dave was a coward about *everything*. When they'd first met, Henry had felt sorry for him. Dave was shy and scared when he moved into Henry's neighborhood. He was always first to snitch and last to join in. Most of the other kids avoided him, but Henry had tried to take him under his wing. A dubious friendship had sprung up between them. But as time went on, Henry realized that Dave was just riding his coattails until someone stronger came along. Dave regularly betrayed his friends and then his coworkers if he thought it would keep him safe, and he and Henry had argued many times about it. But Henry had stuck with him, felt responsible for him, long after their other friends had dropped Dave. He wasn't a bad guy, he didn't *try* to use people to get ahead. Dave was just chickenshit. Henry didn't trust him with a secret, but he wasn't motivated by malice or greed. Just-Plain-Yellow, that's what Henry's father had called him.

And now, Henry was trusting Dave to get him out of a city gone mad. If he hadn't seen the hospital or Mrs. Palmer's corpse-like doll hadn't come flying out the window at him– if he hadn't just heard something growl at him through his door, Henry wouldn't risk Dave's trip. He'd rather hole up and wait it out. Whatever "it" was. He wondered why Dave wanted him to come. Why was he risking himself and his family to come get Henry when he could just drive straight to his brother's cabin, straight to safety? Henry quietly stacked his bags on the fire escape, trying to guess if he had left anything important behind. He looked at his supplies with sudden unease. Was Dave just using him as a quick way to get supplies? Was he going to leave him there with nothing? Henry wasn't going to give him a chance. He picked up his bags, slinging them over his shoulder and began climbing down the slippery fire ladder. The snow was coming fast now, and Henry strained to see if he could see Dave's car or any of the crazy people walking around him. Just snow, sparking in the street lamp's tired light. Henry tried not to look into the apartment windows as he climbed down, equally afraid of seeing a bloody face or a tranquil, twinkling Christmas tree. He kept his eyes on the metal rungs and tried not to make any noise. He dropped down to the ground next to the dumpster and crouched behind it.

He was trying not to move as his legs stiffened in the cold when he felt the phone vibrate on his thigh. He tried to fish it out without banging his elbow against the hollow metal of the dumpster. "Hello?" he whispered.

"Henry? Are you ready? It's Elizabeth."

"Yes, I'm next to the dumpster where the fire escape ends. Is anyone following you?"

"No, we're okay. We'll be there in a few seconds. I'm so relieved you are coming."

Henry hung up the phone. It was Elizabeth then. She'd persuaded Dave that they needed him. Henry couldn't blame her, he wouldn't trust his life to Dave by himself either. The car was almost silent on the snow and Dave had turned the headlights off. It rolled to a stop near Henry and he jumped up and opened the door, throwing the bags in before him. He slid into the warm car and tapped Dave on the shoulder to let him know it was okay to take off. He looked back at the apartment building as they drove away. The soft glow of Christmas trees dotted the building's windows and the snow fluttered and clung, softening the building's edges in the gold street light. Henry wondered how many people would be drawn in by the calm scene only to meet the thing inside. He hoped that his warning sign would work.

He turned back to his companions. Marnie was asleep in her booster seat next to him, her small face a white smudge in the dark. "Everyone okay?" he asked.

Elizabeth smiled at him. "We're okay. We're probably just overreacting. I'm sure things will be straightened out in a day or two, but better safe than sorry, right? We'll just have a little vacation at the cabin."

Henry smiled at her, but his eyes flicked to Dave's in

the rearview mirror. "The cabin is a few hours away. Why don't you two get some rest and I'll wake you up to switch with me if I get tired," said Dave.

Henry was troubled. "And if we–" he glanced at Marnie, who was still sleeping. "If we run into any obstacles, you'll wake me up, right?"

"Obstacles? I think traffic will be light at this time of night," Dave said.

Henry shook his head, thinking of the woman in the traffic accident that morning. "Look, just wake me up if you have to stop for any reason, okay?"

"All right," said Dave.

Henry settled back onto the seat. Marnie's soft breathing and the little halo of heat that her body made in the car caused Henry to drop off quickly. The sound of Elizabeth and Dave fighting drew him out of sleep. He looked over at Marnie who was sitting up and looking anxious. Her teddy bear had dropped into the hollow near her feet and Henry struggled to reach it. He handed it back to her and she gave him a nervous smile, which he returned.

"What's going on?" he asked.

Elizabeth glanced back at him. "There was a couple with a flat tire on the side of the road and Dave refused to stop and help them. The woman was crying."

"But the man looked ready to strangle the next person to look at him wrong," grumbled Dave.

"Honey, it's dark, it's snowing, the police don't seem to be anywhere around. What if no one else stops?"

"Someone will stop," said Dave, glancing at Henry for support in the rearview mirror. Henry's mind flashed to the woman with the remains of a nose in her teeth.

"Do you two have any idea what's actually happening?" he asked.

Elizabeth glanced back at him and then her gaze lingered on Marnie who had fallen asleep again beside Henry. "Only what the news has said. That there is some kind of disease or chemical causing people to act irrationally or become dangerous. No one seems sure exactly *what* is going on."

Henry looked over at Marnie to make sure she wasn't listening. He leaned forward. "Elizabeth," he whispered, "These people, the ones affected by whatever this is, they're crazed. I saw a woman bite the nose off a man's face today before she climbed onto my windshield to try to do the same thing to me. There's some monster in my apartment building– I think it killed my elderly neighbor and then waited for me outside my apartment. And you can ask Dave about the woman this morning at the office." Elizabeth turned pale but still looked unconvinced. With an interior wince, Henry drove his point home. "Look, if you want to keep Marnie safe, it's best if we not trust anyone outside ourselves, even if they look like they are in trouble. Those people back there may have been okay, or they might have been sick. Or they might just have been panicked enough to steal our car and leave *us* on the side of the road in the snow."

Elizabeth began crying and Henry fought the heavy guilt that fell on his shoulders. Someone needed to say it and Dave was too gutless. Otherwise, they'd all be dead in the next few days because of some misplaced kindness. Henry watched the snow building, thick and choking on the road. *Or dead in the next few hours,* his mind amended.

There were no plows and as the highway dumped them onto the side roads, even the tracks of previous vehicles disappeared. The lights of gas stations and little villages disappeared or winked out as the night grew later and the snow heavier. They were swallowed up, lost in a blank world of dark trees and smooth white. As if they were the first or last ever to travel that way.

Henry switched with Dave when they got to the gravel roads. Henry cursed under his breath as they slid from bank to bank, the skids coming so close together that eventually the adrenaline just quit and he let the car scud back and forth as it would, always barely catching on the shoulder and righting itself. They got stuck at last, about half a mile from the lodge. He and Dave pushed the car the rest of the way as Elizabeth attempted to steer. Henry and Dave were both soaked and

Henry was shaking with exhaustion by the time they made it up the hill to the dark house. He began to be really afraid that he had caught the flu that was going around. He tried to push the thought out of his head before the followup panic could set in. Elizabeth carried Marnie into the house and began turning lights on. Henry was shocked to realize that he was still out of breath as he carried the groceries inside. Dave stopped him.

"You okay Henry? Maybe you should sit down for a minute."

Henry waved him off and wondered why his pudgy friend was not as winded as he was. "It's just been a long day Dave, and I've been running on adrenaline for most of it. A good night's sleep and I'll be back to normal." He hoped. They slogged the rest of the supplies in and Dave went looking for the generator, certain that the snow would take one of the lines down fairly soon. That left Henry to find the woodshed. He groaned when he saw it halfway up the sprawling backyard. The open back door made a gold path on the snow toward it, but the trees clustered close to its back and made deep shadows where anything might wait.

Don't be ridiculous, he told himself, *there isn't anything out here, that's why you came.*

"Henry?" Elizabeth called, "Can you close the door, it's getting cold in here."

Henry grimaced. "Sure thing," he called and closed the back door behind him. Now it was really dark. The hiss of the falling snow and his own deep breaths were all Henry could hear. He decided that was a good thing. A *safe* thing. He started out toward the woodshed. His footsteps and his breath seemed thunderous. He tried to force himself to breathe evenly so that he could hear over the sounds in his own chest. The snow melting into his jeans wicked up to his thighs and his breath was a dark wet cloud around him. Miserable and tired and jumpy, the shed seemed miles away from Henry. But when he got there, the trees seemed to lean over it, to strangle the glowing light of the snow. The metal door was pitted with rust and almost a foot of snow had drifted against it. Henry pulled it slowly open. The aching screech it made as it slid over the top of the snow made Henry's teeth hurt. The woodshed was blank, staring dark. Henry took a breath and then fumbled around the wall for a light switch. He began to sweat through the chill when he found nothing. He reached up and found a pull string. He smiled as he yanked it on. But the bulb had burned out a year before when someone had left it on to shine alone all spring. *It's just going to be one of those days I guess,* he thought, *you know, typical Monday.* He stifled a laugh. Henry didn't like to reach into the dark for the wood. He told himself that it was just that he didn't want to be bitten by any rats that may have taken up residence or put his hand into a recluse nest. But he knew he was lying to himself. There was no help for it. Get the wood or freeze.

Henry reached in and grabbed the first log. He almost yelped as he drew his hand back. It was smooth and cold and slid easily out of his grasp like a dead arm rolling into the snow at his feet. He looked down in the dim light. Just a birch log with loose bark. Henry caught his breath and told himself to stop being an idiot. He reached in and scooped up a few more logs. When he had what he could carry he plowed his way back to the porch and the bright house. He looked at the small armful as he placed the logs into the kindling bucket. He groaned and trudged back. The kindling bucket still wasn't full after the second trip. *Screw it,* he thought, glancing back at the woodshed. It squatted and glowered like an evil crone against the dark trees. *I'll get more in the morning. When I can see,* he thought and banged the snow off of his soaking shoes before he walked into the lodge.

FIVE

The snow continued through the next day, but it was dry and slid off the power lines. Neither plow or car passed along the quiet dirt road and since the power stayed on for the next few weeks Henry assumed there were no vehicles to run into the power lines on the main road either. Henry tried to ignore the news reports that Dave was glued to, but it sank into their conversations, pervaded the air. Even Marnie, who spent most of the time sledding or dressing the lodge's stuffed deer with costume jewelry, knew something was very wrong. Within a few days the experts had concluded that the violent attacks were the result of a bacterial infection that targeted the brain.

Elizabeth and Dave pretended that they were only going to be at the lodge for a few days, a week at most. But even the little pieces Henry accidentally gathered from the news told him that things were quickly shutting down. There had been no police on the first day and there had been no snow plow since they arrived. No mailman, no bush planes overhead, no trains sounding whistles on the well used tracks just half a mile down the road. Even the news was broadcast in longer and longer loops. Henry had even tried calling work, but no one in the large building had picked up the phone. He assumed he had worse problems than whether he would be fired for not showing up. He allowed himself to wonder if he even ought to be worried about running out of food before he clamped down on the thought and shook it away.

The lodge was drafty and leaky, not meant for winter living. It was a good-time summer place. Something that was meant to be shut up, its pipes drained, it's light wicker furniture stacked and sheeted until spring. Henry knew they wouldn't last without making some changes. The first thing to go had to be the woodshed. Henry tried to persuade Dave to help, but Dave thought it was pointless. He was too scared to let himself believe the whole thing wasn't going to blow over. Henry privately fumed. His friend would let them starve or freeze before he'd admit to himself that they were on their own. But Henry knew.

He stood on the back porch after taking the swing
down and pushing the patio table to the edge. He looked at the
dark shed with it's chorus of deep woods surrounding it. *No
one else is coming Henry,* he thought. He pushed into the
heavy snow. It took him a few days, but Henry got all the
wood onto the porch while Dave sat glued to the television
and Marnie made snowmen and carried the small sticks to
keep him company. Elizabeth flashed him sympathetic smiles
through the kitchen window, but she didn't lift a hand to help
either. Henry wondered if he were the crazy one.

He stood on the porch in an itchy sweater and pitchy
gloves and stacked the wood in neat bundles, the logs hitting
each other with a satisfying clunk. Marnie was digging a snow
fort at the corner of the raised porch. He could hear the
television droning inside and he tried not to let himself listen
more carefully. He heard Dave swear loudly and call his wife.
Elizabeth shrieked and Marnie came darting out of the snow
cave toward the door. Henry grabbed her before she reached
it. He peered in through the kitchen window, but Dave and
Elizabeth were only staring aghast at the news.

"It's okay Marnie, your mom just saw something scary
on tv."

Marnie relaxed and sat down on the edge of the porch,
biting the packed snow on the top of her mitten. Henry turned
back to the woodpile.

"Henry? What's going on? When can I go back to
school?"

Henry hesitated before throwing another slippery birch
log on to the stack. He didn't turn around to look at Marnie.
"It's Christmas vacation isn't it kiddo?"

"I guess. Christmas is still a few weeks away. We're
only supposed to have Christmas Eve off for break. Our
vacation comes after Christmas."

"Well, I think this year your parents just wanted a few
extra days," he turned around and smiled brightly, "Are you
worried about Santa? I'm sure he'll find us out here."

Marnie rolled her eyes. "I know that Henry. Santa

knows everything. Of course he could find us here."

Henry tried not to laugh. "Right, of course, that was silly of me."

Marnie went back to chewing her mittens and Henry reached for another log, feeling like he dodged a bullet. There were a few muffled shouts from the living room. Elizabeth and Dave were fighting. Henry tried to cover up the sound with the thunk of falling wood. But Marnie heard anyway. "They're arguing about the sick people aren't they?"

Henry felt his chest sag. He didn't want to have this conversation. It wasn't his job. More than that. It wasn't his place.

"What sick people?" Henry kept his voice light and pulled his gloves off and sat down on the porch next to her.

"The ones the lady on the tv talks about. The ones that like to bite."

Henry looked into the dark woods for a moment. He decided the television told the girl far worse things than he might. "Yeah, Marnie, I think they're arguing about the sick people." He looked down at her, the ebbing light turning everything sepia. She was an old photograph, a memory wrapped up on a different day and hidden for decades. "Don't worry. The sick people won't come here. We're safe in the lodge."

Marnie banged her boots together for a moment, the snow curling off her toes. She looked up at him again. "I'm not worried. No one can find us in the deep, dark woods. But Henry, what if we get sick too?"

Henry picked splinters off the back of his gloves. "We aren't going to get sick Marnie."

"How do you know?"

"Because you only get sick by being around other people. And we're by ourselves, so we can't get sick, right?"

Marnie thought for a while. Henry stared at the dark woodshed as the sun sank behind the tall trees and the night hunched around the edge of the backyard. The little girl beside him tugged on his jacket sleeve.

"But if I get sick– or Mom and Dad, you'll take care

of us, right Henry?"

Henry smiled. "Sure, if you'll take care of me if I get sick. Deal?" Henry stuck out his hand. Marnie shook it with a wet mitten.

"Deal," she said.

SIX

The news blared through the lodge's thin glass as Henry stapled plastic over them. He'd been both surprised and relieved to find the large roll of plastic in the back of the wood shed with an old metal toolbox. However it ended up there, in a summer cabin, Henry was grateful. Elizabeth had tacked spare blankets around the inside of the frames, but he knew that wasn't going to be enough. It was only late December and it was already uncomfortable inside. Dave insisted that Henry was wasting his time, that they'd all be back in the city before the month was out. But for all the time Dave and Elizabeth spent in front of the television, they didn't see what Henry and Marnie saw.

The little girl might not have noticed all the subtle clues that Henry had, but she was sensitive to the tones of the anchors and to the increasing amount of violent footage that reeled over the screen. Henry had asked Dave to shut it off for Marnie's sake, but he hadn't listened. Henry watched as the anchors became less and less varied. The channel had been sticking with one camera for a few days now, and Henry wondered if only one cameraman were left, or if it were simply stationary and unmanned. Interviews with doctors, police, even military happened less and less. Most of the footage was from viewers' cell phones now, rough, unedited. The stories looped over and over, the same bits of information. And still Dave sat in a chair shushing his daughter and Elizabeth lay crying on the couch, hour after hour, day upon day.

Henry tried to distract Marnie, feeling ashamed of his friends for neglecting their daughter. He tried to take her with him on his home improvement errands, but it was too cold today. She watched him from the other side of the blurred plastic. Henry flashed her a smile and then went on hammering a thin slat of wood over the plastic sheet. The news blared out at him. Henry pretended not to hear, but it seeped into his brain anyway.

" . . . symptoms include a lack of coordination when

walking, slurred speech, low-grade fever and inability to focus. Those infected become highly irritable and eventually violent as their ability to communicate decreases. While this violence seems to be randomly directed at any other living thing in the area, the real danger is limited as the Infected don't seem to use weapons, but will attack with their bare hands and–"

Marnie's face was pale and turned toward the screen and she had stopped coloring under the window. Henry whistled loudly to get her attention. Dave looked irritated but Marnie reluctantly turned away from the television to face Henry.

"Hey," he yelled through the plastic and the blaring broadcast, "get your boots and jacket. Let's put up some decorations."

Marnie ran to get her clothes. Henry finished the window, slamming his thumb with the hammer as he pounded the last nail. He tried not to swear. *Fifth time today,* he thought, *I've got to pay more attention. Must be tired, I'm never this klutzy.* Marnie came bounding out of the door.

"Come on," said Henry, "I found some party lights in the woodshed. We'll decorate the house for Christmas."

Marnie smiled, but it quickly faded. "What's wrong?" he asked.

"No one will see them this year."

"We'll see them. And Santa will appreciate it. I mean, I know he's all seeing and everything, but he probably doesn't like landing in the dark."

The girl puffed white plumes of warmth as she lugged the heavy box. Henry slid the tall ladder up against the back of the house, where the television was just a soft drone. He locked it into place and then turned to Marnie rubbing his hands together.

"Okay, your job is untangling and plugging them in to see if they work. I'll staple them up, sound good?"

Henry fished the end of a long string of twinkle lights from the box and tucked a stapler under his arm.

"Should we use all of them?" asked Marnie holding up

a small pink flamingo dubiously.

Henry shrugged. "Sure, why not? They have Christmas in Florida too. Maybe flamingos pull the sleigh in the south." Most of the lights were plastic beer bottles or palm trees. Party lights. No one would have been here in the winter. Henry thought about pulling the caps off so only the twinkle lights were left.

"I like the peppers," said Marnie, holding up a string of bright red chili lights. Henry grinned and started climbing the ladder. *I'm going to make a terrible father,* he thought, carefully stapling the little brown beer bottles to the eave. Elizabeth came out at last, while Marnie untangled one of the last strands and handed the end up the ladder to Henry.

"Here for the big reveal?" he asked cheerfully. Elizabeth's eyes were red and tired, but she managed a small smile.

"I actually came to see if you two would like to have some hot chocolate."

"With marshmallows?" asked Marnie.

"I think I can manage a few marshmallows, sure. Henry? How about you?"

"Sure, just let me staple this last bit. You go on in, I'll be there in a moment."

Marnie started running inside and whirled around. "Don't turn them on without me," she said.

"Nope, you're the official switch flipper."

They disappeared inside and Henry managed to attach the last few lights without stapling his hand. He began climbing down the ladder. He frowned and looked down as one foot slid on a rung. They weren't that wet. He went a little slower, but he was still a few feet off the ground when his leg missed the next rung completely and he fell with a thump into the snow. For a few seconds he couldn't breathe and then it came back with a cold groan, as if his lungs were a creaky door. Elizabeth came running out and into the snow.

"Henry, what happened? Are you hurt?"

He sat slowly up. "I'm okay. Just got the wind knocked out of me. I must have slipped." *No I didn't. My foot never even touched the rung. What is wrong with me? I feel like I'm drunk. And not just tipsy either.* The thought struck him almost as hard as the fall had and he sat in the snow as Elizabeth worried over him. Marnie came to the door and looked out, a porcelain cup in her hands. Henry got up and brushed himself off.

"Come on," Elizabeth said, "You should get some dry clothes and warm up. You've been out here all day."

Henry stomped the snow off his boots as he climbed the back porch steps. Marnie gave him the cup.

"For me?" he asked.

"I'll take care of you if you take care of me," said Marnie, her face serious.

"What's that?" Elizabeth asked closing the swollen back door behind her.

"Nothing," said Marnie and ran into the living room. Elizabeth watched her and Henry sank down into a hard wood chair at the table.

"Do you know what she's talking about?" asked Elizabeth, turning to face him.

Henry pulled off a cold boot while he thought about what he wanted to say. He threw a wet clump of snow at the wood stove so he could watch it sizzle and pop. "I know it's not really my place. I mean, I don't know anything about kids Liz. I think the news is making her frightened. It's not making me very comfortable either actually. Maybe you and Dave can– I don't know, shut it off once in a while or turn it down?"

"We're just trying to keep informed about what's going on."

Henry bent over to pull off his other boot. "I know."

Elizabeth sat across from him, the pale kitchen light catching in all the tiny lines around her tired eyes. "I just want to get back for Christmas and have the whole thing behind us. I'm not sure how much longer we can stay out here. We're going to have to go to town for food very soon."

Henry sat up and looked at her sharply. "Do you and Dave have any kind of plan, in case we have to stay?"

Elizabeth laughed, but she started flicking a splinter in

the table obsessively. "Oh Henry, don't tell me you're one of those doomsday people. The government will work it out. I'm sure it will only be a few weeks. The news is still broadcasting, there's still power. Things can't be that bad."

Henry pushed a hand through his damp hair. He took a gulp of lukewarm chocolate. "Yeah, I know, the authorities will sort it out. But, Liz, what if we have to fend for ourselves for a few weeks more until they do? Someone's going to have to go get some supplies and we're going to need to button this place up some more." Elizabeth didn't look convinced. "At least so Marnie doesn't get worried when things aren't normal," Henry continued. It was his last bid for help, the only appeal he thought would snap her and Dave out of their inaction. Elizabeth glanced into the living room where Marnie was playing on the floor behind Dave's chair.

"Okay, Henry, what do you want me to do?"

Henry looked over at Dave. He watched the blue and green images bounce off Dave's glasses for a minute and wondered how much was actually getting through. He turned back to Elizabeth. "Look, I'll go. I know you have Marnie. And Dave– I know he'd rather be here to protect you. But I need some help planning it and getting ready. There's no plow, so I'll have to walk. We're going to need to make a sled or something to bring it back with."

Elizabeth nodded absently, already making a list in her head.

"And I'm going to need some kind of– of weapon. In case."

"We're in the woods Henry, there's no one here."

"I know, Liz. It's just in case. I heard a wolf near the shed yesterday," Henry lied.

"Let's think about it. You don't have to leave tomorrow, do you? Just give me a few days to work things out."

Henry nodded. But as it turned out, they didn't have a few more days.

SEVEN

Henry's bedroom door swung open and hit the wall with a heavy thump. Henry sat up partway and then sank back for a second until his head cleared. He reached for the lamp and the switch clicked but nothing happened.

"Henry?" the small voice floated through the dark room. Henry rubbed his eyes and swung his feet onto the chilly floor.

"Marnie? What's wrong? Where are your parents?"

"In the car. They're fighting."

Henry puffed out a silent sigh. "It's okay Marnie. Can you turn on the hall light? I can't see anything."

"The lights won't turn on. Here." A bright round ball flashed on in the doorway. Henry laughed.

"What is that?"

"Pookta," said Marnie.

"Oh," said Henry and shook his head. Still, the stuffed animal's belly did give off decent light. He got up and went to the doorway. "Okay, let's go find some candles and start the wood stove again. You and Pookta lead the way."

Marnie slid a small hand into his and Henry had to stop himself from pulling his hand back. Where was her mother? Hadn't they noticed the lights go out? Kids were supposed to go to their mom when they were scared.

"At least we don't have to listen to the sick people yell any more," said Marnie as they threaded their way between the ragged armchair and the dark television.

Thank God for small favors, thought Henry. "Check the drawers Marnie, see if you can find candles or a flash light. I'm going to open the stove so we can see. Don't get near it."

He yanked on the swollen back door and stepped, hissing onto the snow-covered back porch in his bare feet. He grabbed an armful of wood and tried not to notice the dark, open door of the wood shed and the hunched shadows of the trees devouring the yard. He could hear raised voices, but they were muffled. He assumed it was Elizabeth and Dave. At least they'd taken it outside. Henry went back in the house and poked the dying fire in the stove. He was glad he'd moved the wood up to the porch. Marnie was lining up small wax candles on the kitchen counter.

"Any flashlights Marnie?" Henry threw a chunk of wood into the stove. His feet ached with the cold. These old houses built on posts just never got warm. They'd have to find a way to insulate it better.

"No flashlights."

"That's okay," said Henry. He lit two of the candles. "Don't touch, okay?"

"I know."

Marnie sat at the table, her legs dangling in the cold air. "Do you want to go get one of your blankets?"

Marnie shuddered. "No," she said, "not by myself."

Henry threw another log into the stove and added some cardboard. He heard the front door open and Dave swore as his shin hit something.

"Are you afraid of the dark Marnie?" Henry was asking. Elizabeth walked into the kitchen.

"Marnie's never been afraid of the dark," she said, confused.

Henry shrugged, his back to them as he coaxed the fire back to life. "It's no big deal, I was afraid of the dark for a long time. And she seemed pretty scared when she came to get me."

"It wasn't the dark that scared me," said Marnie, "It was the face."

Henry felt a cold ache settle into his spine and shoulders. He turned slowly around. He kept his voice even and his face neutral. "What face was that Marnie?"

"There was a man's face looking into my bedroom window," said Marnie, "I think he was hurt. And he looked really cold. But I don't think he saw me, I pretended to be asleep."

"But that was just a dream, wasn't it honey? Sometimes we see scary things in our dreams when we're worried." Elizabeth said, smiling.

Marnie looked doubtful and hesitated. Henry casually pulled on a wet boot and then the other. "Where are you going Henry?" the girl asked, avoiding her mother's question.

Henry smiled and slid his coat over his t-shirt. "We're going to need more wood and its too cold to go out with my bare feet any more." He pulled his jacket from the hook. "Hey, Dave," he called, "Want to help me grab some more wood?"

Dave came scowling into the kitchen. "I need to check the breakers Henry. You and Marnie must have overloaded a fuse with those damn twinkle lights. Can't you get the wood yourself?"

Henry stared at him and thought about shaking him or hitting him to knock some sense into the man, but Elizabeth put a hand on Dave's arm. "I'll check the fuses Dave, why don't you go with Henry. Besides, I don't think its a fuse. Someone probably ran into a pole down the road. There's not much we can do but wait until they fix it."

Dave swore under his breath and pushed past Henry onto the dark porch. "You coming?" he snapped.

Henry glanced at Elizabeth. "You and Marnie stay in the kitchen and get warm. Besides all the candles are in here. We'll be right back," he looked at Marnie. "Stay here," he said and pulled the back door closed with a thump. Dave was piling logs into his arms.

"Why'd you close the door Henry?" he fumed.

"Shh, Dave. I didn't need you to carry wood. Marnie saw someone outside her window while you guys were in the car."

"What?"

"She saw a guy, he looked into the window at her. She thinks he was hurt."

Dave dropped the logs. "Jesus. What if he's infected?"

"He probably just went off the road and had an accident, but I didn't want to find him by myself."

"Does Elizabeth know?"

"She thinks Marnie was dreaming."

Dave shrugged, "Maybe she was."

Henry grabbed a slim log of birch. "You want to chance it?" he asked and walked quietly down the porch steps holding the log like a club. He heard the back door open and looked back.

"Sorry Henry," Dave hissed, "I have to keep my wife and daughter safe." The swollen door squealed shut. Henry ground his teeth together. What was he doing with these cowards? He would have been better off on his own. Then Henry remembered hiding in his apartment as something scrabbled outside, eating his neighbors. He shuddered. Maybe this *was* better. He gripped the slippery log tightly and trudged through the snow toward Marnie's bedroom. The snow was rucked up and piled everywhere from Marnie's play, so Henry couldn't tell if there were fresh footprints or not. He tried to catch his breath before he turned the corner of the house. He shouldn't be this out of breath. He wasn't a gym rat but he was fit and healthy. A dozen feet, even in heavy snow shouldn't have worn him out. Henry told himself that it was just because he was scared. He swung himself around the side of the house in one quick motion, holding the log in front of his face, just in case. The moon was weak and the little piles of snow cast dark shadows in the hollow spots, but Henry could see there was no one next to Marnie's window now. He checked the windows along the side of the lodge. All firmly closed. He looked around near his feet and saw some spreading blackness. A ripple of unease climbed his shoulders and neck. Henry looked around for more. A splash here, a dot there, a trail of night melting the snow. Henry followed it. The man was definitely hurt. Had he been attacked, or just had a car accident? The blood led away from the house and became a clear path of footsteps looping into the untouched field. Henry looked back at the house. There were candles lighting the kitchen now, but no one was even watching at the window for him. An ugly part of him rose up and wondered if he ought to just leave them now. Just walk back into town and take his chances. Let them deal with whatever dark surprise was waiting at the other end of the string of blood beads. But there was the kid. Whatever it was could grab her. It wasn't her fault that her parents were worse than useless.

She's not mine. She's nothing to do with me, thought Henry, even as his feet followed the wounded man's footsteps back toward the dark shed. He glanced back at the house to make sure she wasn't watching. *What's going to happen if I'm not here? Her parents will make a stupid mistake sooner or later.* A deeper thought sprung up at him as he stumbled in the heavy snow. *What's going to happen if I stay? Time to stop pretending Henry. I'm infected. Infected. How much time do I really have left to help them anyway?* Henry looked up from the snow and found himself near the gaping entrance to the wood shed. *Shit,* he thought. He pressed his back against the wall of the shed. He took a deep breath and adjusted his grip on the log. He felt ridiculous and terrified at the same time.

"Hello?" he said. "Is there anyone in there?"

A dull, rattling groan crawled out of the shed and into the still, cold air. "Look, I've got a– I've got a weapon. Just say something so I know you aren't sick."

"Help." Henry wasn't entirely sure he had heard correctly.

"I can't see to help you. Can you come out a little so I can see what's wrong?"

There was a harsh dragging sound and then a sticky hand flopped out of the door frame and onto the snow. Henry looked at the log in his hand and back down at the bloody hand. *Shit,* he thought again. He put the log at his feet and clasped the hand. He tried to be gentle, but the man was large and Henry had to pull him across the snow. At last, he was out of the shed and lying on the snow. The man's right eye was bruised and his nose wasn't much more than a crooked faucet for blood. "What happened?" asked Henry, "Were you bitten?"

The man shook his head. "Almost, but not quite. Snowmobile accident when I almost ran over one of those *freaks* up the road. She chased me into the woods, but I got her. She won't be biting nobody." The man chuckled and the blood from his nose gurgled and spat. Henry pulled him upright. He got the man halfway over his shoulder. He pulled back toward the house while the man leaned on him, his feet dragging against the snow.

"C'mon buddy, you have to help me. You got to stay awake." The man shook his head, trying to clear it and Henry tried not to think of the blood droplets spraying over his jacket. *What does it matter anyway?* he thought, *I'm already infected. Can't really afford to worry about long-term diseases anymore.* The man was cold but he wasn't shivering and Henry could feel his skin rubbing away like an old sticker where Henry's hand held his bare arm. "Stay awake. What's your name buddy? Tell me something about you so you can stay awake." The yard hadn't looked this long when he was lugging wood. He had an impression that he was moving slower and not just because of the added weight.

"Phil. My name's Phil," the words were almost drowned, part of the blood that sprayed from his lips. "Think my legs are broken."

"We're almost there, Phil. We'll get you fixed up."

Henry reached the bottom step of the porch. The kitchen door squealed open. Dave stood there holding a shovel as if it were a rifle. "What are you doing Henry?"

Henry tried to catch his breath. "This is Phil. He was in a snowmobile accident. He's not infected."

"And you know that how? Because he told you? You don't know anything about him. He could be lying."

Henry tensed, his skin warming. He tried to stay calm. "Relax Dave. I know because he hasn't tried to eat me."

"That doesn't mean he isn't sick. Or a robber. Or worse. You can't bring him in here."

Phil groaned and slumped more against Henry. "Dave, he's hurt. He's not going to be able to do anything to anyone for a long time."

Dave shook his head and gripped the shovel tighter. "This is ridiculous," said Henry, putting a foot on the next step.

"Don't make me hit you Henry."

Henry looked up at Dave with a sneer. He took a deep breath and bit his tongue. He pulled Phil up the step.

"Stop Henry, I'll do it." Dave raised the shovel.

Henry sighed. "Let's pretend that you'd actually have the guts to hit me. What is it you want me to do with him? Leave him to die on the porch?"

Dave shrugged. "What do I care?"

Henry squinted at him. "Really? You want your wife to stumble over him when she comes outside for wood? Or your kid to watch him stiffen in his own frozen blood while she eats her corn flakes?"

Dave spluttered.

"Didn't think so. Either get out of the way or come help me. This guy isn't lightweight." Henry grunted as he pulled Phil up the stairs and into the warm kitchen. Dave scuttled in behind them and shut the door.

EIGHT

Henry sat in the road at the top of a hill. Below him was the tiny grocery store that served the dwindling local population. He hadn't seen any movement in the twenty minutes he'd been there, but he was going to wait until dark anyway. If he couldn't see them, then they wouldn't see him.

The man from the woodshed, Phil, had been worse off than any of them had thought. Henry and Elizabeth had done their best to help him. Dave had complained and refused to assist in any way. He had wanted them to drag Phil back to the road and leave him there. In truth, Henry and Elizabeth couldn't do much that would have mattered except to keep him warm and dry. Neither of them knew more than basic first aid. Knowing the man's body would either heal itself or fail completely left Henry restless and frustrated. He had a nagging idea that his own infection was progressing faster than expected, and he imagined that he was having trouble concentrating. So when the brittle, bright morning came, Henry had proposed going to town for food and batteries and medicine. If he didn't do it then, there might not be time to ever get it done. No one but Marnie had wanted to go with him, so Henry shrugged and set out alone, dragging a wood palette with a rope behind him over the snow.

The road was a stripe of blindness. After the first mile, Henry began to notice the harsh rasp of his breath, the echoing crunch of his feet and the slithering shiver of the palette behind him. He had to stop and look around him every few moments to be sure he wasn't attracting anything. His arms and shoulders began to ache from the tension and he ground his teeth almost constantly without realizing it. As the morning melted into noon, the trees began to spring up, flinging the snow from their backs in deep, sudden thuds. Henry jumped and whirled around every time. At last something shattered the smooth skin at the side of the road, a jagged black smudge against the horizon. The smell of spilled gas spread far into the thin, chilled air. The sharp scent prickled in the back of Henry's throat and adrenaline stabbed into his shoulders and legs as he realized what it was.

He hadn't brought any kind of weapon with him. Though he'd been prepared to knock Phil unconscious had he been sick, Henry didn't think he could do it in the clear light of morning, and there hadn't been anything that really fit the bill at the lodge. So far, he'd been lucky, the lodge was on a sparsely populated road and all the houses so far had been silent and dark, closed until summer. He stood still for a few moments watching the snowmobile's corpse as if he expected it to start up again on its own, its mangled frame roaring and chasing him back up to the lodge or into the thick woods. Phil had said he "took care" of the woman who attacked him. Had he killed her? Just knocked her out? Was she waiting for Henry right up there? Henry shuddered, but there was no help for it. If they were going to make it, he had to get down to the town. He waded through the snow to the far side of the road. He wanted to run past, to be already beyond it, but his legs refused to listen. They shook and crept along while Henry's mind and eye raced back and forth over the same small patch and off toward town. Even so, he almost missed her. The wind must have been relentless overnight, dragging snow over the mangled machine and on top of her small, curled up body. The air was still now, and though she was clothed in a light night-dress, it didn't flutter or flap. Her hair clung to the tiny jags of the snow dunes the wind had made. Her face was tilted, eroding into the snow. Henry stopped and watched her.

He had an eerie feeling of having met her before, of trying to mate the face to one in his memory. But that was ridiculous, he'd never even been in this part of the state before. *Maybe we all look the same when we die,* he thought. He pulled the palette closer and crouched beside her, careful not to step on the limbs that were already buried. He was still too scared to wipe the snow from her face, so he slowly blew it away until the round curve of her cheek emerged. He had expected her expression to be one of rage, but it was blank and slack, like a book with all the letters rubbed out. Henry didn't know whether to feel relieved or sad. He could see a deep ring of purple where the skin of her throat emerged from

- 46 -

the snow. He wondered if Phil had strangled her to death or if he had just knocked her unconscious so that he could get away. He didn't think he would have been able to do either, but then he thought of wandering through his neighbor's apartment holding her cane like a bat. Of Dave smashing a woman with a chunk of glass. He shook his head. Henry looked at the thin cotton sleeve of her nightgown. If Phil didn't kill her outright then she must have frozen to death. Who did she belong to? Henry tried to imagine a life around the blank oval of her face. Was she someone's wife? A sister? A mother? He couldn't picture it. Whoever she was, had gone. She was little more than a mannequin and Henry felt guilty for not feeling more. He wondered if anyone would care when he finally went crazy. *Stop it, Henry,* he thought, *they're working on a cure, I'm sure.* But he stood and stared at the dead woman. Then he dug her out of the snowdrift and placed her stiff body on the palette sled. *I can't leave her out here.* He tried to tell himself it was only what a decent human being would do, but the little voice in his head could only keep hoping that someone would return the favor if he needed it.

It was three miles to the hill-top above the grocery store, but Henry felt as if he'd trudged thirteen instead. He paced the hill-top for a while, sweat trickling through his hair and down his neck, the palette jittering and sliding over his footprints, the woman's stiff limbs gently bobbing as the palette dragged over the lumps. At last he sat down in the road and watched the little grocery store until the sun drained away behind the thick trees.

The last orange reflection of the sun evaporated from the store's windows. Henry immediately regretted waiting. He stood up and careened down the hill with the heavy palette rocketing behind him, as if he could take it back, as if he could recall the daylight. He lost control in the deep snow and fell, tumbling down the second half of the hill. The palette with the woman's body kept sliding, crashing to a stop against the store's back wall with a scraping thump. The corpse slid off, landing beside the makeshift sled in a hollow bowl where the snow had melted from the store's roof and dribbled down it's side. Henry groaned and got up. He made his way to the palette and could see the woman's hair floating like tangled weeds on top of the slushy puddle where she lay. He reached to pick her up again and then froze as he heard a shout from nearby. He stood up as it was echoed on his other side. *Not a shout,* he thought, *that's a growl.* There was a hoot now, and then a screech. Henry backed up against the store wall, his hand gripping the palette's rough rope as shadows darker than the surrounding dusk roared and closed in. A hand closed around his arm and yanked him backward. Henry was too startled to fight back, and he fell onto his back and was dragged onto a hard cement floor. A rattling wall descended, cutting the howling shadows off from him. A light clicked on.

"Why did you wait until dark if you were just going to panic and blow it?" the voice growled from behind him.

Henry sat up and winced as the wood palette clattered across the cement floor. He'd forgotten he was still holding the rope. "How did you know I was waiting for dark?" he asked, turning around.

A scowling middle-aged man stood before him, holding a cordless drill as if it were a weapon. "I watched you all afternoon. I thought you must have some smarts since you were waiting. Guess I was wrong. Who was the woman?"

Henry shook his head and tensed as the store's bay door rattled as something hit it. "I don't know. I found her on the road. I couldn't leave her like that. I thought I might be able to find the police or— or somewhere to bury her anyway." He turned toward the bay door. "I need to find out how to get her inside."

"That's decent of you," mumbled the older man, shoving the nose of the drill into a large leather pocket, "but you can't get her now. Anyway, your good turn is why you're alive right now."

"Look, I'm not a looter. I have cash or we can figure out some trade, I wasn't coming to break in—"

"Relax, that's not what I meant. The sick ones— I don't know what else to call 'em, the sick ones went after her body instead of sinking their teeth into you."

- 48 -

Henry's throat shriveled and he tried to stop himself from gagging. The other man looked concerned. "You've been watching the news haven't you? I mean, you did *know* that they were eating people, right?" He put a steadying hand on Henry's shoulder and dropped his scowl.

Henry nodded. "I knew they were attacking people and biting them, I just didn't think they were—"

The older man shook his head. "Best not to think of it more then. Just consider yourself lucky." He stuck a thick hand into the air between them. "Wyatt Reynolds."

The rough warmth of Wyatt's hand and the stale gasoline smell of the store's loading area made Henry think of his father. The thought of the Plague reaching his parents was a wrecking ball bouncing in his chest. He cleared his throat. "Henry Broom. What were you going to do with the drill anyway?"

Wyatt shrugged. "Whatever I had to, I guess."

"You don't have a gun? Isn't this a big hunting area?"

Wyatt laughed. "I'm a shopkeeper. Just because the tourists are crazy enough to tote their guns everywhere with them, doesn't mean that I am. Besides, these people are sick. You going to shoot them just because they caught the flu?"

Henry shook his head.

"Nah, me either. But a good clunk to the head might discourage them if they try to bite. And it was the only heavy thing close to the bay door."

"So what do we do now?" asked Henry.

"I don't know how far you've come but you've been sitting in the cold for at least the last half hour. I've got electric heat still and coffee. And I know you didn't come all this way for nothing."

The bay door banged as something hit it. Wyatt nodded toward it and Henry could see him swallow back his revulsion. "They'll be— they'll be at it and each other most of the night. You can't go out there for a while. As long as we're quiet and keep the shades down in front, we'll be okay."

Henry let go of the palette's guide rope and followed Wyatt through to the front of the store. They sat behind the candy counter and ate stale deli sandwiches.

"You heard any news in the past day?" asked Henry.

"Nope, the cable is out and the police scanner has been nothing but static since last night. I don't know if it's a signal tower or—" Wyatt shook his head and dragged a rough hand down his face. "Been through a lot of storms Henry. Bad blizzards, hurricanes, even a flood in '87. Almost everyone evacuated for that one. But there were still people around, you know? Voices on the radio, helicopters flying overhead even after the power went out, national guard trucks, *someone*. Not this time."

"Maybe there's just nothing to be done. Maybe we haven't seen the guard or Red Cross, or whatever, because this isn't a natural disaster. I mean, what are emergency workers going to do? The most they can do is gather up people to take to the hospital, right? And there's nothing the hospital can do for them. In fact, the last time I drove by the hospital, it was overflowing. But not with infected people. With people who had been bitten. I don't think those that are infected with the Plague are actually becoming weak or feeling ill."

Wyatt tapped his metal travel mug. He shook his head. "No. That's not it." He took a sidelong glance at Henry and then looked into the mug. "You and I may not be willing to shoot sick people, but the military is."

"What? How do you know something like that?"

"A few nights ago, right before the cable went out down here in the village, Sheriff Douglass stopped by. He told me to lock up the store and keep it locked. I asked him why and he said that some of the neighbors were showing signs of infection. He repeated that I was to keep the store locked, no matter what. I asked him what he meant, he said the president had given an executive order that all remaining military and law enforcement were to contain those infected by any means necessary.

'Contain them?' I said, 'They're stark raving mad. How are you going to contain them?'

Sheriff Douglass is a big guy. Kind of a pain in the ass actually. Always busting tourists' chops and showing off. But

I swear Henry, he started to cry. Right there, standing in front of the beer case, not three days ago. And he said, 'I have to shoot 'em Wyatt. There's nothing else to do. I've got to shoot 'em.'"

"But— what if there's a cure?" Henry interrupted, "All those people, it's just a flu, for God's sake. And even if there isn't a cure, they'll shake it off, right? If their bodies aren't worn out, they'll shake it off and be back to normal." He grabbed the thick sleeve of Wyatt's cotton shirt. Wyatt just shrugged and shook his head slowly.

"The infected people are killing healthy people too. What would happen if they weren't stopped? Maybe you're right. Maybe someone will cure it or it'll burn itself out and everyone will wake up sane in a week or two." Wyatt whistled between his teeth. "Then there'll be a reckoning, I guess. There'll be a reckoning for everyone."

NINE

Wyatt loaded the last cardboard box onto the palette as Henry peeked behind the curtain in the loading bay.

"There are still five or six of them milling around," he muttered.

Wyatt nodded. "That's okay. They're full now. They won't bother anyone for at least a day."

Henry looked around at him. "Full? You mean—"

"Looks like karma paid you back. You should be safe to go back now."

"So if we kept them fed, they wouldn't attack anyone?"

Wyatt rubbed the corner of one eye underneath his glasses. "Well, I don't know. I think they are less likely to. But they still seem to get very angry. They fight each other sometimes. But they aren't as desperate, seems like. I saw a few eat a dog the day before you got here. They squabbled some after, especially when they stumbled into each other. They finally stumbled away from each other a few hours later, still okay for the most part. Not like the ones that came after you." The older man shuddered. "Well, I guess that does it for your list, Henry."

Henry turned away from the window and pulled out his wallet. It slipped through his hands and fell to the floor. He looked at it for a second and then bent down to pick it up. His hand missed twice and then closed around the warm leather. He stood up and avoided Wyatt's gaze. "Look," he said, walking toward the sled, "I'll give you everything I have in here and a credit card to cover the rest, but I think we both know it isn't worth very much right now. I don't have anything else to offer though, and I'd be lying if I said the people I'm with could do without it. Why don't you come with me? It's safer together and there aren't any infected up there." His mind added *Yet*.

Wyatt shook his head and held out the hand for cash. "I thought the same last night, and I was afraid it was going to come down to robbery on your part or murder on mine. But after you said you thought the infection would be cured or people would get over it, just like anything else, well, I realized how close to insane I'd got. Of course this is going to blow over. And the best thing we can do is continue to be civilized, right? Besides, if I go, there's no one to watch the store. What if someone needs things, just like you? Or what if Sheriff Douglass comes back? He might have people who need help too. Someone's got to stay. At least until the power gives out." Wyatt looked around at the freezers and coolers around him, "After that, lots of this isn't going to be good for much."

Henry handed him the bundle of bills after fumbling with the flimsy things for a moment. "I hate to think of you down here, when it does go out. And with all those sick people wandering around outside."

Wyatt's eyes sparked with tears as he folded the money and stuck it in his back pocket. "I know most of them, Henry. Some of them grew up from babies right around the corner. The ones that are outside; they're not going to come out okay. Unless the Sheriff can get them back in their houses they'll freeze to death. And the ones he had to shoot." Wyatt scrubbed his face and snuffled, but then he looked up and smiled at Henry. "The rest of them though, they'll be okay, it'll be like a bad flu. They'll just wake up normal and a little hung over in a few days and mosey on in here to get the news and their milk like always."

Henry started to shake his head.

"It'll be okay Henry," Wyatt clapped him on the shoulder, "You take these supplies back to the lodge and have a nice Christmas. By New Year's Eve you'll be making a beer run down here in the car, you'll see."

"And if not?"

"If not, I'll be hiking up there to take advantage of your hospitality. Consider it a down-payment on future supplies, if you need them."

Henry nodded and picked up the palette's rope lead. Wyatt opened the bay door with a loud rattle. Henry peered out, but none of the infected even glanced over. They just slogged in senseless patterns through the snow. It was somehow more unsettling than seeing them bear down upon him. He turned back toward Wyatt. "Thank you. I'll see you later," he said.

Wyatt shook his head. "I bet I'll be seeing you first Henry. Have a safe trip back." The bay door clattered closed between them and Henry began to climb the hill back to the lodge, going quickly in case the infected people decided they were hungry after all.

The palette was heavy and cut deep into the snow, dragging the weight of packed lumps of ice beneath it. Even in his best shape, Henry would have been exhausted after dragging it for three miles. The infection was slow, and it had crept up on him for weeks. It was painless, but he was quickly wiped out now and he found himself struggling to concentrate on even the simplest tasks. He spent most of his energy getting the palette up the first hill out of town. He sat on the crest to catch his breath and was alarmed when he realized he'd sat there much longer than he intended.

He dragged the palette on, trying to remember what the news had said about patients recovering. If he'd heard anything, it was lost now and he eventually gave up chasing echoes in his head. He tried to focus on each step as he passed by the snowmobile wreck, not wanting to see the shattered glass of the headlights or the empty shallow grave of the woman he'd dragged to town. He slipped and fell onto the bare patch that some spilled gasoline had made. He swore as the overloaded palette tipped toward him. It didn't fall and nothing slid off, and Henry scrambled up after a moment. He checked the palette over, his hand brushing the scarlet fabric of the cheap stocking Wyatt had found for him. Henry didn't want to lose it. The kid was expecting Santa. He started off again, an aching creak in his knee where it had hit the pavement.

The snowy path was just as quiet as the day before. No birds, no cars, only a slight breeze catching the snow in streams like broken cobwebs. The trees hunched themselves over the narrow strip of road. The last loads of snow had thumped from their branches hours ago, and they stood dark and thick, like enormous brooding crows on a power line. Henry could feel the little breeze pulsing over his back and through his hair like a great breath, receding and returning. He could see the driveway to the first of the five cabins he'd have to pass before the lodge, and he could feel his heart pick up it's already strained pace. They had been quiet and dark on the way to town, but he still didn't like going past. He tried to slide toward the opposite side of the narrow road, but the palette had built up a mound of dragging snow underneath and it didn't move easily.

They're empty. Summer cabins, he thought, *There'd be dogs barking. Or cars in the driveway.* Henry slunk by the driveway, looking down into the wide front yard. The house was dark, the garage doors closed. The snow still lay thick in the drive, but as he glanced at it, his eye caught on a spattering of dark hollows where the drive met the road. He froze and the palette slid into the back of his calves, but he barely noticed. He stared at the footprints and tried hard to think if they'd been there yesterday. Were they from the woman who'd caused the snowmobile accident? Were they Phil's? Had he tried the other houses before the lodge? *Are they new? Come on Henry, think! You can remember the names and credit scores of hundreds of clients on command, surely you can remember if you saw footprints here yesterday.*

But he couldn't. He didn't know if it was the infection or if he'd been daydreaming when he passed the cabin the day before. Even though the aching prickle in his skin convinced him that his life depended on remembering, Henry simply couldn't. He looked as far as he could down the road. Then he dropped the rope of the palette and waded toward the shadowy voids where someone had passed by. He squinted against the glare of the sun on the snow. The pattern was erratic. Weaving over the drive and yard, into the woods and back out. Henry stopped near the closest footprint. They didn't make it all the way to the house and Henry thought that was a good sign. He looked down at the outline and almost laughed out loud. The moose must have been a large one, it's footprint almost the size of Henry's and much deeper, but the sharp double leafed shape left no room for doubt. Henry felt his heart slow to a quick trot as he released a breath he'd forgotten he was holding. He brushed sweat from his face with a glove and tried to loosen his cramping arms and shoulders. He was getting too worked up. If he didn't relax, he'd burn himself out before reaching the lodge. He slogged back to the palette and grabbed the rope. He tried to calm down, tried to appreciate the warmth of the sun on his face and the sudden cool, quiet patches of shade under the still trees. But the palette drew more and more snow under it and it packed into the hollows and slats, hardening into ice. It made a sound like scraping styrofoam and Henry began to feel a deep ache in his back and hands. He moved more and more slowly, finding himself stumbling more often in the deep snow. He tried walking in his own footsteps for a while, but he found it harder than just slogging through the unbroken part of the road. It took almost an hour to reach the next cabin, already afternoon, and Henry became afraid that he would be caught on the road after dark. He tried to pick up his pace, knowing he was only halfway back. He began to think resentfully of Dave and then Elizabeth sitting warm and dry and comfortable in the lodge. He would have been back by now if Dave had just come with him. But he was too chickenshit. Elizabeth wasn't much better, but for a while he forgave her, since she would have to watch Phil. *Why am I the one doing this?* He wondered, *This stuff isn't even going to help me. I'm sick. I'll be crazy in a few days. They'll probably toss me out to freeze to death.* Henry felt a lump growing in his throat at the thought, but then his anger burned it away. *Stop thinking that. I'll get through this. It's just a flu.* But the doubt wouldn't go away and his annoyance grew with it. *You're sick Henry. Just a day or two away from the lady in the city maybe. You'll muckle on to the first person you see tomorrow. You're sick. And getting sicker by being out here. It's them that's making you sicker faster Henry. It's Dave and Elizabeth. If you'd stayed away from them, maybe you'd be okay. But now, now you're going to freeze or Dave's going to bash you in the head.* Henry shook his head and pulled at his hair. He took a deep breath and tried to concentrate on his feet and the crunch of the snow. *Or else you're going to eat him. You're going to eat Dave all up. And then . . .* The thought stung him suddenly and he sat down in the snow and sobbed before it could get any farther. It made him feel even weaker to cry, but there was no one around, and so he did for a minute, low and shaking. He thought for a minute about not going back, about wandering into one of the vacant cabins behind him and locking himself away. Let Dave come out and find the sled himself. It would be safer that way. For everyone.

But then there was the kid. What would Marnie do without food until her father or mother gained courage enough to come looking? And Phil. Henry didn't know him, had no idea if he were rotten or decent, but no one should die from a simple infection that few tubes of ointment could knock out.

Henry's feet continued toward the lodge even as his mind debated. He pulled a glove off and began absent mindedly biting his nails. Maybe he could return the supplies and then leave again after a night's rest. Did he have another day in him? And then what? Break into one of the cabins and freeze to death inside instead of out here? Who would feed him after he became delirious? And what if there were worse parts of the infection later on?

He hissed as a sharp pain sliced into his thumb. He looked down at his hand and was surprised to see he had bitten all of his nails to the quick. The thumb nail was bitten even deeper and a round drop of blood trembled up from the skin. He pulled his glove back on and decided to get back to the lodge before he worried about what would come next.

TEN

Henry was chilled and his wet pants were heavy and clinging below the knees as he struggled the last few hundred feet up to the lodge's driveway. The trees had eaten the sun, their dark crowns made a great jaw that sank into the sky. He heard the birds at last, calling to each other as they began to roost. He stumbled into the driveway and the lodge leaked golden lantern light from its windows. Everything around it looked darker and colder to Henry. He felt part of the dark, a shadow, a footprint, a memory left behind the living man. He wondered if he should just push the palette ahead of him down the drive and then turn back to one of the empty summer cabins behind him. But then a little shadow jumped up from the front steps and waved to him.

"Henry? Is that you?" asked Marnie.

"It's me. What are you doing out here? Aren't you cold?"

"Not as cold as you I bet," said Marnie jumping down the steps and into the snow between them. Henry kept the palette behind him and hoped it was dark enough that Marnie wouldn't see the stocking. "I was waiting for you," continued Marnie, "I thought it might be scary in the dark. Is it far to the store?"

Henry smiled. "Not so far in the car. But it sure felt far walking there."

"What did you bring?"

"Nope, no peeking."

"Aw, c'mon Henry, it's almost Christmas."

"Almost. But not quite. What's today?"

"Christmas Eve."

Henry felt dizzy. He couldn't make the days add up to Christmas Eve, no matter how he tried. "Are you sure about that?"

Marnie laughed. "I'm sure. Mom showed me on her watch."

"Well what are you doing up then? You need to get to bed so you don't miss Santa!" He tried to sound excited, but his confusion made him uneasy.

"It's not even dinner time. We were waiting for you."

"Okay, run and get your dad and mom, so they can help me unload all this."

Marnie ran back up the stairs and into the house, the door banging shut behind her. Henry swayed and leaned against the boxes on the palette to steady himself. He tried to convince himself that he was only exhausted from the trip, that the sudden dizzy spell, the confusion over a simple thing like the date, it would all disappear after a good rest. Dave and Elizabeth came out of the house carrying a gas lantern. Henry was relieved to see that Marnie stayed inside this time. *I'd better tell them now,* he thought.

"I'm glad you're back," said Elizabeth.

"How was town? Did you hear any news?" asked Dave. He started picking through the boxes.

"No," said Henry, "There's no more news."

Dave looked up. "The power's out down there too?" Henry shook his head.

"What do you mean there's no more news then?"

"The cable and radio have been out for a few days. There are infected people in town too, but the store owner is still well. His name's Wyatt. I tried to persuade him to come back with me, but he wants to wait a little longer to see if people will get better or if someone else needs him. I told him to come here if things get too bad."

"What about the emergency broadcast thing?" asked Elizabeth, "There must be someone figuring out where people should go. Some kind of temporary shelter? Aren't there procedures in place for something like this?"

Henry shrugged. "Maybe, but I don't think anyone is organizing anything. At least not out here."

Dave pushed his glasses up and squinted at Henry. "Maybe we should have stayed in the city. The police would have set something up by now. Or the national guard, or someone. There's always someone in charge of this kind of thing."

Henry slumped down on the edge of the palette. He

pulled his gloves off and rubbed his hands together. He didn't look up at Dave. "I don't think so. Not this time. The sheriff is shooting sick people in town and even though the power is still on, there's no news. Not even anchors filling time. Just— nothing. Static."

"How is that possible?" asked Elizabeth, hugging herself.

"Did you say the sheriff was shooting people?" said Dave.

Henry nodded without looking at them. "You shouldn't have to go to town for a while though. I got enough to last you three for a while, if you are careful. Wyatt will bring more if he comes."

"What do you mean, 'you three'? There are five of us now. I mean, I assume we aren't going to throw Phil out in the snow," said Elizabeth. Her breath was a halo of gold in the light from the lodge's window. Henry thought of the bruises around the dead woman's neck.

"I'm sorry I brought Phil inside. I don't know anything about him. Maybe you should send him to one of the other cabins. They're empty, he could hole up in one of them easily enough."

Elizabeth shook her head. "He's not doing well. There's no way he can leave, at least for a few days. And if we're really on our own, maybe the more of us that are together, the better." Elizabeth picked up the lumpy red stocking with a smile. "Is this for Marnie? Thank you Henry." She kissed his cheek and her breath was warm over his cold skin. Henry tried not to shudder as he thought of how many germs may just have transferred between them. It was too late now. They were all either infected or immune. No use worrying over it any more. Henry stood up and handed Dave the palette's guide rope. He shoved his bare hands into the pockets of his jeans.

"I can take Phil with me if you want to empty the palette. We can put him on it and bundle him up."

Dave squinted in the near dark. "What are you talking about?"

"I think he killed an infected woman on his way here. At least, I hope she was infected."

Dave exchanged a worried glance with Elizabeth. "We'll figure out the Phil thing when he's healthy enough to be a threat. But why would you take him with you? Where are you going?"

"I've got it. I'm infected." He braced himself as Dave backed up a few steps. Elizabeth just shook her head.

"No, Henry. You can't be sick, there's nothing wrong with you," she said.

"There is. I've tried not to feel it, but I know."

"You're just wiped out," said Dave with a nervous chuckle. "You just hiked six miles dragging a few hundred pounds behind you. Anyone would be tired. Just get some rest, you'll feel fine tomorrow."

But Henry shook his head. "No, this is more than that. It's been coming for days. Weeks maybe. This trip just highlighted it. It should have taken less than a day. I can't keep ideas in my head, they just seem to slip away, like I'm on the edge of sleep all the time. I can't walk straight, I've been trying all day. You can look in the morning. The trail just zig zags all over, even though I kept trying to go straight. I get angry at nothing and I have to calm myself down. You know me Dave, I don't lose my temper. But I keep getting closer to it."

"You're just nervous, not getting enough sleep—" said Elizabeth, patting his arm.

"No, I have to go. It's not safe for you and Marnie. I'm just going to go down to another cabin, just a mile away. Wait until I beat this flu and then I'm sure things will get back to normal. I think the owners are gone for the winter, they'll understand."

Elizabeth fell back beside her husband and clasped his hand. Dave looked at her and then at Henry. He pushed his glasses up again. "We can't let you do that Henry. You can't leave while you're sick."

"I have to. Don't you understand? In a few days, maybe less, I'll be one of those— those things. I'll attack anything. You, Elizabeth, Marnie— I have to lock myself away so I can't hurt anyone. And so no one will have to shoot me, either."

"Maybe you won't get as sick as others. Maybe you just have a mild case," said Elizabeth.

"Do you want to take that chance? You want to risk your daughter?"

Elizabeth glanced back at the lodge's bright windows. She was little more than a shadow in front of them now. And Dave was wholly lost in darkness except where the light sparked on the lenses of his glasses.

"We'll figure it out. Maybe we can put you in the basement until you get better," said Dave.

"I don't know if I *will* get better. Has anyone recovered yet? Besides, there is no basement here, remember? It's a summer house."

"Give me tonight to figure it out. I'll find a way. If you are alone you might— you might hurt yourself. People were doing that on the news."

"If I'm not alone, I will hurt you."

"Henry, we've been friends for over fifteen years. Since we were kids. I can't let you just walk out into the snow to freeze. Just give me tonight to think of something."

"What if that's too long?"

"An hour then. Just an hour. Go in the house, get warm, have something to eat," Dave pleaded, "I'll figure it out. And if I don't, I won't stop you. Just an hour Henry."

Henry nodded. "Okay, an hour."

ELEVEN

Henry sank into a chair near the stove. Everything ached. He watched Elizabeth bringing in boxes of supplies and Dave running through the house in an unusual fit of activity, but he didn't offer to help. He'd already expended more energy than he could spare. The stove pulsed with warmth against his side and he could smell something cooking. Marnie sat at the table coloring in the lantern light. Henry couldn't seem to concentrate on anything. The room puddled and merged into a dull sense of comfort. He felt himself sliding into a doze, but fought against it. Something kept telling him not to fall asleep. If he fell asleep would he wake up the same man?

Henry forced himself upright in the chair and looked at the window, trying to see past his reflection and out to the dark road. His throat was swollen with fear and sorrow. Was this what it was like to realize he was dying?

"Henry," said Marnie, glancing over at him.

"Hmm?" he turned slowly from the window.

"Don't be sad Henry. I'll take care of you. You'll be better soon."

Henry shook his head and smiled. "It's not like a cold, Marnie. You need to stay away when I get sick. It will be like the people in the city– like the television. So I need to go away. Just until I'm not sick anymore. Do you understand?"

Her little shadow shook its head and Henry couldn't tell for a moment, whether he'd been talking to her or the shadow. "No Henry. Don't go. We'll take care of you. We won't get close, but we can still take care of you."

Henry felt dizzy as his sight slid in and out of focus. He shut his eyes. "It's too dangerous Marnie. You'll be safe here with your mom and dad. I'll just be down the road a little."

He felt her little girl breaths hit his cheek as she came to stand next to him. She smelled like the light chemical strawberry of plastic toys. He was alarmed as a memory of his younger sister struck him. "Don't leave," Marnie whispered, thick in his ear, "I'm scared of the other man. Don't go Henry, please. And tomorrow's Christmas. Don't you want to be here?"

His brain kept lingering on Phil and the dead woman in the road. He opened his eyes and looked at the small girl beside him. "Marnie, you stay away from Phil. Tell your dad to make him leave when he is well enough. Don't go near him, you understand?" he was yelling without meaning to.

She nodded and started to cry. Elizabeth wandered into the kitchen to check on dinner. "What's wrong Marnie?" she asked.

The girl wiped her eyes with a sleeve. "Don't let Henry leave," she said.

Elizabeth glanced sharply at Henry, but he was too unfocused to notice. "Daddy's trying to figure something out. But Henry's sick, honey. You don't want to get sick too, do you?"

The girl looked up in shock and backed a few paces from Henry. He knew no one would get sick if they hadn't already, but he thought it might be better if the girl stayed scared of him, so he said nothing. "But he went to town. To take care of us. We have to take care of him," said Marnie.

"We're going to try," said Elizabeth with a tight smile, "Come on now, go wash your hands, it's almost dinner time."

Henry stood up as Marnie ran to the bathroom. He didn't trust himself not to fall asleep and he didn't want to have another difficult conversation with Elizabeth. He walked into the living room looking for Dave. Instead he found Phil stretched on the couch in a deep sleep. Henry thought about waking him, asking him about the frozen woman and the marks around her neck. He thought about warning him not to touch the girl or trying to take advantage of Dave or Elizabeth. But a profound sadness came over him as Henry realized there would be nothing he could do if Phil tried something. Even now, Henry was clumsy and slow. He was no match for anyone. He doubted he could even put together a good bluff. So he turned away from Phil and saw a light in the backyard through the window. He headed outside to find

Dave.

The empty woodshed blazed with light. The curved stand of trees behind it seemed darker and closer than ever, a hovering chorus of hunched scavengers over the flimsy plywood and tin. Henry's skin tightened against his warm sleeves as he watched Dave staple plastic over the interior of the empty building. *Not the shed,* he thought, *not like a dog, this isn't how I want to die.*

He walked up to the small shed and tripped at the threshold. Henry fought the panic raking across his chest. "I should just go, Dave." The smell of sap echoed even through the plastic covering the interior of the shed. It made Henry feel cold and achy. A pile of blankets and a sleeping bag slumped in one corner and the camping lantern sat in the center of the small floor. Otherwise, it was empty.

Dave stopped stapling and turned toward him. "Go where Henry? To freeze in the dark? If you are really sick, I don't think you'll be able to take care of yourself."

"You won't be able to take care of me either. I'll just be another mouth to feed. And a dangerous one." Henry shuddered.

"It'll be okay. Elizabeth and I can manage until you get better. We'll be careful, keep Marnie away. Keep– keep the door locked."

"I don't think you've really thought about this Dave. I won't be able to have a fire or even a heater without burning the place down."

Dave shook his head. "No, the plastic will keep your body heat in. I'll make sure there are no gaps. We've got lots of blankets. You won't freeze. Look, I know it might be uncomfortable, but even if you made it to one of the other cabins and were able to get inside, you really would freeze. At least now I can keep an eye on you and figure something else out if this won't work."

"What happens when I'm delirious and begin attacking people?"

Dave kicked the pile of blankets over and exposed a snaking bundle of rope and thick cargo straps from the car. He didn't look at Henry. "That's what these are for."

Henry was startled and brushed away sudden tears with the back of his arm. "Like an animal Dave? You want to tie me up like a wild dog? Someone would have to feed me. And– and clean me. And I would be trying to hurt whoever was helping me the whole time."

"It's only for a little while, you'll either beat this thing in a few weeks or they'll start developing a cure."

Henry shook his head and swiped at the tears still escaping him. "We don't know that. We don't know what's going to happen. Maybe I'll die. Maybe I'll be ill for months or permanently damaged if I survive."

Dave slammed a fresh staple into the wall. "What do you want me to do?" He shouted, "If you leave, you'll starve or freeze for sure. At least here you have a chance." He sat on the floor suddenly, shoving his glasses up with a gloved finger. "I know I haven't been the best or bravest of friends Henry. I know I've made stupid mistakes in the past few weeks. But we've been friends a long time. Can't you trust me to do this for you? If things are as bad as you say, if there are people shooting the infected and no one is reporting any news or directions on where to go and what to do, we're going to need each other Henry. You are going to need me. And if– when you get well, I'm going to need you."

Henry slumped against the cold plastic. "This isn't like running Trevor Harmon off when he was going to beat you up for lunch money. I can't save you from this. I can't even save me from this."

Dave nodded. "I know. But stay anyway. Just stay." Henry just shook his head.

"Don't decide now. Have some dinner with us, so at least I know you've had something to eat. Eat and warm up at least, for my sake. Then, if you feel the same after dinner or in the morning, I won't stop you."

Henry sighed. "Okay," he said, "I'll go after dinner."

It was a relief for Henry to walk away from the tiny woodshed and into the warm kitchen. Dave followed him in and Henry barely paid attention to the bustle of Elizabeth and

Dave over the stove. He sat down as Marnie set the table. The meal was filling and the stove was very warm. Henry felt more and more drowsy. He tried to fight it, but his body seemed more and more unresponsive and at last he fell into a heavy doze in his chair.

He woke in the pitch black and he was shivering on a floor. He tried to sit up, but his hands were bound behind him. There was a weight on his chest and Henry tried not to panic as he struggled to shrug it off. He twisted until he was sitting. His hand damp plastic behind him and he realized where he was. A blanket slid from his chest and hit the plastic beside him with a soft crinkle. He tried to twist his knees underneath him so that he could stand, but a thick rope around his waist grew tight when he tried. He realized he was tied to the wall. Harnessed and leashed like a wild dog.

The little room was warm and the dark pressed in like water. Henry wondered if he would suffocate. He began to struggle to at least sit up. The slick plastic made it hard to press himself up and he was out of breath and sweating by the end. He sat for a minute to rest. The sound of his breath washed against his ears, drowned out anything else. He strained to hear anything outside of the shed, but there was nothing. Not even wind rustling the great trees that surrounded him.

He began to yell for Dave. The sound bounced around him and he wondered if it escaped the shed at all. He yelled louder. But no one came. He kicked out with his feet, searching for a wall. After a few tries he found it and banged his foot against it while he yelled. He had no shoes on and his feet became sore quickly so he stopped. He realized he was tired. And his thoughts were muddy. He tried to concentrate on getting out of the ropes, but his heart wasn't in it. He gave up and tried to grab the fallen blanket with his teeth and then with his foot. He managed to snag a corner of it and worked it slowly back up his cold legs. Henry lay on his side, his arms prickling painfully as they lost feeling around the ties. *Like an animal.* He thought it over and over, like a skip in a record, each time making the groove deeper, more natural. He forgot to think about anything else. He felt warm water on his face but he wasn't sure if it were the condensation from his breath on the plastic or if he were crying. He decided it didn't much matter and fell asleep at last and dreamed he was in the lion's pen at a circus his father had taken him to as a kid.

A raw wind splashed over him. Henry squinted and slid backward as the light from the open door hit his face. "Henry? Are you awake?"

Henry struggled to sit up. The door banged behind Dave as he squeezed into the shed. He put down the plate he was holding and helped Henry up.

"What did you do?" Henry asked as he twisted his hands behind him, trying to wake them up and get the blood circulating again.

"I had to," said Dave, "I couldn't let you just walk out into the woods to die." He squatted next to Henry and pulled a piece of foil off the plate. "I'm sorry about tying you up, but I wasn't sure how much time we had." He fiddled with a fork while Henry glared at him. He held a piece of toasted waffle up to Henry's face. "I'd untie you now, but your hands are in bad shape. Why do you keep biting them?"

"What? I wasn't biting them." But the memory of the blood oozing out of his thumbnail came back to him. He shook his head. "I can't stay here like this Dave. I can't die like this."

"You aren't going to die," sighed Dave and waved the piece of waffle in front of Henry. Henry felt the back of his neck begin to heat and the skin of his face began to burn.

Like a dog. Or an infant. He kept his thoughts to himself. "It's not safe," he said.

Dave shoved the waffle into Henry's mouth while he was talking. "It's fine. We'll be careful. You don't need to worry about anything."

Henry turned his head and spat the dry piece of waffle out. "You aren't listening to me Dave. It's not safe. I'm not safe." His voice rose as he spoke. Dave shook his head and poked another bit of waffle.

"It's not safe, Dave!" Henry yelled. Dave looked up,

mildly alarmed. Henry shouted again. "It's not safe. Not safe."

Dave backed up slightly, his rear brushing against the damp plastic wall. "Calm down Henry. It's going to be fine."

"Not safe!" Henry lunged toward him, sliding across the plastic floor. Dave dropped the plate and stood up. He backed toward the door as Henry continued to yell.

"I'll come back when you calm down," he said, pushing his glasses up with a shaky finger. One leg was already out the door and the cold air blasted through the small space and rattle the foil still sticking to the plate. "It's all for your own good you know Henry. It's just for a few weeks. Just till you're better." He tried to yell over Henry, but gave up at last, sliding out the door. A heavy scratching came from the outside as Dave locked Henry in.

Henry just kept yelling, "Not safe!" and couldn't seem to stop himself. This time, even though it was almost as dark as it had been the night before, Henry knew the damp on his skin was from crying. He couldn't seem to stop that either. At last his shouts became one long roar, whether of warning or grief at his loss of control, or just rage at being left to die penned in the cold, even Henry couldn't have decided. It lasted until he had worn himself out and he drifted into an aching, restless sleep.

TWELVE

Eight years later

Henry could smell them even before he opened his eyes. The smell overrode any thoughts he might have had of dreaming it all. It was a putrid gassy mix of rotting meat and mildew that hung over him, pulsing, undeniable, and *real.*

He tried to focus. What was the last thing he could remember before the reek? He had chased a man and a woman across a field. She was wounded. He had smelled the blood even over his own stench. Henry had been hungry. So hungry. He had ached with it, he still felt hollow, but the pain had subsided. He realized he could taste the rotting meat on his tongue as well as smell it and his stomach clenched, but there was nothing to vomit. When he thought of what he had meant to do to the woman, to the man too, if he caught them made his stomach cramp again, but whether it was from nausea or hunger he couldn't tell. *Have I shaken off my madness at last?* He wondered.

And what about the others? Henry had seen them from the corners of his eye as he ran across the field. They had been only competition then, and he would have eaten any one of them if they had been easier to catch. Were they still sick? Had he awakened only to be devoured by them instead? His muscles stiffened painfully as a weak splash of adrenaline hit them. Not enough energy to run now. If they didn't eat him, he'd die of starvation anyway.

Henry risked opening his eyes just a crack. A mountain of brown hair shuffled around about an arm's length from him. He stopped breathing. It seemed to sway for a moment and then a thin brown arm reached out for something. The hand was missing its last two fingers and the arm was little more than a wrinkled stick. He opened his eyes a little more so he could see what it was trying to grab.

Henry started to sit up as he saw the hand reaching for a pile of boxed food on a nearby table.

"I wouldn't do that," growled a thick voice to his left. The hairy thing's arm and Henry both froze. Relief wrestled with wariness in him. At least the man could talk and the mountain of hair could presumably understand. Not infected then. But what did they want with him? Why were they here? Henry turned his head. The man next to him was naked, except for the spackling of mud and grass on his skin. His gray hair tangled into his straggly beard and hid everything except one watery eye and a ragged socket where its mate ought to have been.

"Oh please," said the voice under the hill of brown hair, "I'm so hungry, I just want a little. Just a little. I'll do whatever you want."

The hair began to sob and the gray man leapt out of his chair and knelt beside it, surprising Henry with his energy. "It's not mine," the gray man said, "I think it's for all of us. I won't try to keep it from you, but if you eat it, if we eat it, we'll get sick."

"I don't care," snivelled the woman next to him, "I'm too hungry."

"What was your name?"

"Molly. And I used to work in a grocery store. And there were impossible amounts of food just ready to pick up and eat. I've been hungry for so long. Months? years? I had to eat. I had to." The woman slumped down on the floor and cried harder. "Oh God! What did I eat? What did I eat?" she sobbed. The gray man wrapped a skeleton arm around her shoulder and tried to help her get up.

"It's okay. It's okay. It's done now. We don't have to do that any more," he said.

"We?" asked the woman.

He patted her gently. "I was Vincent. And I was a priest. Listen, Molly, we can eat real food now, but we have to be careful. If we eat so much that we get sick, we may die. We have to start small, with a little broth or some milk. But I need help," Vincent held out his emaciated arms. "I can't lift very much water by myself and there are a lot of us." He turned toward Henry. "Now that you're awake, maybe you can help?" His remaining eye squinted and Vincent drew back hesitantly. "That is, if you're– if you're not still sick."

For the first time in almost a decade Henry felt himself smile with relief. "I'm not sick any more," he said, his voice crackling with thirst. He pushed himself slowly off the wooden floor.

"There's a kitchen and a few soup pots, but the water is out. There's a pond behind the house."

"Shouldn't we call someone? A hospital?" said Molly pushing aside the matted curtain of hair in front of her face.

Vincent shook his head and reached for a fluttering piece of paper on the table. "I'm not sure when you got sick, or if you know what has happened since, but I don't think there's anyone to call," he said, handing her the paper. "It's not all bad news," he said as he saw Henry's grin collapse. "And we're alive and sane again." Henry helped Molly up and followed Vincent into the kitchen.

"How long have you been awake?" Henry asked.

"Only about an hour longer than you. There are the other three that haven't woken up yet too."

Henry looked doubtfully back into the living room. "Are you certain they are alive?"

Vincent clattered around in dusty cabinets looking for pots. "Yes. I checked you all. So far, we're all alive. But without food and water, we aren't going to last very much longer. None of us are in good shape."

Henry looked out of the kitchen window at the thick whorled grass still silver with frost. "It's cold. We should find some clothes."

Molly stumbled into the kitchen, still holding the paper. She stood next to Henry and looked outside. "It's all gone, isn't it?" she asked.

Henry looked over at her, tried not to see the tarry stripes of old battles on her thin arms or the maggots wriggling on the surface of a new wound near her chin. He tried to smile. "Someone woke us– cured us. It can't all be gone, someone must be making medicine still. And they didn't just shoot us, so they probably weren't looters. Not that we had anything valuable anyway."

Molly twisted the mat of hair back with her mangled, clawed hand. She looked up at Henry. "I guess that's true," she said and she smiled a little too. Vincent emerged from the cabinet with two large stock pots. He looked over Henry's shoulder at the gray, frosty day and shivered.

"There must be clothing here somewhere." He placed the pots near the door. They heard sounds of people moving from the living room.

"I'll check upstairs if you want. There must be a bedroom here," said Henry, "If you'll check on whoever is waking up."

"Be careful," said Vincent, "I haven't been upstairs yet. I don't know what, or who, may be up there."

Henry shuffled toward the dusty entrance hall. His legs were rickety, like unoiled wood and he wondered how he had been able to chase anyone when he could barely keep himself upright. He stopped in front of the front door. The man had shot him with a dart as he banged on the front door trying to get to the woman. *That* was the last thing he remembered, not the field. There must have been a sedative in the dart. He wondered how long he'd really been sleeping. If the past several years had just been an awful dream. Maybe this was the dream. He turned toward the dark stairs and almost groaned as he counted them. Dark spots and splashes wove across the treads and Henry hoped whoever was bleeding had gone away long before. He went up slowly, leaning on the wall, but he was still out of breath when he reached the top. There was a pile of bloody clothes and sheets in the hallway corner. They were so soaked that the blood was still wet and a heavy copper smell hung in the top of the stairwell. Henry's stomach roiled and he was horrified to find his mouth watering. He hurried past the pile and into the first bedroom. He wiped his forehead and tried to push away his stomach's reaction. Tried to push out the memory of all the other times he'd given in to that particular desire. He wasn't ready to think about it. His body couldn't afford for him to become overwhelmed by grief and guilt. He could hear long sobbing wails rising up from downstairs and knew someone else had just woken and realized the past was real and not the nightmare it seemed.

The dresser was askew and the bed unmade but not dusty, though everything else in the house seemed to be. Henry assumed it was the wounded woman and the man who had shot him, but where had they gone? And why had he been brought inside? Henry struggled with the swollen dresser drawer. It squealed open at last. Men's clothes. He hesitated, thinking of the grime and blood and acrid sweat that covered him. He'd never wanted to bathe so badly in his life. He had to eat first. Before comfort and definitely before vanity. Henry pulled on an old pair of jeans and a shirt. He looked at the shorts and socks, but it was too personal. He grabbed armfuls of clothing and walked back to the stairs, throwing the clothes down ahead of him. He didn't want to come back up here if he could help it. The heavy copper smell made his stomach cramp again. He turned toward another bedroom. The curtains were drawn and only a gray glow outlined the furniture in the room. Henry crossed to the window, relieved to be away from the bloody clothing. He opened the curtains and watched a flurry of dust specks settle lazily back onto the windowsill. The room had been closed for a long time, everything neatly tucked into place, it still smelled lightly of pine needles. Henry looked around and saw the naked trunk of a Christmas tree, tiny glass lights slung over its bones, here and there a shining ornament clung to the thin wood claws, a pile of dark needles and shattered sparkling glass at its base.

Henry walked around the carefully made bed to the stenciled white dresser. He began rummaging around the drawers, pulling out armfuls of women's clothing this time. A shadow caught his eye and Henry looked up, catching his reflection in the dusty vanity mirror. He stumbled backward and the withered tree snapped underneath him, ornaments shattering with a musical tinkle around him. He got up, brushing himself off and blushing, realizing the reflection was his. His face was almost entirely hidden, dark, matted hair covering all but his eyes and nose. He tried not to look, but he caught a glimpse of himself anyway. His bones seemed to be rising as the rest of his face sunk away. His nose had a crook that he didn't remember and there were white wriggling maggots in the muck caught in his long beard. Henry shuddered and picked up the clothing. He hurried away from the mirror and down the stairs, away from both his hunger and revulsion, toward the safety of the others.

He carried the large bundle of clothing into the kitchen where the whole group now milled around. The three newly awakened people argued tearfully with Vincent and Molly for food.

One of them, a weaselly looking man, whose hair only remained in patches of long tufts stood very close to Vincent, his eyes squinting and his chest thrown forward. Henry thought there might be a fight and wondered if he had enough energy to stop it. "Look," said the weaselly man, "how do you know all this stuff? Maybe you just want all the food for yourself. Why should we trust you?"

"What's your name, son?" Vincent asked calmly.

"Rickey. And I'm not your son."

"Rickey. I was a missionary before– before this. I worked in places with severe famine. I've seen people die because they were allowed to eat too quickly. We need to start with this powdered milk."

"We're not starving," sneered Rickey, "We had that cow just a few days ago, don't you remember?"

Henry watched Molly put her good hand to her mouth, as if she could stop the vomit that wasn't going to come. It was a dry heave instead. He tried to block out the image of the rotting cow, but he could feel the slick, spoiled mush of the meat between his teeth even now. One of the women behind Rickey spoke up.

"I don't think that was a few days ago. I think we've been asleep a while. I fell and scraped my hand on the porch when we were chasing those people. It was very bloody and I was so hungry. I– I kept licking my hand until I passed out. And now, the scratch is almost gone." She held out a small hand where a large scab was flaking off and leaving clean skin behind.

"Even if it was only a few days ago," said Vincent, "we haven't been eating properly for a long time. Probably since we got sick. And the little we got from Phil's men stopped, what? Three months ago now? Our bodies aren't meant for that. We have to be careful."

Henry held up the bundle of clothes. "Then let's get dressed and get that water so we can at least have some of the milk." He dumped the clothing onto the tiled floor and picked up one of the soup pots. He didn't want to hear them argue about food any more, it made his whole body ache. He opened the back door and walked carefully onto the cool, overgrown yard. The dead grass was matted down in great silver whorls from where the snow had lain. A few patches of early clover had begun to poke through. Henry trudged slowly down a small slope to the pond. He had to push through thickly clustered reeds and yellowed lily pads to get to the water. He felt the chill of the water on his ankles before he realized he had stepped into the water. He backed up in surprise and looked at his feet. He touched them, poked his heel, pinched his big toe, but he couldn't feel anything. He wondered when he'd had shoes or even socks on last. It was like trying to remember an endless bad dream, but he thought it must have been at the lodge. Marnie had made sure they had things like that. His feet must have been frostbitten sometime in the last three months. Henry wondered what else he didn't know about his own body.

He watched his feet carefully as he filled the pot with the gray-green water. He didn't want to make them worse. He'd have to remember to find some shoes to protect them. He wondered where Marnie was as he struggled back to the house with the heavy pot. She had come to visit him after Dave had stopped. Henry could remember her pushing a plastic plate full of food toward him with the handle of a broom. He had lunged at her, but the little girl hadn't even flinched. She just looked sad. "I told you I'd take care of you if you got sick, Henry," she'd said. She was the only one who'd called him Henry after a while. Henry sat down on the back porch, the heavy steel pot between the knobs of his knees. His memories were blurry, angry things, a smear of bloody rage populated by strange voices and faces. He hoped they would stay indistinct, locked away. But Marnie stood out, sharp and vibrant. He remembered every time he'd seen her. Something in his infected brain had built a barrier around her, as something separate, untouched by the madness that swallowed him. He hoped she had escaped the carnage at the lodge. He could still feel the warm pressure of her weight on his back as she unhooked the chains that held him and he could almost feel the warm panic in her breath as she'd said goodbye. He had been gnashing his teeth, roaring, straining to leap at the men beyond his pen. She probably thought he hadn't heard her, but he had. He had to find her. Had to protect the little girl who'd been abandoned to the world by the people meant to care for her the most.

The back door creaked open behind him. The weaselly man, Rickey, came out holding an empty pot. "You ever going to bring that in man?" he asked.

"Yeah, sorry, it was just heavier than I expected," said Henry standing up.

Rickey snorted. "It looks bigger than you are, man. I mean, no offense, but you look like you're hung together with spit and a prayer." He glanced down at Henry's soaked pant cuffs. "And if you're taking a bath, I think you missed a couple spots."

Henry laughed. "And you're such a model of excellent health."

"You're okay. I'm Rickey." He stuck out a thin hand.

Henry shook his hand. It felt good to be doing something human again. Even if he was wary of the man's intentions. "Henry, nice to meet you." He bent over and picked up the heavy pot. "Well, I better get this into the house. We'll have to figure out a way to clean it I think. The pond's mucky."

Rickey nodded and headed toward the pond. Henry opened the back door and slid the heavy pot slowly across the kitchen floor. One of the women grabbed it and lifted it onto the stove top with a grunt. Vincent and Molly were portioning scoops of dry milk into empty cups. The other woman was sitting at the table reading the letter that had been left for them.

"How do we clean the water? Is it safe the way it is?" asked Henry.

Vincent shook his head, but it was the woman standing next to him that answered. "This is a gas stove, I think," she said, "If it's hooked up and we can find some matches we can boil the water."

"Good idea Pam. If we can't get it to work, there's a fireplace in the living room," said Vincent.

Henry opened the drawer next to the stove. Fishing around under the dish cloths and pot holders, he found an old box of matches. "Think they still work?" asked Pam.

Henry shrugged. "I'm not even sure how long it's been since I got sick let alone when these people left." He handed her the box. She turned the burner dial, but there was no thick hiss and she sniffed close to the range.

"The gas is off, I think."

Henry remembered the neatly made bedroom. "I think these people evacuated. They must have closed up the house first. I'll see if I can find the propane tank." He looked around. "Anyone seen any shoes lying around?"

The woman reading the letter looked up. "There's a laundry room with coats around the corner. I think I saw some boots in there."

"Thanks," said Henry and made his way into the little windowless room, tripping on objects in the dark. After fumbling around for a few minutes he found a mismatched pair of boots that fit him. They were both right feet, but Henry didn't care. He just wanted to eat. As he passed the table on his way out, he slid a finger along a small spill. It was stale and musty, but he didn't think he'd tasted anything so good in a long while. He immediately regretted trying it. It only made him hungrier. He hoped the gas tank's nozzle hadn't rusted, he didn't think any of them had enough strength to fight with it. He found the tall cylinders just around the corner from the back door. The people that had lived there were careful, the hose was disconnected and carefully coiled and covered with a plastic tarp. The propane cannister was turned off and capped with a snug plastic piece. Henry sighed with relief and reconnected the hose and turned the gas on. Rickey was stumbling back toward the house, trying not to spill half of the water. Henry helped him bring the heavy pot back inside. Pam was already heating the water. Henry tried not to watch the stove or the glasses with their drifts of tiny powdery balls. He walked over to the woman who had been reading the letter. It sat in front of her now as she watched Pam at the stove.

"Hi," said Henry, "Do you mind if I read this?" She shook her head and handed him the paper and went back to staring at the stove top. Henry retreated to the living room.

THIRTEEN

"I wish I could be here to tell you this instead of leaving a letter, but this is an emergency. I hope you can forgive us for leaving you to recover by yourselves. My name is Nella Rider. I'm a psychologist who worked for a long period in a Cure camp with the Infected– people like you. I'm traveling with Frank Courtlen, the man who administered the Cure to you. He was also Infected once. We've both seen what you will be experiencing in the next few weeks and months. And we both regret not being here when you woke up.

I don't know how much you knew about what was happening before you became infected, or how much you can remember about it. The world has changed since you've been ill. There is no easy way to tell you how much it has changed, not even if I were able to speak to you face to face as I would like. The first news of what we call the December Plague came roughly eight years ago now. I know that people who have been cured remember most of what has happened in the intervening time since infection, but those memories can be blurry for the first few weeks. For better or worse, they will return with greater clarity after a while."

Henry looked away from the letter. He buried a hand in his filthy hair and clenched his jaw. He wasn't surprised that it had been so long since he had been infected. He'd watched Dave and Marnie grow older and Phil grow meaner without realizing what he saw, but he understood it now that his head was clear. He didn't want to remember. He wanted it to stay a vague whirlwind, to never resolve itself into definite focus. He heard spoons clattering in the kitchen, but he didn't go back in. He looked back at the careful words on the page.

"For two years there was terrible violence between the Infected and Immunes. Many, many people died. The federal government is gone. Contact with the world beyond a fifty mile radius around the City is non-existent. At last, only a small immune population was left, kept safe behind the Barrier. But then the Cure was discovered. Six years ago the military began using sleeping darts to administer the Cure to groups of Infected. We tried very hard not to miss anyone, but there are so few of us left. There were bound to be blind spots as we expanded from the City. I'm sorry that we passed you by somehow, until now. It's been a long crawl back towards normal life, and we are nowhere near finished. The Cure has helped hundreds of people over the past few years, but the military began finding fewer and fewer groups of Infected as more and more succumbed to exposure or starvation. They've all but wrapped up their Cure operation now, which is why they didn't find you."

The others must have been shocked to realize they had lost six years needlessly. If they'd known how close the early Cure camps had been, they might despair. But Henry knew. It had been Elizabeth who had told him. He wondered if Marnie knew, even now, what had happened to her mother.

Elizabeth had fed him first, so he would listen. Even Marnie hadn't been able to sneak him food that week. Phil had thrown the corpses of a rival camp over the palings, but he'd allowed none of the Infected to be fed anything else. He'd even threatened to tie those that violated his order to the central pole of the pen and release the Infected from their leashes.

But Elizabeth had walked into the pen at midday, brazenly holding a platter mounded with real, warm food. She'd ignored the howls of the other Infected, just skirting the reach of their leashes. She'd come straight to Henry. She'd put down the food and shoved the platter with her foot into his small, worn, dirt ring so he could reach it. Then she had squatted and watched him while he stuffed himself. This memory was like a clear photograph among hundreds of blurs. He remembered how dark her bruised eye had been compared to the blond hair falling across it, the twisted puff of her split lip in the smooth, drawn lines of her pale face. She'd watched him until his growling and lunging had stopped, until he was full and the mild sedative she'd put into the food took effect. He swayed and looked at her, glassy eyed, like a tired child. And then at last she had spoken to him.

"I should have picked you, Henry, all those years ago.

Even knowing what you've become. It still would have been the better choice. Instead I'm yoked to a coward." Elizabeth turned her head and spat. It had been a pink stream in the black dirt of the pen. "I know you can't answer me. I don't even know if you can understand what I'm saying. But sometimes I wonder if I still see a flicker of the old Henry. I wonder if you are still trapped in there. So I came to tell you that there's a Cure."

She leaned in, close enough for Henry to bite. But he was no longer hungry and the sedative muted his normal aggression. He snarled, but he didn't move toward her.

"There's a Cure. And it isn't far away. But Phil doesn't want you cured. He wants to keep his guard dogs. He wants to stay king of scenic Cannibal Lodge." Elizabeth laughed and Henry had backed away. A chill cut through even the confusion of the infection, his sick brain sensing an even sicker one in her.

Elizabeth's eyes streamed tears even as she continued to smile and speak calmly. "But I'm going to the Cure camp anyway. And when I come back, I'm bringing the army. They're going to cure you all. And then you and the army, you can give Phil what he deserves." She covered her breasts with her arms as if she were cold. "Oh yes, Henry. Then you can do what Dave will not and make sure Phil pays for everything he's done."

Elizabeth stopped and swiped at some of the tears and her face became threatening. Henry began to pace his dirt circle, the mild sedative overridden by his increasing agitation at her presence. She backed out of his reach.

"Marnie told me you have a deal. Henry, if you can hear any of this– if you understand or remember or even dream any of this, pay attention. I know you have a deal. I know you promised to take care of her if she got sick and she promised to take care of you. I know you didn't really mean it when you said it. I know you didn't expect to get sick. But Dave won't protect her. *Doesn't* protect her. And if something happens to me– I'm taking care of you. I'm getting the Cure for *you,* Henry. So I'm going to hold you to your promise. I'm taking care of you for Marnie. So you need to take care of Marnie when you can. No matter what, Henry. Don't leave her alone here with these people. Even if Dave stays with them. I'm taking care of you, so you'll take care of her when I'm gone. Remember Henry."

He started as Vincent handed him the hot glass of reconstituted milk.

"Drink it slowly. Sips at a time. Or it will hurt," he said.

Henry nodded and set aside the letter and Elizabeth's memory. He held the cup with both hands as if it would give him more control of himself. Hunger rumbled through the aching echo chamber of his gut and he raised his cup in front of his face. The steam was a warm, sweet breath on the small patch of his face not buried in hair. The slightly soured smell of the stale milk made Henry salivate. He was relieved that he could still find something besides meat appealing. *This is going to be difficult,* he thought, and pulled the cup to his lips. It took a superhuman effort to stop drinking after just a small gulp. His hands were shaking as he lowered the cup to his lap. Most of him wanted to tilt the glass all the way back, fill the cold hollow of his belly with a the warm slosh and gurgle of too much milk. But he knew Vincent was right and forced himself to stop and count slowly to five before the next sip.

Pam crept up to him, holding a small spoon. She held it out to him as if she expected him to slap it from her hand. He took it, confused.

"It will help you not drink it all at once. The priest said just a spoonful at a time. It will stop you from gulping."

"Thanks," said Henry. She sat down across from him near the fireplace. The clothes he'd brought down were so large, she almost disappeared into them, a bundle of sticks inside a parachute. He wondered if he looked the same.

"Are you going back for your daughter?" she asked as she lifted her spoon.

"What?"

"Your daughter. The one that untied us. Are you going back for her now?"

Henry looked down into the flat white of the milk. "She's not my daughter."

"Oh. I'm sorry. I just assumed, she seemed to bring you things."

"Her parents were friends of mine."

"Oh." Pam sipped another spoonful and avoided looking at him.

"She couldn't still be there. She would have run away during the confusion, don't you think?"

She shrugged. "I had babies. You know, Before. But not as old as her. I'm going back home to find them."

Rickey shuffled into the room, his pants puddling around the knees and feet. He flopped down next to Henry and eyed his almost empty glass. "Didn't you read that letter? It's been eight years. Almost everyone's dead. Your babies won't be home," he said, downing the last few drops of his milk and sliding closer to Henry.

"You don't know that," said Molly from the doorway. "The letter also said there was a city with lots of people. Even people like us, and families that reunited. I'm sure your kids are there, Pam."

Pam smiled at her. "They were away when I got sick. They went on a school skiing trip. I can't wait to see them again."

Rickey snorted.

"What's so funny?" asked Henry, with a warning look.

Rickey shrugged. "Well, it's just– Let's say this city is real and that they allow people like us inside–"

"People like us?" asked Vincent wandering in with Melissa in tow.

"Yeah. Infected. Cannibals. Zombies. Uh, Cured or whatever it was the psychiatrist chick called us. People like us. Let's say they allow us to come in. And let's even pretend that Pam's kids here, are actually alive and living in this city. You think they're going to want to see her? You think they're going to kiss and hug her and pretend everything is okay, when they know what she's probably done in the past several years? You think *anyone* will want to be around us?"

- 84 -

"Hey," said Henry quietly, "relax."

"We don't know what is normal any more. If there are enough– enough Cured around, if we outnumber the Immunes then maybe what we've done isn't really that unusual. Maybe it's not even surprising," said Melissa, throwing a scrawny arm around Pam's shoulder.

Henry scrubbed at his itching, crawling beard. "Murder's not normal," he said quietly and felt his eyes prickle with tears. "There's nothing normal about what we've done."

"We just did what we had to do to survive," said Molly, "We didn't know what we were doing."

"We do now," said Rickey, "and so does everybody else. Why would they let us in? Why would they want us back after that?"

"The people that cured us were willing to accept us," said Vincent, holding his hands out toward the pile of supplies spread on the coffee table between them, "They've left us directions straight to their home. And if things are as bad as Dr. Rider's letter says, I can only assume the things they have left us are scarce and valuable now. They could have killed us or left us to fend for ourselves, but they didn't."

Rickey shook his head. "It's a trap. You think they are just going to give us this stuff without expecting something in return? Have you people forgotten the past several years? Have you forgotten what Phil and his gang did to us?" he waved at Pam, who shrunk backward into Melissa, "did you forget what he did to you? No one came to help us in all those years. What makes you think this city is any different? This guy," he flicked the letter with a finger, "What's-his-name, Frank? He's probably this woman's slave. That's all we'll be. First guard dogs and whores. Now servants or slaves. Pam's kids hope she's *dead*. That's the best anyone can hope for. We have no friends. We have no families. Their lives and memories are happier if they continue to believe we're dead."

Henry stood up. He shoved his almost empty cup into Rickey's hand. "Shut up and drink your milk," he said and walked toward the kitchen.

"You know I'm right," Rickey called after him, and picked up the spoon to finish Henry's food. Pam got up and followed him into the kitchen.

"Do you think he's right?" she asked.

"I think he's kind of a jerk. I don't know what to think about the City or the people that left us that note."

"Aren't you worried about going there then?"

"It's a little early to worry about that. I don't think any of us are going anywhere for a while. We'll have to wait until we're stronger." He started rummaging through the kitchen drawers.

"What are you looking for?"

"Scissors. I can't stand this hair any more. Although, if I come across soap first I'll be equally happy." He could feel bugs and debris wiggling and itching and it made Henry want to scream. Now that the overwhelming pain of his empty stomach was gone, it was all Henry could think about. If he didn't get rid of the itches soon, he thought he'd scratch himself until he bled.

Molly heard them and walked over. "I could die happy if I could brush this foul taste out of my mouth." Henry nodded. The taste in his own mouth was the congealed memory of all his sins.

"I think there are two bathrooms," said Pam, "but they might have been cleaned out already. I'll go look."

"Want to get some more water with me Henry? We can warm it up on the stove." Molly picked up a large pot.

"I'll go too," called Vincent from the other room. There were no scissors in the drawers. Henry could feel himself building into a panicked frenzy. He grabbed a steak knife from the drawer instead and picked up a soup pot on his way out the back door.

FOURTEEN

The knife was dull and pulled more hair out than it cut away, but Henry was beyond caring. He sawed away at his beard first. It was a mass of rotten meat and clumped colonies of fly eggs and maggots. The knife kept slipping in the slick mush that stuck to the hairs or sticking in the crusted clots of mud and gore. Henry wept as he chopped at it. It was as if he were seeing his memory of the past eight years in physical form. Blood and dirt and pain all bunched together. The hair on his head was easier. Cleaner even. He was able to calm down as the cold air hit more and more of his scalp and the weight on his neck lightened. The smell of rot receded into the background. He sat next to the pond, unwilling to bring the mess back into the house. It took him a long time to get rid of all of it, the sun was beginning to set and his hands were shaking with cold by the time he'd cut most of it. The others came and went with pots and basins of water, but they let him be, passing silently back and forth to the house. He looked at the dark mass next to him. He kept worrying about whether the maggots would crawl into the pond and infect the water, even though some part of him knew that the idea was insane. He thought about burning the hair in the fireplace, but he didn't want it in the house. Now that it had been shorn, now that he was free of it, he recoiled from the thought of touching it again. Even to move it. He looked around the darkening field. There was a snow shovel leaning against the back door of the house. Henry grabbed it and came back to the tangled, matted chunks of greasy hair. He scooped it up with the shovel and then hesitated.

Where was he going to go? Why was he worrying about this? But it was no use. The hair bothered him and he wouldn't be able to rest until it was gone. He walked to the far fence, holding the shovel as far from him as possible the whole way. He set it down near the post and then chopped away the dead grass and stiff, cold dirt with the steak knife, until he had made a small dent in the ground. Tipping the hair in, he hastily covered it with the chunks of earth he had cut away. Strands stuck out here and there, and Henry's mind flashed to the frozen woman he had found in the snow so long ago, her hair barely fluttering against the drift. *I should have known then,* he thought, *I should have gone back to the lodge and killed him before I got sick. What's he going to do to Marnie? What's he already done?* Henry's sight was suddenly blurry with tears. He tore up the grass around him and stuffed handfuls onto the little grave of hair, trying to hide it, pressing it into the chilly mud.

"Hey man, you okay over there?" Rickey was calling him from near the pond. Henry sniffled into his shoulder, then picked up the shovel and knife and turned back to the house.

"Yeah," he called back, "Just taking care of something." He walked slowly back to the pond and traded the snow shovel for his pot of water. Rickey's tufts of hair were trimmed and combed over the bald patches and his beard was gone. His nose stuck out like a log splitter's wedge and the scars on his bare neck shone purple and smooth even in the dim light. Henry wasn't sure if it was an improvement or not.

"Man, I thought you looked like shit before. Did you pull all that hair out or what?" Rickey asked him.

Henry held up the steak knife.

"That priest found some razors and the chicks found some bars of soap in the bathroom. You could use both. C'mon, let's get this water inside. The priest says we can have another cup of milk, and he says we can put a little oatmeal in it. One of the girls is cooking it right now." Rickey rubbed his long hands together before picking up his pot of water. Henry followed him into the house without comment.

Someone had made a fire and the kitchen glowed in the light of three fat candles. One of the women was stirring a small pan of milky oatmeal. Henry wondered if it would feed them all before he remembered how little they were meant to eat. He looked at the woman, but her hair was chopped short, spiking like needles from her head, and he couldn't tell who it was, having seen very little of anyone's face before.

"I'm going to have to introduce myself all over again,"

he said to her, "I can't recognize anyone without their hair."

The woman smiled, "Melissa. And since you aren't running at the mouth or missing an eye, you must be Henry."

He laughed, feeling ten times lighter without the halo of filth surrounding his head. She eyed the choppy hair that was left. "Did it hurt to cut it with the knife?"

Henry blushed. "Yeah, but I had to get rid of it."

"I understand. You might want to clean it up a little though. There's no one in the bathroom now, if you want it. Dinner will be a little longer."

"Thanks," said Henry. He found Vincent trying to tape a gauze pad over his empty eye socket in front of the mirror. "Here," he said reaching carefully for the tape, "it can't be easy to see what you are doing with your hands in the way." Vincent held out the soft pad with a tight smile.

"You aren't bothered by it?" he asked.

Henry shook his head. He washed his hands in the water someone had filled the sink with. It was warm and the soap stung his nose in a pleasant way. "I think the only thing that can bother me any more are the things I've done." He dried his hands on a towel and took the gauze from Vincent's hand. He carefully straightened the tape. "Do you think it matters that I didn't mean them? Would it have been better if I had died before I got sick?" He gently pressed the tape across Vincent's brow and then at the edges of the socket.

"Why are you asking *me*? Haven't I done the same sort of things?" Vincent's brow wrinkled and Henry pressed the tape down a little harder so it would stay.

"Well, you said you were a priest. The church must have something to say about violence while a person is not in control of themselves."

"Are you a Catholic?"

"No, I mean, I wasn't. But I'd feel better knowing anyway."

Vincent slid down, making room for Henry at the sink. "You're asking about sin?"

Henry nodded and tried to hide his embarrassment by bending to wash his face.

"For someone to sin, they must have free will. You have to *choose*. We weren't operating under free will. If we could have stopped, we would have. But we didn't even realize what it was we were doing at the time. At least, I assume it was the same for you as it was for me."

Henry straightened. "Yes," he said slowly, "if I'd known what would happen, I would have found a way to end it before it began."

Vincent shook his head and looked distressed. Henry held up a hand. "I know, that would have been suicide. I know. I still would have done it. But–" He glanced at Vincent and picked up a razor. His hand shook as he brought it to the patchy stubble on his face. "Father, I feel overwhelming guilt for what I've done. But while I was doing it– every time I bit someone, every time I *fed,* it felt *good.*" Henry nicked his chin as tears once again blurred his sight. Vincent put a hand on his shoulder and handed him a towel. Henry pressed it against his cut.

"Henry, we were little more than beasts. Don't you think lions or hawks or wild dogs feel the same– the same *satisfaction* when they catch their prey? But that is just the body's reaction to food. You are back to your rational self now, and you would not choose to kill someone now. You could not have sinned, because you had no choice."

Henry turned to look at the old priest. "Is that really what you believe?" he asked, "That it was something separate, divorced from us, and that now we can go on, untarnished by what we've done?"

"Are you asking me what I believe as a priest or as a man?" Vincent sat down on the closed lid of the toilet and rubbed at his chest, as if he ached there. "Doctrine says that I needn't repent of something that's not my fault. But as a man, how could I not? How could I not spend every day trying to lessen the harm I've done?"

Henry shook his head. "How can we lessen it? We will never lessen it by even a hair, no matter what we do."

Vincent stood up, and squeezed Henry's shoulder again. "No," he said, his old voice creaking, "we can't. But maybe we can stop any more harm from happening."

Rickey knocked on the door frame. "Uh, dinner's ready. Better let Henry finish up."

Vincent nodded and let Henry go. He left the bathroom. "Just 'cause you cut it off doesn't mean it wasn't real you know," said Rickey, still leaning on the frame.

"I know," said Henry, "I'm not trying to pretend it wasn't. I just had to get free of the mess. Just wanted to feel human again."

Rickey shook his head. "Don't be long or you'll miss dinner" said Rickey, "Oh, and we found the toothbrushes. Bad news, there are only four. Just try and clean it really well after. Don't want your cooties, man." He grinned and held out the four brushes like an apology.

Henry nodded and took them. The bristles were already bent over and dingy from the vigorous use they'd gotten from the others. Henry chose the newest looking one and looked for the toothpaste. The tube was empty and Henry groaned, but there was a box of old baking soda sitting next to the sink. He decided to shave first and then refill the sink with clean water before dipping the brush in.

The face that emerged from the stubble was one that Henry didn't recognize. His nose had been broken in a few places and his teeth didn't line up the way they used to, a combination of wear and a badly healed break. His neck was circled with a dashed line of welts where his chain collar had choked and cut him whenever he had lunged at something. Still, he'd been luckier than most, protected in his little shed and then in the pen. He didn't have scars as severe or noticeable as the others, and it wasn't the damage to his face that shocked him. It was his age. Henry felt as if he were looking at his father and not himself. Exhaustion and thin, loose skin from recent starvation made him look as if more time had passed than the eight years since he had last seen his own reflection.

He felt like a living Rip Van Winkle, outliving his friends and family, waking in a shattered world, a stranger even to himself. Henry turned from the mirror and began scouring his teeth with the gritty baking soda and a dirty toothbrush. *Everything is wrong,* he thought, *everything. It's as if I've woken up on another planet.* He washed the toothbrush as well as he could and passed through the darkening living room into the kitchen with the others. They were eating silently, none of them looking at another. Five people with whom Henry had spent the past eight years living, who'd seen him at his sickest, darkest moment. And they were still perfect strangers, each completely alone in the silent, vacant world. *But I'm **not** alone. There is someone I know out there. And I made a promise to take care of her.*

Pam stood up to get him a bowl of oatmeal and milk. He smiled as she handed it to him, smiled as he realized there was a reason he had been cured. "Yes Pam," he said, "I'm going back for Marnie."

FIFTEEN

"You know you're batshit crazy right?" Rickey thumped his dusty pillow and flopped onto the couch . Henry shoved a new log into the fire, pushing it far to the back with the bottom of one bare foot, forgetting he wouldn't feel it until too late if he got burned.

"You think I should leave her? She's the reason we're here and cured."

Rickey rolled his eyes at the ceiling. "Yeah, you can thank her for that too, when you see her."

Vincent sat up from his blanket on the floor. "You don't want to be cured?" he asked.

"C'mon Father, are we really better off this way? A few days ago we weren't worried about what anyone else thought or what happened to them. We didn't know we were cold or hungry, had no guilt, no responsibility, no pain. Or if we did, it didn't register. We wake up here, to what exactly? An empty belly, an empty world with no future and all of us dragging our memory with us. We have no friends, we have no food besides the little that's here, we're wounded– hell, you're missing an eye and we've got nowhere to go. What's better about this?"

Henry turned around to face the two men. "We aren't killing and eating people."

Rickey sat up. "Oh please. We didn't even know we were doing it. It was just another meal to us. It helped us survive didn't it? You think what we did is any worse than what Phil's guys did?"

"Are *they* the example you want to judge your life by?" asked Vincent.

"Oh come on, Father. You never felt guilt at what they or we were doing until this morning. You going to drag your past with you for the rest of your life? We killed a lot of people. A lot. You remember them all? You going to whip yourself for every one? I don't even remember the first person I ate. It's all a blur, all the faces like melted wax. Seems like if it were important, a person would remember their first one.

Do you?"

Vincent looked at the ground. He smoothed the edges of his makeshift eye patch. "No," he said quietly.

But Henry did.

He had still been in his tiny shed. In the dark. It wasn't cold any longer, and he could smell the crushed grass whenever someone opened the door to feed him or to splash him with buckets of clean water. But it had been days since anyone had done either. Henry raged, smashing himself against the walls, straining against the choke chain, chewing on the thick utility gloves that covered his hands. At last, Dave opened the shed door, a round shadow in the sharp spring light that Henry never saw. Henry roared until the metal collar cut off his breath.

"I'm sorry Henry. Phil says we aren't to waste food on you any more, since the store owner won't give us any more on credit. Elizabeth went to the other houses on the road to scavenge, but Phil grabbed it all." Dave slumped down to the ground, ignoring Henry desperately scrabbling and clawing to reach him. "I never meant it to be like this. I should have listened to you when you told me to get rid of him. He strong arms everyone now. He's even collecting people, says we need to band together to survive. But the people he's choosing, I don't think they are good people to have around Marnie. We're supposed to visit the store tonight. Phil says we need to do some heavy persuading. I'm scared Henry. But I'll bring you something to eat tonight, I promise."

Henry's rage had at last worn out and he had fallen asleep in the hot, smelly little shed, still chewing on the leather gloves that protected his hands. Men's shouts drawing close to the shed woke him and he immediately flung himself forward and joined the noise with guttural snarls and the lurching clang of the chain leash and collar. Something metal dragged along the outside of the flimsy plywood wall. "You hungry zombie?" Phil's thick voice oozed into the shed. The men with him hooted and laughed like hyenas, banged on the walls of his shed. Henry growled and pulled on the chain until he almost fainted from lack of air.

"Why are you doing this?" Dave's voice whined through the door. "We have what we want. Just let him go."

"No," growled Phil, "he could have made this easy on himself and us, we could all have been friends. But instead, he sets booby traps for my guys. He broke Sam's arm. He needs to pay."

"You're nothing but a band of thugs. We would never have been friends. The people left in town– they'll have nothing now. You think they will go quietly away and starve? I'm not the only one that's going to pay."

"You see Dave? He doesn't want to cooperate even now. Besides, your buddy sounds pretty hungry in there, you want him to starve?"

The door flung open and bright flashlights jittered and slid over the interior of the shed, finally resting on Henry's face. "Well Wyatt, you don't want to be friends with me, maybe you can make friends with Henry here."

The man was shoved inside. "Here," laughed one of the men, handing Wyatt a flashlight, "this way you can see his pretty face." The door slammed shut and the padlock snapped shut with a clunk. Henry lunged, reached out, his fingertips brushing the man's shirt, but he pressed himself against the far wall, just out of reach. There was a metallic tang to the air and Henry knew the man was already bleeding. Henry began to salivate.

The flashlight beam shook and blinded him. "Henry?" came the man's voice, "Oh Henry, I'm so sorry this happened to you. When the men came, they said they were staying here and I asked them to let me see you. I knew you'd protect me, if you could. You seemed decent and honest last winter." There was a low sob from behind the light. "I know you can't remember me. Or maybe you do, but you can't help yourself. I've seen it lots over the past few months. It's me, Wyatt, from the store. I should have come with you then. I wouldn't have let this happen. I know you would have gotten sick, but I wouldn't have kept you in a flimsy woodshed. Like an animal."

Henry growled deep in his throat and strained against

the chain. It cut into his neck.

"Do they even feed you? The Sheriff was right. It's a mercy to shoot you. You wouldn't freeze or starve that way. This, this is worse." Wyatt sucked in his gut as Henry's glove caught on the buttons of his shirt. "Aw Henry, I would have shot you," he sobbed. Wyatt sucked in great, ragged breaths for a moment. Then he clicked the flashlight off.

"I know what you're going to do. I don't know if there is any part of who you were left in there or if you'll get better someday like we thought so many months ago. But in case some part of you understands, I know what you're going to do. I know you can't help it. I forgive you Henry, I want you to remember that if you ever come back to yourself. I forgive you."

There was a rusty screech and dull cracking as the ring holding Henry's chain came free of the flimsy wall. "I forgive you Henry!" Wyatt screamed into the dark. Henry fell forward with a thud as the chain loosened. "I forgive you! I forgive you!" Wyatt kept screaming until Henry found the soft, sagging folds of his neck. Henry's teeth ached with want as they closed around the wrinkled skin and he drooled freely. Even eight years later he would remember how intense the salt taste of that first bite had been, the dull, rubbery snap as tendons broke, and the deep, secret heat of blood splashing onto his face.

Phil's men left him there for several days. There was nothing left of Wyatt except bone and hair and cloth. The days were hot and the shed, still lined in plastic, was a stew of waste and rotten meat. But the men could hear Henry bashing against the walls, and they knew he was loose. They eventually forced Dave to take care of it. He waited until Henry was quiet and then shoved a plate of drugged food into the shed and locked the door.

Henry woke up as ice cold water jetted over him. Dave was hosing him down in the overgrown front yard. His leash was attached to a wooden post now, where he would stay for another six and a half years. It only took about a week to wear a dirt circle around it as he paced, hungrily, as far as the chain allowed. Marnie cried when she saw him there. It wasn't long before he had company.

SIXTEEN

Vincent shook him and Henry woke with a start. "Bad dream," whispered the priest.

"Thanks." He sat up.

"You want to come in the kitchen? Melissa is up too. We can be a little company for each other at least."

Henry nodded and stood up to follow Vincent to the kitchen. Melissa handed him a cup of boiled water. He sat at the table and watched the wax candle sputter and flare.

"Did you figure out how to get there?" Vincent asked Melissa. She pushed a map closer to the candles.

"He marked us as here. The shortest route would be this way. Should take us two days on foot, but we don't know how bad the roads are. I can't recall seeing any pavement in a while, can you?"

Vincent shook his head and they both looked at Henry. "Not since we left the Lodge," he said, "but I wasn't exactly following roads, I was chasing Phil's men. Does it matter?"

Melissa shrugged. "I guess for healthy people it wouldn't. One or two days more hiking might make them a little thinner but none the worse for wear. But we can't afford that. We need to get it right the first time or find supplies on the way."

"Can't we just hole up here until we're back to normal?" asked Henry.

Vincent glanced doubtfully at the small pile of supplies on the counter. "I don't think we have enough food for more than another day or two here, even with us not eating normal meals."

"These people can't walk in their condition," said Melissa, "let alone carry the water we'd need."

"There's a barn. Maybe we can see if there's grain or a car or anything that can help us tomorrow," said Henry.

"And if not?"

"I guess we scavenge and hope for the best."

"It's been eight years Henry, don't you think everything will be ransacked?"

He bit at his ragged, filthy nails and stopped himself, shuddering with disgust. "We're in a fairly rural area, right? And there were lots of cows left. We wouldn't have made it otherwise. Maybe these houses got missed."

Melissa nodded. "This was farmland all through here," she pointed to a large sweep along their route, "Lots of them were dairy, but I remember farm stands on some of them during the summer. Maybe there are still gardens at some. We might find potatoes or carrots that didn't freeze from last year. Or canned stuff in the basements."

Vincent rubbed a hand across the gray stubble on his head. "This is going to take forever," he said.

Henry wondered bleakly if Marnie had forever to wait or if he were already too late.

"Where exactly are we going?" he asked. The other two looked at him as if he were insane.

"The City. Where else is there to go?" said Vincent.

"You sure everyone is going to want to go the same place? Rickey seems dead set against the City. And I need to go back to find Marnie."

Vincent shook his head. "Henry, she's dead."

"You saw her die?"

"No, but how could she still be alive? There were a lot more of us in the beginning, remember? And if one of us didn't get her as she was letting us go, then Phil's men must have. Even if she survived the night, she would have been on the run, alone, with nowhere to go and nothing to eat or protect herself with."

"She's clever and quick. She'll be all right until I can find her."

Vincent and Melissa exchanged a doubtful glance and Henry saw it. "Even if you're right," he continued, "even if she's dead, we have to go back. What if there are still people like us trapped there? What if Phil has gathered more of us?"

"Look, I have no love for those thugs," said Melissa, "But what do you expect six starving people to do? Even if we could make it back to their camp on foot, we have no weapons and we have no medicine to cure the Dogs."

"Don't call them that," Henry said more loudly than he had intended. He rubbed the smooth scars around his neck. "Don't call them that," he said again quietly.

"That's what they are. That's what we were. There's no reason to get upset about it. We didn't make ourselves that way." Melissa tightened her lips into a thin line and turned away.

"We have to get help before we do anything else. We have to get to the City," Vincent broke in.

Rickey stumbled into the kitchen, rubbing his eyes. "What if we don't all want to go?" he asked through a yawn.

"What do you mean? Where else are you going to go?"

"Why go anywhere? This place is quiet, no one will mess with us out here."

"We're almost out of food," said Melissa.

"Oh these old farm houses always have basements filled with stuff. And if not, we'll go find more. And I bet the deer population has exploded."

"You remember seeing any?" asked Melissa, putting a hand on her bony hip.

Henry stared at her. "Why *didn't* we see any? I doubt there's many hunters out this far."

Vincent started up from the table. "Maybe there's another big camp around here. We need to find out–"

"Relax. There's no one out here. They would have taken the cows instead of leaving them to fend for themselves. It was us. Well, people like us. Infected I mean."

"Impossible. There would have to be hordes of people to wipe out the entire deer population of the area. How many of us did it take to bring down one cow? Weren't there eight of us last time we did it?"

"Yeah," said Rickey grinning, "we're just missing the guy that attacked the people that cured us and the scrawny chick that Henry had as a snack."

Henry felt heat rise into his face. He rushed to the door as he choked on bile.

"What?" he heard Rickey say behind him, "It's not

- 100 -

like any of us wouldn't have done the same. You guys got to lighten up. Are you going to drag this along with you forever? It wasn't our fa–"

Henry sucked in a great gulp of cold night air and blocked out the conversation. He tried to think about the deer so he wouldn't think about the girl. There couldn't have been that many people infected, could there? He had seen several before he got sick, sure, but nowhere near enough to wipe out all the deer. Who had been left? He felt dizzy as the emptiness surrounding them hit him.

"Hey," he said, turning back to the others, "Why didn't they eat the cows?"

"What?" asked Rickey.

"If there were so many people infected that they ate the entire deer population, why didn't they eat the cows?"

"The fences kept them out. They couldn't figure it out. I don't remember climbing over anything while I was sick. Falling over stuff, maybe, but not climbing," said Melissa.

"But we ate the cows."

"The fences are down now, rotted away or knocked over. The cows just stayed close to what they knew. But in the beginning, when there were lots of people wandering around, the fences would have mostly been solid. I'm sure some fences broken and some cows were eaten. Or some starved or froze if they were stuck out in the fields. But there were a few left for us."

Vincent shook his head. "Where did they all go? Did they kill each other? Is there anyone left? What are we going to do?" he asked. Henry closed the back door, shutting out the still night, the enormous silence that swallowed everything.

SEVENTEEN

"Sweet," exhaled Rickey as they opened the barn doors. Henry walked over to the large SUV, eyeing it doubtfully. "No, not that," said Rickey and kicked the misshapen tire. It wheezed a little. "This isn't good for anything but scrap. But this beauty," he turned toward the enormous dusty tractor in the back, "might get us all out of here if we're lucky."

"How lucky?"

Rickey walked around toward the back of the tractor and Henry followed him. "Well," Rickey called over his shoulder, "if we're lucky, it's diesel instead of gas. If we're really lucky, Farmer John has a sealed supply of diesel that's still good because it was too much of a pain in the ass to ride down to the local feed store and get it every month. If we're super extra lucky, Farmer John was also smart enough to winterize the thing before the Plague hit and he disconnected the battery. We'll probably have to find a way to clean the filters though, if it's been sitting with fuel in it all this time." Rickey rummaged around a large tool chest he had found.

"Well? How lucky are we?"

"First thing's first," mumbled Rickey and fished around some more in the tool chest, "Hey, pull those doors open on the other side. It's pitch black in here."

Henry moved carefully through the dark back end of the barn and shoved hard on the back doors. They squealed and stuck on the overgrown grass. Henry put his weight against first one door and then the other, wedging them farther open. Bright spring light filtered in. "That's better," called Rickey. Henry found the ladder to the second floor. More out of curiosity than anything else, he climbed up into the loft. Things scuttered out of his way and he hesitated. He could see the outline of another window on the far side though, so he carefully began crossing the floor.

"Careful Henry," called Rickey, "If there are any roof leaks at all then that floor will be soft. Besides, there's probably nothing up there but mice."

"There's another window," yelled Henry, "I'll be careful." The floor was covered with scattered strands of straw and baling twine. It reminded him, perversely of what the castle must have looked like after Rumpelstiltskin was finished. It was still very dark up in the loft, even with both sets of doors open. He gingerly tested the floorboards with each step. Coming at last to the window, he pushed against the wooden shutter and had to catch himself on the frame as it fell completely away with a loud clatter.

"You okay?" Rickey called.

"Yeah, it was just the shutter." Henry turned around, the morning light turned an afternoon gold as flakes of hay made the loft into a swirl of dust around him.

"Anything good up there?"

"Nope. Just some old hay. And probably rats." Henry made his way back to the ladder and down into the now bright barn.

"Got it!" Rickey waved a dented pack of cigarettes triumphantly.

"That's what you were looking for? You realize that might be the last pack you're going to find in a while right? And they probably taste like crap."

Rickey shrugged, tapped the case on his wrist and pulled one out. He grinned and held it up to his mouth. "You know what's weird?" he said before putting it into his mouth and talking around it, "Haven't had one in eight years, you'd think I would be over them. Eight years. And there's other stuff more important. We're starving to death, haven't gotten laid in almost a decade, but the first thing I thought about when I woke up was having a cigarette." He shook his head and grinned, the cigarette bobbing from the corner of his mouth. He held up a rusty lighter. "You're probably right. I'm going to regret this." He lit it and took a short drag. Henry winced and Rickey coughed and laughed. "Yeah, it tastes like crap all right." He took another drag. "But I don't care. C'mon let's look at the tractor."

There was something comfortable about the stale smoke mixed with the ghost smell of gasoline and diesel and the thick scent of motor oil. Henry had never been a smoker, but there was something lived in, familiar about it. Rickey climbed a stepladder next to a steel drum and looked in. His lit cigarette dangling perilously close to the opening and the crazy patchwork of hair sticking out from his scrawny head made him look like a crazed scientist from an old movie. "Well, it's diesel," said Rickey and Henry tensed as the cigarette bobbed between his lips over the steel drum's cover. He closed the cover and came down from the ladder. "It looks okay, but we won't know until we try it. I'll have to check the tractor first though. See if you can find the battery. I doubt it's held it's charge all this time, but maybe we can figure something out."

There was a metallic squeal as Rickey opened a panel on the tractor. Henry picked his way through extensions and wicked looking farm tools to a workbench, hunting for the battery. "Hey, were you an auto mechanic before?" he called back to Rickey.

"Sometimes. I grew up on a farm. I know about tractors. I won't blow it up."

"I was just curious."

"What were you?"

Henry laughed to himself. "Office worker. I was one of those people that called if you didn't pay your credit card bill."

"Shit. You were a debt collector? No wonder you're so depressed all the time."

There were several batteries on the bench. Henry had no idea which one he was supposed to grab. They all looked the same to him. He tried to lift one, but his arms had lost most of their muscle over the past several months of privation. He looked around for a dolly or wagon to help him.

"Hey, Henry, did you hear about the two cannibals who decided to split their dinner evenly? They decided to start at opposite ends and work toward each other. Partway through, the cannibal who started at the head said to the one that had started at the feet, 'how you doing down there?' and the second cannibal said, 'Great! I'm having a ball!' The first

cannibal got mad and shouted, 'Stop! You're eating too fast!'"
There was a wild laugh.

"You're disgusting Rickey. How can you laugh about that?" said a woman's voice. Henry realized that Rickey'd told the joke for her benefit, not his, but he didn't respond.

"Relax, I'm just trying to get Henry to lighten up a little." Their voices floated through the barn and Henry tuned out the words, just appreciating the company, the presence of other people around him. He wondered if he would be able to leave the City to find Marnie once he got there. To turn his back on civilization and go back out alone into the empty world. But he had promised. It was why he'd been spared. And when he and Marnie returned to the City together, what had happened in the past wouldn't matter quite as much.

Henry found a toboggan hidden behind some old bikes. It would have to do. And if they couldn't get the tractor working, at least he'd found the bicycles. He stood looking at the batteries for a minute. He didn't want to drop them and crack them. He looked around again until he'd found a wide plank of scrap wood. He set it against the bench to use as a ramp down to the toboggan. It took a few tries, but he lifted the first battery and slid it down the plank. It left a smear of brown liquid behind it. Henry frowned. Maybe it was just rainwater. He inched the plank over in front of the next battery. His arms already ached and he was breathing harder than he would have expected. He took a rest. He hefted the next battery and plunked it down on the ramp a little harder than he had meant to as his arms gave up. The wooden bench behind the ramp collapsed in half, spilling tools and batteries onto the floor with a loud crash. Henry stood dazed, looking at the mess. The bench was little more than a cinder, a thin rod of charcoal where the batteries had been. An oily gurgle came from one of the larger batteries and Henry groaned as he realized it was leaking more.

Rickey came running over, followed by Melissa. "I didn't do it on purpose," Henry snapped before they could say anything.

Rickey grinned and threw a bony arm over Henry's

shoulder. "Well ain't that a pissah," he said.

"Are you okay?" asked Melissa.

"Yeah, just frustrated with myself," said Henry.

Rickey shrugged and winked at Melissa. "Don't sweat it. They were cracked anyway. Probably froze at some point. The acid must have eaten right through the bench." He took his arm back and leaned forward to look at the batteries. "These have been no good for a while. Eh, it was a long shot anyway. If it wasn't the batteries then the diesel might not have fired. Hell, I don't even know how to drive the damn thing."

Henry laughed, feeling better. "I thought you said you grew up on a farm."

"I did. I didn't stick around long enough to drive the tractor though."

"What are we going to do?" asked Melissa, "the others are inside packing. They expect to be leaving in the morning."

Henry pointed to the toboggan. "I found some bikes next to this. I don't know if there's a pump or anything, I'm sure the tires are flat by now. We could carry our stuff on this though."

Rickey shoved the remaining battery off with his foot. "We're going to want to clean off that acid. Henry, you too, you need to change or it'll itch and burn."

Henry helped them get the bikes out. There were only four. They found a bicycle pump nearby. Henry left them to figure it out and walked back to the house to find another set of clothes.

EIGHTEEN

The second floor creaked in comforting patterns as Vincent and Pam shuffled between the bedrooms, looking for backpacks or suitcases to take with them. Henry poked the fireplace with an unlit log and then threw it in, sinking onto the old dusty couch. It was hard for him to stay warm. He felt light and battered like driftwood. Like there was no cushion between himself and the world. He basked in front of the fire and started to doze. A low groan from the nearby bathroom woke Henry with a start. He sat up. "You okay?" he called, no knowing which of them was there.

"Yeah. I'm all right," came a shaky voice. Henry got up and walked over to the bathroom.

"What's wrong?" he asked through the door.

"Nothing really, I think my hand has a little infection is all."

Henry didn't know much about medicine, but he was beginning to realize how dangerous any injury could be in this new, ruined world. "Can I come in?" he asked, "Maybe I can help. Or I can go get Vincent, maybe he'll know better…" The door opened a little. He found Molly sitting on the edge of the tub, her face red and swollen from crying. He sat down next to her and gently turned her wounded hand toward the little window. "How long ago did it happen?" he asked.

Molly shrugged. "A few weeks ago, I think. I'm not sure. After the last cow."

Henry let her go and stood up to look in the medicine cabinet. "How did it happen?"

"Is it important?" Molly asked, already tearing up again.

"Sort of. Did your fingers freeze? Did they get cut in rusty wire?"

"They got eaten," Molly sobbed, "but you can't tell anyone."

Henry froze, a bottle of old vitamins in his hand. "Did one of us do it? Did I—"

Molly shook her head. "Not you. It was Pam. Don't

- 107 -

tell her. She already feels so badly about having to tell her kids the things she's done. I know she didn't mean to. She was hungry. We were all so hungry. Please, Henry, don't say anything."

"I won't. But if we can't stop the infection we'll have to tell the others so they can figure out how to help." He shoved the vitamins back into the cabinet with a rattle. "This place has been cleaned out. Probably for the psychiatrist. She was bleeding."

"So what do we do now?" Molly sniffled.

"We'll clean it as best we can and hope that we can find some supplies tomorrow. I can't see in here though." He pulled her out into the living room in front of the fire. The gold and red of the flames only made her swollen hand look worse, but Henry was relieved to see that thick scar tissue had already grown over the wound. He pulled a warm pot of water out of the fireplace and looked around for something clean.

She was watching her hand intently. She flinched before the wet cloth even touched her skin. "You don't have to do this, Henry. I know it's awful, I can go do it myself."

"You don't have to do it by yourself. That's why we're all here together. Don't look at it, it'll only hurt worse."

She flinched again as the cloth touched her. "What did you say you did before? You worked in a grocery store, right?" asked Henry, trying to draw her eyes away from her hand. She took a deep breath and then focused on him.

"Yeah. I mean, I was still in school, but my weekend job was at a grocery store."

"What'd you do there?" asked Henry somewhat absently.

"I was just a stocker. I hated it. The palettes were always so heavy and sorting the produce was the worst. We had to pick out the stuff that wasn't perfect before we'd put the rest out. I used to think it was icky." Molly let a slow sob out and Henry looked up. "Now I'd give anything to touch all that food again."

Henry started wrapping her hand tightly in a strip of clean t-shirt. "You know what I miss?" he said. Molly shook her head, like a kid. "Grilled cheese sandwiches. I haven't had a piece of cheese in a decade. I used to eat a grilled cheese almost every day since I was little boy. How about you?"

Molly winced as he tied the strip but tried to play along. "Peanut butter," she said.

"Peanut butter? I'd bet we can still find peanut butter," said Henry with a grin. But she burst into tears.

"I don't want to be the last person to eat peanut butter. I don't want to be the last person to do anything. Everyone is gone. What does the rest matter? Why did they wake us up, Henry?"

He looked up from her hand. "You didn't want to stay the way we were, did you?"

"No. I just wanted to go with everybody else. Why did Phil have to keep us? Why couldn't we just die like everybody else? Why didn't those people just shoot us? What did we do to deserve waking up alone in this dead world? Why do we have to be the last ones Henry?"

"We aren't the last ones. There are other people out there. We'll find them."

Molly shook her head. "We don't deserve to. Rickey was right. Nobody's going to want to live with murderers and cannibals. Everyone would be better off if we were dead."

"Rickey's an idiot," said Henry, yanking a little too hard on the bandage, "Molly, that Cure cost a lot of time and resources. Maybe, in the beginning, they made it to save themselves, to stop sick people, like us, from attacking them anymore. But that was a long time ago. It would be easier to shoot us now. In fact, the people who did cure us had a gun. They shot the guy that bit them. But they didn't shoot us. They could have left us to starve or freeze while we were sleeping. Instead they brought us in near this warm fire and left us a good supply of food. They even promised to come back if they could. Does that sound like someone who would rather we died?"

"No," she said quietly.

"I can't tell you why we woke up and so many others died. I can't tell you why you wound up in Phil's camp. But we *are* here, whatever things we've done in the past. Maybe there are only a few of us left. Maybe the world finally ripped itself apart with this disease. If that's true, then we better stop thinking of ourselves as the last people. We better start thinking of ourselves as the first people in a new, better world. Cause nothing's going to change otherwise. You understand, Molly?"

She nodded and swiped her face clean with one arm. "Good," he said, turning back to finish bandaging her hand. She was silent for a while, watching the flames. She leaned her head back on the couch. "I'll tell you what I never want to try again," she said.

"Oh yeah? What's that?"

"Beef jerky. I never even want to see the stuff again."

Henry grimaced. "I can agree on that one. Even thinking about the texture makes me queasy." He stood up. "Okay, I think that will do for now. Try not to knock it around and we'll check it in the morning to see if we need to clean it again."

"Promise you won't tell?" she asked.

"I promise," said Henry.

NINETEEN

Henry worried how they would divide the bicycles and gear. He really knew nothing about the people he was traveling with. He knew they had been chained to posts for the past several years, feral, sick, starving. Even if he'd known them before they'd become infected, the experiences of the last decade were enough to change anyone. Henry was startled to realize that he didn't even really know himself any more. He was chasing someone else's daughter because of a promise he'd made when he was a different man. He wondered if he'd ever become that person again. He thought again about the supplies. He was too weak to defend himself if any of the others tried to force something. He looked around at the exhausted, emaciated party. They were too weak as well. It made Henry feel strangely more comfortable to know this.

In the end, it wasn't the supplies or the bikes they fought over anyway. Everyone seemed to sense that sticking together was better, and everyone agreed that they had to leave the farmhouse and at least find more food. They sat on the front lawn eating their powdered milk and oat mush in the morning sun, arguing about where they should go.

"I don't really think we have a choice. None of us are cut out for this," said Molly, scratching at the bandage on her maimed hand, "I mean, it'd be nice if one of us was one of those die-hard living off the land types, but none of us are. We don't even have a doctor if things go wrong or even a way to get food except by scrounging and thieving. Am I wrong?"

Henry eyed the group, but they were silent, no one wanting to admit just how helpless they were without the cushioning of modern society in their daily lives. Rickey fumbled with another stale cigarette.

"Why are you all hesitant to go to the City? The note says we can find help there, maybe find our families. Why are we even arguing about it?" said Pam, already moving to pack the last bits onto the toboggan.

Vincent glanced at Rickey, but it was Melissa that

spoke up first. "Pam, we don't know what we are going to find in the City. All we know is what the note said. We don't know how bad things are other places, maybe there are other cities, better places. Or maybe this city is really just a group of scavengers living on the edge of starvation, constantly battling people like Phil's band."

Rickey snorted and shook his head. "You guys don't get it," he mumbled around the cigarette, "You think people are still going to treat each other the way they did before, like Phil was just a bad egg. You all thought his band was awful, the way they treated us, the way they treated people who happened into their path. Well, I got news for you, folks. Phil was piddling. He was a simple thug with a couple of buddies. This city is organized. They have food. They have medicine. They have a fucking military force big enough to not only protect all that, but to go out and 'cure' mobs of infected people. The City could make life under Phil's lazy rule look like paradise. This isn't the freaking soccer mom convention we're talking about Pam. No one is going to hand us the stuff we need." He flicked his ash into his empty cup in disgust.

"But they cured us, Rickey. Why didn't they just shoot us if they didn't want us?" asked Vincent. He leaned on a bike next to Henry and watched Rickey intently.

Rickey shrugged. "Maybe they needed slave labor. Melissa said there had to be hordes of us to wipe out the deer, maybe there just aren't many regular people left. Someone's got to make the place run. And if they make it look attractive enough, they don't have to round us up, we just walk into it willingly. Don't forget, these people left us for dead for years. Or they shot at us themselves. If you think you're just going to waltz into this town and be greeted with open arms, you're crazier than I gave you credit for. Molly just laid it out clear as day- none of us have any skills in this world. The fact that we've been infected is obvious to anyone with eyes, and as far as we know, we have no friends left alive. We have no value to these people. And I think you'll find Vincent, Christian charity seems to dry up where it's most needed in hard times like these."

"What's your big plan then?" asked Melissa, crossing her arms.

Rickey shrugged. "Who said I had a plan? I just think this one is stupid. Why don't we take our time, look around first. This place isn't so bad. It's not leaking, it's got a fireplace. Even we can probably figure out where the well is. We can forage for food until spring and then see if we can scavenge some vegetable plants from neighboring farms. We might even find a cow or two we haven't eaten yet."

"And when someone like Phil comes along, and decides he wants it for his own?" asked Henry.

"Look Henry, I know you have it in your head to get a posse together from the City and go after Phil's band, but I'm telling you, it's not going to happen. And I sure as hell am not going to get dragged into an ass kicking just because you have a hard-on for some little girl–"

Henry shot up, and Vincent put a hand on his shoulder to keep him from leaping at Rickey who just smiled and sucked on his cigarette.

"We obviously all have different ideas of where we want to go and what we plan to do next," Melissa said quickly, to forestall a fight, "and there's certainly no law that says we have to stick together. But I think it's better if we do, at least for now. I'm going toward the City, but not directly. There's a strip of hotels a few miles to the east in what used to be the suburbs. The stores and restaurants will probably be all cleaned out, but maybe no one thought of the hotels. We can hit the houses around here too, this one hasn't been looted yet, maybe the ones around us have food and supplies. That's where I'm going. You can come with me, or you can keep on arguing. It's up to you." She held the handlebars of her rusty bike and steered toward the grassy lane that used to be the road. Pam and Molly followed her.

"Shit," said Rickey grabbing the last bike, "They might be the last broads in the world. I can't let 'em leave without me." He wheeled after them. Henry grabbed the toboggan's rope and slung it over his shoulder and began pulling it over the dead grass.

"I understand why you need to go back for the girl," said Vincent, "and I'll go with you when you do."

Henry stopped and looked back at him. "Why?" he asked.

"I was the one that killed her mother," said the priest. Henry shook his head and began pulling the sled again.

"I appreciate the sentiment, but I wouldn't recommend it," he called back over his shoulder, "I don't intend on leaving a single one of those monsters alive. And this time, Father, it will definitely be sinning because this time, I'll mean it."

TWENTY

The thin rope bit into Henry's shoulder every time the toboggan bounced over the uneven ground. Vincent fell back from the others to take a turn. Henry handed him the rope. "You killed Elizabeth?"

"I didn't have a choice Henry."

"I know. She came to tell me there had been a cure found. A long, long time ago. She said she was going to get it for me. For all of us, so we'd get rid of Phil. She never came back. I didn't know what happened to her."

Vincent pulled slowly on the sled. "She came back," he said quietly. "I was in the pen at the front of the camp. She came up the hill and she had a gun. She started shooting the other people in the pen with me. I think she must have had the Cure. She must have been shooting them with darts, like the people at the farmhouse. She had to keep reloading and Phil's guys caught her before she could get to me. I was the only one left, the others just slumped down on their posts and fell asleep. Phil came up to her and started yelling. I was too far away to hear though. He came up to the palings and looked at the other people in the pen. I heard him say she'd ruined perfectly good 'dogs,' that he'd have to kill them now, because how was he supposed to let them live? They'd know what he'd done to them." Vincent paused to wipe his eye.

"He *knew*? He *knew* it was a cure and he knew how it would work. And he still let us stay sick. How many years were we sick when we could have been better? How many more people did we kill?"

"He didn't just let us stay sick. He killed the people she cured. Shot em. Left them in the pen. Then he pushed her in and shut the door again. He hooked my leash and pulled me back to the palings. Then he unclipped the leash." Vincent stopped and sobbed, his face in his hands, the toboggan rope forgotten, hanging loose on his arm. "But she ran, and the people he'd just shot, they didn't. So I didn't get her first. I wish I had. I wish I'd killed her first before I ate those others. It took days, because I was the only one left. Phil's guys did come and get most of the dead ones after the first few days, but it still took me a long time to bother with her. The first day, she cried and cried. The girl came out and screamed and cried and stuck her little fingers through the fence to touch her mom. Phil threatened to throw the little girl into the pen too, so Elizabeth told her to go away, begged her not to come back. And then she just sat in the farthest corner from me and cried. I don't think she slept. But I did. After I gorged myself, I fell asleep. After the first day, she didn't cry anymore. She didn't try to escape. The girl's father came once to the fence. Elizabeth asked him to kill her, before I did. Asked him to shoot her. He was too scared of Phil to do it. She spat on him and turned her back on him and he went away. Finally, after a few days, she fell asleep. She wasn't given anything to eat and refused to drink from the same trough as me until the last day or two. She must have been so hungry. But in the end, I was hungrier."

Henry watched the others disappear into the slumped wreck of a house down the lane. He didn't want to think about Elizabeth. He didn't want to think about the terrible pens where they had spent the last eight years, and he didn't want to think about Marnie screaming for her mother. He squeezed Vincent on the shoulder, feeling awkward and nervous, and then walked toward the rotting house without saying anything at all.

Henry walked around to the backyard so he wouldn't have to see the others and to look for a shed, a garden, anything that would help them. There was a broken window in the back, so he could hear the others talking behind him. It was pleasant background noise. He knew that he should feel sad for Elizabeth, for Vincent, but it was distant, like an old scar, long healed. He was overwhelmingly relieved that she hadn't come to find him first and that she hadn't been thrown to him to eat. An old wood shed sat in one corner of the yard. Henry suppressed a shudder as he started toward it. He ought to have left Phil to die in the first shed, to bleed to death after his "accident." The shed door was padlocked. Henry tugged on the rusted hasp. It pulled loose after a few yanks but he hesitated before opening the door. Part of him insisted that there was someone infected behind it, kept like him. He opened the door. An old riding mower and a few garden tools were all that lay inside. There was an old red gas can but it smelled like turpentine and Henry didn't have anything to put it in anyway. He shut the door and turned back to the house. The others had found some old shoes to replace the layers of socks some of them had resorted to, but not much else. They walked on to the next house without really speaking much. Melissa led them over fields and through fence gaps, somehow knowing where they were going without following the crumbling road. It was only a few hours before they'd left the rural farms behind and began seeing small clusters of houses as the neared the suburbs outside the City. They'd found very little in the farms, most of the food was gone, eaten by animals or long rotted away, even the one basement they found lined with jars of preserves had mostly crusted with rust or turned to vinegar inside the glass. The group had turned glum, as even Rickey started to realize how helpless they would be without outside help. Henry had taken the toboggan back from Vincent and lagged behind the others a few paces. They reached the first small cluster of houses, and Molly suggested that they split up, since the afternoon was quickly wearing away. Melissa looked doubtful, but everyone else seemed too weary to care much. The only thing that moved was an old plastic ribbon that flapped from one of the porches, the corpse of some long ago birthday party. Henry had an overwhelming desire to tear it off. There were no birds, no dogs, no car horns. He had been able to push it out of his head before. There had at least been bird song at the farm. He hadn't expected much more from the other farms, they were isolated, rural. But here– he had a dreadful, passing instant where he feared he had gone deaf. The spring wind still sounded in the hollow places between the houses. When Henry was little, his mother had read him the story of the Pied Piper. It had given him nightmares for years. Standing in the suburban street, Henry realized that the scariest part was not the fate of the children who got swallowed up by the mountain. It was being the little lame boy who had to turn back all alone. And here they were, the leftovers, the gleanings. He understood now, why Molly had been crying.

"All right," said Melissa, interrupting his thoughts, "leave the sled here so we can just dump what we find onto it. Ten minutes and then we'll meet back, if anyone finds a jackpot, call out."

Henry stood next to the toboggan for a moment as the other wandered away. He was reluctant to leave it. What little they had was all packed on it. *There's nothing there, Henry. A few cans, a box of milk, some old rags. Let it go.* He looked around him. Everything was quiet except a few curtains rustling where the others were hunting for more. He turned away from the sled and walked to the house next to it. It was blue once, now beginning to peel in spots. The roof looked solid though. Feeling foolish, Henry knocked on the front door. He waited for a moment and then tried the door. Locked. He began walking around the house. The living room window was one solid pane. He felt badly about breaking it and decided to find another way. The bathroom window was too small and the kitchen window was too high off the ground. He looked around for a rock, but on his way back he found the basement bulkhead doors. They were loose. He opened them onto a very dark hole. "Hello?" he called, and swung himself down onto the ladder.

For the first time, Henry got lucky. In the thin gray light from the bulkhead he could see several flashlights hanging neatly from a post. He tried one and was relieved to find that it worked. He gathered up the rest without even checking. He swung the flashlight around until he found a cardboard box. It was filled with empty jars. He pulled them out and dumped the other flashlights in. Placing the box on the wood stairs, he walked around the basement. Tools and a furnace, a washing machine and dryer. Just a typical house. He wondered for a moment whether he ought to go through the tools. He decided anything other than the essentials would be too heavy for their wasted frames for now. He dragged the box up the wooden stairs and into the kitchen. There was a rustling and scrabbling as he shut the basement door. Henry froze. "Hello?" he said. There was a squeak and Henry laughed at himself. He prepared himself to be disappointed, expecting that the mice had gotten to any food left in the house. Most of the cabinets were empty, the contents carried away either by the former owners or looters or in tiny bits over the years by rodents. But he found a few ceramic cannisters sitting on the back of the sink. Rice, coffee, sugar, pasta noodles. He smiled to himself as he put them in the box. He had no idea whether they would still be okay, but for the moment, it didn't matter. A jar of bouillon cubes and a few containers of spices were swept into his box as well. Other than that, the kitchen was empty. Henry took one more moment to sift through the silverware drawer until he found a can opener. His flashlight sparkled on the silver refrigerator front. Henry put his box down on the kitchen table and moved closer to the refrigerator. There were photos of a family taped over the front, but they didn't bother him. It was like the photos that used to come already inside of picture frames. Not real, distant, strange. And it wasn't the crayon Christmas cards or the clunky homemade magnets covered in seashells. They weren't connected with anything. Just something to pack away in a box. Someone else's history.   It was the torn envelope that made Henry stop. Just a normal business envelope, it's little cellophane window peeling inward, the top flap ragged where it was opened. The return address was what caught his eye. It was his old work address. There was a yellow sticky on the front of the envelope. "Last Payment! Let's celebrate!" it said. That was all. Henry hadn't thought about his job much. Not even when he was working there. It wasn't something he really liked or disliked. It was just a job. He wasn't terrible at it, though he didn't much like harassing people for money they didn't have. He'd still done it. Regularly. People that managed to pay off their debt completely just didn't happen very often. Closing an account had always been one of Henry's secret joys, though it meant less money for his company. He imagined the utter relief these people must have felt with that last payment. Like a thousand pounds lifted off their backs. And then– Henry shook his head. He hoped they had celebrated before it didn't matter any more.

He turned away from the refrigerator and made his way with his box into the living room. There wasn't much of immediate use, and Henry was getting nervous about the others, so he hurried past and into each of the home's bathrooms, emptying the medicine cabinets into the box without even looking at what he was doing. He wondered if anyone else would remember toothpaste and soap and grabbed them too, narrowly avoiding a nasty bite from some mice that had made a nest in old toilet paper under the sink of the upstairs bath.

Henry opened the door to the first bedroom, looking for blankets and towels, but then quickly backed up. The curtains were torn down, letting the deep yellow of late afternoon in. The room was purple with dried blood, the whole coated in a stiff, chalky layer of it. Furniture was tipped, bedclothes torn to streamers and dragging nail marks raked the walls. A heavy wall mirror lay smashed, face up, where it had fallen, reflecting the gore and the terrible, breathless stillness in a thousand different pieces. "I'm sorry," said Henry, as if he'd caught someone naked in the bathroom. He shut the door. He looked toward the other bedroom, but decided to skip it and headed quickly down the stairs. He unlocked the front door, took a quick glance around the room to make sure he wasn't missing something vital and then picked up his overflowing box and opened the door.

There was a small boy climbing over the toboggan, pulling things off. He couldn't be more than five or six, probably not even born yet when the Plague had hit. An odd sensation of missing time hit Henry again. He put the box down on the front step, just as the boy looked up and saw him standing there. The boy froze, a dented can in one hand, his knees already tensed to spring away. Henry held up his hand, "Wait," he said.

The boy began running. "Infected!" he screamed, "Infected! Infected!"

"Wait!" Henry called after him and began running down the steps. He made it halfway across the street before he heard gunshots blast around him. He should have run back to the house. Instead he threw himself over the sled, as if they were trying to shoot the supplies instead of him. Henry held his arms over the back of his head and winced into the pavement. The cans jittered and clunked and poked him as his stomach tensed over them with each shot. Whoever was shooting wasn't very good at it, and they didn't waste many bullets on him, for which Henry was very thankful. He wondered if it was actually the little boy himself. He pushed the thought aside and sat up, still shaking. The others were running toward him, and Henry's relief that they hadn't just abandoned him almost overwhelmed him.

"Are you hurt?" asked Pam as she reached him.

"No, but I think we're missing some stuff."

Rickey scowled and picked up a shovel from the sled. He brandished it and made a move to go after the kid. "No, don't," said Henry, "it was just a little boy. I think he might be alone. He probably needs it more than us. I tried to talk to him, but I guess I scared him." He picked himself up from the street and rubbed the side of his face with one hand. "I guess I look worse than I thought," he said with a rueful smile.

"We all do," said Melissa. "Let's get out of here before the kid's big brother shows up. Everyone grab your stuff, we're going to find a place to hole up for tonight at least."

"Wait," said Henry, "did anyone find a wagon or a wheelbarrow or anything? This sled is starting to splinter on the broken tar."

"I found two of those bike stroller things," said Molly, "And more bikes. But I need help hooking them up."

"I'll pull this stuff to you then," said Henry, jogging back to retrieve his box. The others drifted off to get their things. Henry followed Molly back to a garage and felt immediately better as they pulled the sled inside. In the end, they had found so much that it filled both of the small trailers and a hiking pack that Molly volunteered to wear for a while. The sun was setting as they headed out of the small suburban street and onto the main road. Melissa assured them that they'd be at the hotel by the time the light was gone, so they put their tired legs through a little more and rode into the thickening dark.

TWENTY-ONE

Melissa led them into the alleyway between two hotels. "We'll go in the back way, far from the lobby," she said softly, "by the pool. We can lock ourselves in there if anyone else is living here."

They wheeled their bikes through the glassed in hallway. The pool was empty long ago, but it still smelled faintly of chlorine. Henry felt a little exposed in front of the large plate-glass windows, but they overlooked an empty courtyard between them and the lobby, and everything looked dark and still. Melissa led them into the large, windowless women's locker room. She swept a flashlight beam over the area before Pam flipped the light switch. There were a few gasps as the light flickered on. "I thought so," said Pam, "I hope no one else knows."

"How did you know?" asked Vincent.

"There was a really bad storm several years ago," said Pam, "everyone in the area was without power for weeks, except this place, the hospital and the high school. Those got power back first. This hotel just happened to be on the same line as the hospital. They could have made a killing. Instead they housed the electricians who were fixing the lines for free and opened their doors for anyone that wanted a hot shower or to do laundry while they waited for the power to come back on. I brought my kids swimming here for a few weeks."

"But why would it still be on now after all these years?"

Pam shrugged. "I assume the City restored power at least to itself. It's been a long time. Someone would have figured out how to get it running again. And they'd probably power the hospital first. We aren't that far away. We're just lucky that the hotel happens to be on the same line."

"You mean we can have hot showers and sleep in our own rooms in an actual bed? Maybe we can figure out how to run the hotel videos," said Rickey excitedly.

Melissa shook her head. "Sorry, but we can't do any of those. The boiler probably ran out of oil ages ago, so the showers will be cold, if we're lucky and the pipes haven't burst yet." She walked over to the sink and twisted the tap on. It chugged for a moment and then spat brown water that gradually ran clear.

"Why can't we sleep in the hotel rooms?" asked Rickey.

"The battery packs on the door locks are all dead. That's why we were able to get in here. We couldn't lock any of the bedroom doors either. And every one we open to sleep in, we risk finding someone hostile. Plus we'd be farther from a quick exit."

"And separated," said Molly, with a panicked look.

"The pool entrance and these locker rooms have manual locks, and we're close to an exit with all of our gear nearby. And–" Melissa walked over to a wooden door and opened it, flicking another light on. "There is a pass through here that used to be a sauna, so we can use both locker rooms and still be together."

"Why are you so convinced that other people are here?" asked Rickey, "we didn't know about the electric until Pam turned the light on. And what are the chances that anyone else is left alive that knows or would expect that the electricity has been restored out here too?"

"The only reason we didn't know is because we came during the day," said Henry with a dull groan. He sat down on a changing bench. "The parking lot lights, the lobby lights, any lighted signs that aren't broken, they're all on timers aren't they? And now the sun has gone down. This place must look like Vegas in the middle of the desert. We should leave now–" he started to stand up, but Melissa shook her head.

"There's nowhere to go Henry. This place is warm, we can lock ourselves in, we can even use the camp stove that Pam found in the shower room if we use the vent. The hotels around us are already dark and they don't have back entrances like this. If we're quiet and don't go wandering around, no one will know we are here. There's no reason for anyone to come down here. We'll be okay, and in the morning we'll sneak out the back again."

"I agree. Let's get the other room set up and all of our gear safe and locked in with us," said Vincent, and he pulled Henry up onto his feet.

Henry gradually felt better about staying, after the doors were locked and the cracks under the door were stuffed with cloth to keep the light from shining out. Rickey made a casual survey of the old lockers where members and hotel guests had left an assortment of mostly useless junk. Vincent rummaged through the food trying to choose something that would fill them up without killing them. Henry hoped it would be more than oatmeal mush this time. He went to take a shower. Cold or not, it would still make him feel more himself if he could get really clean. He covered the shower room mirror with an old towel from the lockers. He'd seen his face as he shaved, but he had tried to pretend it was someone else. And he wasn't ready to see the scars over the rest of him. He didn't want to know what the kid had seen that made him run screaming away.

The water started a dark brown and Henry waited for it to clear. He waited a few extra seconds before he realized he had been waiting for it to heat up out of sheer habit. He stood under the water and it was colder than the pond had been. He didn't care. He stood under the water and smelled the ghost scent of bleach and soap and hair gel. He found his own soap and the smell of his own patches of rotten, broken wounds disappeared underneath the bar. He tried not to wince where it stung his cuts or where his too tight skin felt sorely pressed between the bones jutting out from inside and the water tapping down from outside. Gradually, an aroma of food cut through the water and Henry turned off the shower. He sighed as he pulled clean clothes over his clean skin. For the first time in as long as he could remember, he felt good. Not just an absence of pain, but really good. He even pulled the towel off the mirror and faced himself. He still didn't recognize himself. Too old, too thin. He wondered if Marnie would scream and run away like the boy did. She had more reason to. She'd seen what he'd done.

"C'mon handsome. Chow's on," Rickey snickered and

elbowed him. Henry shook his head and went back into the women's changing room. It was warmer in there, not just because of the camp stove's recent use, but because everyone was already sitting there. Henry didn't understand how six walking bundles of bone had the energy to produce body heat, but they did.

"Careful Pam, we still have to be careful," said Vincent as he watched her ladle food into bowls.

"We have to eat or we won't be able to walk," said Melissa.

Vincent nodded. "I know, but take it easy. Otherwise we won't be going anywhere."

Henry jumped as a toilet flushed behind him. The noise was so foreign, so loud. Molly walked out of the stall, scratching her hand loose of it's bandage. Henry could see the stumps of her fingers had blackened and shriveled even more. She looked up and saw him watching her and burst into tears. He hurried over to her. The rotting smell clung to her, even though they had all scrubbed every inch of themselves. "It's going to fall off," she said.

"No, I'm sure it's just infected. I think I found a first aid kit in that house. Let's find it." She waited by the sink, suppressing a sob and unwrapping the remaining bandages while Henry rummaged for the first aid kit. He frowned when he found it. It was old, hadn't even been new when the Plague hit. And it was very basic. He doubted there would be anything of use inside, and if there was, it would probably be spoiled. But he glanced over at Molly, still looking at her blackened hand, shoulders pulled up and in, a cave of loneliness and fear. He hoped whatever he did wouldn't make it worse. Or kill her. He walked over, opening the case as he went so he could avoid her eyes. At least there were fresh bandages inside. He pulled out a packet of antiseptic wipes. The foil paper was creased and soft, but it wasn't broken. Henry hoped they'd still be good. He held out his hand and she lay her wounded one in it. He hesitated and then pulled out the wipe. "Does it hurt?" he asked, and gently applied the wipe. She flinched but then relaxed. "A little," she said, "but it's mostly numb. I think it's dead." A low sob escaped her.

"Vincent might be better at this-" Henry started.

"No! No. I don't want anyone else to know until they have to. You already know. You can do first aid right?"

"I'm an office clerk Molly. I just have basic work safety type training. This is not that." Henry shook his head and hissed through his teeth as the blackened skin crackled and puffed under the wipe. "We need something stronger. We need to find a doctor too." He fished around in the kit. She put her good hand on his arm to stop him.

"Maybe we shouldn't waste this stuff," she said.

"It's not a waste, you're hurt."

"But you can't fix it. Maybe there's nobody left that can fix it. Maybe we should just let it go."

Henry stared at her. "We can't 'just let it go,' you'll get very sick. It might even kill you."

"I don't think I'm cut out for this. I was a student. I can't fix anything, I don't know how to build anything or where any secret bunkers are. I can't shoot, I can't fish, I've never even had a garden. I didn't survive this long because I'm smart or resourceful or valuable to anybody. I just got lucky. I don't think that's going to work any more. Maybe we should just let it go. Survival of the fittest."

"That's crap Molly. Sure, we're all still here because we're lucky. There are people that were much better prepared than we were that are dead now. But that doesn't mean we can't learn how to grow food or build a shelter or bandage a wound. We aren't dead yet."

"I've only got one hand, even if we stop the infection. I'm not going to be any good to anyone," she sniffled.

"And Vincent's only got one eye. And Rickey has a smoking problem. And we're all depressed, starved, and weak. Look what we've survived through. If we give up now all those years were for nothing. All those people we killed to survive, died for nothing."

"Maybe they did," whispered Molly, "This is all too big and too terrible. It doesn't *mean* anything. There's no lesson here. We didn't deserve to suffer. They didn't deserve to die. There's nothing to learn. It was misery. It *is* misery. That's all that's left."

Henry shook his head. "I don't believe that. I *can't* believe it. But let's pretend for a minute that you are right. Let's pretend the world would be better off without us. Let's pretend the rest of our lives will be nothing but suffering and that we'll be better off if we end it. Look at your hand Molly, do you know what that is?"

She shook her head.

"I'm not a doctor," he continued, "but I'd be willing to bet that is gangrene. It smells and looks like it. It's not a good way to die. You'll be in pain, more than you are now. You'll struggle to breathe. You'll get confused, maybe do something dangerous for the rest of us. Or we'll have to sit and watch you die for days. If you sit down and die, we aren't going to just abandon you. Look around, Molly. Look at them."

Molly watched the others gathered around the little camp stove. "They're walking skeletons," said Henry, "but they'll still stay to help you. And by the time you die, we'll be out of what little bit of food we have. We'll starve and die too. You don't want us all to die, do you?"

"No, of course not."

"We all have to choose whether or not to go on in this world. I'm not trying to change your mind. You're right, some people truly won't be cut out for this life. And some won't be able to live with the things they've done to survive this long. I don't know if I'll ever be able to move on from what I've done. But this is a bad way to go. This isn't an easy death. So I'm not just going to let it go. In a few days, we'll be in the City. We'll go our separate ways and make our own decisions. Let me think that I've helped you for now. Just for now. Let me sleep a little easier knowing I did one good thing against the balance of so many bad. Okay?"

Molly covered her face with her hand and sobbed. "Okay," she mumbled.

He pulled out a small bottle of hydrogen peroxide and some foil packs of antibiotic cream. "Is there soap in that dispenser?" he asked.

Molly used her good hand and pressed hard on the dispenser. A dribble of soap oozed slowly out. "It must be almost all dried up," she said. Henry reached over and caught the small bubbles of soap.

"Good enough. This peroxide's probably no good. Almost all water now, but we'll try it anyway. The soap might help some too." He glanced up at Molly. "Sorry, this is going to hurt. I'll try to be gentle." He tried the peroxide first. It fizzled halfheartedly and Molly didn't even seem to notice. He'd hoped it would take away some of the dead skin. He scrubbed her hand gently with the soap and water from the sink. She tried not to yell, but her arm was shaking by the time he was done. It was cleaner than it had been, and fluid leaked from several blisters. Henry hoped that was a good sign. The smell still made him want to gag. He did his best to wrap it in sterile gauze. "Do you think we should put a glove over it to protect it?" he asked, holding the ghastly purple plastic up.

Molly shrugged. "I guess so. It probably can't make it worse. It'll keep the dirt from the road out anyway."

Henry stretched the glove as much as he could so that it wouldn't snap on her fragile skin and guided it over the gauze. It was a lumpy mess, with loose plastic fingers where hers were missing and it was anything but subtle. At least it was done. Molly looked doubtfully at it, her eyes still oozing slow tears. Henry squeezed her good hand and caught her eye. "It's going to be okay, you know. We're going to find a doctor tomorrow. The City will have medicine to help."

Molly nodded but didn't say anything. Henry turned and packed up the kit, trying to put the blackened skin and the smell from his mind as he rejoined the others. Pam handed him a bowl. He looked up as a sharp crackle filled the room.

"Shut that off," hissed Melissa, "someone will hear it."

Rickey fiddled with the volume on the dusty television. "I just want to see if there's anyone broadcasting. A hotel movie on a loop or something. Public access, a technical difficulties screen, anything. I just want to see something human."

"It's been eight years. There's no generator still running. You aren't going to find–" Melissa stopped suddenly as a well-groomed woman appeared on the screen. Rickey almost fell off the bench he was standing on. Everyone else was utterly silent.

"...Farm is warning of a frost overnight tonight, so if you've already plowed, it should be a good day for rock picking tomorrow. Double shifts are requested at the Farm for the next few days in preparation for the growing season and to ensure that everyone that wants to has the opportunity to attend the trial without production falling behind. We've received fresh news from the prison on the December Plague Trial, the warden reports that Dr. Gerta Schneider, long sought in connection with this case, has turned herself in to the authorities without incident. Judge Hawkins has asked us to report that she will stand trial at the same time as Dr. Pazzo and Anne Connelly when court resumes on Monday, her defense having been prepared by her attorney in her absence." The woman's voice was calm and clear, practiced.

"It must be coming from the City," said Molly, her spoon still hanging in the air between her mouth and the bowl.

"Shh," said Rickey.

The newswoman continued, "In other recent news, the final Cure team has sent word back to headquarters. There have been no new survivors found on this trip. The Cure team has been ordered to come home. There will not be another team sent. The Military Governor asked us to air a special address on this matter." The screen stuttered for a second and a tired, middle-aged man at a cluttered desk appeared on the screen.

"Good evening. It's been almost nine years since the December Plague began. I know how much you– we have all suffered, but with determination and cooperation, we've made great strides in recovering. Our City is safe. Our people are fed and warm. Electricity and communications have been restored. The people that were responsible for the outbreak are in custody and will face justice in the coming weeks. Hundreds and hundreds of Infected have been cured and

- 130 -

returned to their families. But we will never be able to restore even a fraction of all that we've lost as a city, a country, a species. Our security has been hard won. Thousands of good men and women have sacrificed themselves to protect us. Their lives have consecrated this small bastion of civilization. The outside world has become a violent, wild hell. But our City remains safe and strong even in the heart of that hell.

I know how many of you still cherish secret hopes that your loved ones will be found and returned to you, even after all this time. But it is time to face the truth now. Our former way of life, our neighbors, our family members, even some of the beliefs we strove to exist by– have all perished." The man cleared his throat and reached for a clear cup of water. He wrapped his fingers around it and turned it back and forth, but didn't pick it up to drink. He looked back at the camera. "The Cure was a noble cause, and very effective. Without it, we would probably have been overrun long ago. I heartily salute and thank the medical teams and our militia for doing their work so thoroughly and for so very long. But our City is small. And yet, it may be that we are the largest gathering of humans remaining in the world. Within our wall lies all the remaining knowledge of centuries of human life and advancement. I know we aren't naive. I don't think there is one of you out there that truly believes anyone else is going to swoop in and save us after all these years. So our responsibility is great. And our resources are very limited. As much as I wish it could be otherwise, there is no one left to be saved from the Plague. No one has been found for several months, and those found in the past few years were people that avoided the first infection only to succumb much later as they emerged from their bunkers. Exposure, starvation, conflict with healthy folks or wild animals have carried off the rest. So I have recalled the Cure teams. Their expertise is desperately needed here."

"I know what a blow that must be for some of you. Like you, I expected my loved ones to be discovered in a Cure camp every day. I checked the Found Lists every morning along with all of you. For all of us, there will be a period of mourning, one that has been long delayed by uncertainty. Though it feels as if you've just received fresh news of your loved ones' deaths, today is the beginning of a safer, brighter future. With the upcoming trial, we will see our wrongs redressed, and our questions answered. The Infected are gone. We no longer need to fear them, our conflict with them is over. We can turn our attention to expanding our resources, to securing ourselves against bandits, and to restoring and repopulating beyond the Barrier. We have a great task before us now, and it is up to us, who remain behind, who live on after the fever has passed, to expand what others have fought so hard to shield. It is time for us to begin reclaiming our world, to dedicate ourselves to advancing civilization in the outside wastes."

"That is the second reason I've asked to speak tonight. Scouts have reported that electricity has been restored to places beyond the boundaries of the City, either through makeshift means of generators, unconventional sources such as windmills and solar panels, or by tapping into the City lines. So some of you listening may be outside of the City itself. I want you to know that the City will welcome anyone into it's borders. As long as you are willing to work, you will be safe, clothed, fed, housed, have access to medical care and school for your children. We have many things to offer that the outside world is now bereft of. And as I have said, we will be expanding beyond the walls of the City, now that the Cure teams have finished their work. You don't even need to change your residence. There is nothing required of you except that you treat others with decency— both Immunes and Cured. We have all had to do things we regret, things maybe, that go against our natural beliefs and morals, just to survive. We have all stolen, looted, killed. In the past. But those things are not necessary any longer. If we work together we have more than enough. This City— I— will no longer tolerate looting or raiding. There will be no more 'hunting parties' targeting the Cured, there will be no more abuse of the weaker members of our society. This is your one chance. At this moment, the slate is wiped clean. Whatever you've done in the past is over. What you do from this point on, however, will determine your fate." The man's face lost it's calm kindliness. It tightened, hardened as he stared now, directly into the camera. "When we arrive, and we will someday, no matter how far you are from our walls, if we find pillage or murder or torture, we *will* wipe the perpetrators out as well as any who aided them in their cruelties. Our former way of life may be gone, but we are striving to resurrect what was the best in our society, the good in our natures. We cannot turn a blind eye to those that would use our vulnerability to sway us to our worst actions toward each other. We are coming. If you'd rather live in barbarism and misery than participate in a regulated, decent society, then you had better flee as far away as you can and hope that we are too slow to catch up with you in your lifetime. We will show you no more mercy than you have shown to your victims."

"Holy shit," breathed Henry and then quickly added, "Sorry, Father."

"What?" asked Rickey from his spot underneath the television.

"Rome just declared war on the rest of the world. He better hope there aren't more organized groups listening in."

"You sure you still want to go there?" asked Rickey.

Henry stared at him. "You heard him, you sure you *don't* want to?"

The pretty newswoman reappeared, looking somewhat nervous. "We have just a few more announcements for the night, before we run tonight's movie request. Immune men and women who are unwed and are between the ages of thirty and forty are reminded that they are required to register this month with the DHRS for the new Cupid Service program that began its trial run last week. Residents on the dockside are reminded to boil their water before consumption…"

TWENTY-TWO

Henry walked back into the men's changing room, out of earshot of the television. He didn't think he wanted to hear any more. He almost tripped over Pam who was sitting on the floor, her back to the lockers.

"Pam? What's wrong?" Henry asked. *What a stupid question,* he realized as he sat down next to her. She shuffled over a little to make room for him.

"It's just– all this time, I assumed that my kids and my husband were okay. That they were immune and living somewhere waiting for me. But now that seems ridiculous."

"Why?"

"Well, if I wasn't immune, then my kids probably weren't either, right? That's how it works. And my husband wouldn't have left them, even if they were sick."

"I'm not sure how it works. But maybe, if your husband was immune, the kids have just as much chance to be immune as sick, I'd think."

"But what if they weren't? What if there isn't anyone waiting for me in the City? What if I never find out what happened to them?"

Henry hesitated, then put an arm around her bony shoulder and gave it a light squeeze. It felt odd, foreign, to touch anyone without feeling the overwhelming need to bite. Henry was relieved that he didn't feel it any more. "Hey, even if they weren't immune, it doesn't mean we won't find them. You heard that governor guy, he said hundreds of people were cured. Maybe they were cured and are waiting for you right now."

Pam shook her head. "I hope not."

"Why?"

"I think I'd rather they were dead than that they had to go through what we did."

Henry sighed. He was silent for a moment, one arm still around her shoulder, his face turned to the ceiling. He looked back at her. "I hope nobody went through what we did. I hope Phil and his men were utterly unique. Your family wasn't with you when you arrived at the Lodge, were they? When did you get separated?"

"I think I got sick early. I only remember one thing on the news– just something about the hospital and police seeing lots of people who had gotten into fights or who had hurt themselves in home accidents. Was there more than that?"

"Lots more. You must have been one of the first ones."

"My kids were on a ski trip with their school a few weeks before winter break. I didn't notice anything, except that my husband scolded me for being clumsy for a few days, and I kept forgetting to turn things off. I just thought I was tired. One day, my husband went to work as usual. It had snowed a little, overnight, so after he left, I went outside to shovel the walkway. The mailman had left a package by the door, something that wouldn't fit in the box. It was a present I'd ordered for one of the kids. And when I came outside, the neighbor's dog was peeing on it. That *damn* dog. I hated that dog. It marked everything in the neighborhood. And I got really angry. Really angry. I don't get angry, Henry. Never had a fight with my husband or even my parents, never even raised my voice with my kids. Even when they were going through their tantrum phases. I just don't like being angry. So I try really hard to stay calm."

Henry nodded, because she seemed to be waiting for some response.

"But I was angry at that dog. And I chased him with the shovel. I just wanted to smash him with it. I'd never hurt an animal or person in my life before. Never, ever wanted to. I never even spoke to the neighbor about her dog's bad habit. We just shooed him away and figured stuff like that was going to happen. But not that day. I chased that dog all over the neighborhood, waving the shovel and screaming at it. I couldn't catch it though. Finally I got too tired to chase it anymore. So I turned around. I decided to go to the neighbor's house and tell her to control her dog. That's all that I meant to do, I swear on everything sacred, that's all I intended when I went there. I got to her house and banged on the door. She let me in, of course. Why wouldn't she? We'd always been

- 135 -

friendly. She shut the door and looked at me expectantly. I started to yell about her dog, but all that came out of me was this scream. This endless scream of anger and hate and wanting to hurt."

Pam brushed her face with the palms of her hands. She didn't look at Henry. He looked away from her, feeling vaguely as if he'd caught her doing something private, as if he'd walked in on her in her bedroom, rather than listening to a story she was willingly telling. A story he had lived too.

"And my neighbor just stared at me, confused for a second. 'What's wrong, Pam? Are you hurt? Are you sick?' she asked, and she tried to touch my shoulder, to guide me to the couch or something. She was saying something about calling my husband or an ambulance when I bit her hand. She yelled and smacked me, but I didn't let go. Even then, there was some part of me that thought it was a wrong thing to do. But it was as if I'd been craving that exact sensation for– for forever, and finally feeling her skin dimple and split under my teeth. It makes me nauseous to think about now, but then– it was like my worst pregnancy craving tripled. I couldn't let go. And when she finally forced me off, I just bit her again, in the leg. I just kept biting, all the time she's struggling to get me off, her skin tearing more and more in my mouth as she struggled. Eventually she was quiet and still. And I– I still kept biting. I should have been caught right there. I'm sure someone on the street must have called the police by then. But that damn dog came running up to the back door and kept barking and barking. Finally, I was so angry, I left my neighbor's body lying in the hallway and ran to the back door. It had a weak latch, had for years. My husband tried to fix it for her a few times, but the door needed replacing. So I just bashed into it and it opened. And there was the dog. It bolted and I chased it out into the backyard and then into the woods behind. I chased it for a while until I lost it. I wandered around in those woods for a few days I think. I'm not sure how long. The nights were cold, but I didn't freeze, probably because I was still bundled up from shoveling the walkway. Eventually I stumbled out onto a road. A sheriff saw me after a few hours maybe someone called him to come out, I don't know. But he could see I was covered in blood. I wasn't hungry enough to attack him yet, so I don't think I could have been out there that long. But I was still stumbling and only screamed instead of spoke. I think he thought I was drunk or high. He put me in the back of the cruiser and then put me in his little jail cell. I think things must have gotten worse then, because he was gone more and more. He brought me food a few times, kept talking about bringing the doctor, but it never happened. One morning I woke up and he was standing at the cell door looking at me, with his gun drawn. I scrambled up, hungry now for him, though he'd been giving me food, and he backed up. He raised the gun. 'We're supposed to shoot you,' he said, 'I've been doing it all morning. Dozens of you. You keep attacking people. I don't want to, I know you're just sick, but I don't know what else I'm supposed to do.' The gun was shaking a little and I could see his eyes getting red. 'I'm sorry, it's orders,' he said, and would have shot me right then, except an angry man came barreling in through the door behind him. 'He was my son! You shot my boy!' he was yelling. The sheriff didn't even try to defend himself. He just stood there and cried. He dropped the gun onto his desk and just cried while the other man beat the living daylights out of him. Didn't even try to fend him off. But the father must have had something wrong with his heart, or something. He just collapsed after a while. The sheriff said he was going to get help and took the gun and ran out. I never saw him again. But the other guy, he was close enough for me to reach. And he was big. I lived on him a long time. Until Phil and his men raided the police station and found me."

"Your family could be just fine Pam. Maybe your husband picked the kids up from the ski trip and took them somewhere safe, or maybe the teachers on the trip did. You can't give up on them yet. We'll find them when we get to the City."

"Who's that?" asked Vincent as he wandered in.

"Pam's family," said Henry, "she was telling me how she arrived at Phil's camp."

Vincent sat down on the other side of Pam. "You were both there before me," he said. Henry pulled his arm back from Pam's shoulder. She looked over at him.

"You were the first weren't you? That's how you know the girl?" she said.

Henry closed his eyes and rested the back of his shaved head against the cool metal locker. "Her name is Marnie. And yeah, I was first. It's my fault that Phil kept us, that Marnie's parents are dead, and my fault she's still trapped with him." He heard Pam shift away from him, but he kept his eyes closed.

"What do you mean?"

"I knew I was sick, for days before I finally lost it. I did what I could to get Marnie's family ready. If I'd been paying attention I never would have come out to the Lodge with them. I would have hidden in my apartment until it happened. But I didn't realize I was infected yet. By the time Phil wandered in after an accident on the road, I knew I was sick. I was actually relieved. Can you imagine? I was relieved that Phil showed up, because I thought he could help them after I got really sick. As much as I loved Dave, he would never have been able to protect Elizabeth and Marnie on his own. They were so *useless*." Henry banged his head on the hollow locker for emphasis. He looked over at Vincent. "I dragged Phil inside, gave him first aid, did what I could because I thought he could take my place. I thought he'd return the favor. But if I'd known then– I would have left him outside to freeze. And I wouldn't regret it. Even though I know it would have been wrong."

Vincent sighed and shook his head. "I'm not God, Henry. I'm just a man like you, you don't have to defend your feelings to me."

"I don't understand. You and this family were there first and they were your friends, but Phil ended up using you as a guard dog and the rest of the family allowed it?" Pam said.

"Like I said, Marnie's parents were useless. But so was I. I wanted to leave when I felt myself slipping away. I knew I didn't have much time left, I don't know how, I just knew I was getting worse and fast. But I let them persuade me into staying another night, mostly because Phil was still recovering, out of it. He couldn't protect them, and I convinced myself I still could. But Elizabeth drugged my food and they tied me up and put me in the shed." A shudder at the memory of the damp plastic worked it's way up Henry's skin.

"Why?"

"They thought they were protecting me. They thought I'd freeze to death or starve if I left. I was just sick. If they took care of me until it passed, everything would be okay. So they kept me tied up there, in the dark for a long time. I'm not sure how long. Eventually, the food must have run out, and Phil must have recovered, because they stopped feeding me. Until one day, they brought back someone that refused to give Phil something he wanted. And they shoved him in there with me." Henry closed his eyes as Wyatt's cries echoed in his head. "After that, I was basically a garbage disposal, chained to a post, just like the rest of you. Every time an infected person wandered by, they were added to Phil's collection. Some of them had it worse than me. Some of the women– I hope you were just a guard dog Pam."

She blushed and looked away, knowing what he meant. "Your friends just allowed this?"

"Phil kept telling them it was for their protection. But Elizabeth tried to stop it. She went after the Cure when she found out about it. But he killed her. And that kept Dave quiet and obedient until the end. And Marnie- well, she let us go, didn't she? She never gave in to him." He crossed his arms over his thin chest. "Not yet anyway. I have to go back to find her. I left her alone with him."

"She wanted you to get away. She wanted us all to escape, that's why she let us go," said Pam, putting a hand on his shoulder.

"I can't leave her there. She's just a little girl. I have to go back."

Pam and Vincent exchanged a worried glance, but Henry didn't notice. "Go with us to the City. We'll get help.

You heard the broadcast, they'll be happy to help us stop people like Phil. You can't go back alone, half-starved with nothing to defend yourself and nothing to bargain with." Vincent watched him for a long moment until Henry nodded his agreement.

Henry ended up passing out in the center of the blue felt-like carpet of the men's locker room. Someone came along later and covered him with a sleeping bag, and then the others wandered in eventually, when Rickey could bear to silence the television, and slumped down beside him. The warm jumble of bodies around him was foreign after all the years alone in the yard, and it made him restless even in his sleep. Henry dreamed of the night they had escaped, the last night he'd seen Marnie.

It was midwinter, the snow outside the leaky thatched shelter a crunching shell dirty with soot and muck from the Infected that trod in it. A bonfire was all that kept them from freezing to death. Henry's clothes were little more than rags, a worn second skin of mud and dried gore with bits of cloth stuck in by mistake. He hadn't been fed in days and he howled and roared any time someone passed too close to the fence or came into the pen to break the ice off of the water trough, their smell throwing him into a frenzy. That night, Henry was stretched as far as his chain allowed, straining toward the fire, choking himself with his collar in a futile attempt to get warm. At last his eyes caught something moving past the flames. It was Marnie, sitting inside the pen, watching him. Henry growled and tried to lunge farther. Marnie stood up. Not a little girl any more. Thirteen, skinny and quick, far more clever than her parents, more even than Henry had been. She survived first because her mother protected her from the cruel caprice of Phil and his men. Later, after Elizabeth had gone, she was old enough to learn how to stay out of the way. She survived on the edges of the camp, unnoticed by anyone but her father. She watched Henry lunging at her, standing still, her eyes red and swollen from crying. She waited until Henry slipped in the mud at his feet and fell face down, his arms still stretched toward her trying

- 140 -

to grab. Then she leapt onto his back, holding his head still with one arm. Henry was weak, mostly starved and very slow. She was younger, faster and better fed. It wasn't hard to hold him. He lay on his stomach, one ear in the mud, still snapping his teeth at her, though she was well out of reach.

She leaned over him, her small white face just an inch or two from his cheek. "They got Dad today, Henry," she said softly. She was close enough that he could hear her even over the snuffle and growl that came from him. "There's no more food. Not for miles. Dad was supposed to do a supply run, but he came back empty. There's nothing left. Phil threw him into the front pen. I should be grateful that Dad was already dead when he got thrown in." Warm water trickled down Henry's cheek and evaporated from his skin. Marnie was crying. "He threw one of the women he uses– one of the Infected he pulled all the teeth from, he threw her into the pen alive at the same time. Said he was going to start feeding the deadweight to his guard dogs. That means people like me, Henry. The older people, the sick people. The babies. I can't let it happen. You're all I have left Henry. But I have to let you go. I can't let this happen any more, the fragile people are all inside, safely tucked away. Phil's men are drunk. They split Dad's supplies that he had left and had a party. You're the last one to free. I wanted to give you a fighting chance. Some of them must have escaped the front pen by now and I let the others from here out earlier, without any noise. I didn't want you to get shot. Find the Cure Henry. I wish I could take better care of you. Remember your promise. I'm sorry I have to use you like this. Don't leave any of them alive."

Henry heard the chain clank against the wooden post as it fell away from his neck. The pressure on his back was lifted and he sprang up, but Marnie was already gone, disappearing over the back of the wooden fence. Henry wasted no time looking for her, but ran for where the smell of food was strongest. The rest of the night was heat and blood as the Infected chased their old masters through the thick woods and at last collapsed near their bodies after eating their fill. But Henry didn't dream that part. He woke up with

Marnie's soft voice in his ear, "Remember your promise."

He was surrounded by the others, packed too closely to slip away. Where would he go anyway? Henry realized he only had a vague idea of where the camp was. His escape had been a frenzied blur of biting and running through winter woods. Henry lay back down. There was no knowing if Marnie was even still there. Maybe she'd led the people she was protecting somewhere safer. Maybe Phil had caught her. Maybe she was dead. Was he really going to spend weeks or months on a futile search for someone who had most likely been shot or starved to death months ago? What did she really expect him to do? What did he really expect himself to do? Henry closed his eyes. He had tried to leave when he knew he was sick. He'd tried to protect them. He didn't owe them anything. He was ill. Not in control. Even the priest had said that.

But then there was Phil. Henry had tried to tell himself that even without Phil there, Dave and Elizabeth didn't have what was necessary to survive. In his heart Henry wondered though. If they'd kept quiet, if they'd never picked Henry up from his apartment, they might have made it until a bigger group of people picked them up. It was Henry that saved Phil. It was Henry that brought him into the house and didn't question his "accident" or anything else for that matter. And it was because of Henry that Phil got the idea to use the Infected around him to terrorize his neighbors, his enemies, and his own camp members. It was because of Henry that Elizabeth went for the Cure and died. And he had promised her he would take care of Marnie. Somewhere, in the deep, quiet part of his mind, the part that was still him even at his worst, the part that remembered what he'd seen and done, that part had promised Elizabeth that he wouldn't leave Marnie to Phil and his men. It was no use debating with himself. Henry already knew he would spend the rest of this borrowed lifetime trying to find her or what happened to her, this little girl who had grown into a stranger long before she released him. It had been decided years ago. And when he found Phil... the better part of him hoped Phil was already dead. Henry was secretly afraid of what his own soul was capable of doing. He drifted off again, chasing the vague memory of the roads to the Lodge.

TWENTY-THREE

It was harder to slip out of the hotel in the morning than it had been to get in unseen the night before. The courtyard seemed to be an impromptu marketplace in the morning. Rickey suggested they simply blend into the crowd, but one look in the locker room mirrors told them all that there could be no blending in. It was obvious that they had been ill, that they were starving. And starving meant they looked desperate. Desperate was dangerous for everyone. The people in the courtyard were thin and their goods few and mostly broken, but they weren't starving and they were each conspicuously armed. Melissa and Vincent spent the morning peering through a small crack in the doors, watching the crowd. Rickey turned the television back on until Molly forced him to shut it off, terrified the sound would draw others. Pam kept packing and repacking all the gear, scared they would leave some trace behind. Henry was a little relieved that they couldn't start yet, still struggling with everything that lay ahead. He studied Melissa's route, trying to see how far they were from the City's borders. If they didn't make any more detours for extra supplies, they might make it that evening or sometime tomorrow morning. Henry realized he didn't like the idea of spending another night outside of the City's protection. Regardless of what that protection might cost. He sighed and folded the map, trying not to dwell on all the future nights he'd be spending out here looking for Marnie.

He got up and went to the door, tapping Vincent on the shoulder. He pulled the door open a crack and peered through. The courtyard was full of people, but no one was looking inside. All the activity was going on out there. Someone had made a massive bonfire on the concrete patio. The smoke was blowing their direction, concealing them for a few moments. "Let's go," said Henry and slid himself and his bike through the door. He didn't wait to see if the others followed, just wheeled the bicycle to the exterior door, unlocked it, and rolled out into the midmorning sun. The crackled, weedy parking lot was empty. The market people must have been entering from the front. Henry rode the bike down the back lot and back onto the road toward the old highway. He tried to make himself go slowly, to look like he belonged, just a guy going home from market. He hoped he looked normal from a distance.

He chanced a glance over his shoulder as he pedaled up the on ramp of the highway. The others spread in a long line behind him. Henry smiled, relieved he wasn't alone. He turned back to the road. It was immediately clear that this road, unlike the others they'd taken, had been maintained, at least for a while. Mostly tarred, and absent of abandoned vehicles, the highway was a smooth ashy ribbon in the morning light. The wind made a comforting silence in his ears. Henry felt as if he could ride for miles. But they were still weak, underfed and exhausted. They had to stop several times to rest and eat. It stayed warm and quiet. The open air seemed to have lifted their spirits, the marshy green smell of young grass pushing through the mud and the occasional sweet chorus of frogs in nearby ponds and ditches made Henry suddenly realize that he was happy. He wasn't frenzied or scared, his stomach was full and he had no serious injuries. He was free of the pen and headed for a better life. Even if it were one of constant travel and searching. It was still better.

He fell back near the others as the sun sank and the tar became a dark, cold river cutting through the trees. They hadn't had a view yet of the City, the trees had overgrown the median and shoulders, even though someone had cut a few back. But just as the trees were swallowing up the last of the day, the road took a turn and Henry stopped. They were at the top of a long hill and below them the City was just beginning to flicker and pulse with light. It was shocking, after so long in the dark, to see that electric gold spilling everywhere. Henry felt alien and primitive, as if he were witnessing the discovery of fire. He could see the ocean, a great dark emptiness beyond the tiny harbor lights. Around the City was a massive black barrier. The highway led directly to the lone gate in the wall, which was brightly lit, though not very welcoming. Henry wasn't sure whether it was meant to make him feel safer or more frightened of what lay outside the walls. Or both.

Henry put one foot back on its pedal and leaned forward to take off. Rickey grabbed the handlebars. "No way. No fucking way. I'm not going down there. Look at it. It's a prison." Henry stared at him. Then he shrugged.

"Okay. Don't come."

Rickey didn't let go of Henry's bike. "Come on, we can make a life out here, all of us. We'll find a farm. Hell, there was enough leftover stuff in that suburb to last until we can figure out the whole garden thing. We don't need them." He waved his arm at the City's barrier. "They don't want us anyway."

Pam wheeled her bike up to them. "My family might be down there. I want to see them again. And I'm tired of being scared and hungry and cold all the time. If seeing my kids means I have to live by a few rules, work a little harder, that's okay. Sorry, Rickey." She got on her bike and started rolling down the hill.

Rickey turned to look at the rest of them. "Well, what about it? We've got no one waiting for us down there. We can make a good life out here."

Molly shook her head. "Maybe you're right Rickey, maybe we could be okay for a while. But someone's going to get sick or hurt eventually. Or raiders are going to come along and take everything. Or the City's soldiers will. I'm not as naïve as you think, but I'd still rather be on their side than against them. I don't want to die because I poked myself with a rusty can opener or because we're trying to defend a small stockpile of old cans. I'm not cut out for this. I just got lucky that I made it this far. We all did. I don't want to rely on luck anymore. I'm with Pam."

They watched Molly disappear down the dark hill. Rickey turned to Henry, becoming desperate. "You owe me. You owe us. I heard you, it's because of you that we were kept by Phil and his men—"

Vincent put a hand on Rickey's shoulder. "Henry is no

more to blame for what happened to us than we are to blame for what we did while we were sick. Whether he believes it or not. In fact, as awful as the pens were, we probably wouldn't have survived as long as we have without them."

"C'mon Rickey," said Melissa, "You really want to stay out here? What's out here? You'll struggle the whole time. There's electricity in there. Food, medicine. Maybe some cigarettes and beer." She grinned, her teeth flashing in the dusk, "Definitely a wider variety of 'broads' as you'd say. If we don't like it, we can leave."

Rickey turned toward her. "How do you know? What if we're walking into a trap? What if people like us are slaves down there?"

Melissa sighed. "I'm sure Vincent would tell you to trust in the better nature of people, but I know you won't. The truth is, I don't think there are actually enough immune people left to make us slaves."

A flicker of doubt woke in Henry's mind at that. But he stayed quiet. Rickey still looked doubtful. Vincent shook his head. "You have to take a chance sometimes Rickey. You can't live up on the top of this hill and wonder forever." He got back on his bike and rode down the hill with Melissa, leaving Henry and Rickey alone on the chilly dark road.

"I know what I owe you Rickey. I know what I've done and I'm not as sure as Vincent that surviving is really the better alternative. But I made a promise before I met any of you. I know you don't understand it, you think I'm crazy or have some other motive. I owe someone else more. And to help her, I have to go down there and get help. If it's as bad as you think, I'll help you get out, somehow. We can't stay here Rickey, we're sick, starving. We wouldn't even be able to plow a field if we knew how. We have to try this first. Let them fatten us up. Then we'll do what we both need to do." Rickey's hand dropped away from Henry's handlebars. Henry looked at him for a long moment. "I don't want to leave you alone out here. But if you make me, then I will."

Rickey was quiet for a moment. He anchored himself on his bike and looked down at the electric glow of the City.

"Shit," he said at last, "I'm out of cigarettes. Might as well run to the store while I'm here."

Henry smiled to himself in the dark. He pushed off, feeling the brisk wind press into him with a green, new washed smell and watching the light of the City reach out and pull him in.

TWENTY-FOUR

The group, even with their bikes and trailers of supplies, was dwarfed by the massive cement barrier. As they drew closer to it, the light from the City disappeared behind it. The gate looked devoid of people until Henry entered the tight circle of cold, stark white light where the highway met the Barrier.

"Halt!" came a voice from above him. Henry stopped, the others pulling close together behind him. "Come forward into the light please," continued the voice. Henry squinted up into the light but he couldn't see anything. He stepped farther into the circle. The others pressed in beside him.

"Is this all of you?"

Henry glanced around. "Yes," answered Melissa.

"You have weapons?"

"A shovel and uh– a crowbar I think," said Henry. A soldier dropped down from a ledge out of view. He was carrying a gun, but his attitude was casual.

"You coming to stay or just passing through?" Another soldier appeared from behind him and began circling them, inspecting their gear. Henry heard Rickey's breathing behind him speed up and rasp.

Vincent shook his head. "We aren't sure. We were– sick. But someone tranquilized us and when we woke up, we were okay again. She left a note that told us to come here. A Dr. Rider?"

Henry watched the soldiers exchange a rapid glance. "You were Infected? How did you survive this long?"

"Maybe they were Cure camp runaways Steve," said the other.

"It's a really long story," said Melissa, "and as you can see, we aren't doing so hot. We just need a place to stay for the night. If there's paperwork or interviews or whatever, we'll do them, but I'm dead on my feet."

Henry glanced around at the others. The bright light on the gate didn't do them any favors. The ridges of their brows and cheeks, the jutting blades of their noses cast deep shadows where there ought to have been rounded skin, raised scars that ought to have been smooth, protruding skull caps that ought to have been softened by hair. He thought of how close they had come to dying, how close he had come. He shuddered and turned back to the soldier.

"You'll have to stay in the barracks for tonight. And your bikes and supplies will have to stay with us."

Rickey started to protest. The soldier held up his hand. "I know how that sounds. You probably had a lot of trouble getting these supplies. I promise that no one will touch your bikes, but we have to keep our people safe too. I know a person's word probably doesn't seem to mean as much to you as it did before, but that's how things work in the City. If you want, you can turn around and find a camping area for the night and come back in the morning. We won't stop you. But you sure look like you could use a night in a warm bed and some decent food."

There was a deep clanking sound and the metal gates opened slowly. The road behind the gate was quiet and lit by street lamps. There was a large brick building nestled against the Barrier, it's windows brilliant with electric light and someone's music floated out toward them. Henry felt like crying with relief.

The soldiers walked through the gate without bothering to look back at them. Henry turned around and looked at the others. "What do you think?" whispered Molly, her eyes fixed on the gate, her body leaned forward as if it had already decided for her.

"It's a fair deal," said Melissa, glancing at Rickey.

"If they hold up their end," said Rickey glumly.

"It doesn't matter if we go in tonight or in the morning, we're still going to have to let them search the supplies," said Henry, "and I'd honestly rather sleep in a bed if I can."

Pam was already walking up to the gate, her face streaming with tears. "Where are you going, Pam?" hissed Melissa.

She turned around. "I don't have to think about it. I

can be home in a few minutes if I want to. *Home*. What is there to discuss?" She followed the soldier through the Barrier. Henry shrugged and followed her, not bothering to see if the others were coming or not. He'd see them sooner or later either way.

The talkative soldier shook Henry's hand as the other gently took his bike and wheeled it away. "What was your name?" said the soldier.

"Henry."

"Nice to meet you Henry. Name's Steve. You got family here too?"

Henry shook his head. "I think Pam's the only one expecting to find anyone." He looked around him at the bright electric lights, tilted his head toward the rock song sliding out the barracks window. He looked at the soldier. "How is all this possible?"

"You mean the City? Or the electricity?" asked the soldier scratching his chin.

"All of it. The Barrier, the City, the electric. Jesus, you've even got a working television station."

Steve nodded. "Yeah, kind of makes the outside look pretty basic, huh? The electricity did go down for a while in the middle of the Plague, but the plant never got overrun or anything. Most everything just needed people to flip it back on. Don't get me wrong, it took a while, because we didn't really have anyone who knew exactly what to do. But after about six months and some good luck, we got it going again. Kind of been learning how to make things run again since then. The electric was always priority one though. We needed it for everything. It took a lot longer to get what limited phone lines and towers we have working again. Dunno why. But that's the reason for the television station. It didn't really get too damaged and we still had people who knew how to run it. The head honchos thought it was good for giving out orders or issuing attack warnings. Once the electric was restored, it was easy to make sure everyone had tvs. I mean, it's not like they've ever been scarce. Turns out more people had tvs when the Plague hit than they had radios."

"But so fast…" murmured Henry.

"Not really. It's been almost a decade. It's not like we had to invent anything. Everything's just lying around ready to be turned on again. The real problem's the stuff we've run out of. Medicine, batteries, wood planks, gasoline. We're just starting to figure out how to make new stuff now."

Henry felt dizzy as the length of his illness dawned on him again.

"Listen to me, going on and on. You folks are tired and hungry. Come on inside, forget about all that stuff. There'll be time later for history lessons."

Steve led him into the building. "Sarah will get you set up for the night, I know you'll be comfortable. I've got to get back to the Barrier." He shook Henry's hand one more time. "Everything's going to get better from now on. I mean, it's never going to be what it was, but it sure is a heck of a lot better in here than anything out there."

Henry nodded with a tight smile. He turned to see where Pam had gone. She was talking to a young woman who was nodding sympathetically and patting Pam on the back. Henry hung back until they were done. He heard the others filter in, Rickey already had a wrinkled cigarette hanging from his lips, looking far calmer than he had just moments earlier. He saw Henry and grinned. "Homegrown," he said, holding up the cigarette. "Shhh, not supposed to tell anyone though."

Henry smiled and shook his head. The building was warm and filled with the quiet bustle of people, something Henry hadn't heard in almost a decade. He sat in a plastic chair, waiting to be told where to go, while the others milled around in the hallway. He realized how tired he actually was and drifted in and out of a doze as he sat.

Molly shook him awake. "Henry, they're getting us dinner but we have to see the doctor first."

Henry yawned and rubbed a bleary eye. "A doctor? That's good news though."

"They're afraid to feed us until then."

"Are you nervous? Want someone to come with you?"

Molly shook her head quickly, but she started to cry and clutched at the dusty purple glove over her hand.

"I can come with you if you want. Stop them from doing anything you don't want them to do. Or Melissa or Pam if I'd make you more nervous."

"Did it look really bad to you this morning? I didn't think it looked so bad, did you?"

But Molly's arm had smelled so badly that morning that Henry's eyes had watered. And the glove's empty fingers had been filled with fluid. He didn't know if he should lie to make her feel better for a few more minutes or prepare her for the worst.

"I don't know Moll. I'm not a doctor. I just hope I didn't make anything worse."

"What if I have to lose it?" she sniffled.

"They aren't going to do anything that major unless they have to. They'll do everything they can to fix it first."

Molly led the way slowly down the hall. "Maybe it would be better if you did come. You know, to tell the doctor what it looked like before."

They stopped in a carpeted classroom where the others were sitting or lying on the floor.

"Okay," said Henry, "we'll go together."

The doctor finally arrived, just as Henry was beginning to drift off again. He paused as he stood in the doorway, talking to another soldier. "Uh, don't you think a Cure doctor would-"

The soldier shook his head. "They're all still out. Due back by tomorrow. These folks need treatment today."

"But I'm not familiar with– with people in their condition. I just do well checks for you guys."

"Did you go to medical training?"

"Of course."

"Then you are the most qualified person here."

Henry hoped he was the only one who had overheard the conversation. The doctor entered the room with a cheerful smile. *At least he's good at faking it,* Henry thought.

"Okay men, we ought to have this over with quickly.

Get undressed and form a line," said the doctor.

The others glanced at each other, confused. Henry watched them with new eyes. They had shaved themselves bald to get rid of the lice and matted hair and gore. Their faces were all bone and shadow, androgynous in their want. Even the shape of their bodies was the same, absent of hips and breasts and bellies, just a string of bones balanced atop one another in a long line from foot to crown.

The soldier nudged the doctor and whispered in his ear. The doctor blushed and Henry saw Melissa and Pam blush as they saw it. Molly was still chalk white with worry.

The doctor cleared his throat. "Ahem. Sorry about that, Officer Smythe tells me there is another exam room ready, we can see you one at a time. Let me start with– you." He pointed to Vincent and walked out of the room.

Molly and Henry were last, going together for Molly's sake. The doctor looked shaken even as they entered the brightly lit room. Henry guessed that it was harder to act unfazed than the doctor had imagined.

"Oh," said the doctor, "are you together? I thought we were going one at a time."

Henry held Molly's good hand. "I'm just here to help. I'll leave after you look at Molly's arm and you can finish her exam."

The doctor nodded and Henry watched him swallow as Molly lifted up her purple gloved hand. He gently cut off the glove with a pair of surgical scissors and unwrapped the gauze. Something about seeing the tray of clean and shining instruments made Henry immensely relieved. Surprisingly, the doctor didn't even flinch when he looked at Molly's black hand. It was even darker and more twisted than Henry remembered. The stumps looked smaller. Henry couldn't tell if they had just shriveled more, or if some of the skin had actually fallen away.

"Can you fix it? Will you have to cut it off?" asked Molly, squeezing Henry's hand with all her might.

The doctor actually grinned. "This is something I can actually fix," he said, "We just have to clean some of the dead skin off and give you some antibiotics. Oh but-" he glanced up from Molly's hand at their faces. "Antibiotics are expensive now. Hard to make."

"We don't have anything! We've been sick. Slaves! We have nothing." Molly cried.

"We'll give you what we've got. Work it off, something. We'll find a way," said Henry grimly.

The doctor nodded. "I understand. We can bill it to the government and then you can work it off gradually. I'll get the treatment set up and be right back." He left the room and shut the door.

Molly looked at Henry. "You'd do that for me? Help me work it off?"

"Of course. I'm not going to let them take your hand off just because of– of money, or whatever they use now."

"What about your little girl? Don't you have to go after her?"

Henry nodded. "Yes, but I'm going to get help for that. And when I get back they can work me to death in payment if they want. For right now, we are all we have. You five are all the people I know in the world."

"I'm not sure I can let you do this. I'm not sure I want to–" Molly began.

"I told you I wouldn't stop you, but maybe you should wait a few days. See what the doctor says. Try on this new life for a little, before you decide you don't want to live it. This world is bad, Moll, I'm not pretending it isn't. But killing yourself isn't going to make it any better. Just *try*, Moll. Take your turn. Then you can quit if you want to."

The doctor returned. "The antibiotics are coming. The surgery I can do myself." He handed Molly a pill and some water. "We've been reduced to rudimentary methods of sedation, but in your condition, this should be enough." He guided her onto the exam table. "Just let that work, and when you wake up, your hand will be much, much better."

The doctor put a hand on Henry's shoulder and guided him out of the room. Henry wanted to push him off, but he submitted. "This is going to take a long while," said the doctor, "I wonder if we can do your exam in the morning? I'll send word that it's okay for you and the others to be fed. The girl—"

"Molly," said Henry.

"Molly can eat when she wakes up."

"You aren't going to amputate are you?"

"It isn't that severe, we can save her hand. I've done it dozens of times. It happens often these days."

"Will it hurt her?"

"The sedative should be strong enough. It will be sore when she wakes up, but not excruciating. Unfortunately, with current drugs and technology, I can no longer promise no pain."

Henry nodded. "I understand." He turned to go, but the doctor stopped him.

"I'm sure that you think I'm cold, insisting on payment for a lifesaving antibiotic. But I do care, I've heard a little of what you've been through, and I wish I could do more. But once you've been here for a while, you'll understand how rare good medicine is now. You'll understand why I can't just give it to you."

"I understand," said Henry, "I appreciate that your City is taking us in, no matter what the rules might be." He walked down the hall back to the others and the first full meal he'd had in eight years.

TWENTY-FIVE

A soldier woke Henry before it was light. He was led to another exam room where the doctor was waiting. The doctor handed him a funny smelling cup of coffee.

"It's just grain coffee. The real stuff is worth almost as much as chocolate now. But I figured it might help perk you up. It does me."

"Thanks," said Henry. He took a gulp. Not even hot enough to burn his mouth awake. Still, it was warm and something for his cramped stomach.

"We're going to start early with your exam and then you've got entrance interviews. That is, if you're staying."

"I told you I'd pay off Molly's treatment and I will." Henry tried not to growl, knowing it wasn't the doctor's fault.

"She did fine, by the way, her hand will recover nicely."

"She must be relieved."

"I think so. I had your friend– Pam? Stay with her last night in case she needed anything but she seems pretty optimistic this morning and not in too much pain. Well, let's get this over with then."

Henry put down the cup and stripped off his clothes. The doctor began writing on his pad and it made Henry nervous. The room felt cold, but Henry wasn't sure if it was the actual temperature or because he had no fat between his bones.

"Do you remember how long it's been since you were infected?" the doctor asked.

"You mean do I remember being infected or do I remember when I lost control of myself?"

The doctor glanced up. "The latter."

"It was Christmas day eight years ago."

"You turned eight years ago?"

"Yes. Well, a little over eight years I guess, if the date on that letter was correct."

"And you survived because of this bandit camp, like the others?"

"Yes."

"Did they feed you or . . ."

"In the beginning they fed me, like a normal person. Then, they let me attack their enemies."

"And you escaped this camp how long ago?"

"It's hard for me to tell. I think it was a few months ago. There was snow at the camp."

"What did you eat between then and now?"

"At first, we attacked the people who had enslaved us. Then we kind of spread out. The group that was with me stuck together because we found a farm with cows. It took more than one of us to take down a cow. There were a few cows, a horse I think. I remember attacking another girl, she was sick like me. That's all I remember."

Henry tried to pretend he didn't see the doctor shudder. "Were you clothed when you escaped?"

"I was. At least partially. I don't think I had shoes. I don't know about the others."

"Do you have any numbness anywhere, tingling or wooden feeling in any extremity?"

"I think the bottom of my feet have frostbite, if that's what you are asking."

"Hmm. Sit up here please."

Henry was silent as the doctor checked him over and cleaned small wounds on his arms and legs and feet. He hadn't even realized most were there, the pain of his hungry belly vastly outweighing any other concern.

"Did you do this?" asked the doctor indicating his shaved head.

"You mean the nicks? Yeah, I didn't have the greatest razor. But I had to get the hair off. It was a nest of bugs and bacteria." Henry shivered and gagged a little thinking about it. The doctor handed him a small trashcan in case he needed to vomit.

"Good job," said the doctor, "it probably kept you from infection. What's this from?" He touched his pen to the red ring around Henry's neck.

Henry rubbed the smooth scar self-consciously. "A

collar. Didn't the others have one?"

The doctor shook his head. "One of them did, but the rest didn't have them around their necks, they had them at their wrists. They said they were restrained at the wrist. Some of them have long-term injuries to their shoulders because of it. But some of them said it was to stop them from chewing on their own hands. Why aren't yours chewed?"

Henry smiled. It was the one thing Dave did for him, long after Phil told him to stop. "My friend taped heavy wood gloves onto my hands. I escaped shortly after he died."

"You didn't chew through them in eight years?"

"Yeah, I did. They lasted about a month. My friend would replace them every so often."

"That's a good friend," said the doctor shaking his head and writing. Henry didn't bother to correct him. If that's what he wanted to believe, who was Henry to disparage Dave?

"Do you remember your weight before you got sick? It doesn't have to be exact, just an estimate."

"Uh, about 210, but I wasn't the best eater and I had a desk job."

"Would you step on the scale for me?"

Henry hesitated. "Do I have to look?"

"Not if you don't want to."

He stepped onto the scale and turned to face the doctor. He didn't have to look. The doctor's face as the little weights settled behind Henry's head said it all. But Henry didn't want to know more, so he didn't ask. The doctor wrote without comment.

"You can get dressed now, if you like. You're healthier than the others and your frostbite is only mild. It will mean a loss of sensation but not much else. Just be sure to wear shoes and inspect your feet for damage often, they can still get infected by stepping on something sharp, but you might not feel it. You are more underfed than the others, I suspect because you didn't– partake as often as they did. I'm going to recommend a special diet for you for the next few weeks, I want you to follow it. It will help you get what you need without causing your body to shut down." He pulled a few vials out of his pocket. "I need to do some blood work, it's only to be sure you are healthy. It has no bearing on your being admitted to the City, it's just so we can make sure we've treated you for everything that we can."

Henry let him take the blood, feeling exhausted and a little woozy after. The doctor gave him a chipped mug with lumpy apple juice in it.

"Drink this, it will help with the nausea and the tiredness. Do you need a wheelchair?"

Henry shook his head. "Well, when you are ready, go down the hall to the first office on the left. You'll have to fill out some background history with the secretary. I'm going to check on your friend. I'll have your blood work results and diet recommendations sent to the apartment they assign you." The doctor offered him a tight smile and then left the exam room. Henry felt as if his head was whirling. He drank the juice slowly while he finished dressing and then walked unsteadily down the hall to the next office. He knocked on the dull metal door and it opened to let him in.

The secretary wore a soldier's uniform and unlike his younger, more casual counterparts from the night before, this one looked like he actually belonged inside it. He didn't smile or hold out his hand to Henry, just opened the door and then returned to his desk.

"Have a seat," he said without looking up. Henry folded himself onto the cold plastic seat. He noticed that the other man's hair lay perfectly straight, held there with some kind of dark grease. His hands were thick but clean, as if he'd been doing this type of work for a while, but not for always.

"Name?"

"Henry."

"Full Name."

"Oh, uh Henry Steven Broom." An old typewriter clacked into life. Henry wondered why they didn't just use a computer. Maybe they could make typewriter ribbons easier than ink cartridges. He was so used to a paperless society. The stacks of pulpy recycled paper around him made him feel small, lost in the clutter.

"Social?"

"Huh?"

"Social Security number." The secretary sounded irritated.

"I don't– does that even matter anymore? I honestly don't think I remember all of it."

"It's how we find surviving family members. Do you remember any of it?"

"I don't have any family." Henry felt a brief pang when he thought of his sister and father, but they had lived states away. If they weren't dead, it didn't matter. He'd never find them.

"Very well. When did you succumb to the infection?"

"Christmas, eight years ago."

"How long have you been Cured?"

"Four days I think. I woke up sane four days ago anyway."

The secretary finally looked up at him. "I thought the Cure camps kept you folks for a month."

"We weren't at a– what did you call them? A camp."

"How did you get the Cure?"

"We were chasing a man and a woman across a field toward a farm house. One of us, another man, bit the woman and was shot and I think he died. The man and the woman made it to the farmhouse and then the man went up to the second floor and shot us with darts. The next thing I remember I woke up in the farmhouse with the others and there was a letter left for us, telling us to come here. Melissa has the letter I think, if you need it."

The secretary squinted at him and then clacked away at the typewriter, shaking his head. He looked up again. "How did you survive for so long? We haven't found an Infected in almost a year. Most of the Cured who come in now are runaways from the camps that couldn't make a go of it out there." He jerked his head toward the Barrier.

Henry shifted uncomfortably. "Is this part of the report?" he asked.

"No, why?"

"It's a long story."

The secretary shrugged. "Suit yourself. What occupations have you held?"

"I was a debt collector with a credit card company. Office work."

"Anything else?"

"In high school I washed dishes for the local diner."

"Did you have any hobbies? Fishing, gardening, hunting, that sort of thing?"

"You mean stuff that would help with survival."

"Yes, we're looking for skills, no matter how old. Could even be cub scouts if you remember it."

Henry shook his head. "Sorry, I was a pretty modernized person. Movies, video games, trips to an air conditioned gym, that's about it."

"You ever shoot a gun?"

"Nope. Not even sure I'd know how."

"Do any first aid?"

"Nothing beyond very, very basic stuff. I took a course for work, but it's probably nothing more than the average adult would pick up from normal life anyway."

The secretary looked grim. Henry felt like he was failing some sort of test. He started to sweat through the thin clothes he'd been given. "Look, I'm sure there's some kind of clerical work I can do to contribute. And I'm willing to learn a new trade. Maybe if I knew what you need–"

The secretary waved him off. "Never mind. I'll put you in the All-Work pool. Someone will find something for you to do. You can talk to your supervisor about apprenticing if you find something you'd rather do. But you have to work. In here, if you don't work, you don't eat, that's just how it is." Henry started to interrupt but the secretary spoke over him, "I'm not saying you won't. I'm sure you will be a hard worker and always were, but I have to give the same speech to everyone." He scribbled something on a gray piece of paper and slid it into a folder with Henry's name at the top. "Here is your assignment. Take this folder down the hall to housing.

Don't lose your folder. It's hard to find replacements."

"I need to talk to someone in charge."

The secretary barked a short laugh. "About your assignment? No one is going to see you about that. Besides, I told you that you could apprentice if you wanted–"

"Not about that. I need to see someone in charge about the people we were with all this time."

"Oh. Well, the Military Governor sees citizens every afternoon between one and three when he can. But he's pretty busy managing security for the trial, so I don't know if he'll see you. Housing will have a map of the City. They can show you where to go."

"Okay," said Henry standing. "Thanks," he said, because it was something to say, though he wasn't sure he meant it. He opened the heavy metal door and slid out into the hallway. The secretary didn't bother to say anything, just clacked away on the typewriter as Henry left. Pam was waiting to go into the office after him.

"How's Molly?" he asked.

"Much better, but the doctor says she'll have to stay here for a few days to make sure the infection is really gone."

Henry nodded. "You better go in, the guy is kind of testy. I think he has a list of people in the City though, so he can find your family."

Pam's face brightened and she hurried over to the door. Henry turned and walked to the next office. This one was brightly lit with children's drawings hanging in the window and an odd feeling of displacement overcame him. It was like a post-apocalyptic kindergarten. Henry shook his head and opened the door. A plump woman sitting at a large round table smiled at him and stood up.

"Hello," she said, "My name's Maureen." She extended a hand toward him. He shook it.

"Henry."

"Nice to meet you Henry, please have a seat."

Henry sat in another plastic chair, this one cherry red and too short for the table. Maureen sat across from him in an office chair almost a foot higher. He felt ridiculous.

"Welcome to housing and reproductive services."

"Reproductive services?"

Maureen smiled. "Yes, well, that's just part of my spiel, I'm sure you won't be needing that part, you're Cured right? Reproductive services is just for Immunes at the moment. But let's get to work finding you a new home."

Henry was a little offended without even knowing why. But Maureen turned to the side and sorted through some cracked binders. "Let's see, not these–" she pulled the top three off and placed them below the table. She glanced back at him. "What's your work assignment?"

"Allwork? Miscellaneous I gather."

"Good," she said cheerily, almost clapping her hands, "that means you have a broader choice. And you've retained all your limbs (bravo), so we can give you something that isn't handicap accessible."

Henry blushed with embarrassment for her. How could she openly be this rude?

"Do you have children?" she asked as she flipped through the first binder of plastic covered pictures.

"No."

"Wife?"

"No."

"So just a single occupancy then."

"What if I need something bigger later?" Henry thought of finding Marnie.

Maureen smiled and nodded her shiny bob cut bouncing around her full face. "That's right, nothing attracts like confidence Henry. Goodness knows I've seen lots of far more scarred people come through here and later find someone. If you find yourself needing more room, you just come back and see me and I'll find you a nice family home. Maybe even move you up toward the north side of town if I can manage it."

Henry blushed, humiliated. He couldn't remember ever being this angry except when he was sick. He fought it, fearing that the cure wasn't complete for him or that it would reverse itself.

Maureen placed a small pile of pictures in front of him. "Most of these are over near the docks but there are one or two with space for a garden or some chickens by the far barrier. Of course, you might have to walk farther to work that way."

"It doesn't matter," Henry muttered, too angry even to pick up the photos. She clucked and shook her head.

"You all say that, but it's a big decision. Why don't you look through these. I'll get you an appointment with Furnishings while you decide."

Henry flipped through them, finally deciding on one small house that was close to the school, hoping not to have to return once he found Marnie. He'd sleep in the living room for the rest of his life if he had to before he'd come back to get a bigger place. He wondered absently what this was going to cost in labor. He was already feeling the weight of future servitude heavy on his neck. *It's better than where you were,* he thought, *nothing could be as bad as that.*

"Is that the one you've chosen? It's a darling little house and so close to everything on the dock side of town," said Maureen cheerfully, bustling up behind him with a cloth sack that clunked and clattered with something and a small pile of gray papers. She plopped down across from him and took the photograph. She was silent for a moment as she wrote in her records. Then she spilled the contents of the cloth bag onto the table. It was a small pile of brass tokens, the kind Henry remembered from the local arcade he went to when he was a kid. They were spray painted different colors and the paint was beginning to wear off from the touch of hundreds of fingers. "It's a little clunky and primitive, but it works," said Maureen, picking up a green token. "Green coins are for produce from the Farm." She pulled one of the grey lumpy papers from her stack. It was a crude hand drawn map. Henry was surprised to see it wasn't a photocopy but an original. Ink must be at a premium. He wondered if there were a cluster of monks somewhere in the building hand copying all the records. Maureen circled a large triangular space on the map. "This is the Farm. It used to be the city park, and there are still roadsigns up in case you get lost. They are open for food distribution from ten to four. Your green coins will get you a box with enough food for a day for each, or you can trade in enough for a week at a time. Remember though, your house is quite far–" she circled another small square, "here, so you'll need something to carry it with. If you are ill or you are on work duty during all Farm hours and can't be excused you can ask for delivery. However, we're short on delivery personnel at the moment so we ask that you only utilize them when truly necessary. Understand?"

"Green coins for food. Got it," said Henry drily.

"Green coins for *Farm* food. If you go to a diner or a butcher, those are the red miscellaneous coins. You'll use those for almost everything and your work will pay you mostly in the red coins. They'll give you seven green coins a week as well, of course. If you are excused from work for any reason, your green coins will be delivered to you, but you'll receive no extra red coins. I'll be giving you some of each to start you off and the rest you'll have to earn."

"What about the blue coins?"

"Clothing allotment. You'll start with a good amount, but I suggest you take good care of them. Blue coins are only rarely distributed, usually when a scavenging team finds an unlooted department store or something and once on Christmas. Clothing is a precious commodity here. Try to keep yours clean and free of tears. You can go here to pick up your first batch," she said circling a third square near the Farm. Henry wished now that they'd stuffed more clothing into their gear. Then again, he wondered if they'd get their gear back at all or if it was just going to get tossed in the community pot. He wondered how Rickey was going to react to all this.

"Do you have any more questions?"

Henry leaned forward to look at the map. "Yeah, where are we now?"

"Silly me," said Maureen and drew a thick black box around the building hiding behind the curved line of the Barrier.

"And where's the guy in charge and how do I talk to him?"

"Well, City Hall is here," she pointed to the silly half circle and box that were meant to symbolize a graceful capitol building, "You can make an appointment to see the Military Governor there, but it might take a while." She frowned as if she wondered what he could possibly want to bother the governor for.

"Thanks. Is that everything?"

Maureen swept the tokens into the cloth bag and handed it to him, then slid the map and the photo of his new house into the folder.

"Oh yeah," said Henry, "what about rent? And the furnishing place you were talking about?"

Maureen smiled sweetly, as if she were talking to a small child. "Furnishings is in the same building as Clothing. And the City is happy to provide housing for its inhabitants at no cost."

Which means I'll find out later what rent is, Henry thought. He nodded though, and took his bag and folder.

"One more stop and you'll be on your way," said Maureen. "Go two doors further on to orientation for a brief presentation on your rights and responsibilities in the City and then you'll be free to go find your house and work supervisor."

Henry felt a chill run up his spine. He wished the others were going with him to this orientation. He felt too vulnerable alone.

TWENTY-SIX

Henry loitered in the hall for a few minutes, hoping to see Pam or Vincent coming behind him. Eventually he moved on to the orientation classroom. There was a young man in an apron putting out food for lunch and a soldier helping him.

"Hello," said the soldier, "why don't you make yourself at home and grab some lunch, we're going to wait for the others to finish their interviews. It shouldn't be long now, I gather most of them went together. When they get here, we'll start orientation."

Henry was relieved that he wouldn't have to go through the presentation alone. He relaxed and waited until the two men left the room. He picked a grainy sandwich and some vegetable sticks and sat at the conference table. He ate without really thinking about it, looking instead at the picture of his small house and wondering how he was going to persuade the governor to help him. Vincent wandered in and sat next to him picking at a salad. "Where's Pam?" asked Henry.

Vincent grinned. "They found her kids. Called them to come down and meet her. She'll finish all this stuff later."

Henry leaned back and smiled. "That's great, I bet she was happy."

"Ecstatic. She couldn't stop crying. She says she'll track us all down once she's settled."

"Just four little Indians left," said Melissa as she walked in, overhearing them.

"I'm glad Pam and Molly had some good news," said Henry. He felt lighter, less nervous, as if the news were his instead of theirs.

Rickey sauntered in to the room a few minutes later and propped his feet on the table, chewing on a sandwich. "Gah, everything is vegetarian here," he said. Henry was secretly glad he hadn't had to face meat yet. "Henry, where'd they put you for work?"

"Miscellaneous I guess. It's supposed to be where ever I'm needed I think. How about you?"

"Electric plant. What about the rest of you?"

"Delivery system," said Melissa, "I'm a supervisor. Because I was a postal worker before I guess."

"Teacher at the school," said Vincent. "And church duties if I want to."

Henry leaned forward. "Do you want to?"

"Good you are all here," said the soldier from before, interrupting them. "We just have a short video and I'll be here afterward if you have questions. We want you to get off on the right foot, there's nothing to be nervous about," he continued, patting Rickey on the back. Rickey took his feet off the table with a guilty look. The soldier rolled a television into the room and flipped the lights as the video started. The woman they had seen the night before on the news appeared.

"Congratulations on your arrival in the City. Whether you were immune to the December Plague or have just come from the Cure camps, you are welcome here. We've made this video to help get you settled more quickly. Since you are watching this, you already know that we've restored power, at least in this area. We also have limited telephone and cell service, an operating hospital and police and fire department services." The screen switched to a shot of the Barrier.

"For security purposes the City is bordered by a concrete barrier on three sides and the bay on the fourth. Military personnel work diligently to make sure you stay safe. While you are free to leave the confines of the Barrier at any time, we ask that you do not, for your own security. You may feel that you have a compelling reason to leave, but the City asks you to consider carefully whether it is truly worth the risk. Scavenger teams are escorted by military personnel every month. If there is an item you need that you think may be got out *there* please make a request with the scav team. They are trained to go into unsecured locations. Most items that are still available are already within the City itself."

A busy office filled with embracing people lit the screen now. Henry wondered if that's where Pam had gone. The woman's voice continued, "If you are thinking of leaving to locate loved ones, consider that they may be looking for you at the same time. The best thing for you to do is to stay put where it's safe, so you don't miss each other. You can register yourself in the Displaced Family office, if you didn't already do this in the Cure camp. Our DF office has a stellar record of reuniting people and tracking down the fate of those who have become unfortunate casualties of the Plague. Our Cure teams and military are spreading from the City outward in very tight grids. We can assure you that no one will be missed. It is best to wait for trained personnel to locate your friends and family and bring them safely home to you."

The woman appeared again. "Attacks on the Barrier are rare, but in the event that one happens, please follow the instructions of the military personnel. Attacks by Infected are usually solitary events, since they lack the ability to coordinate with each other. These happened regularly in our early years but have since subsided as the Cure's distribution has moved farther from the City. Attacks by Looters, while infrequent, are more dangerous and you may be called upon to help defend the Barrier. Invalids, the elderly and children under thirteen are excused from service. Anyone else who refuses a direct order by military personnel during a crisis may face expulsion. Anyone with knowledge of an impending attack who does not alert the proper authorities will also face expulsion or execution."

Henry felt his stomach grow tight. He hoped the other rules didn't carry such harsh punishments. Rickey raised his arm as if he were in a classroom. "Hey," he said, trying to get the soldier's attention. The video paused.

"Yes?" said the soldier.

"Look, do we really have to watch this broad? I mean, can't you just give us the rules or something, tell us how things really work?"

The soldier shrugged then walked to the door and peered into the hallway. He closed it and flipped the lights back on. "I guess it'd be okay, most of this stuff is for Immunes anyway. They don't care so much what we do."

"We?" asked Melissa.

The soldier rolled up his pant leg to show them and ill-fitting prosthetic leg. "We. I was Cured a few years ago. Thought I was one of the last actually. We haven't seen many more roll in and never ones that didn't get the run through at a Cure camp." He sat next to Henry at the conference table. "You guys must be so messed up. No offense, of course. But I mean, you wake up eight years later with no one to tell you how things are or what to do, with all those memories. I've got 'em too, but at least at the Cure camp they help you try to deal with them. Explain things, sort of." He shook his head. "I can't even imagine how confused you guys are. That video is supposed to run another two hours so we've got time if you want to ask me anything."

"How about what else gets us tossed out or executed?" asked Rickey.

"Well, about what you'd expect. Violence or theft will get you one or the other. There's no tolerance for either here. Even if you're starving, you don't steal from other people around here. And even if the guy that ate your wife or kid is living next door, you don't attack him. Well, I guess in our case it'd be the guy that shot at us or our wife and kid. The City would fall apart otherwise. It was really bad in the beginning I guess. Cured folks would come in and be hunted down for stuff they did when they were sick. But this Military Governor took over eventually and he's kept a tight control over that sort of thing. If you have a problem with someone, you take it to the police. We have courts, just like before, for things like vandalism or shady trading, small stuff like that. The big things go before the Governor himself."

"What happens for the small stuff?" asked Rickey, as if he were already contemplating doing something not-quite-legal.

The soldier scratched at the back of his neck. "Mostly extra work or repairing the damage that you caused. But breaking the vice laws are usually just extra work penalties."

"Vice laws?" asked Vincent.

"Yeah, but like I said, they mostly only care if the Immunes do those. Alcohol is illegal and so is smoking," he said pointing to the cigarette behind Rickey's ear, "but as long as we don't get drunk in public and cause a problem, no one cares too much. If we were Immune though, we could get in trouble. They don't want to lose any of that precious Immune DNA, so anything that causes bodily harm is not allowed. So drugs, alcohol, we're all tested for STDs when we get here—"

"Us too?"

"Yeah, that's what the blood work was for, among other things. If you have one that's not treatable (and they're mostly not treatable these days) you'll be monitored by someone from DHRS and if they find out you're interested in a healthy Immune, they'll warn that person away. Not that Immunes and Cured get together that often. Some stuff is more scarce than illegal. Like the cigarettes and cars— they just let us sort of run out and then it's not a problem anymore. Only military people and emergency workers get gas for cars and alcohol is reserved for medical use at the hospital. But everyone knows where the closest moonshine bar is and you can get all sorts of contraband from them, not just alcohol. Like I said, for us, those rules are far more relaxed. We're allowed to endanger ourselves as long as we do it in private." The soldier looked like he wanted to spit, but didn't.

"So we're second class citizens then?" Henry asked.

"You asking me what the official orientation would say or what I would say?"

"Both I guess."

"It's not overt. I mean, there's no rule to put us in our place or tell us we can't be friends with the Immunes or have the same rights, in fact it's clearly written in the code that we all have the same rights and are meant to be treated as equals. But things are different when you give actual people a say. I mean, I guess I can understand how it all started. All of a sudden, these people that have forced them to the brink of extinction wake up and realize what they were doing was wrong. Not only do these people need massive amounts of medical care, but they need food and shelter and jobs too. And there's no place for them to go but right alongside their old enemies behind this wall. I can understand putting them down on the dock side. There's lots of empty, ready to go houses down there, and it's near the hospital which they'll need on an almost daily basis. And then, there's not *quite* enough food to go around, so maybe the new people get skimped a little bit. After all, they've just woken up after eating your relatives. Why do they deserve to eat more than someone who never did those terrible things? Yes, yes, they were sick, they were out of control and wouldn't have chosen to do it- but still, the fact remains that they committed murder. Part of what the City needs is more laborers. There are thousands of 'em, just been Cured. You don't know what's really happened in their brains. Are they functional? Will they revert? Are they even capable of skilled tasks? So they get put into grunt work, even if they are skilled at other things. Just in case.

I can see how it started. Doesn't have to be rabid zombie hunters to make things go south for us. You just let these things slide by long enough and it sort of gets ingrained in how people think. You get people like Maureen down the hall there. People that *should* know better, but truly don't see things the same anymore."

Henry grinned ruefully at the name. "So none of the people in charge are Cured?" Melissa asked.

The soldier shook his head. "Not unless you count people like me. This is about as far up the ladder as we get, and I had to work for years to get this far. There are a few former doctors that are allowed to do simple procedures at the hospital. You know, stitch up a small wound, mix ointment for rashes, check on older folks. But that's it. Former surgeons and obstetricians and cancer doctors reduced to activities a housemom would routinely do. Just because they got sick. And it's like that pretty much everywhere. There are a few Cured engineers at the electric plant, just because the City was so desperate for them and there's that lawyer, Frank Courtlen, in the trial, he's Cured. He's only there because no one else would defend Robert Pazzo though. Other than them, we're pretty much all in the lower paying, harder jobs. We live segregated from the Immunes in fact if not by law, in the most rundown pieces of town. The police take their time responding to emergencies down there as do the utilities people. In fact, eight years after the power came back on, we still have to boil our water because no one has bothered to restart the filtration system on our side of town. We aren't welcome in the north side restaurants and some people will outright refuse to trade with you. Sometimes, if you aren't paying attention or you are too scared to say anything you even get stiffed at the Farm if there's a bad harvest. Even though the overwhelming majority of the people that work there are Cured. Just not the food distributors."

"Should we leave?" asked Henry, knowing what the others were already thinking.

The soldier shrugged. "Where are you going to go? You saw how things are Outside. Even without constant threat of Looters, there's nothing left to live on for miles. And as unfair as things are, it's still better than that. In fact most Cured would be upset with the idea of leaving. This is the City that cured them and took them in after what they had done. Any family they have left is here. There's been talk of expanding the City. Developing a satellite sort of colony or something, but there haven't been many people interested. It just hasn't got off the ground. Maybe in a new place we would do better, but no one wants to take a chance on it."

There was a knock at the door and the soldier stood up to answer it, rolling his pant leg down again. He stepped outside to talk with someone. Henry looked at the others.

"I told you," Rickey grumbled.

"We can't change anyone's mind by running away, Rickey," said Vincent.

"I don't want to change anyone's mind. I just want to leave. Why should I live with people that look down on me, that treat me like crap?"

"You heard him," said Melissa, "There's nowhere else to go. For miles. Everything's picked clean. Even the houses we hit were scavenged, we got lucky to find what little we did. You'd rather starve than put up with a few inconveniences?"

"It's not just an inconvenience–" Rickey started, but Henry interrupted him.

"Look, at least here we have food and shelter and medicine. Even electricity. I hear you Rickey, and the first opportunity I get I'll volunteer for whatever new town they want to set up in order to get out. But for now we need them. Until we can get enough together to make it on our own, we have to live by their rules." *And until they help me find Marnie,* he thought, though he didn't say it out loud. "So let's just keep our heads down in the meantime. Besides, we can't leave until Molly is better at least. She may want to come with us."

"And Pam?" Vincent asked.

Melissa shook her head. "No way. She found her kids she'll never go anywhere else no matter how bad things get here. The world could end again before she'd leave them."

The soldier returned. "Sorry about that, we have the last Cure personnel coming back this afternoon and they need us to help with the supplies. Did you guys need anything else?"

Henry shook his head for them all.

"Well, look me up when you get to the dock side. We stick together down there, more than the Immunes do anyway. I'll introduce you to the best moonshine bar in town."

Rickey grinned and the soldier left them to their own devices.

TWENTY-SEVEN

"I'm sorry, sir, but all the government offices are on skeleton crews. It's the trial. Even the Military Governor has gone for opening statements. He won't attend the entire trial of course, but he won't be back today." The pretty secretary turned back to her files.

"Everyone keeps talking about this trial. What is it about?" asked Henry. He really didn't care. He was just buying time, hoping someone important would walk through the office so he could grab them. The secretary looked at him as if he were crazy.

"Uh– I just got to the City two days ago," he said quickly.

"Oh, that explains it then. It's the Plague trial. The military found some scientists holed up in a lab and they are supposed to be the same ones that started this whole thing."

"The first ones? How did they survive that long?" Henry was interested in spite of himself.

The secretary shrugged. "The typical way I'd guess." She eyed him and added, "how did you?"

"Look, I just want to make an appointment to see someone. Anyone. I came from a bandit camp full of really bad people. There are kids and innocent people trapped there too. Some of them are just sick– like I was."

"All right," sighed the secretary sitting down at her desk and picking up a pencil, "But I don't think you're going to get much help. The world's full of really bad people right now. Can't chase them all down, you know?" She scribbled in an appointment book. "What's your name?"

"Henry Broom."

"Okay, Henry, three o'clock tomorrow, the Governor has a fifteen minute block. You need permission to leave work early?"

"I don't know," said Henry, blushing. The secretary glanced up at him.

"Jeez. You *are* new. You supposed to be at work now?" Henry shrugged. "What's your assignment?" she asked holding her hand out for his folder. She pulled out the work assignment and picked up her phone.

"Hi Steph, it's Cheryl over at City Hall. You expecting a Henry Broom today . . ."

The secretary's conversation trailed off as Henry's mind drifted off into it's now familiar rut of frustration and worry and desperate planning. How many days was this going to take? Every day was one more that Marnie was trapped or worse.

"Okay," said the secretary, "you're late but you've been excused. Go to the All-Work Station now. You're excused for tomorrow afternoon but don't miss any more work or you'll be short rations."

"Thanks," said Henry, halfheartedly. He headed out of the massive empty building to his bike and took off for work. He was glad the soldiers had given him the bike back. He hadn't seen very many since he'd entered the City and it had already proved very useful, since he lived so far from everything important.

The All-Work Station was an unimpressive little brick building near the docks. Henry opened the door, where a woman in a threadbare jacket was sorting sooty work orders onto bulletin boards. Everything was dusty or grimy. The floor, the counter, the windows. The only bright thing in the place was a little gold bell on the counter. Henry found that oddly funny.

"Hello," he said, and the woman turned around.

"You Henry?" she asked.

"I'm sorry I'm late, I'm still finding my way around."

"Don't worry. All-Work isn't exactly a high pressure environment. Most times it's a hurry up and wait kind of place anyway. I'm Stephanie. Normally I just lead a work shift, but Bernice is at the trial with everyone else. She's the one that really runs things."

"How come you aren't at the trial Stephanie?"

"Someone has to keep the doors open. If you are really interested we can listen to the broadcast. The way I see it though, those scientists are either already living the worst kind of hell just knowing what they did, or they don't care. And if they don't care, a trial won't even come close to making them care. It's just a lot of heartache for everyone else."

"Don't you want to know why they did it?"

Stephanie shook her head and Henry could see the smooth, melted scar of a missing ear flashing under her long hair. "It can't change anything. People are still dead, no matter why. It won't bring anyone back and it won't make their dying worthwhile." She dropped the small stack of papers. "Come on, I'll give you the tour." She came around the counter and led Henry through a squealing metal door. Behind the little office was a large warehouse. It was stacked to the brim. Everywhere Henry looked was something different. It made him dizzy and a little nervous.

"So, we're All Work. Obviously. And that means we have to have tools for everything. We're kind of the back up for the regular departments. The good news is you could be doing something different every day. The bad news is that everyone knows you're temporary and gives you the worst tasks that no one else wants to do." Stephanie grinned. "The good news to *that* is that you only have to do it that day and not every day."

"Where do I even start?" asked Henry, "I thought I was sent here because I didn't have any skills that they found useful."

She laughed. "That's just because we're Cured. They never think we can do anything right. Like we haven't quite got out of our drooling idiot stage." She gently elbowed him and he smiled but it didn't feel funny. "Don't take it personally Henry, they don't even know you. You're just a number, it's not a judgement. Besides, there are lots of good things about this job. Don't get me wrong, it's not for everyone, and if you decide to apprentice out, there's no shame in it. But if you stay, you'll learn a lot more. You'll see parts of the City no one else ever bothers with, you'll make friends with people in all sorts of positions. People that can get you things. And between you and me, if the poop meets the pin wheel again, you'll be ten times the survivor that you were when you started."

"So, what do I do first?"

"Well, there's not much to do today, since everyone is at the trial. Why don't we work on organizing some of the warehouse, that way you'll kind of get a feel for the layout. It gets really sloppy in here really fast with everyone checking tools in and out. Oh yeah, meant to tell you that too. Obviously, there's a *lot* of valuable stuff in here. Everyone checks their tools out for the day and back in when they are done. We have a big chalkboard." Stephanie walked toward the back wall and Henry followed her. The chalkboard was huge. It was like the old betting board at Henry's favorite sports bar. There was even a ladder to reach the top. "It looks confusing now, but you'll get used to it. This is where we keep track of assignments and tools. I already added you, see?"

Henry's name sprawled in metallic stickers about a foot from the bottom. "So your first column would be your assignment for the day, and then you'd just sign or x in the tool column for the stuff you need. Everything is in packets, so you don't have to worry about specific tools. You just grab a bundle and it should have everything you need for the day. That's kind of why things get messy in here, but it's so much faster than digging through everything or making three trips back to the warehouse for forgotten tools. Bernice is kind of in charge of all that too. Most of the time she'll have everyone's bundles lined up by the warehouse door by the time they come in, so you just pick it up and go."

"How many people work here?" asked Henry, awed at the number of names.

"Right now, about seventy. We had a big group apprentice out to the water works last month. They were desperate for new workers. But it'll fill up again."

The idea of seventy people in the same small warehouse at once after so many years of solitude made Henry's stomach twist. But it was quiet now. Either everyone was at the trial or already out at work. He and Stephanie sorted bundles of tools for the rest of the day. He was surprised at how complete each one was, holding parts and pieces that could only be occasionally called for. But, after years of trial and error, he supposed they must know what was going to be most valuable. They only got a few sections done before people started flooding in. Some exchanging bundles for ration coins, others coming in to talk about the trial. The extra noise made Henry flinch and he stood awkwardly in an empty part of the warehouse. Stephanie found him still sorting bundles a little later. "Hey," she said, "why don't you go on home. We're done for the day and it looks like you're still bulking up. We don't want to wear you out."

Henry blushed, humiliated and unable to deny his exhaustion. "Don't be ashamed," she continued, "We're all Cured here. We all came in most of the way starved and weak as kittens. You have to take it easy for a little while or you'll collapse. I've seen it happen. No one expects anything superhuman here. Come back in the morning and we'll do some more sorting, I'll introduce you to the guys before your meeting."

Henry just nodded, too embarrassed to thank her. He ducked out of the tiny office and climbed onto his bike, riding through the long shadows the ramshackle buildings made in the empty afternoon. He sat on the cracked wood step of his house as the chill of the afternoon tightened into proper cold. Rickey and Vincent found him there as the sun was setting.

"Well? Did you get your posse?" asked Rickey. Vincent looked concerned, the last of the afternoon light filling up the drawn lines in his face.

"No, he was at that trial thing. I'm supposed to go back tomorrow."

"It's not going to happen, man. We don't even know if he's still alive. Maybe the whole camp is wiped out. In fact, I'm not even entirely sure I remember how to get back there."

"I asked Melissa. She used to deliver mail in the area, she found me a map."

Henry stood up and opened the door, motioning them inside.

"What are you hoping will happen, Henry? Find the

girl and take revenge? And then what? Are you even sure if you find Marnie that she'll want to come back with you? She didn't exactly see you at your best."

"I know you aren't interested in helping me Rickey, I'm not asking you to. But I have to know, one way or another, that Phil's not doing the same things to other people and that Marnie is free of him. Even if she doesn't want to come back with me." He flipped on a light and the empty room glowed. The furniture delivery sat in a sad, spare pile in the center. Rickey walked over and pulled a kitchen chair from the pile, lighting a cigarette without asking.

"What exactly are you going to do if you find him?" asked Vincent.

"You want me to spell it out for you?" Henry asked, turning to look at him.

"Actually, yes. Because no matter what you do, it's never going to be enough."

"Wow. I didn't think a priest was supposed to say those things," said Rickey between puffs.

"You want a crack at him Father?" asked Henry, surprised. Vincent shook his head.

"No. No torture would ever be enough. And it would only make me into something like him. It won't make you happy, Henry. Not for long."

"For long enough. I don't care if it *destroys* me. He has to pay for what he's done."

"He *will*. Maybe he already is."

Henry could feel his heart beginning to pound, his chest become hot. "I don't mean in the afterlife, Vincent. I mean here and now. With these hands. God had His chance. For eight years. Maybe longer. And He did nothing. It's my turn now."

"Calm down," said Rickey, rising from his chair. Henry could feel all the short hair on his head prickle as it stood up, as if he were a dog with hackles.

"What if he's changed? What if he's not the monster you remember? What if he even had good reasons for doing some of the things he did?" Vincent asked.

"It doesn't matter," said Henry, brushing past him and joining Rickey near the pile of furniture. "He could be a saint now, but it doesn't change what he did. And there's no reason good enough. There are plenty of people here that survived without doing the things he did."

"Are there?" Rickey asked, squinting up at Henry, "I'm not so sure that's true. At least, not on a general level. I just think people don't talk about it here."

"What about the girl?" asked Vincent, so quietly that Henry almost missed it.

"Marnie is tough. She knows what has to be done in order to survive now."

"This isn't about survival Henry. You're out. You're free. You say you don't care if this destroys you, that you will have your vengeance, come what may. But what about the girl? What if it destroys her too?"

Henry was quiet. Rickey stood up and pushed the chair back into the pile. "Relax, both of you. That military guy isn't going to help him anyway Vincent. And there's no way he'll be able to take a whole camp on by himself, even if there is a camp left to take. At least, not till he's much stronger and has, you know, some kind of weapon. By then it'll be fall and too late for him to go. There's no reason to argue until then. It makes my head hurt."

No one said anything for a moment. Rickey put out the last of his cigarette on his boot. "Come on. I'm starving. Henry can't even be bothered to unpack let alone cook. Let's go to that diner near the old tracks. We can pick up Melissa on the way."

But Henry was still fuming and refused. Rickey shrugged and walked out the door with his slow saunter. Vincent watched Henry for a moment longer and then offered his hand. Henry shook it reluctantly.

"I'm not your enemy Henry. I just don't want to see a good man ruined by anger. Whatever you are planning– it's not going to make anything better for you or for Marnie or for anyone else."

"I'm sorry, Father. But I'm not so sure that I *am* a

good man."

"If you weren't a good man you wouldn't be looking for the girl. You're all she has left. Let it be a good man that finds her and not a monster."

Vincent left the house and the last of the afternoon sun went with him. Henry was too angry to follow them. He spent his frustration in labor, dragging the few pieces of furniture around the house until he burnt his temper away.

TWENTY-EIGHT

The pretty secretary watched a man in a perfect black suit walk out of the office. She glanced over at Henry and gave him a brief and pitying smile. "You can go in now, Mr. Broom," she said.

He tried to ignore her look, but he felt under-dressed and overwhelmed. If the Governor wouldn't agree . . . He couldn't think about that now. He smoothed the clothes he had been given, they were too large by two sizes, but they were clean and had no holes. He stood up with a brief tight smile to the secretary and walked into the Governor's office.

The man behind the desk was even more shrunken and tired than he had appeared on television. Henry guessed that all the pomp and fashion was reserved for the secretary. Here was where the real business happened. And he could see it took its toll here too. "Mr. Broom is it?" said the governor, standing to shake his hand.

"Yes, Henry Broom."

"Please, have a seat. You're a new arrival. Dorothy didn't say what this appointment was about. Why don't you go ahead?"

Henry sat and then adjusted uncomfortably. "I'm not entirely sure where to start. I saw your broadcast a few nights ago. I don't know what kind of files or information you have on me or my friends, I don't know what they said in their interviews or what your soldiers reported back to you. We were kept, these past eight years– we were slaves. Most of us were used as guard dogs for the camp–"

The Governor leaned forward, his ancient desk chair squealing. "Guard dogs? What do you mean? You mean you were soldiers?"

Henry shook his head. "No, not soldiers. We were Infected. Mad. We were chained to posts in the front and back of the camp," he slid the fabric of his shirt away from his neck and the smooth red scar glimmered under the florescent bulb. "We were starved, without shelter or medical care. One of the people in the camp, my friend, found out about the Cure. She

- 184 -

went to get it. The men in the camp threw her in the pen with us when she came back. It took her days to die. They knew about the Cure, but they wouldn't help us. They used us to scare locals into giving them what they wanted. They'd throw anyone who stood up to them into the pens with us. That's what we ate for eight years." Henry's eyes started to leak and he turned deep red. "And the women had it worse. All their teeth were removed so they couldn't bite. The were tied up and *used*. And then the food started to run out. So the men that ran the camp started getting rid of the dead weight. They started by throwing those women into the pens with the rest of the Infected. Only they couldn't fight. They were planning on feeding the older people and the kids to us, so they didn't have so many mouths to feed and so they could keep us. But we escaped before they could. One of the kids let us all out." Henry stopped, the knot in his throat now too tight to speak around.

The Governor coughed. "I'm sorry that you went through that. But you are free now, son. You're safe here, all of you."

Henry shook his head. "I'm not here to give you a sob story and get a pat on the back. Those men are still out there. Maybe keeping more Infected, people who didn't escape. Maybe just killing the people who depend on them and the people around them. Terrorizing survivors for miles. There are people up in that Lodge that need help. I came to ask for help."

The Governor leaned back, his chair squeaking again. "What kind of help?"

"You said in your broadcast that you wouldn't tolerate bullies and looters. You said the war with the Infected was over and it is time to turn your attention to retaking land, expanding. These are the worst kind of bullies, Governor. Thieves, rapists, slavers, murderers. It doesn't get any worse. And they have innocent people in their grasp who they'll squeeze until there isn't anything left, not even a corpse. You have to send someone to stop them." Henry found himself half standing, breathing hard. He sat quickly.

"Do you have a location for this camp?"

Henry pulled out the wrinkled map that Melissa had found for him. He handed it to the Governor. "It was here when we left. Here for eight years. They were well entrenched, I doubt they abandoned it."

His knee wiggled restlessly as the Governor studied the map. At last he put it down and looked at Henry again.

"This is a very long way from the City. It's a long way even from the farthest our patrols have been."

"But this is the only civilization left. This is the only place with enough people and firepower to help."

"It would take a great deal of resources. Supplies and men that may be better used here or closer to us, to help protect the people we already have."

Henry felt a little claw of panic piercing his arm, climbing with little jumps up toward his neck. "But there's no one else to help them. They've already lived almost a decade in the worst kind of fear and pain–" The Governor held up a hand to stop him.

"Henry, if you don't mind me asking, were there any Infected left when you escaped or did you all leave together?"

"I– I'm not sure. She said I was the last one to be freed, she wanted to give me a running start so I wouldn't be shot."

"She?"

"The girl that let us out. Marnie, my friend's daughter. She let us out so they couldn't use us anymore."

"I see. And when you were escaping, did you flee immediately or was there some fighting?"

"There was fighting. Lots of fighting. We were hungry, most of us hadn't eaten in days."

"Don't you think there's a good chance that everyone is dead? Would you, in your starving state, have left anything standing?"

"I don't know. Maybe. Maybe all the bandits are gone. But what if there are still Infected in the pens that didn't get released? And the people Marnie locked away in the Lodge– they were already hungry. They might be starving. Or some of the men may have been inside or out looting. We need to go back and make sure."

"I understand from your interviews that it's been months since your escape. Dr. Rider finally administered the Cure, what, about a week ago now? If there was anyone left at your camp, they've either moved on or they've starved. I'm not trying to be harsh, but that's the way things are. I can't spare any men to go so far out of our current zone to take out someone who may or may not still be there. Not even to rescue a handful of survivors. I'm sorry."

"It would be different if I was Immune and sitting here wouldn't it?"

"Actually, Henry, I'd be far less likely to believe you if you were Immune. I'm trying to be as kind as I can about this, but we've walked into ambushes before trying to rescue people. I don't know you. You just showed up a few days ago. Until I have a chance to speak to Dr. Rider or Mr. Courtlen to verify your story, I have no way of knowing if what you say is true. They are unfortunately both busy with the trial right now, too busy even for me. I can't risk it. Try to understand, my first duty is to the people that already live here."

"Then give me a weapon and some supplies, I'll go myself and bring back whoever is left. I can't just leave them there."

"Have you ever even fired a gun?"

Henry shook his head.

"You are in no shape to go tramping through the outer zones again. You're half starved, you don't know the first thing about the dangers out there. You've survived mostly by dumb luck. If I gave you permission and supplies, I'd be responsible for losing a gun, not a small consideration these days, and probably for your death and the death of anyone you actually shoot. I can't do it."

"Look, I saw your broadcast. I know there are still people waiting for their loved ones. You've told them they're all dead, not to hold out hope for them any more. But they might be. Some of them might be up at that camp. Immune and starving or Infected and enslaved. If I can't get you to help me, I'll have to go to the citizens of the City for help."

The Governor sighed and scrubbed his face. "I know that's supposed to be a threat. And if the man who had this job before me were still here, he would have had you and your friends executed and hidden before you even walked through the gate because he would have believed you could convince people. I'm not him though, and even if I thought you could get people on your side I'd still let you go on as you have. But I know how things work here. Better than I ever wanted to. You're one man. Even if you could get people to sympathize with you, they wouldn't help. They're too scared of what's out there. Too comfortable in here. And who is going to believe a newly Cured stranger over the government that has protected and fed them for years? I'm sorry, Henry, but there isn't anything I can do. We should be headed toward that sector by the fall, if everything goes well. Why don't you come to see me then, if you are still convinced you can help."

Henry shook his head. "There won't be anybody left by then," he said quietly and stood to go.

"Oh, and Henry, in case you're thinking of doing something silly like going after them yourself, I have to remind you that vigilantism isn't tolerated here. If you leave, don't come back."

Henry walked out of the office without responding. What was left to say?

- 188 -

TWENTY-NINE

He didn't sleep, just paced the floor and moved furniture across it. He didn't answer the door when the others came by. He didn't want to hear Rickey gloat because he was right or endure the pitying relief of Vincent and Melissa. He felt a pang of guilt for not visiting Molly after the meeting with the governor, but it wasn't enough for him to make the trip to the hospital.

He tried to plan, but he didn't get very far before he stumbled against the probability that they were already dead. Over and over, as if he were on a circular track and the thought only moved farther along to meet him again later. He got as far as planning to steal tools from his work, but had no real idea of which or how. He forgot to eat, the thick, greasy lump of impotence in his chest choking him. By the time the City's bells rang for wake up, Henry was haggard and bristling with hair and he was stumbling, aimlessly, as if the Cure had never happened. He'd figured nothing out and his frustration had not abated. He resolved to watch the assignments and the tools that went in and out of the warehouse. He'd have to start saving up food and tokens for supplies. He wandered into his bathroom and caught a glimpse of himself in the mirror. *Successful thieves don't already look like criminals, Henry. Clean yourself up. Pretend this didn't happen. That you've forgotten the idea, even to yourself for a while. Watch, wait. You're only going to get one chance.*

He took a shower, shaved, put on clean clothes, though he didn't want to do any of those things. And then he went to work with a placid smile on his face, biking through the breezy City's bright morning to the low, dirty brick All-Work building.

He was unlucky when he got there though, immediately assigned to the Farm instead of the warehouse. He'd have to wait to find a weapon for his journey.

"You normally wouldn't get thrown into it this fast," said Stephanie, "but everyone is at the trial, it's the defense's opening statements today. Don't worry though, I'll be with you. I don't think we'll be doing anything complicated. Probably rock picking or stubble burning. It's too early to start planting."

There was a long sling filled with a shovel, a hoe, a rake, and a few other tools Henry didn't recognize. He arranged it on his back and picked up the thick plastic bucket Stephanie handed him. He was shocked at the mob of people walking in the opposite direction as he and Stephanie made their way to the Farm. The street was actually crowded and the noise shocked him. Stephanie didn't seem to notice and Henry tried to pretend like he didn't either, but he kept stopping to watch the people and at last she had to wait for him to catch up.

"It must be odd. Seeing so many people after all that time," she said, "does it make you nervous?"

"No. Not nervous. Excited maybe? Happy I guess. Were you sick for a long time too?"

"No, I've been here a while now. I was a kid when it happened. Twelve. So I was small. Most people were holed up or locked away. The ones that made it here anyway. I wasn't. I was just quick. I was faster than most of the other adult Infected, so they had a hard time catching me when they were hungry. I was too small to attack another person on my own. I mostly survived on animals. Cats, rabbits, squirrels. Sometimes on leftovers. I think the Immunes wouldn't shoot me because I was a kid. No one wants to kill a kid, not even when they have to. I was pretty close to the original Cure camp, so I was one of the first ones. I was fourteen then. I think if I'd been sick much longer things might have been different. I was starting not to look like a kid anymore, I was getting bigger, going after wounded Infected on my own. It was only a matter of time." She pushed open the large wrought iron gate to the old park. "Let's find the foreman," she said. There were a handful of people scattered over the dull brown field that used to be the park. Some were marking plots and others were hoeing up large stones and dropping them into buckets. A team of horses pulled an old plow down the field, the dark furrows bulging in their wake. Stephanie found the foreman drinking grain coffee and sorting seed packets.

"Good morning Amos," Stephanie waved at the large man as they approached.

"Mornin' Steph. Only two today?" Amos shook his head. "You'd think eating would be more important to people than a couple of lawyers jawing about nothing all day. Well, we're mostly rock picking today. We just started, so take your pick of sections. The Governor gave the okay for bonuses until the trial is over, so for every bucket of stones you cart off, I'll give you an extra red token."

"Hot dog!" exclaimed Stephanie. Henry smiled.

"No cheating now. Full buckets," said Amos, giving Stephanie a stern look. He turned toward Henry. "You just come in from the camps? You look like a stiff breeze could blow you over. You sure you're up for this? You can stay and sort seed packets with me if you'd rather."

Henry shook his head. "Thanks, but the only way I'll get stronger is with good, steady work."

"Good man," said Amos, nodding his head in approval, "well you and Stephanie get to it, and I'll make sure someone gets down to you both with fresh coffee and something to eat by break time."

Stephanie elbowed Henry gently as they walked down the field. "Good job," she said, "It's hard to make friends with Amos. He's a good guy to have in your corner though, especially if you end up working the Farm a lot."

They settled about halfway down the field, intending to work their way toward the others. It was still cool, but Henry was grateful for the breeze anyway, picking his shirt off his skin as he dumped the sling near where he was working and grabbed the hoe and bucket. They'd started on opposite ends of the same row, working in toward each other. It meant they couldn't really talk to each other, but that suited Henry just fine. The work was almost mindless, a twist with the hoe, the gritty cold of a wet stone and the satisfying hollow thud and then click as the stones hit the side of the bucket and then each other. It let Henry's racing mind rest. He tried not to think about Marnie or Phil. Tried not to plan or eye the sharp blade of the shovel or imagine its weight on his back for miles. He remembered the smell of dirt. The way the rain sizzled as it put out the campfires, soaked through his rags. The soft flow of the mud as he paced a circle around the post. He was covered in it more often than he was clean, even though Dave tried to splash him with water every day. He was used to the smell, it was almost part of him. Henry's shoes felt too tight and hot. He stood up and pretended he was stretching. Nobody was looking. He crossed to his bundle and pulled his shoes off, wrapping them carefully in the canvas of his bundle. He blushed, embarrassed. He wondered if he were doing something wrong. But it felt like burying the hair. An intense compulsion, now relieved by the feel of the damp soil brushing the top of his feet, cool and soft. He tried not to worry what the others would say if they saw, and went back to pulling the dark rocks, like teeth from a rotting jaw.

He was sore and sweaty by the first break, but he never let on, refusing another offer by Amos to sit and sort seeds. The sun was beginning to shine with real force and he'd stopped for water more than he meant to. Still, he'd filled two buckets by lunchtime, a horse cart coming slowly up and down the rows to empty the buckets and truck away the load. He and Stephanie had worked through four rows, but they were still a good distance down the field when the City bells rang. Henry's breath was too loud in his ears for him to hear them, but Stephanie stood up and shaded her brow with her hand, looking toward the tall metal fence of the park. "Did you hear that, Henry?" she called. He stood up and shook his head. She looked at her watch, then held it to her ear. "It's too early to be afternoon break," she yelled.

The others were already drifting toward the gate. Stephanie walked down the row toward him, her forehead wrinkling with worry. "Something's wrong," she said as she reached him, "we should go find out. It might be a fire, they'll need us. Grab your shoes and tools." She walked past him and picked up her bundle. Henry sat on the unplowed turf at the edge of the field and brushed his feet off, slowly pulling his shoes on and watching the other farm workers as they began to hurry toward Amos. He took a minute to wipe his face, nervous and suddenly shy of the others.

The others were crowded around the iron fence watching as a string of military vehicles passed them. The City bells were still ringing and Amos pulled himself together first. "Okay folks," he rumbled, "grab your buckets and follow those trucks."

"Is it a fire?" asked one of the farmhands. Amos shrugged. Stephanie was squinting at the skyline again, her dusty hand making a shade.

"There's no smoke," she murmured.

"Maybe we just can't see it," said Henry.

"Maybe– but it's not like it used to be. There's no smog or traffic exhaust for it to get lost in. We can usually see fires for miles, even past the Barrier."

"Maybe someone's attacking the City."

Stephanie shook her head and bent to pick up her bucket. "The soldiers would have stopped and told us to get home or to our stations. We used to do drills all the time."

The iron gate clanged behind them and they started jogging down the road, following the convoy of trucks. Here and there someone would come out of a nearby house or business, joining the flow of people, but the street was still mostly empty.

"Where is everybody?" growled Amos. The big man was beginning to sweat though he hadn't even started breathing heavy yet. Henry began to become nervous. If the foreman was getting scared then something must be very wrong.

"They're at the courthouse," called someone farther up.

Amos's face split into a nasty grin. "Good. Maybe that Pazzo guy finally got what was coming to him."

"No, that's not it," puffed Stephanie, "They wouldn't send all those trucks just for one assassination."

Their conjectures were interrupted by a wall of

uniformed soldiers telling them to stay back. Henry remember Amos's smile though, saved it for later like a secret note, just to him. Someone else in the City understood vengeance.

THIRTY

"We came to help," yelled Stephanie, holding up her bucket. The soldiers looked nervously at each other and at the small crowd that was forming around them. Henry guessed that it was a good thing almost everyone was inside. Otherwise the crowd would be much larger. But then he noticed the soldiers standing on the steps. They were facing the doors of the courthouse, not the crowd outside. They were dressed in plastic suits with breathing masks. As Henry watched, a soldier with a cart began handing more of the suits down the line of the soldiers closer to him and to the crowd. The panic was almost immediate. The crowd backed away, and some of the people shouted. There was a broad space between the soldiers and the crowd now. An officer stepped into the space, the hood of his suit still not on, his face still a human one. He held up a hand for quiet and Henry was shocked as the crowd fell silent.

"There has been an accident in the courthouse. A bacterium has been released– we don't know what it is yet, but given the nature of the trial, we want to isolate it. We're going to move the people inside to the hospital and we need you to go to your homes and stay inside until the Military Governor gives the all clear. There is nothing you can do to help. The work day is finished, please return to your homes. We will broadcast an update as soon as we can and give you information on friends and family as soon as it's available. Please let us do our jobs and return home safely." He pulled his suit on and stepped back through the perimeter of soldiers. The crowd began to disperse, fleeing farther into the City, scattering like ash.

"I guess we should go back to the All-Work Station and drop off our tools Henry," said Stephanie, her eyes still wide, strands of hair slicked to her brow with sweat, "and then go home."

"Forget that," said Amos, "I'll meet you at Margie's in ten minutes. The 'shine's on me." He wandered off, looking a little stunned and directionless.

"Margie's?" asked Henry as they walked toward the All-Work Station.

"The only bar where Immunes and Cureds can drink together without any fistfights breaking out. And the only one not regularly raided. I think the Governor turns a blind eye to it as long as there's no trouble."

"Is Amos an Immune?"

"Yeah, but he's one of the Immunes that refuses to treat us like crap. His wife and his kid were Infected."

"Are they Cured?"

"No, they died in the Plague. I don't know the whole story though. But he blames the people who made the bacteria, not the Infected. Or the Cured."

There was no one at the station when they got there. "I'd better leave a note, just in case," said Stephanie, "I hope Bernice wasn't in the courthouse. I have a feeling that she was though. And a lot of our guys were using some of their saved up tokens to take days off and see it too." She suppressed a sob and against his will, Henry felt a pang of sympathy for her and a suffocating blanket of loneliness in the silent office. He tried not to think of the giant blackboard with its list of names. He touched her shoulder.

"Hey, don't worry. We don't know anything yet. Maybe it was a false alarm. Or maybe it was just one small part of the courthouse that was exposed. The officer said they didn't know what it was, either. Maybe it's just an experiment or something. Not a disease at all."

Stephanie sniffed and nodded. "You're right, I shouldn't panic yet." She wiped her eyes with a small clean spot on her sleeve and tacked the note to the door. "Let's go meet Amos."

Margie's turned out to be a badly lit bakery with a banged up pool table and a few televisions. Someone had tried to add some style though, lining the top shelves with wildly colored jars of pickled vegetables interspersed with tangles of twinkle lights. The glass cases were filled with sandwiches wrapped in stained cloth napkins and lumpy loaves of bread. The whole place smelled of fermenting yeast. Henry found it comforting. He was relieved to see Rickey already losing to Vincent at pool. He wondered how they found the place, but the crowd that was quickly forming around them told him that pretty much everyone had naturally made their way here. Amos saw them and waved from a far table. Stephanie headed toward him while Henry stopped to let his friends know he was there.

"Hey," said Vincent, looking concerned, "have you seen Melissa or Pam?"

"No, I'm just relieved to see you two. I think Pam went to the trial. And Molly is still at the hospital. Has the news been on yet?"

Rickey shook his head. "No, I think the chick that does the news was probably there too. She was there yesterday." He twitched his head toward Stephanie and Amos. "Those people from your work?"

"Yeah. Well, at least for today's work. Come over and meet them when you're done."

Henry moved away, uncomfortable with the way Vincent was staring at him. He hadn't told them about his meeting with the Governor yet, and he didn't really want to. But Vincent would be suspicious until he did. He'd try to stop Henry's plan, and that was something Henry couldn't allow. He retreated to the relative anonymity of Amos's table. "Why a bakery?" he said, sitting on a cracked leather stool.

Amos grinned. "Beer."

"What?"

"It's the only place with beer. Wheat beer. Everyone else just has moonshine of various potencies. But I like beer."

"Why doesn't anyone else make it? Everyone gets a wheat ration right?"

"Yeah, but they're the only ones who know how to make the right yeast. Margie's husband was a microbiologist before. Kind of his thing. It's a family secret now."

Stephanie sat down with two cracked mugs. She handed Henry one. "Thought you better start with the beer," she said, "the 'shine still lays me out and I've been drinking it for a few years now." She turned to Amos. "Hear anything yet?"

"Nope. But if they had to move everyone into the hospital it'll be a few hours until everything is settled. Still, you'd think they'd warn people away or something."

Henry looked around, losing the thread of the conversation in the gentle hum of the place. Every few seconds the string of bells on the door rattled as another group came in. Vincent and Rickey gave up the pool game as the bakery became more crowded and wandered over. The pool table was appropriated as seating. The smell of cooking food filled up the spaces between bodies and Henry was sure Margie's was going to have a record sales day in both alcohol and food. The employees didn't look any happier than the other people though. At last the televisions crackled loudly and the bakery fell dead silent. The screens stuttered and at last focused on a sparsely furnished cinderblock room where soldiers moved constantly around at various tasks, though none of them were in bio-hazard suits, which Henry took as a good sign. The Military Governor stood at a table strewn with papers talking to another soldier.

"Sir?" called someone from behind the camera, "We're ready for you."

The Governor looked up and nodded. He walked around the table toward the camera. The skin on Henry's arm crawled with tiny sparks as the Governor came into sharp focus. The man looked exhausted. In the space of a day he seemed to have aged another ten years. Henry suddenly didn't want to hear what was going to be said. He looked around for an exit but he was crammed in by motionless bodies, all eyes on the bakery's two screens. He could see the panic on other faces too and he knew he wasn't being irrational.

"Good evening. This afternoon, the prison uncovered a plot by Dr. Robert Pazzo to release a new strain of the December Plague into the public. Through hard work and quick thinking, Officer Stan Kembrey and his team were able to alert the officers of the court that Dr. Pazzo was likely using himself as the incubating host for this bacteria."

There was a collective gasp around Henry. He could

smell burning toast as someone forgot the oven.

"The team at the prison believes that we caught him in time to prevent transmission. As a precaution, however, we have isolated the potentially infected inside the hospital. It's too soon to determine the length of the quarantine, but we will get that information both to those of you watching outside the hospital and to our people who are waiting inside.

"Since I took this office, I've prided myself on our transparency. I will not hide any information that we know from you. In a moment Dr. Lang will tell us what is known about this strain of bacteria and what we can expect in the next days and weeks. In return, I must ask you not to panic. The phones in the hospital have been turned on and will remain so throughout. Please use these to contact your loved ones. Do not try to break quarantine. There are soldiers stationed both inside and outside the hospital. The last thing anyone wants is to use force to keep the quarantine secure, but we will if we must. For those of you outside the hospital, we will need your help especially during this crisis. Please do not flee the City, your work is going to be vital to keep everything running. You are safe here, the bacteria has been contained. We all must work together to get past this. I'll turn it over to Dr. Lang for the moment."

There was a murmur around Henry as a short man in a patched lab coat fidgeted his way into view. "Margie!" someone yelled, "Bread's burning." Someone else opened the door and a cool breeze threaded it's way in between the bodies, barely reaching Henry before it became a tepid splash of air. There was a little shifting, but then everyone was quiet again as the doctor began to speak.

"I was hoping that Dr. Carton would be willing to do this, but his health is failing, and he refused to speak on camera." The doctor held up his hands in a calming gesture. "I want you to know he is working closely with us on this though. It will take time to verify our information– we have to be careful of course, but I will tell you what we know so far." He pulled out a thick fold of papers from his oversized pocket. "Most of what we know so far comes from Dr. Pazzo's attorney, Frank Courtlen, Officer Kembrey at the prison and a– Dr. Rider. They've apparently known about the bacteria for a short time and were working with the authorities to find it and stop its release." Vincent nudged Henry.

"Think that's why they couldn't stay when they cured us?" he hissed.

"The lab that Dr. Pazzo worked for was responsible for the development and accidental release of the original December Plague, which was subsequently cured by Dr. Carton, of course. What only a few people knew though, was that another strain of the same bacteria was developed at the same time. This strain was more powerful because of a certain plasmid . . ." The doctor trailed off for a second as he saw the Governor shaking his head. "Anyway, you don't need all that medical speak, the point is, the other strain was stronger because it is incurable. There is no antibiotic that can treat it, not now and not in the future. The bacteria were frozen in three vials and locked away in a vault. It's unclear at this point how Dr. Pazzo got his hands on it, but he did and smuggled it into prison at his arrest. At some point in the past twenty-four to forty-eight hours, we believe that Dr. Pazzo infected himself with the bacteria and walked into the courthouse today, intending to infect as many people as possible.

"Fortunately for us and all the people in the courthouse, we probably caught him before he became widely contagious. Chances are very good that Dr. Pazzo himself is the only person infected. We also don't know if this bacteria would have the same mutation as the last strain. It maybe as harmless as its creators originally meant it to be. However, it would be foolish not to keep an extra watchful eye on ourselves and our neighbors in the next few weeks in case the contagion has somehow escaped. If it follows a similar path to the December Plague, then symptoms would be very similar, and may not be apparent for some time. If you or a loved one is stumbling more than usual or seems clumsier than normal, is slurring their speech, acting drunk or impaired, has strange cravings or compulsions, or becomes unusually or inappropriately angry, please go to the dental clinic near St.

Agricol church, it is being converted to an alternate quarantine station and there will be medical staff ready to help you. Please do not try to approach anyone displaying these symptoms or enter their house. If you were immune last time, do not assume you will be immune this time. It is highly unlikely that you are. We have yet to determine if this is airborne or not, we will let you know as soon as we do."

The world swirled and warped to Henry. As if this better place, this City, were just a dream in the unending misery of his illness. Just a vision of food and warmth and human contact that his brain had erected as an escape. A dream he was about to wake from.

"Thank you Dr. Lang," said the Governor, shaking the nervous man's hand. "A few last things. First, everyone who is not already assigned to the Farm, Medical, or the Electric and Water Plants will report to All-Work Station tomorrow. We need to make sure the lights stay on and the people in the hospital get fed. Everyone will be assigned essential tasks until this is over–"

"Shit," whispered Stephanie.

"What?" said Henry.

"Bernice was at the courthouse. That means you and me and the ten guys that aren't in the hospital have to manage all these people."

"Me? I don't know anything about– well, anything."

"You're two days ahead of everyone else," she hissed, "be there early tomorrow, we're going to need to organize."

"–and lastly," Henry tuned into the Governor's voice again, "I will remind everyone that our rules will be enforced even with our smaller patrols. Looting will not be tolerated. Brawls, riots, vandalism are not acceptable. We are all that's left. We won't survive by adopting an 'every man for himself' attitude. Everyone must pull together for us to get through." The Governor took a deep breath. "All right, we will broadcast again when we know anything new. Goodnight everyone."

THIRTY-ONE

Margie's cleared out pretty quickly after that, each customer looking at the people around them as if they expected each of them to already be crawling with infection. Stephanie decided to get home early and warned Henry to be ready for the morning. Amos finished his beer and clapped him on the shoulder. "Hope you get assigned the Farm some more, Henry. We need more like you. Going to have to hear your story sometime. Some better day than this." He nodded to Vincent and Rickey and wandered out into the dark. The bakery workers wiped tables and counters with tired, frightened expressions.

"Let's go home," said Vincent, "These folks want to go to bed."

But suddenly Henry was afraid to be alone in his house. They stumbled out into the dark street, the wheat beer overwhelming their reduced frames. "I'm not going home," said Henry to Vincent.

"Me either," said Rickey, "Time to get out of Dodge."

"What? You can't leave– these people need us," said Vincent, "Even if you haven't made friends here yet, there's Pam and Molly. They're both at the hospital. Are you going to leave them?"

Rickey shoved his hands into his baggy jean pocket. "You want us to stay and do what? Get sick again? Eat them? I'm done Vincent, I'm not going back to that. I'll kill myself first." He drew a shaking hand out of his pocket. It was holding a cigarette.

"Where are you going to go? It's a disease, if it's out it will spread everywhere."

Rickey shook his head, the burning red eye of the cigarette making tiny trails in the dark. "Not anymore. I'll go as far west as I can, to the coast if I have to. There aren't many people left, it can't travel if it doesn't have people to infect. Maybe I'll live in the Great Empty, wherever I can find it. Maybe find another city, just as isolated. Where there aren't insane scientists trying to murder us all."

"What about bandits or wild animals or other Infected?"

"Sorry to break it to you, Father, but I'm pretty sure we're the last survivors of the Infected. Everyone else starved or killed each other a long time ago. Sure, there'll be the odd camp like Phil's or someone nursing along an Infected hoping for a cure and never hearing of it, but most of them are gone. Alone, or with Henry, we'll be able to avoid most big camps and we can stick to rural areas, places no one wants. There's probably enough stuff out there that a man could live out all his days never needing to go near another person for help or to trade."

"You've *seen* what's out there. There's nothing left. Nothing. You'll starve."

"I've seen what's a few miles from here, Vincent. That's it. There's a whole big world out there—"

"It's a dead world!" cried Vincent.

Rickey sucked on the cigarette.

"Maybe," Henry said, "but even if you're right, I'd rather starve than go back to what I was. It wasn't so bad. The starving, I mean. It didn't hurt so much after a while. But waking up was the worst thing that's ever happened to us. We have to relive the eating every day. Forever. I don't want anymore of it."

The three of them began walking toward the Barrier.

"You could come with us Vincent," said Henry quietly.

"And abandon the people who took us in, fed us, healed us? I can't Henry. You shouldn't either."

"Is it better to turn back into what we were?"

"We don't know that's what will happen. Maybe we'll be resistant to it, since it's already happened to us once. Maybe it's our turn to take care of others."

Rickey snorted. "You mean like Phil 'took care' of us? Feed them to each other, cage them, beat them? No thanks."

"Henry's friends cared for him when he was sick. They made a choice to protect him even when they knew what was likely to happen."

"But they didn't!" Rickey was shouting and waving

his arms for emphasis. "They turned him over to a thug. They turned us all over to him. They were cowards. So was everyone here," he turned around pointing to the dark houses with his glowing cigarette. "They sat behind this wall and let the world tear itself apart. And now, when they are set up nicely, they can't even be bothered to clean up the mess that's left. Can they Henry?"

"What are you talking about?" asked Vincent.

"The Military Governor said he couldn't spare the men or the resources to go after Phil's camp. He won't even give me a weapon so I can go myself."

"Well, at least someone here has some sense," grumbled Vincent.

They could see the lights of the Barrier now, could hear a bustle from its direction.

"We're not the only ones who are leaving," said Henry, pointing to the big gate where a small crowd milled around.

"Henry, you asked me if you were damned for what you had done while you were ill. But you are not ill now. You know what is right. And the man who knows the right thing and does not do it– that is sin. A good man would not leave."

Henry stopped and turned to face Vincent. "I'm not a good man any longer. I don't know if I even *want* to be a good man any longer."

Vincent shook his head. "Then you are truly lost. Is there anything I can say to persuade either of you to stay and do your duty to these people?"

"I'm sorry Father," said Rickey, "I can't do this all over again." He shook Vincent's hand. "Coming Henry?"

Henry nodded and began to walk after Rickey into the lighted street in front of the Barrier.

"Henry," called Vincent, "if you want to find the girl, you have to stay."

Henry stopped. "Her name is Marnie," he said over his shoulder.

"Fine. The only way you're going to find Marnie is if you stay."

He turned around. "How do you figure?"

Vincent sighed and his shoulders sagged. "Because Phil is in the City."

Rickey spat a stray thread of tobacco. "Lying now, Father? I don't think that's allowed," he said. But something in Vincent's manner made Henry's heart hiccup.

"It's not a lie," Vincent said, his voice weary and cracking, "He's a gravedigger for the City. I saw him when I went to help with some church repairs this morning."

"Shit." Rickey spat on the pavement again.

"Does he know we're here?" asked Henry, his skin tingling and sparking with adrenaline.

"I don't think so. I mean, I barely recognize myself and he never paid attention to any of us particularly. You maybe, but I doubt you look the same. I wasn't even sure I recognized him, but Melissa saw him too, on one of her deliveries."

"You weren't going to tell me."

"No, I wasn't."

"Why are you telling him now? Why are you so desperate for him to stay? Why couldn't he have come with me? What's it to you?" Rickey walked quickly toward the priest. It looked like he was going to start a fight. Henry wasn't sure he wanted to stop him. But Vincent grabbed Rickey's shoulder before he could swing.

"Because Rickey, as tough as you think you are, as bad as you think you've been, I'm confident you're good at heart, that you'll do the right thing eventually. And that you're lonelier than you say. If Henry refuses to leave, then you won't go. But Henry– I'm not sure he'll come out right in the end. He's far too concerned with damnation to deny that he feels himself already headed there."

Henry shifted uncomfortably and felt anger heat the center of his belly. Vincent glanced past Rickey at him. "I know it's a risk telling him that Phil is here. But if he ever wants to see Marnie again, he'll have to restrain his taste for revenge. And if he stays, it will give me– *us* more time to convince him to stay a good man."

Henry walked off into the dark in the direction of his house without speaking to either of him. A small part of him regretted not saying goodbye to Rickey, but Vincent was probably right. Rickey wouldn't leave alone. The greater part of him raged. He was angry with Vincent for not telling him immediately about Phil. He was angry that Vincent had seen Phil but not Marnie, even though he knew it was irrational. He was angry that he was being manipulated. He was angry with himself for not just walking out the City gate and never looking back, for not forgetting Marnie or the past decade of his life.

What was he supposed to do now? Vincent would know if Phil died who had killed him. And he probably knew where Marnie was. Henry struggled with himself, trying to convince himself that he cared more about where Marnie was than about revenge. He didn't quite succeed. But as he tripped over the dark stoop outside his door, he suddenly grinned. Grave digging wasn't essential. Phil was going to be at the All-Work Station in the morning. And somehow, no matter what he had to do, Henry was going to get himself assigned to the same job. He flicked on the living room light and looked around. He had to get the house ready. In a few days, he was sure, Marnie would be living with him and he wanted to have her room ready.

Henry collapsed on the couch, falling asleep without even considering whether Phil would see him coming or not.

THIRTY-TWO

The sun was barely leaking into the horizon when Henry arrived at the All-Work Station. The work bell wouldn't ring for another hour, but there were still a group of people milling around the station. A few of them belonged there, the few who had taken a vacation during the slack time instead of attending the trial. Most of them were new people who'd been too nervous to sleep. Henry wondered absently whether many had fled the City overnight, or if most everyone had friends in quarantine to keep them. There was a little lonely chime in the back of his head as the Barrier passed through his thoughts. He wished he knew what Rickey had decided. The small crowd was silent, not even a whispered conversation or greeting as other people drifted in. Normally, it would have sent a chill through Henry, but now he was too absorbed in trying to recognize Phil among them to even notice.

Stephanie arrived a few minutes later and herded them all into the warehouse. He wasn't there. Henry fought an irrational rage. *It's still early. Calm down*, he told himself, *It's been eight years. Wait just a little longer. Just a little while. Have to do it right. Have to do it so I don't get caught, so I can take care of Marnie.*

He helped Stephanie sort tool bundles, all the while watching the door for a sign of Phil. The warehouse was soon crammed with people and the work bell was still ten minutes away. "We have to get these people moving. There are a lot more coming. Hank, can you take most of this group to Electric?" Stephanie asked one of the men helping them. He nodded and moved off, bringing people bundles and directing them out the door.

"You want me to do the farm today, Steph?" asked a lean, tanned woman. But Stephanie shook her head.

"I think Henry and I will take people to the farm. Why don't you get a security team together. The Barrier is short because of the hospital barricade. And Gwen, try to find people who at least know how to hold a weapon without shooting themselves."

The woman grinned and lost herself in the crowd. Henry was becoming anxious. It didn't get any better when Vincent and Melissa walked up to him. "Let it go," hissed Melissa.

"I can't. Simple as that. Is Rickey gone?"

Vincent shook his head, "At the power plant. Can we be on your crew?"

Henry shrugged, but Stephanie overheard. "What's your normal assignment?" she asked.

"Postal service," said Melissa.

"Perfect, we need someone to head up food delivery to the hospital. You won't have to go inside or anything, just deliver a truck of prepped meals to the soldiers at the barricade. You interested?"

"Sure, how many people do I need?"

"You better grab ten or so, there are a lot of people in there and some of them may make requests for items from relatives or their homes. Again, don't go into the hospital, just give it to the soldiers."

"Can I keep the same crew until this is over?"

Stephanie sighed with relief. "That will make things *much* easier. Tell them to meet up with you instead of here."

Melissa pinched Henry's elbow before scouting the crowd. "You have to let it go," she whispered, "you think he's going to tell you where the kid is if you threaten him? He's protected here. You have to play nice to get what you want." Henry shook his head but she was gone. Vincent was being swept away by a flood of kids whose school had been forgotten in the crisis. Henry panicked for a moment looking quickly at each small face, but of course Marnie wasn't there. She was a big girl now. Vincent herded them toward the door with another adult.

"There's the bell," said Stephanie, "Want to help me get these tool bundles to everyone that's left? We'll head to the Farm a little late in case there are any stragglers."

Henry leapt at the chance to get a closer look at the remaining crowd without Melissa or Vincent watching him. He pulled the heavy bundles over, one after the other, faster than seemed possible for his wasted frame. He paused to look at every face as he handed out a bundle. *Is this him? Have I forgotten his face?* Flashed through him each time, until dozens of faces later, he determined that yes, he had forgotten. His memories all ran together with the faces he saw now, muddied the waters. Henry felt a pang of despair. Phil could have walked right by him without being noticed. He could have been in one of the other crews. He could still be assigned to the graveyard. Maybe they were expecting that job to be in demand shortly. Henry shivered at the thought. Or Vincent could have been lying to keep him in the City.

"You want to stay here and wait for anyone that's late?" Stephanie asked, "Just hang out for ten minutes and then come over to the Farm. Anyone later than that will just have to fend for themselves."

Henry nodded dumbly, still circling the thought of Phil escaping him. The warehouse emptied around him. The air cooled in the vacant building and there was no shuffling or coughing. Finally, when Henry was shouldering his bundle, already weary now that the adrenaline had worn off, he heard the door to the office open.

"Sorry I'm late. Took forever to find the place. Hello?" Rumbled a voice from the office.

"In here," called Henry irritably, picking up another bundle. He looked up as boots clomped into the warehouse doorway. And there stood Phil. Henry had expected him to be diminished somehow. Wounded maybe, from Marnie's attack. Or sunken from losing power over others. Or just smaller, weaker in the face of Henry's recovery. But Henry knew he'd never be the man he had been before the Plague, and neither would Phil. Phil seemed to grow larger, be more threatening, filled with a creepy jolliness the worse things got. Henry had withered over eight years, not just because of the deprivation he'd been forced to undergo.

Phil's bulky work clothes filled the frame of the doorway and he looked as healthy and spoiling for a fight as he always had. The only sign that anything had changed was a deep purple scar that twisted across his thick jaw. But it was

like a tar seam on a patched road, it belonged there, only
made him seem more dangerous than he had before. And for
the first time, Henry began to feel a little frightened that
things were not going to go exactly as he had planned.

"Hello?" asked Phil.

"Uh, hello, sorry, I was just closing up to go to the
Farm." Henry had no idea what he was doing. He hadn't
planned this far ahead and now he was floundering. And you
didn't flounder in front of Phil. Not if you wanted to live. He
handed Phil a bundle of tools and tried to catch up.

"Name's Phil. I don't recognize you, but then I don't
come over to the Cured side of town much," Phil grinned as if
he'd said something funny. Henry was strangely encouraged
by the sight of Phil's patchwork of missing teeth. "Are you
new?"

"Yeah, got here a few days ago."

"You Cured?"

Henry began walking toward the door. He hadn't
considered what he would say about himself. It was no good
lying, he guessed. Other people knew who he was and would
tip his hand for him. It was easier to tell the truth and hope he
was changed enough that Phil couldn't recognize him.

"Yeah, I'm Cured."

"I thought everyone from the Cure camps came to the
City months ago."

"Yeah, well, I wasn't ready yet."

Phil laughed behind Henry as he closed the door. It hit
Henry like a roll of thunder. "I hear you. Had a sweet setup
until recently myself, decided to come to the City this winter
though. Times are tough out there. What'd you say your name
was?"

He turned around and stuck out his hand as if he were
greeting a friend. "Henry."

Phil shook his hand and gave him a greasy grin again.
"Henry. Kind of old-fashioned isn't it? Don't meet too many
Henrys anymore–" Phil interrupted himself with a snort of
laughter, "well, I guess you don't meet too many of anyone
these days, but you know what I mean."

"Family name," Henry said dryly as he turned back toward the Farm.

"I knew a Henry once. You know, Before."

Henry nodded and chewed on his nerves, ready to swing the heavy bundle of tools at Phil if he had to. "Where is he now?"

"Eh, you know how these things are. Dead most likely. He got sick. I tried to take care of him but he was out of his head. Ran off one day in the middle of winter. He must have frozen."

"That's too bad," Henry said through his teeth. His knuckles gleamed around the dirty canvas. He focused on the iron gate of the Farm.

Phil trotted to catch up with him. "Yeah, I looked for him, you know, he was my buddy. I owed him. But he was long gone."

"He give you that scar?" Henry asked. There was a vicious little thrill in his core as Phil reached up to touch it gently.

"Nah, that was someone else." Henry flinched as Phil clapped a heavy hand down on his shoulder. "I'll give you some free advice. World's changed since you bought your seat at the long pig buffet. Can't be kind anymore. Got to look out for yourself. You find yourself extending a helping hand to someone, you just remember the scar on my old mug and pull it back. People are ingrates. They'll take what you'll give em and then kill you to climb over your corpse and find whatever else you got."

Henry longed to ask him if this was about the Lodge, desperate to find Marnie, but they had reached the gates of the Farm. Amos waved to him, and Henry felt the balance of power shift without Phil even realizing it. They parted ways, leaving Henry with mixed feelings of relief and urgency. He had to find out about Marnie, but he'd have to be more collected next time. He'd already given away too much.

"That guy giving you trouble Henry?" Amos asked, pulling him over to the seed sorting table, "I can tell Stephanie to assign him to Electric if you want."

The thought of Rickey's big mouth made Henry answer too quickly. "No, no. I don't want to cause any trouble. It's an old thing, not worth worrying about." He smiled in what he hoped was a reassuring way.

Amos looked at him for a few seconds. "It sure *looked* like you wanted to cause trouble. You're new here. I won't say whatever he did isn't worth it; chances are it probably was. But they take fights very seriously here. You can get thrown out or worse for things like that. And with everyone being on edge now, the punishment's likely to be stiffer if you get caught. Things don't work in here like they do out there." he said, jerking his head toward the Barrier.

Henry stared hard at Phil. "Things don't work *out there* at all. I'm not even sure they work so well in here either."

Amos shook his head. "Whatever you're planning, keep it out of the Farm. I've had enough of all of it."

"Don't worry. I'm not planning anything. And if I were, I'm not stupid enough to do it in public."

THIRTY-THREE

The yeasty smell of bread and beer hit Henry's stomach a full block before he and Amos reached Margie's. Smells, sounds, even lights carried so much further now. Henry supposed it was the lack of exhaust from cars, or the missing cushion of people that made it seem that way. The world was hard and bright and brittle now, without complex society to soften the edges. It was the silence that bothered Henry the most. Even when people were together, they mostly didn't talk. Nobody swapped jokes or gossip, not even about the trial. No one laughed or shouted. So Henry thought he'd wandered into a past life when Amos opened the door to Margie's and a blues song tumbled out into the street. Unlike the previous night, the employees were the only ones inside. The music was coming from the televisions, the screens showing picture after picture of faces in happier times. Amos smiled at the music but he avoided looking at the screen. Henry sat next to him, his eyes glued to the photographs. They fascinated him.

"What is that?" he asked. Amos grudgingly glanced up from his beer.

"Missing people. The DJ runs 'em while he plays music for work or whenever they don't have a movie to run. Probably no one at the station but him. Most everyone was at the courthouse I'd guess."

"Missing people from the Plague?"

"Yeah. Relatives who want to know what happened post pictures asking if anyone has seen them. Maybe you're up there."

"How many are there?"

Amos shrugged. "There's something like ten thousand people in the City. I think more than half probably know what happened to their families. Or know enough. Some more won't have brought pictures with them. In fact, the Cured won't have had anything with them at all for the most part. Still, say two thousand Immunes want to know. That's a spouse, an average of two kids, parents, maybe two siblings;

- 213 -

seven people that each person wants to know about. So fourteen thousand pictures around? That's what I'd guess anyway."

"Has it ever worked?"

"You mean have people found information or each other? I think people have probably found out information on some of them. But you're not just talking about finding one or two survivors out of fourteen thousand, Henry. You're talking about finding one or two survivors out of eight billion dead. You'd have had a better chance playing the lottery when there was one."

"But doesn't Immunity run in families?"

Amos cleared his throat and Henry sensed he might be treading near sensitive territory. "Yeah. It runs in families," he stared at Henry for a minute. "Just 'cause someone's Immune doesn't mean they survived."

Henry was silent for a minute. Melissa walked through the door to the kitchen, carrying a load of boxes. It was the dinner delivery for the hospital. She caught his eye and it looked like she wanted to say something to him, but another delivery worker walked out behind her with more. Amos caught the glance between them though.

"So, you going to tell me what's stuck in your craw today? Or we going to sit here until your friends spill it for you?"

Henry was quiet, considering what to say.

"Yeah. That's what I thought. I get it. I don't know you, you don't know me. I'm trying though. Seems like you've already made up your mind that this place isn't for you. That's too bad. If it's 'cause you got a beef with that greaseball gravedigger, I get it. But you're hardly the first one. The City's a big place, getting bigger all the time. You never have to see him again if you don't want to. We've all done bad things Henry. All of us. If we hadn't, we'd be dead. Whatever you did, it's over and done. There's no going back and fixing it. Whatever he did, that's in the past too. There's nothing, *nothing* either of you can do to make up for it or atone or right it. You understand? Nothing's gonna come close to what's been lost. Not revenge or trials or blood money. *Nothing.* It's useless to expect that. It's a bad old world out there, Henry. We can keep chewing at each other and making it worse, or we can move on and try to make it better for people that come after."

"That's what I'm trying to do, Amos. He's an evil person. The world would be better without him in it any more. He didn't just do– he was cruel because he enjoyed it. Not because he was trying to survive. I don't know why or how he came here, but he's not someone who should be here. He'll destroy this place from the inside out, just for the fun of it. In fact, when he remembers who I and my friends are, he'll happily dispose of us himself. We're not talking about a guy that just took potshots at Infected or hunted us for sport. He's far, far worse than that. How can I live in the same city with him? I can't even stand to live in the same world that he does."

"Then go to the Governor. There are other things that can be done besides killing him."

Henry scowled as if he'd tasted something bitter. "I did, before I knew Phil was here. I told the Governor what he'd done, what he was still doing. That he was in control of innocent people. People that belong here. The Governor said he couldn't spare the men to go after him. Not until after this trial. And if I told him now that Phil was here… you said it yourself. The attitude here is forgive and forget. But I can't. Not him. And I still don't know what happened to the people who were with him. Some of them were kids. People who've done things like he has– he's worse than the people they have on trial now. People like him shouldn't be forgiven. You're right when you say there's nothing he can do to make up for what he's done. There is no punishment severe enough to satisfy me. But he can be stopped."

Amos shook his head. "I don't understand. What is it that this guy did that's so much worse than what we've all done? I don't like to assume, but I don't think there's any way that you survived Infection for eight years without getting some blood on your hands."

They both looked up as Rickey slid a wooden chair over the floor toward them. "It's true then? You saw him Henry?" he asked, tumbling into the chair. Henry just nodded. Rickey looked like he want to spit, but a large red-faced woman behind the counter was eyeing him suspiciously. He turned to Amos instead. "Listen, did you hear about the cannibal who attempted suicide and then changed his mind halfway through?" Amos looked confused.

"Not now, Rickey," Henry groaned. He knew Rickey was nervous, but he had no idea what the other man would think.

"Seems he jumped out of the frying pan into the fire," said Rickey, ignoring him. He didn't wait to see if Amos would laugh. "Sure, we've done things. Killed people. Eaten 'em. Some of us even waste time feeling bad about it. Right Henry?" he said, nudging Henry's arm with his. He looked over at the red-faced woman and lowered his voice, "But Phil– he didn't just kill people. He kept us, like dogs. On chains. He fed people to us, tortured people that didn't give him what he wanted. Even stopped us from being Cured a long time ago. And he didn't stop there. He had this shack for most of the Infected women . . ."

Henry blushed and turned away from them, letting the television's music drown out Rickey. He'd lived it once already. He didn't need to hear it. What happened after they had escaped? Those women must surely have died. Without teeth they would have starved even faster. Was Marnie in that shack now? Did the little girl have to take their place? Was he keeping her just the same way, somewhere secret in the City even now? Something much more terrible than rage filled Henry then, an overwhelming, paralyzing wave of grief replaced the anger that had energized him for so long. He was exhausted and panicked. He was free, but was the girl?

Vincent and Melissa came in when Rickey was still droning on behind him, and Henry quickly rubbed his arm across his face. They pulled two more chairs up to the table. Henry decided to order dinner from the red-faced woman, so he wouldn't have to hear them add anything to the story. He watched the endless loop of pictures while a dead man sang the virtues of the equally extinct and wonderful world.

"You know any of them?" asked the red-faced woman, looking up from chopping vegetables. Henry shook his head. "You in any of them?"

"I doubt it."

"Least you got friends now," she said with a significant nod toward the table, "It's not everyone who can say that these days. Lord knows we all got things to bring us down mighty low these days. But you just remember you got friends. They'll help pull you back up again when nothing else will. New people always want to run off and find someone they lost from Before. Most times, they don't find anyone. Whatever it was, whoever it was, it just isn't where they thought they left it. Protect what you already got first, or when you come back, it may not be where you left it either." She handed him the plate of wrapped sandwiches.

"Thanks," he said, offering her an extra red coin. She shook her head.

"Advice is free. We don't take returns on it."

He smiled and walked back to the table, setting down the platter. Rickey was the only one that was hungry. Amos was silent, but his face was ashen and grim. "Does he know who you are?" Melissa asked. Her eyes were puffy and Henry knew she must have been crying.

"No. I couldn't lie about my name, someone would have called my by my real one, but he didn't make the connection. Still, I don't think he should see all of us together. Do Pam and Molly know he's here?"

Vincent shook his head. "Both in the hospital. Even if we can somehow reach them through the phone or something, I don't see what good it will do. It'll just make them more nervous while they wait out this quarantine thing."

"I told you we should have left last night," Rickey mumbled around a sandwich.

"And leave the rest of us behind?" asked Melissa, "Thanks for that."

"Even if we had everyone, I'm not leaving until I find

out about Marnie."

Melissa sighed and shook her head. Vincent's lips tightened.

"Don't you get it, man? She's dead. They're all dead. There's nothing to find out," said Rickey hitting the table with his palm, "how many times do we have to go around on this before it gets through that thick stubbly head of yours?"

"I have to know," said Henry. "That's just the way it is." Amos looked over at him with an expression of pity and grief. It scared him and he looked quickly away. "You can all leave for a while if you want. I'll find a way to get rid of him one way or another."

"Go to the Governor," rumbled Amos, "Try one more time. He's here, that changes things. And you're right. People like him shouldn't be forgiven."

"Everyone can be forgiven," said Vincent in a gentle tone.

Amos shook his head. "Sorry, Father, but not this one. Not if he's done the things you all say that he has. There are always men like him around, but they stay hidden mostly. Bad times bring em out though. Some people do terrible things just to get by. Others go a little crazy, get swept up in a thing and can't stop themselves. I've seen it before. I did a peacekeeping tour in Rwanda, you know, Before. Met a lot of people who weren't proud of things they'd done. Met a lot of people managing to live together after it all. But not with people like that gravedigger around. They were all gone. Escaped to do more harm or already dead. Men like that, they thrive on times like these. Start them even. They're the ones that know exactly what they are doing and enjoy it. He'll keep going until he's stopped. He can't stay here. The Governor has to see that. I'll make sure he stays on the Farm tomorrow. You can go see the Governor together, I'll arrange it with Stephanie."

Henry shook his head. "If we see the Governor, it'll tip our hand. If he doesn't do anything, then Phil will know who we are. If he does, Phil will be dealt with but I'll still miss my chance to find out about Marnie. We have to wait until I can get him to talk."

"How can you be so damn thick Henry?" cried Rickey. Melissa shushed him. Vincent looked hard at Henry.

"I hope you're right. I hope she's alive. But we don't know. And right now we're all in danger. The six of us are in real trouble if he finds out who we are and what we remember. We have to do something before that happens. It's one thing to risk your own life in a desperate mission, but Henry, we're all at risk. Will you trade all of our lives for a girl that is probably beyond help? Pam and her family? Molly who is fighting so hard to recover? Us?"

He refused to look at Rickey and Melissa, concentrating instead on Vincent. "She's just a kid," he whispered, "you're supposed to tell me to do what's right, not confuse me."

"Henry, how would you get him to tell you where the girl is? By threats? Torture?"

Henry was silent.

"How can either of those be right?"

Henry looked around at the others. "Just one day, a few hours in the morning even. He might have her in his house. She might be in the City. Give me that long to go look while Amos keeps him at the Farm. Just a few hours."

"How are you going to find his house?" asked Rickey.

Melissa sighed. "I know where it is. I looked it up this afternoon at the delivery office. Just in case."

"We're going tomorrow afternoon," said Rickey, "with or without you Henry."

"I'll be there," said Henry, his chest expanding with relief.

THIRTY-FOUR

Henry waited in the shade of a mausoleum doorway watching the caretaker's cottage. He'd been there before dawn. It was five minutes past the work bell and he still hadn't seen Phil. The thought of Marnie being inside the old house, at Phil's mercy, looped relentlessly in Henry's mind. He decided to chance running into Phil and get into the house one way or the other. He couldn't wait any longer.

Just before he stepped out of the doorway and into the plain light of the weedy cemetery lane, Phil stumbled down the slumped wooden stairs in front of his house. He wore dirty coveralls and a dusty hat shoved partially over some cowlicks. He coughed and spit into the grass, then set off at a leisurely pace toward the Farm. Henry waited until he was just out of sight, then darted down the sunny lane and up to the rickety screen door. He could hear voices inside and hesitated. He crept back down the steps and around the corner of the house, peering carefully into the windows. The shades were drawn. He listened for a long moment. There was a shovel sitting in a rusty barrow next to the house. Henry picked it up, careful not to scrape the blade along the metal barrow. He gripped it tightly and had a disorienting flash of holding a cane in Mrs. Palmer's apartment. He shook it off and walked up to the door.

He'd just knock. Pretend he was here to get Phil for work. No need for violence. Not yet. Not unless they didn't let him in to get Marnie. He opened the screen and knocked on the heavy wood door. It sounded too loud to him and he winced. Nobody came. He turned the knob and opened the door a crack.

"Hello?" he called, his voice full of neighborly cheer. His hand was sweating around the wooden handle of the shovel. Nobody answered and the steady drone of voices from inside didn't change. He opened the door wider and stepped inside. He looked at the shovel. If he took it and found someone, it would look suspicious. If he left it and found someone he'd be defenseless. He glanced around him, but there was nothing in the small hallway that would work better.

"Hello?" he called again and after a few seconds, "Marnie? Are you here?" When nobody came, he tightened his grip around the shovel. He felt better with the wooden door open, so he left it hanging that way and moved farther inside the house. The hallway opened into a small living room where a television blared. The shades were thick and kept out almost all of the morning light. It was hard for Henry to make out anything in the flickering light of the television. There was a hulking shape of a couch facing away from him, but he couldn't see if anyone was on it. The television had been turned up, as if someone a few rooms away were trying to listen. Henry pressed himself against the peeling wallpaper and inched toward the couch until he hovered just behind it.

"Marnie?" he asked in a hissing whisper. No one sprang up. He looked over the couch back. It was empty. He tried to listen around the noise of the television, but it was too loud, spilling out some old action flick that had been scrounged up. He reached over and switched it off. He waited to see if anyone would come, but no one did. Henry was almost certain that he was alone in the house. If Marnie wasn't here, there had to be some way to find out where Phil had put her.

He opened a few of the shades, reminding himself to put everything back before he left. There was a pair of muddy boots tumbled onto the floor near the couch and a grimy set of work gloves tossed onto the arm of a chair. A few moldy plates and a scuffed up coffee table were everything else there was to see. Henry shut the blinds again, disgusted. He moved into the next room and flipped on a light. The kitchen sink was overflowing with dirty dishes and the refrigerator was almost empty. *If he's keeping her here, he's not feeding her much. Not that that is anything new,* thought Henry, his stomach aching with the memory of so many years of hollowness. His throat tightened with panic at the thought of the girl starving to death.

"Marnie?" he called loudly, "Marnie, it's Henry. Call out if you can hear me. I've come to get you." But nobody answered. He shut off the light and propped the shovel at the bottom of the stairs, convinced that he was alone now. He ran up the steps trying to find anything personal, anything from Phil's life before the City. Anything that might give him some idea of where Marnie was, or how she might have died. In a corner of the bedroom a half-emptied hiking pack leaned on its side. Henry headed straight for it, shoving dirty clothes out of his way. He sat beside it and opened the canvas flap. On top was the same folder Henry had been given when he entered the City. It showed Phil's medical exam results, his housing assignment, his work assignment and most importantly, the date he'd arrived. Henry tried to remember what day it was. He counted back and tried to figure out what day Marnie had let them loose. He scraped a hand over the stubble on his head, frustrated at how vague it all seemed. Phil had arrived in January. Henry thought it was late March, but time hadn't meant so much to him in a very long time. It had been snowing the night Marnie unchained him. It couldn't have been much earlier than January. He had to have come soon after Henry and the others had escaped. Had the whole camp been wiped out? Had Phil found out who had done it?

Henry flipped to the medical record. He didn't understand most of it, but the notes said that Phil had to have stitches and was treated for tetanus. Henry wondered if it was the scar on his face. It could have been from the same night that Henry and the others escaped. He had a time line, but Henry still didn't know what it meant. He flipped through more of the folder. There was a psychological evaluation. Henry wondered why he and the others hadn't received one until he saw the signature at the bottom. Dr. Rider, the same woman who had cured them. Must have been the only one on staff. Still, he wondered if it was standard procedure or if something about Phil had been wrong. The evaluation read like a transcript, the bare skeleton of a story, no notes from the doctor. It frustrated Henry that all that Phil's words were all that were there. Whether his story was true or not, it didn't matter. These people had let him in. Henry hoped he'd be able to pick out the truth.

"Subject arrived at the Gate mid-morning January 12. Name: Phillip Grant Previous Occupation: Construction This is Phillip's statement when asked what he had been doing since the outbreak of the December Plague: 'I was just finishing this job down south when the news started about the Plague. The foreman wanted us guys to stay and finish. He said he'd give us a bonus on top of the one we were getting for the holidays. But something felt hinky. We were finishing this foundation for some new movie house or something. All we had left was cleanup, so I agreed to stay with a few of the other guys. I could always use the extra money. The news was getting worse all the time, but you didn't see it outside yet. The last day, I show up to the job site and didn't see a soul. Not only were the guys from *my* crew not around, the framing crew hadn't shown up either. I was pretty ticked off, because even the foreman wasn't there and I wanted my money.' Subject laughed. 'Money. Like it was going to do me any good. But I didn't know then. So I went over to the office trailer to leave a nasty not. I heard this scrabbling noise next to me as I circled the foundation.

See, that's why the next crew was supposed to come in as soon as we finished. They needed to lay the floor right away so animals or kids don't fall into the foundation and hurt themselves. So I leaned over to look. And there was the rest of my crew. Most of them were already dead. Torn apart. It looked like eight bodies instead of the three that were actually in there, limbs just scattered and blood everywhere. Sinking into the new concrete in dark stains. But the foreman, Chuck, he was alive still. He was the one that was scrabbling on the wall. He was a mess. I think his jaw was broken or something. It was sticking out wrong and he was covered, *covered* in blood. Even his hair was plastered in the stuff and he left streaks where he was trying to climb. I thought he was trying to escape. I yelled down to him to wait, that I'd grab the ladder and get help. He didn't say anything, so I just thought he was in shock. I jogged to the truck and tried to call an ambulance on the way, but it was the weirdest thing. I just kept getting a busy signal. No dispatch, no answering machine or robotic switchboard. Just– nothing. Just that empty, endless beep.' Subject seemed agitated, I asked if he needed a break but he refused.

'So I pulled the ladder down from the truck and grabbed our first aid kit from the front seat. I don't know what I thought I was going to do with it, but I had an idea it would be useful. So I extended the ladder right near Chuck. That was when I noticed there was already one in the foundation. It was lying on its side though. Nothing wrong with it, just lying there, where they had probably stowed it while they worked the night before. I wondered why Chuck hadn't just propped it up again, but I thought whatever happened must have rattled him hard enough he just plain forgot it was there. He started flying up the ladder. He climbed so fast I had to hold onto the ladder so it wouldn't jitter its way free and collapse. He got to the top and just stared at me for a minute. 'What the hell happened?' I asked. He didn't say anything. He was just breathing really heavy, his broken jaw working back and forth like it didn't hurt him at all. 'I'm going to get you some help, okay?' I said and started toward the trailer. That's when he growled and leapt at me. He caught me off guard and I stumbled and fell. He was on top of me, but I still didn't understand what was going on. I tried to push him off a little. Not hard, 'cause I thought he was hurt and confused. But he kept lunging at me, trying to bite me, even though his teeth wouldn't meet. 'Chuck,' I yelled, 'It's me, Phil. Stop, it's me.' But he wouldn't stop, so I pushed a little harder and tried to roll free. He held on though. He held on tight. I kept pushing and we kept rolling. After a few turns, we were at the edge of the foundation again. But I didn't know it. I swear. I was getting tired. So I gave one really big push to get him off me. He rolled and fell into the foundation. I heard his bones snap. It was like green wood breaking. I didn't even have to look to know that he was dead.

I panicked. If I'd thought about it, I'd probably have stayed there waiting for the police or something. I'd probably be dead. But I panicked and ran to my truck and left. I knew I couldn't go home or to any of my family, that'd be the first place someone would look. But I had this old girlfriend. From way, way back. And her dad had this camp in the woods way up north. Not so far from here, actually. Her dad never used it, only once a year during deer season. We used to go there when we wanted some alone time. I figured things wouldn't have changed too much. Christ, her dad would have been tottering around on a cane by then. What need would he have of an old hunting camp? I could still remember the way, so that's where I headed. The roads weren't bad until I hit Hartford. By then it'd started to snow and other people were getting the hell out of – well, everywhere I guess. There were accidents but no police and no ambulances. Trust me, I was looking for them. That's when I realized something bigger was happening and I turned the radio on and started listening to the news. It was hard to find. FM was mostly that canned holiday crap. But there were people talking on AM. By the time I cleared the suburbs I knew I wasn't going to be in trouble for Chuck. I also knew I wasn't stopping until I got to that camp. But the truck was meant for southern weather. By the time I crossed the state line I was fed up. It was dark by then, but that didn't mean I was safe.

I'm– I'm not proud of the next part, but I did what I thought I had to do. I stopped at that camping place. You know, the one just off the turnpike. They were closed by then. I broke in and stole some gear. And I took one of the new snowmobiles out in the lot. Alarms went off everywhere, but I knew no one was coming. I took my time. I didn't take everything I wanted. I only took some clothes and the snow machine. I figured I had a long way to go and I wanted to travel light.'"

Henry rubbed his forehead in frustration. *This* is what Phil was ashamed of? Stealing a snowmobile and a jacket? Not killing his boss? Or the woman on the road? Not letting people starve while he kept them in chains and used them? He wanted to throw the folder across the room. But he couldn't. He needed to find out what happened to Marnie.

"'I made it almost all the way to the camp. There were no plows and very few cars so the snowmobile did fine even on the major roads. It was really isolated, way up in the mountains. I stopped to get gas from this old geezer at the local bait shop in the village just before the camp. He gave me the hairy eyeball, but everything else seemed quiet. Like emptied-out-summer-town-quiet. But that's exactly what it was, so I wasn't worried. About a mile from the little bait shop there was this woman standing in the middle of the road. I didn't see her until it was almost too late. I crashed the snowmobile in the ditch and blacked out for a minute. Broke my leg, my nose. When I came to, the woman was hovering over me. I thought she was going to help, but she jumped onto my chest instead. She was small, but she kept trying to bite. I was in a lot of pain and I couldn't have run from her. So I knocked her out.' Subject is silent for a moment. 'You knocked her out?' I ask him.

'Yeah. I didn't know what else to do. I choked her until she let go and passed out.' Asked Subject if he killed her. 'No, no. I just put her to sleep for a while.'" Henry gasped as he bit through his thumbnail. The tiny drop of blood on his thumb made him shudder and look around to make sure of where– of *when* he was.

"'I don't remember much after that, until a few days later. I was in this cabin with a family. Didn't know them, but they were taking care of me. Took a long time for my leg to heal and the family was kind of helpless. You know, city type. Used to having other people take care of things. Except I guess the guy that took care of them before, he got sick. So I decided to step in and take care of things for them. To repay them for helping me after the accident. They were keeping the first guy in the woodshed.' Asked Subject what he meant. 'The first guy, the one that got sick. The family didn't want anything to happen to him. So they kept him in the shed, where he couldn't hurt anybody. They fed him and cleaned him, like a family pet. Said they were waiting on a cure for him. So whenever I went out to find supplies I looked for people, sick or well, didn't matter. Figured the more we could keep safe, the better. Over the years, the camp got pretty big. People heard about us and joined up or we found sick folks wandering in the cold. Brought 'em back to camp so they'd be out of the elements and have food till we could figure out if they could be cured.'" Henry could feel the cold mud and the burning chill of his metal collar on bare skin as he read it. He didn't know which made him more angry: that Phil's whole story was a lie, or that the doctor believed him without question. He clutched his short hair with one hand and tried to convince himself to skip to the end. He couldn't do it. He had to see every word, if he missed something, he'd never forgive himself.

"Asked Subject how he fed all these people. Did he steal? Go to war with other camps? Subject shakes his head. 'Nah, we didn't have to. We just took what was left behind. Lots of empty camps. Even the storekeeper in the bait shop ran off after a while. For a long time there was plenty of stuff if we scrounged for it. Nobody had to get hurt and people were happy to join us and throw in their pool of resources too.'" A parade of agonized faces flashed through Henry's mind. They started with Wyatt, but it went on and on. All the people he'd killed for Phil. All the people who had resisted him. But Henry's overwhelming feeling was no longer one of guilt. He was profoundly sad that all those people, not just the ones that had been thrown in his pen, but all the people Phil had killed, would never be found. Never be buried. Never be mourned by anyone but him. No one would ever even go looking for them. It was as if they had never existed at all.

"Asked Subject why he had come to the City, if things were going so well at his camp. 'Things got tight this winter. We'd cleaned out most of the empty shops and houses for miles. Most of the remaining gas had spoiled. Couldn't go farther to get more. I did my best, but we were going to have to move the camp, and soon. I was coming back from scouting a new location when all hell broke loose back at the camp. Remember that family that originally helped me? Well the parents had gotten sick with the flu or something a few years back. Nothing we could do, we didn't have any doctor or anything. They passed away and I took care of their kid, a girl. Well this girl wasn't so stable, growing up in the end times and losing her parents and all. Poor kid. She got it into her head that I was going to let the sick people we were keeping starve–' Interrupted Subject to ask if he had really not heard about the Cure after six years, and if all of the Infected had remained that way all that time. 'No. I never knew there was a cure until I got here this morning. We were way up in the mountains, remember. We didn't get too many folks passing through with news. All the sick people were still sick. And this girl decided I was going to let them starve. She had a soft heart, you know, and maybe a soft head. She let them all go. Just let 'em loose. The people in the camp fought back as best they could. They had to, you see, since the sick people wouldn't stop attacking. But most everyone just scattered and died in the woods around camp. When I got back from scouting, there wasn't anybody left.' Asked Subject how he knew it was the girl that let them loose if everyone was gone. 'I found her down by the road when I was leaving. She was dying, got bit and had to kill on of the sick people herself. I tried to stop her bleeding, but it was too late. She told me what happened, said she was sorry. What could I do? She was dying. I told her I forgave her. When she was dead, I just started walking. Saw your lights at night when I got out of the mountains and headed here.'"

There were a few more paragraphs from the doctor, but Henry didn't bother. He knew what he needed to know. Marnie wasn't with him. He'd either killed her or she'd escaped, Henry wasn't sure he believed the end of Phil's story. Still, he'd been confident enough that she wouldn't show up to contradict him that he'd flat out lied about everything in the camp. She had to be dead. Henry shoved the folder back into the bag. He didn't bother to look for anything else. She wasn't here.

His relief was immediate. He didn't have to worry any more. She wasn't being tortured, neither were the others that had been left behind. It was all well and truly over. He never had to think about it again, the deep rut anxiety had worn in his mind was gone. He never had to see Phil again, if he didn't want to. He never had to go back to the terrible, dark, plastic covered shed or the muddy post with his chain threaded through it. He was free.

He was halfway down the stairs of his enemy's house when he realized he was feeling relief at a child's death and that her killer was going to walk away unscathed, and guilt overwhelmed him. He wandered through the house to the door, numbly shutting off lights and turning the television on again. He was out in the sun again, out among the fallen stones and weedy grass of the cemetery. A warm breeze rumpled the grass, twisting it silver to green and back again. He walked out of the graveyard without looking back toward the house, never realizing that he'd left the shovel standing at the bottom of the stairs. He turned down the road and came to the church. The stained glass windows had been broken long before and they were boarded up now. Shards of blue and red glass crunched under his shoes. He could hear Vincent inside teaching a history lesson. He opened the heavy doors and stood in the dark vestibule as a chorus of children's voices answered Vincent's question. Henry sat on the cool brick floor and finally understood that Marnie was dead. That they were all dead, everyone he had ever known before the Plague. His parents, his friends, coworkers, neighbors, they were all gone. Even Henry, the Henry he'd been before, was gone. Wiped away, like they'd never been. He wanted to cry, to expel the loss and grief, it was like the need to vomit, insistent and agonizing, but the shock was too great. Henry couldn't cry. So he sat in the dark church until the kids filed past him into the warm afternoon and Vincent found him.

He sat down beside Henry. "Did you find anything?"

"He came into the City alone. Not very long after we escaped. There was no one with him."

"You said that already," Vincent said gently.

"I know. What happened to the people we left behind?"

"Maybe they escaped too. Maybe they found a better group."

Henry shook his head. "Why haven't they come here then?"

"Maybe they don't know about this place."

"It's the only light for miles and miles. They must have seen it. Phil did."

"Maybe they are afraid. You and Rickey weren't too keen on coming here. Rickey still isn't very comfortable."

"Everybody is dead."

"Probably. But you aren't."

"Why aren't you angry? Why aren't you sad? Some priest thing?"

Vincent shook his head and leaned back against the dark paneling. "Who should I be angry with? It was a disease, not a villain."

"How about Phil for a start?"

"Maybe Phil believed he was doing what he needed to survive. Who could have known we would get better? Who could have known we were still human inside there?"

"He knew. He stopped Elizabeth from curing us."

"I know. I think about that day all the time. He was frightened."

"That doesn't make it better."

"No. But maybe if she'd done it with his knowledge, he would have come around. Maybe if he'd treated us better to begin with, he wouldn't have been so scared of returning us to sanity."

"So why aren't you angry? Can't you see that he is evil?"

Vincent sighed and rubbed his eyepatch as if the socket beneath ached. "Maybe he is. But look at the things I have done. Am I less evil?"

"You said what we did when we were ill was not our fault, that it wasn't a sin."

"You asked what the *church* would say about what we did. I'm not the church. I'm just a man who knows what kind of horrors he's really capable of. Like you. Like Phil. Like everyone else left alive."

"Are you going to come with us to see the Military Governor?"

"Yes."

"Why?"

"Because you're my friend Henry. You and the others. You're the only people I know. And you can't seem to be able to live peacefully with Phil around. So either he's got to go, or the rest of us do. It's safe here, and organized. We aren't starving. But I know it's not perfect. If you leave, then I will too."

"It's not enough to just let him leave."

"What do you want to happen?"

"I want him to suffer as much as we did."

Vincent was silent for a moment. He stared at Henry. "Even if it were possible to do that, Henry, it would make you into a mirror of him. Isn't one of him enough? You wouldn't be able to do it. You might think it, but you couldn't actually do it. You're a good man, whether you believe it or not."

"I *was* a good man, once. Before. But everything from then is dead. Even me."

"I didn't know you Before. I know you now. You worry about the things you've done, the people you've left behind. You're moved enough to try and rescue them. That's more than I can say for myself or the rest of us. You kept Molly going when she wanted to lie down and die. You didn't let the others chase down a starving little boy who stole from us and shot at you. You're willing to care for someone else's child in a world where things like that can get you killed. You're a *good* man, Henry. Don't let Phil turn you into something else."

Henry was silent, feeling the aching sorrow of the day as if it were a hollow socket in his chest. Vincent stood up and brushed the dust from his pants. "We'll be late for our appointment. We need to go meet Melissa and Rickey."

Henry nodded and stood up.

THIRTY-FIVE

Melissa was sitting in the waiting room pretending not to know Rickey, who was doing his miserable best to seduce the pretty secretary when Henry and Vincent showed up. Rickey gave up and sat next to them within seconds.

"Did you find her? Did you find anything?" asked Melissa.

Henry shook his head. "He came alone. In January. I can't remember dates so well. I think it must have been close to our escape right?"

Rickey shrugged. "I haven't had use for a calendar in almost a decade."

"At least he came alone," whispered Melissa, "maybe that means his men abandoned him."

Henry picked at the fraying upholstery on his chair. "Maybe it means that everyone else is dead."

Melissa squeezed his hand gently and was quiet. The waiting room was silent and they were the only ones there. Even the secretary excused herself after a moment. Rickey's knee started bobbing up and down. It drove Henry slowly toward madness. Rickey elbowed him in the ribs.

"Hey, what do cannibals make out of politicians?"

"Not now, Rick. Just calm down and wait."

"Wait for what? What are we even here for?"

Melissa leaned in as if waiting for Henry to answer. He looked around at them. "Why should I decide? It's not like I suffered any more than you. What I want will never happen."

"We're not here to ask for anything," said Melissa suddenly and sharply. "We aren't here to beg or to make trades or to offer solutions. Why should it be us that has to solve anything? We were the ones wronged. This man was elected or took power or whatever in order to fix things like this. You all need to stop acting as if this is a personal vendetta. Phil is a monster. He doesn't belong in any sort of decent civilization. He's a destroyer. Not just of us. Not just of the people at the Lodge. He needs to be expelled from every society he tries to blend into. We're here to tell what's left of the world what he's done."

"And if nothing is done?" asked Rickey, his hand tapping his lips nervously.

"If they want to live with someone who is worse than a murderer, then that's their business. We'll have done what we meant to."

"But what about us? Are we going to live with someone like that?" asked Henry.

Vincent held up a calming hand. "Let's just get through today. Maybe this military governor will be reasonable. Maybe the situation is changed now that he won't have to expend resources to catch Phil. Let's just see what he says. We can worry about the worst if it happens."

The secretary bustled back into the office and they all fell silent again. Still, the woman noticed a change in the atmosphere and quickly tapped on the interior door. She disappeared for a moment into the Governor's office.

"How long have you been waiting?" asked Henry when she was gone.

"She told us he was in another meeting about the hospital," said Melissa, "I told her we would wait as long as necessary to see him."

Rickey snorted. "She must have decided she looked at our ugly mugs for long enough."

The secretary walked briskly back out again, followed by some grim looking people in uniform and an exhausted looking little man in a lab coat. Henry felt a small shudder curl up and over his neck. He wondered again if they should just leave, let this new disease take its course in this dark little bastion of a City and start fresh somewhere new.

"You can go in now," said the secretary, almost shooing them out of her waiting room. They stood up and Melissa turned to them one more time.

"We aren't here for sympathy. We're here to get justice. You understand?"

Henry realized she had been as angry as he this entire time. He stood straighter. Vincent put a hand on Rickey's shoulder to steady him. The Governor was as tired and shrunken as the last time Henry had seen him, and the office felt smaller with all of them in it. Henry felt larger, stronger. The Governor stood up and shook hands hesitantly with each of them, either not recognizing Henry or choosing to pretend that he didn't.

"Please, have a seat, tell me what brings you here today. It must be important to take you away from work at such a crisis point for the City."

"I was here a few days ago, asking for help in capturing the leader of a camp a few days distance from here," began Henry, ignoring the barb.

"Ah. Mr. Broom. I believe I made myself clear last time we met, and if anything I have even fewer resources to spare since the incident in the courtroom. Bringing your friends won't change my decision I'm afraid. As I said, I'm very sorry for what you all went through but I can't justify sending men and supplies after every petty criminal–"

"This isn't a petty criminal!" Melissa banged her hand on the large wooden desk and the Governor flinched. "He isn't a simple looter or thug. He's a monster. This man doesn't kill and steal for survival's sake. He does it because he enjoys it. He draws it out, extends the suffering. Weak, ill, children, makes no difference to him. But he's vulnerable now. All alone. You need to arrest him before he rebuilds, before he starts making friends again."

"I don't understand. I thought you folks escaped that camp some months ago. How do you know this man is alone now?"

"Because he's in the City," said Vincent quietly. The Governor looked over at him in alarm.

"Are you sure?"

Rickey stood up. "Are you accusing a priest of lying?" he asked loudly.

"N– no, no of course not. It's just, people change, memories get blurry. Are you sure this is the same man?"

"We've all seen him," said Henry, "we're all certain."

The Governor nodded slowly and pulled a lumpy pad

- 234 -

of pressed paper toward him. He cleared his throat. "What was this man's name?"

"Phil," said Henry.

"His last name?"

Henry looked around at the others but no one knew.

"You don't know his last name?" asked the Governor sharply.

"It's not like we were formally introduced," said Rickey, "we just know what his men called him."

"Fair enough, but how are we going to find him? There must be a dozen Phils in the City—"

"He's the gravedigger," said Vincent. His face and voice were still calm, but Henry could tell that Vincent was becoming upset with the Governor's reticence.

"The gravedigger? But I remember authorizing a full time hire for that three months ago."

"What difference does that make?" asked Melissa.

The Governor leaned back. "I declared a general amnesty only a week ago. It was time to stop dredging up the past over and over. The Plague Trial was meant to be the capstone on the tension between Immune and Infected— excuse me, Cured. The City can't live in this constant state of uneasy peace forever. We need to be one society, or we'll collapse."

"And you thought a general amnesty would make people just, what? Forget everything that's happened over the past several years? Burying your head isn't going to make memories disappear. If you want to have true peace and rebuilding there has to be justice."

"Justice? For which people?" The Governor leaned forward and pointed at Melissa. "You want me to arrest this man, hold him accountable somehow. Okay. He did things that were wrong. Maybe evil. So did everyone else. What happens when someone realizes you killed their parents? Should I arrest you too?"

"We didn't torture anyone. We did what we had to in order to survive," said Rickey jabbing a finger back toward the Governor.

"You sure about that? I think the people you devoured alive would probably disagree. It's an awful way to die. I've seen it too many times in the past."

Vincent tilted forward, burying his head in his arms, his thin back shaking with suppressed sobs. Alarmed, Henry tried to calm him down. The Governor ignored him and continued, "and this Phil guy, he probably did what he thought he had to in order to survive as well. We all tell ourselves that these days. What makes him so different? If I'd had the idea to use Infected as guards rather than innocent men, I would have done it too, before the Cure. We didn't know you were going to recover. I needed every man that I lost in those years."

"Would you have used the women for sport? Chained people in the freezing cold without shelter or clothing? Let them slowly starve to death? And after you knew about the Cure would you have prevented the survivors from receiving treatment so you could continue to use them?" Melissa was almost shouting. Henry found himself growing calmer as his friends started giving way to despair. He spoke quietly, still kneeling next to Vincent.

"I don't know if we were more human or animal when we were ill. Maybe you're right. Maybe we were more dog than man. But even animals deserve either better care or a more dignified death than we received. I have not tried to use my illness as a shield to pretend I've done no wrong. Why should this man, who had the presence of mind to act like a man, unlike myself, be allowed to use it to deny doing evil? Do you want him among you, working with your friends? Speaking to your children? Leering at your spouse?"

The Governor stared at Henry for a long moment. Then he scrubbed his stubbly cheeks with his hands. "Look, if I arrest Phil, we start down a slippery slope. One that could cause a permanent split in the City. My job is not to allow that to happen. There is too much depending on the people here. We've all been through so much. But terrible things happen during war. It's part of the cost—"

Melissa stood up. "It was a disease. We aren't the

enemy, you can't treat us like captured soldiers. This wasn't a *war*!"

The Governor too, shot up, his rolling chair hitting the wall behind him with a bang. "Yes it fucking *was!* You people always say that, but you don't know. For years we fought people like you. Years! You pushed us back into this small City until there were only a few thousand of us left. I watched people like you tear apart my men, piece by gory piece. Men caught beyond the wall when a cluster of you would hit. They'd scream for us to shoot them so they didn't have to feel your terrible claws and teeth any longer. I had to bury you. Hundreds, thousands. Every day for years, so that the City's water didn't make us sick. So rodents didn't eat you and bring in disease. We starved behind the Barrier for months between scavenging efforts. All things you've been blissfully unaware of for almost ten years. And now you come here, to the place *I* sweat and bled for, and you complain about what's been done to you. It absolutely *was* war, of the bloodiest, most desperate type. It's bad enough we have to find work and food and shelter for you–" the Governor stopped himself and took a deep breath. Vincent had recovered enough to look up at him in shock and Melissa was speechless standing across from him. Rickey, alone, looked unsurprised. The Governor turned around and found his chair. "I'm sorry," he said wheeling it back, "I shouldn't have lost my temper. It's been a very long week, but that is no excuse. Again, I'm sorry for what you have been through. The best thing for us all to do is to move forward and try to leave the past behind us. Life is better here, and you need never repeat your experiences. I hope you will stay. But I cannot risk tearing this entire society apart just to punish one man."

Rickey laughed and it was a bitter, dry snort. "Yeah, you already did that this week."

"I'm sorry but that's my final word. I've already warned Mr. Broom, but I will reiterate for the rest of you; the City does not tolerate vigilantes. If I find out that any harm has come to the gravedigger, I'll know where to look. Avoid him. Forget that you ever met him. Pretend he died in your escape. Whatever you need to do to get by. If you cannot, I suggest you leave now, before you commit a criminal act that would result in your own execution."

Henry helped Vincent up. He felt dazed, as if something had shorted out, missed the connection within his brain. Melissa's face was slack and expressionless, as if she felt the same. He grabbed her hand and began leading her and the priest out of the office. Rickey was still fuming though. Henry nudged the door open just as Rickey began shouting. "You just remember that we were here, that we warned you. You remember when your asshole itches and burns because you refused to wipe that piece of shit out. We warned you. You think this City is going to survive? Even *you* can't hide how you really feel about living with the Cured. Others have a lot less reasons to pretend to be polite than you do. If this new Plague doesn't kill us all, you're going to have a *real* war on your hands in a few years."

The secretary was staring open mouthed, at them as they left the office. Henry blushed and hurried them out into the street, away from everything that had just happened. Melissa sat down on the building's worn stone steps. Rickey sauntered down them and sat next to her, pulling out a flimsy hand wrapped cigarette. He lit it and held up his hand toward the building, flipping off the blank windows.

"Well that didn't go quite as I expected," said Henry, scratching at the back of his neck.

"Really?" Rickey grinned and half closed his eyes against a puff of smoke. "That's pretty much exactly the reaction I thought we'd get."

Melissa started to cry. "What do we do now? We can't stay here. We can't live like this."

"Aw, now, don't cry," said Rickey, putting a scrawny arm around her neck. "Let's go somewhere else to figure it out. These government buildings give me the creeps. What do you think, Vincent, you up for a round of pool?"

Vincent shook his head. "I'm going home. I don't want to be around strangers just now. You can come if you want. I'll make dinner."

They stood up and walked away from the cold, granite building. Henry was the only one who didn't spend the walk wondering why he hadn't stayed at the farmhouse. A new desire was taking place in Henry's head. Free to think of alternatives now that the civilized courses had failed him, a dark plan began to solidify in his chest.

THIRTY-SIX

Henry stared out of the rectory window toward the church. It was too dark to see the cemetery but he knew it was there. He imagined Phil slumped on his couch, his thick boots flaking mud in the corner, the television blaring. Henry wondered what the man thought about when he was alone.

"We can't leave without giving Molly and Pam the chance to go with us," said Vincent as he lit the stove. Henry turned to look at him.

"Pam's family may decide to stay. But I don't think Molly knows anyone except us. Of course, after all this time at the hospital she may have made better friends with the nursing staff. Still, we should give her the option."

"How long's this quarantine thing supposed to last?" asked Rickey.

"I'm not sure. I haven't seen another broadcast, have you?"

"The soldiers at the barricade said at least a week, probably closer to a month," said Melissa, setting the table with tiny clinks in the corner.

"A month?" groaned Rickey.

"We still have to figure out where we're going and how we're going to make it work. That will probably take us about that long." said Henry, turning back to the window.

"Why are you so calm?" asked Melissa, "Out of all of us, I thought you'd be the one in a rage."

"Because after meeting the Governor the first time, I was the only one that didn't expect anyone to help us."

Melissa sat in a chair with a sigh. She clicked her silverware together on the table. "How can they live like this? All piled together in a heap, each pretending as if everything were normal. Meanwhile each knows they are working with, trading with, maybe even sleeping with people that killed those they loved. How do they do it?"

Vincent looked up sharply. "Because they have to. What's the alternative? Should the Cured be forced to live separately from the Immunes? Should we all live apart from each other, just in case? We can't survive that way. And we aren't the first to do it either. Passions, wars, diseases, violence all pass. Neighbors still must live together, rely on each other, afterward. You think I'm old fashioned– you think my calling makes me naïve or vulnerable," he turned toward Henry, "but there are real, effective reasons that concepts like turning the other cheek have lasted so long."

Henry stared back at Vincent, feeling a hot bubble of anger fill his chest. "An eye for an eye is even older, Father."

Vincent nodded. "There is of course, a place and time for justice. You've asked how we can live among murderers. We too, have murdered. If we expect to take a life from those who have taken one from us, shouldn't we pay with ours as well? We're all guilty. We might as well lie down and die right now, because if we stick with an 'eye for an eye' then the species is doomed."

"I can't forgive him, Vincent. I can't see him healthy and thriving every day. It will destroy me," said Melissa.

"I know. That's why we need to leave. I wish we could stay, I think we could do very well here. I confess, I expected more from the Governor. An investigation at least, some kind of help. But it seems he blames people like us for all of the City's troubles. Even if Phil were not the issue, I know now that we are not welcome here. Not really. We could spend the rest of our lives fighting for acceptance here or we could spend it fighting for existence out there. I will choose what you choose."

They were all silent for a few moments. Vincent went back to cooking. "Can you find your way back to that farm?" asked Rickey.

"Yes," said Melissa, "it should be easy to get to."

"We're no better off than when we left it in the first place Rickey," said Vincent, "we face the same problems we did before we came."

"In a month Henry and I will be strong enough to plow a garden at least."

"It may be too late to plant in a month."

Rickey nodded. "I know, that's why we should go back

to that suburb. We only made a quick check. There is probably more we could use."

"There were already other people there," Henry reminded him.

"Just a kid, maybe a few kids. We can save up any extra credits we have and buy supplies on our way out just in case we can't find anything. If we pool all of our credits we should have a lot."

"You don't think someone will try to stop us if they see us stockpiling?" asked Melissa.

Rickey shrugged. "Why should they? There's no law against leaving is there? And if we are open about why we're leaving, maybe other people will be interested in joining us. After today, we're going to be watched. Why not just be honest? At least we'll have some people on our side then."

"Because I still don't want Phil knowing who we are," said Henry, "He's still dangerous. Just because the Governor has scruples about revenge doesn't mean that Phil does. If you must talk, let it be about Cureds versus Immunes, not about what happened to us."

Melissa scowled. "He should be exposed. The whole City should know what he's done. If he decides to attack me out in the open, so much the better, it will be more proof."

Henry sat down across from her. "He won't attack you in the open. He won't attack you at all. He'll go after your coworkers, your friends. Pam's kids. Vincent's parishioners. That's how he ran his camp. He held onto something dear to everyone, always threatening."

"So we're just supposed to leave and let him continue this better life without any consequence at all?"

Henry leaned back in his seat and looked steadily at her. He could hear Rickey and Vincent a few feet away dishing out food and talking in low voices. "No," he said, his voice a spare, distant rumble traveling toward her, "that isn't what's going to happen."

Melissa shifted and leaned in toward him. "What are you going to–" But Rickey slid a plate of food in front of her and they talked no more that night.

Henry wandered back to his tiny house a few hours later. He flipped on the lights and closed the door. He looked at the couch where he had been sleeping. He stumbled into the lone bedroom, the twin bed neatly made, waiting for Marnie. He sat on the edge of the bed, his mind constantly shuttling between his broken promise to Elizabeth and everything, everyone he'd lost. He slept in the bed, dreaming of his father and sister, of Dave and Elizabeth and Marnie, of Wyatt and Mrs. Palmer in her shattered apartment.

THIRTY-SEVEN

Henry paced inside the All-Work warehouse ten minutes after the others had left for the Farm. Phil was late again. Melissa had offered Henry a spot on her delivery team so he wouldn't have to meet Phil again, but Henry had refused. He told her it was so that one of them could keep an eye on Phil, warn the others in case he started to suspect them. But the truth was that Henry was determined to know if Marnie had really died, whether she'd suffered, where Phil had dumped her. Henry was going to find out in the next month. And then Phil was going to pay, limb by bloody limb for what he'd taken.

Phil lumbered into the warehouse, yawning. "Oh," he said, realizing he and Henry were the only ones left, "You didn't need to wait for me, I know the way now."

Henry felt a grin eat away at his clenched jaw. "No problem," he said, "It's not like the seeds are going to notice a few minutes either way." He slid a bundle over toward Phil.

"Where were you yesterday?" asked Phil as he shouldered the tool bag.

"One of the delivery crew was sick and they really needed someone to take his place. Why?"

"The little split tail that runs this place got her panties in a bunch when you weren't around. But then that darkie farmer said he knew where you was and she cooled off right quick."

Henry felt a tremor of revulsion pass through his gut to hear Stephanie and Amos talked about that way. But he just grinned wider and said, "Ain't that always the way with women though? Always poking their noses into other people's business before they take care of their own."

"Tell me about it," said Phil, "some of 'em just need a man to put 'em back in their place. Especially now. Thank goodness that whole women's lib thing's gone the way of the dodo, now that they need us again."

"Have you got a woman?" Henry asked, hating himself as he did so.

Phil walked toward the door. "Nah, not since the camp I was in before," he rubbed the scar on his jaw.

"Didn't she come with you to the City?" asked Henry. He said it casually but his heart banged and popped in his chest like a string of ladyfingers. They stepped out of the cool building into the shimmering spring morning. Phil squinted against it.

"No, she didn't make it. Most of my mates didn't make it."

"Jesus, what happened? I though you brought all your people here."

Phil nodded. "I would've. I really would've Henry, but remember how I told you I was taking care of my sick friend, the other Henry?"

"Sure," said Henry, his muscles beginning to ache with built-up adrenaline.

"Well I was taking care of a lot of sick people. You know, keeping them safe so they wouldn't run off and freeze or starve or get into fights with each other."

"That's mighty kind of you," said Henry.

"Aw, any man would've done the same if he had the chance."

Henry's hands shook around the rope of his bundle. Phil shrugged. "Anyway, this little *twist* got it into her head that I was abusing them. She couldn't understand that without me, they'd have been dead months before. So one night, she gave my men some drugged food and extra alcohol. And then she crept through the camp and let all the sick people out of their– their rooms. She didn't warn nobody. She locked away some of her little friends in the big building and left my men out in their tents, all fast asleep and drugged. The sick people didn't know what they was doing. They just did what come natural. By the time my men woke up, it was too late. They had to shoot most of the sick people and some of my men got hurt pretty bad. My woman too, she got killed."

"What happened to the rest?" Henry asked.

But Phil lifted his chin toward the Farm gate. "Looks like the darkie's calling you. We'll talk again later."

Henry tried to calm down before he reached Amos who was staring at them intently. He took a spot at the seed table without saying anything. Amos didn't ask him anything, just went back to sorting. It was a good hour before either one spoke.

"We need to get these seed packets out to the workers. It's time to start planting the early stuff. Next week I'll take you to the greenhouse," said Amos, handing him a tray of seed envelopes.

"Any particular order these should go in?"

"One tray is one crop and should do one square of the field. Light and water's pretty even, so doesn't matter which plot gets which crop. Except these," said Amos, pushing a few trays to one side, "those are corn and wheat. They go in back, too tall for everything else."

"Have you been doing this a long time? Farming I mean?"

"Since before the Plague. Not always here though. Been all over the world building irrigation ditches, finding high yield plants, fighting vermin." Amos grinned.

"Think you can teach me some? Not everything, I know I can't learn it all, but say, enough to start my own garden?"

Amos squinted at him. He seemed about to ask something, but then he waved Henry away. "Go start trucking those seeds out and we'll talk about it later. You can buy me a beer."

Henry jogged out into the sunny, sweet smelling fields. He tried not to look over at Phil, tried to forget the dark, frozen past and look forward to the quiet, hay filled barn and the unfurling leaves of a wide garden near a still pond at the farmhouse he had woken in.

Henry tried to corner Phil again, but they were never left completely alone. He didn't dare to ask anything else around other people, so Henry just shrugged and assumed Phil would be late again the next morning anyway. Most of the workers bolted at the last bell, but Stephanie, Amos and Henry stayed until dusk covering the planted plots with thin, tattered tarps.

"Going to have to patch these again," scowled Amos.

"What do you patch them with?" asked Henry.

"We used to just sew the holes closed, but when the tears got too big we'd patch them with other old tarps. Past few years I've started using rags. Plastic's kind of hard to come by now. I don't like the cloth, it rots in the rain, but it gets the job done for one season anyway. Keeps the seeds from freezing in case we planted too early."

"Is that my first tip?" asked Henry.

Amos stopped fiddling with the tarp and looked intently at him. "When are you planning on planting this garden?"

"Next month. Maybe the month after."

Amos nodded and looked disappointed. "You won't need tarp then. You'll have to worry about frost at the end though." He studied Henry for another minute. "Do any of you have a clue how to do any of this? Or you just trying to wing it? 'Cause this isn't the Mayflower Henry. No one's going to come bail you out in the spring with a big shipment of food. Or in the middle of winter for that matter."

"I know."

"I'll teach you what I can, but there's a big difference between hearing and doing. And between gardening as a hobby and farming for survival."

"I know, and I'm grateful for the help."

Stephanie walked up, shaking the soil from her jeans. "Why are you two so serious? What are you talking about?"

"Whether this quarantine's going to slow beer production," rumbled Amos.

"Oh, that *is* serious," said Stephanie, "We better get to Margie's before they run out."

"Race you," said Amos, locking the iron gate behind them.

THIRTY-EIGHT

Rickey was already at Margie's by the time Henry arrived. He was sitting with the soldier that they had met during orientation. The soldier looked exhausted but greeted Henry warmly and shook hands with Stephanie and Amos.

"You look like death warmed over," said Amos.

"I've been assigned to the dental clinic, I just rotated off."

"The one they made into a quarantine station?"

"Yeah. You wouldn't believe how many people thought they had it. Hell, tired as I am, you could almost convince me that I was infected too, if I didn't know better."

"Was anyone really infected?" asked Henry.

"Nah, I doubt it. We ruled out most of them anyway, just because they didn't have any contact at all with anyone involved. There are a few family members, friends of people in the courtroom, that sort of thing, but the doctors tell us they've pretty much narrowed down the window of infection to that one court session. Still, we're holding on to a few of them, but they don't have any symptoms that they didn't cook up in their own heads."

"It's just people getting scared. Can't blame anyone for that," said Amos.

The soldier nodded. "The symptoms are so vague, too. Someone doesn't sleep enough, has kind of a clumsy day or is a little cranky and they suddenly panic. A person could go crazy just from a few suggestive incidents."

The words echoed like tossed rocks in Henry's head. He didn't say anything, but he saw the glance that Rickey shot him and knew he wasn't the only one who would remember what the soldier had said. Amos finally spoke up when the others got up to play a round of pool and the bartender turned the television up a level.

"I take it the Governor isn't going to pursue the matter of the gravedigger?"

Henry shook his head.

"So you're leaving. How many people are you going

to take with you?"

"I hadn't really thought about it. I assume just us four plus Molly. I don't think Pam will want to go, her family is here. But we'll take anyone that wants to go and is willing to work I guess."

"You know there's been talk of starting a colony somewhere outside the City, right?"

"Yeah I heard. I don't know if we'll have any way to defend that many people. I wasn't planning on starting another town, just leaving this one. We don't even have a doctor. Or a farmer. Unless this is you angling for an invite. In which case, pack your bags."

"No one has ever left the City before, Henry."

"What? That can't be true."

"I don't mean no one has ever gone beyond the Barrier. Plenty of people have. No one's ever made a permanent break with this place though. There are people from Cure Camps that took a while to come in, but once a person is here, they tend to stay."

"I saw people at the gate the night they announced the new Plague risk."

"Yeah, those people would have been turned back or gone to stay outside for a few weeks. They won't stay gone forever, I guarantee that they all left most of their possessions here. And this isn't the kind of world where you leave what you own."

Henry shrugged. "Okay, so no one has left before. What's your point? If you are trying to warn me that I'll regret it, believe me, we've discussed it at length. It's better than living here with *him*."

Amos shook his head. "I'm not trying to persuade you of anything. No one's ever left before, but there's been plenty of talk about it. Especially among the Cured. People are tired of being treated like they caused all of this. I don't blame them. I'm just saying, if you go about this open and honest like it seems you want to, don't be surprised if there are more people waiting at the gate to go with you than you expected."

"Why would anyone decide to come with *us*? If there

are people talking, then there are people planning. Which is better than what we're doing."

"Planning and doing are two different things."

"I don't even know if we'll make it through one winter, just the five of us. How would we do it with *more* mouths to feed?"

Amos shook his head. "You *won't* make it, just the five of you. Even if you raise or scrounge enough food, you'll just get raided by looters. Or one of you will get sick or have an accident. There's power in numbers. It may be the only real power left in this tired out world. That's why people have waited for so long to make a break with the City. We aren't stupid. We know things are rotten here. And getting more rotten by the day. But we're scared. A group like yours– it might seem small to you, but it's a start. Like a piece of grit in an oyster. You let enough people get drawn to you, and you'll have a real shot. Of changing things. Or just starting over." Amos looked around at the tired, sad faces watching the television screens. "Yeah, that's what we all need. It's time to start over. Pull out the leftover weeds from the old world. Burn off the chaff and be left with a blank field."

"So you're coming?" asked Henry.

"It's going to be hard to give up Margie's beer," he said leaning back in his chair. He looked over at Henry and his face broke into a slow grin. "It's going to be rough you know. Not just the farming part. All of it."

"I know."

"And you haven't the slightest clue what you're doing."

"I know that too."

"Yeah, I'm going too."

Henry laughed. "Why?"

"Because I'm tired of looking at that damn Barrier and wondering if there are more people behind it somewhere. And I'm tired of living under someone else's rule. I grew up a free man in a free society. My kid– if my daughter were here, I'd want her to be able to choose what she wanted to do when she grew up. I'd want her to be able to decide when she's ready to have her own kids, if ever. Not assigned to a mate at thirty by some government department just to reproduce her immunity. I hope she'd be upset by the way we treat the Cureds. I hope she would understand that I did terrible things to survive, but that she didn't have to and that it wasn't acceptable any more. That people like Phil don't belong among good men. And that good people don't do the things we've done. Not now, not again. I want to be a *good* man again. Live among good people. So I'm going with you."

Henry stared into his beer. Amos chuckled. "Don't start sweating. I'm not hitching my moral star to you or anyone else. I just want the chance to try to be someone different. You can still keep your nefarious plot, whatever it is."

"Why do you think you aren't good?"

"Because I've seen too much and stopped too little of it. I've seen the food distributors short Cured families in skimpy harvests, when we should all be shorted. But Immunes never are. I don't say anything, because I always figured maybe they should stand up for themselves. But they never had anyone to appeal to. I never hired a Cured to be a food distributer or a supervisor. I just wanted to go with the flow, not cause waves. Figured it would be bad for whoever I hired first that wasn't Immune anyway. Didn't want the hassle for me or for them. My wife would have been ashamed of me for that. I'm ashamed of that. Then there's this place," he said, glancing around.

"What's wrong with this place?"

"Nothing. It's just– safe. It's neutral ground. I can pretend I'm not friends with any Cureds even if they show up here, because this is the Immune side. I don't have to defend my actions or claim anything but a passing acquaintance with Cureds here. If I was really friends with people like Stephanie, or you, I'd visit your houses, babysit your kids, meet you at your speakeasies. If I really value you, that's what I ought to do."

"Being friends shouldn't be anyone's business but ours."

"It shouldn't be, but it is. It also shouldn't be true that Cureds can't get jobs they are qualified for or homes that aren't falling to pieces. It shouldn't be true that the Immune kids get to go to highschool but Cured kids and kids who were born on the Cured side of town can't find a desk past elementary. Or that Immunes who get caught stealing from a Cured or beating up on them are given far less severe punishments than the other way around. But some places have seen so much bad, there's just no fixing them. No matter how much you want to. You either let em stay bad or you destroy them trying to change it." Amos shook his head, "It's time to start over. Somewhere new. Somewhere with less bad memories. It's a big empty world out there. There has to be some space to try again."

The pool game broke up and the others rejoined them. Henry kept thinking of what the soldier had said about the people at the dental clinic. He started to form a plan that night, surprised at how very simple it seemed. He slept in the bed meant for Marnie without waking until the first bell.

THIRTY-NINE

The red tokens clinked halfway up the old bell jar and Henry smiled. *Halfway home,* he thought. Phil and he had not crossed paths in weeks. Almost everyone had been released from quarantine, but a few workers had been kept at their special assignments for the remainder of the month. People like Phil, who had no graves to dig and Melissa, who still needed to deliver meals to the people left at the hospital. Henry wasn't sure if Phil was avoiding him or if Stephanie or Amos had finally forced the grave digger to start showing up on time.

It rankled a little, having to wait to find out what had happened at the Lodge, but at least Henry didn't have to pretend to be friendly. He hadn't been merely biding his time either. This was the day that his plans for Phil would begin.

He walked through the hazy gold of the late afternoon to Melissa's small apartment. The row houses around it had all had their tiny yards plowed and planted with herbs and vegetables. Henry and Amos had been helping while so many of the owners had been quarantined in the hospital. Henry had been practicing for the coming months. It gave him a pleasant surge of pride to see the neat green rows of uncurling plants like stitches in a new shirt. Many Cured families would have an easier summer and fall because of Henry and Amos.

He knocked on Melissa's door. "Hi," said Melissa, opening the door. He heard Rickey yell something about cannibals from farther within and ignored it.

"Is Vincent here?" he asked, trying to look over Melissa's shoulder.

"No, just Rickey."

"Good. I need your help."

Melissa led him to the living room where Rickey sat at a table covered in a pile of red tokens. He was counting them with an unlit cigarette hanging from his lips and a spare behind his ear.

"Here," said Henry, handing him the glass jar.

"What the fuck is this?" said Rickey, shaking it. "You

been blowing it all on loose women and horse races or what?"

"Relax," said Melissa, "Henry's been paying for Molly's medicine. It's not cheap."

"We won't get any from her either. She's still doing physical therapy every day," grumbled Rickey.

"It's not like it's any good to us out there. What are you going to do with it all?"

Rickey raked a hand through the wild tufts of hair left on his head. He looked at Henry and winced.

"What?" asked Henry.

"We're up to twenty now."

"Twenty? Where are we going to put twenty people? How are we going to feed them?"

Rickey shook his head. "It looks like all of Amos's savings is going to go for seeds and saplings. We still need tools for farming, for building, for everyday life. One farmhouse isn't going to cut it any more. I don't think we can afford lumber, not usable stuff anyway, so we'll have to get woodworking tools too. That's not even mentioning transportation, storage bins, medical supplies– there's so *much* to do. But the thing I'm worried about this second is water purification tablets. They're rare and expensive."

"Don't worry so much about finding everything here. Those houses in the suburbs had lots of tools, no one seemed to want them. And the farm itself must have a few, it's not like we were looking for those things when we left. And we can boil the water instead," offered Henry.

"Those propane tanks will run out faster than you expect. And then we'll have to cut wood every time we need water."

"There has to be a well. A farm like that always has a well."

"And if not?"

"There were other farms out there," said Melissa, "a few needed only slight repairs. One of them has to have a well. It's warm enough now, we can use tents until we get something permanent. But I'm not staying in this City for a moment longer than I have to. I hate the thought of that monster walking around free to do what he wants day after day."

Henry felt the warm glow of anger shared between them. Rickey sighed and scrubbed his face. Then he grinned at them. "If my poor Ma could see me now, she'd have the shock of her life. She'd never have guessed I'd be responsible for the survival of twenty people. She'd be horrified."

"So am I," teased Melissa. Henry elbowed her.

"Why's that so hard to believe?" asked Henry.

Rickey started stacking tokens in little columns, clinking and wiggling them between his fingers. "Well, I wasn't exactly the most obedient kid. I told you I grew up on a farm right? My dad's ticker stopped cold when I was fourteen. He was out driving the tractor. It just kept going until it smashed into the barn. He was already dead by then. Anyway, my Ma wasn't able to run that big place by herself, and she wanted me to stay in school, so she let a neighbor buy the place for a song and we moved near my Ma's folks in the city. It was a stinking, loud, bright and beautiful place to me. I didn't stay in school long. Found some friends and we got our kicks stealing cars and breaking into apartments. We never really did much, just went joyriding and ate people's food and rented movies on their cable. At least, not till I was older. I was really good at stealing cars. Really fast. So some of the older kids got me into a group that had it's own chop shop. My Ma, she never let on that she knew what was going on, but I know that she knew. She used to beg me to go back to school, not hang around with the bad kids anymore. I always promised I'd do better, and for a while I would, but eventually I'd go back to it. I finally got caught. I mean, I'd been arrested before, but I could always talk my way out of charges. Not the last time though. Didn't have that kid face any more. I got sentenced to seven years. *Seven years*. But honestly, I was lucky I didn't get ten, the way I acted in court. Such a stupid kid. I was six months from getting out when the Plague hit.

"Prison's a funny place. It's this isolated world where everything that would seem trivial out here take on this huge importance in there, while the world could actually be ending out here, and no one would really notice in there. Not until the staff stopped showing up anyway. You wouldn't realize how little daily life depends on contact with the outside world until you aren't in it anymore. My buddy noticed first. He said the guards were different one day. But I was on my way out and I wasn't paying attention anymore. I figured they must have been fresh out of training or something. But a few days later, my friend noticed there were less of them around. Every day, less and less. We counted. Finally, one morning, we woke up and there was no head counts. There are *always* head counts in prison. For everything. But not that morning. But the cell doors released, just like always, so someone must have had pity on us. Someone immune, cause none of the prisoners got sick, not then. It only took a few minutes to realize something was off. Things got really bad, really fast. My friend pulled me into his cell and we blocked the door with the mattress and hid. You'd think hundreds of guys that just found themselves without guards or locked doors in the way would just walk out of the prison and rejoice in their good luck, wouldn't you? But that's not what happened. For a few minutes people did just start running for the doors, but only for a few minutes. Then fights started to break out. There was nothing to stop them. Years and years of old arguments just spilled into this riot. It was like the whole place had gone mad. Like it was full of Infected. But it wasn't. Nobody was sick yet. They just tore each other apart out of plain old human meanness. My buddy and I hid for a few days, but we didn't have any food. We finally snuck out of the cell one night when it seemed quiet. There were dead and dying guys everywhere. It was like one of those old war movies. We could hear other people hiding in their cells. We tried to get a few of our buddies to come with us, but they were too scared. Some of them were scared of the other prisoners, but most of them were scared of whatever had happened outside. I should have been scared too. But I was a dumbass. Why would a prison just be left unlocked? What could be worse than letting hundreds of criminals loose? I should have thought first, but I didn't.

We got out okay, my buddy and me, but we both

wanted to go check on our families. So we split up. I never
saw him again. No idea if he was immune or if he got sick
like me, later on. I went straight to my Ma's. There was no
one sick yet in my town, but we saw on the news that it was
coming. My Gramps had a fallout shelter from when they
used to worry about the bomb, but it was winter and he and
my Gram were in Florida. So I got it ready for me and my
Ma. We didn't have a lot, but Ma always helped Gram put
away preserves and pickles and stuff every year, so we were
okay for a while. We stayed in the house for a few months, I
put plastic on all the windows and doors and stuff. I didn't let
Ma go to the store or anything, we just sat in the house until
the power went out. We would have stayed longer, but the
neighbors kept knocking on the door looking for help or food,
I don't know. It was only a matter of time before they broke in
and we would be exposed to the air. So we went downstairs
and locked ourselves down in the shelter. There wasn't any
power and we only had one of those little potties for camping
and a little propane. So every day I'd listen at the door until I
was sure it was okay and then I'd open it for a while and I'd
go dump the potty as long as no one was around." Rickey
glanced around at them, "It wasn't all bad you know. Ma and I
had some good talks in the shelter. We played cards and
dominoes. She told me stories about when she was a kid. We
spent more time together than we ever had before. But we
were only in there maybe six months. Then Ma had a stroke
or a heart attack or something. Don't know for sure. Just woke
up one morning and she wasn't able to move right and her
face kind of sagged on one side. She tried to get me to stay in
the shelter, but I knew she needed a doctor. So I brought her to
the hospital. But it was gone. Burned to the ground a long
time ago. So I drove to the next one. We didn't see anyone.
No people on the street, no cars, no police, no lights on,
nothing. My Ma started crying halfway to the next hospital.
She kept saying 'We're the only ones left. Everybody is gone.'
I kept telling her they were probably in their shelters or
evacuated, we'd find out at the hospital. Our radio had
stopped working a few months before. I thought it was

broken, like I cranked it too hard or something, but now I know there was nobody left to broadcast.

So we got to the next hospital, it was a big one, like the one here. I got the creeps as soon as I saw the empty parking lot. But I thought maybe I'd find *somebody*. A janitor, a security guard, *someone*. Or a sign telling us where to go or something. So I parked right where the ambulances are supposed to be and told Ma to wait in the car. I went in the emergency section first. All the lights were off, even the battery backups. You don't realize how dark hospitals are until there's no power. There were no windows in the emergency wing. I yelled a few times, but nobody came. There was furniture tipped over in the waiting room and papers scattered everywhere. Patient folders and flyers about smoking and release forms all over the floor. No signs though. Nothing. Just dark and empty. I don't know why I didn't leave then, but I was convinced there had to be somebody, so I walked down the hall toward the labs and the coffee shop with it's overpriced, tacky get well gifts. There was a receptionist desk there, and I guess I was thinking there had to be some kind of sign or something. I kept calling out, trying to get someone's attention. Nobody ever answered. There were a lot more windows at the front entrance and it was a sunny summer day, so I could see pretty well. The floor was white rubber or something, you know, like those cheap linoleum jobs they put in high schools that are easy to clean. In front of reception though, it was black. Dull black with no shine. I got a little closer until I saw that it was dried blood. Yards of the stuff just spread out down the hallway and out the door. Like it had been painted there. I got real scared then and I stopped yelling for anyone. We'd heard reports of the Plague, but not anything like this. We'd just heard that people were getting sick and dying. Not how. I went running back for the car. When I got back near the Emergency Room, I heard a little yelp. It sounded like Ma yelling for me and I raced out to the car. Her door was open and the car was still running, but my Ma was gone. I yelled for her, but she didn't answer. I looked everywhere for her. Hours and hours. I went back into the hospital and searched, I drove all the side streets and parking lot, pushed through all the little hedges, but I never found her. I spent the night at the hospital hoping she'd come back. I didn't know what to do. So I went home again. Just to check. Maybe she'd got back somehow. But the shelter had been broken into while we were gone and everything was gone. My Ma wasn't there. I thought about checking on the neighbors or even going back to the prison, just so I could find some people. Anybody. But I was too chickenshit. I decided to go see how my buddy was doing. If anyone would help me, it'd be him."

"I thought you said you never saw him after the prison," said Melissa.

Rickey shook his head but didn't look up at them. "I never did. But that was my plan anyway. I drove the car until it ran out of gas and then I stole another one that was outside an empty house. The gas stations were already dry. The groceries too. I had to break into a lot of houses to find food. I used to get real happy when an alarm went off. I thought, good, the cops will show up and this whole shitty nightmare will be over. But the only time anyone came, it was an Infected. He was pretty desperate so he was fast, but he was also already weak. I didn't know what he was going to do. I kept talking to him as he came at me, I thought maybe he was looking for help. 'Man,' I said, 'am I glad to see you. It's like fucking Christmas.' But the guy didn't say anything, just kept running at me. I had time to think that he either wanted my stuff, or he was so glad to see someone he wanted a hug. I was so *stupid*. I started backing up real quick. 'It's okay, man, what I got is yours too. We can share, I don't need it all,' And he stopped. Like he heard me. But he didn't say anything, just stood there, breathing real heavy and looking at me. I wasn't in many fights in prison, I just stuck to myself mostly. But I'd seen lots of them start. And I knew this guy was going to attack me. I could see him tense up, but I wasn't quick enough. He jumped on me and we fell over. He was on top of my chest scratching at me with his fingers, like he thought he had claws or something. He tried to lean down and bite me, but I got an arm in between us and held him off. I managed to roll out from under him, but I think that's how I got infected too. We were in this restaurant kitchen and I had one of those massive cans of tomato sauce. I had to hit the guy in the head to stop him. I don't know if I killed him, I ran away and I stuck to unlocked doors after that. I didn't go straight to my friend's house. I didn't want to go empty handed and be a burden. It took a couple of weeks for me to get all the things together I thought I'd need or would help. By the time I made my way to my buddy's house I was pretty sick. I couldn't seem to steer right and I kept forgetting that I was driving. It wasn't a problem because there wasn't anyone else to hit. Until I ran into Phil's scroungers."

"Oh Jesus," swore Henry.

"They were parked outside this run down bar, a big line of motorcycles a tow truck and a station wagon with one of those trailer things on the back. I guess to carry everything. Nobody was outside. I saw the bikes. I always had a thing for bikes. Anyway, I wanted to get a closer look and I forgot I was driving. I drove right into them. Took out four or five by the time I realized I'd hit em. Phil's guys come running out and I'm just sitting there in my car, complete space shot. I didn't even get pissed when they pulled me out of the car. But then one of the guys started waling on me, just pounding the living hell out of me. And it was like something snapped. Like one of those glow sticks I used to have as a kid. Like some glass vial in me snapped and the right chemicals mixed together and I was something different. Angry. Glowing. I killed the guy that hit me by the time they were able to stop me. There was a fat, balding guy with glasses that had a gun. I thought he was going to shoot me. But somehow, I wasn't scared. I didn't care at all. All I cared about was the way his fat little wrists were going to slide around between my teeth."

Melissa winced. Henry thought he must have been talking about Dave.

"But Phil stopped him. Said I must be Infected and he wanted me to replace one of the dogs he'd lost. That's how he said it too, I was going to replace a dog. They tied me behind one of the bikes and made me run up the road until we got to the Lodge. I fell a few times. That's how I got this lovely patchwork," Rickey pointed to the wrinkled purple splotches between tufts of hair on his head, "but Phil didn't let them kill me. Then he put me in the same pen as Pam. And the rest is history I guess." He crossed his arms over his bony chest. "Couldn't survive in prison, couldn't take care of my Ma, couldn't even take care of myself. Now I got to take care of twenty people."

"Not by yourself," Henry said, "we're here to help."

"I thought Pam's pen was the one they took the women from," said Melissa quietly.

Rickey glanced at her quickly and then away. "Not just women," he said.

"But you both have your teeth–" she began. Rickey jumped up.

"Yeah, well some of them liked it rough, okay? They got a kick out of extra risk. You want to know more?" he snarled.

Melissa turned to Henry. "I hope all of those men were eaten alive. We're supposed to just let Phil die comfortably in bed decades from now, an old man, maybe with kids and grandkids, no one ever knowing what he's done?"

"No," said Henry, "but if you want me to do something about it, I'm going to need your help."

FORTY

Henry sat in the front of the delivery truck with Melissa. The others rode in back or walked. "Just do your normal thing," said Henry in a low voice, "let me do mine."

"What is it you are planning to do Henry? If it's dangerous–"

Henry shook his head. "It's not. Not this part."

"This would be much easier if you just told me what we were doing."

"No. I'll tell you all when everything is done. No one is going to stop me or interfere or try to persuade me that I'm wrong. You're going to have to trust me. We aren't ever going to have to think about Phil again."

Melissa pulled up to the hospital and parked. "I don't want to stop you," she said quietly.

"I know. But you have to be able to sleep at night afterward too." He reached for the door handle.

"So do you," she reminded him.

He turned back to her with a grin that was too easy, too loose on his tight face. "I'm going to sleep just fine afterward. Better even." He opened the door and got out of the truck. Melissa felt a shiver wriggle from her fingertips to her shoulders.

Henry walked slowly around the barricade to the back of the hospital, the grin already faded away. A few bored-looking soldiers were standing near the back door.

"I'm here to pick up empty food trays," said Henry, "boss told me they'd be back here."

"Sure," said one of the soldiers. His voice sounded hollow behind his plastic bio-hazard mask. He pointed to a metal cart stacked with trays sitting outside the door of the hospital. "Right there."

Henry fidgeted. "You– you want me to come past the barricade?"

"Yeah, it's fine," said the soldier, "everyone is confined upstairs, no one's even tried to come out. We're just here as a precaution."

"But you have suits."

The other soldier chimed in. "Don't worry about it man, there's nothing contagious out here, it's just part of the uniform."

Henry started forward and stopped in front of the cart. The soldiers had turned back toward the road, ignoring him. "Hey," he called. They turned around again. "They been eating off these right? Breathed on em and stuff."

"This your first day man?" asked one of the soldiers, "sure, they ate off em, the trays have been cleaned and disinfected already. They're fine, really."

"How do I know? I got no protection, not even a pair of gloves and you want me to pick them up?"

There was a long shhhhhhhh as the soldier sighed into his mask. "Look, you want protection? There's gloves, masks, entire bio-hazard suits in that bin over there," he said waving to a plastic crate farther down the building, "if it makes you feel better, knock yourself out, I don't care."

"Thanks," said Henry. The soldier shook his head and went back to the road. Henry pulled a suit out of the bin. He started pulling it on then looked around. The soldiers weren't watching. He grabbed another plastic package from the bin and gently stuffed it into the baggy leg of his suit. He finished putting the suit on, complete with mask and gloves, and then casually wheeled the cart of cleaned trays past the barricade and down the road toward the truck. He could hear the soldiers laughing at him as he passed them. He didn't care what they thought. Hell, he felt like laughing too. But this was the easy part of the plan. The next part was going to require either luck or patience or some incredible fakery. Henry just wasn't sure which yet. They were getting close to the end of quarantine for the people who'd been most at risk now, and he had to finish this before then. He loaded the cart into the delivery truck and then sat up front, carefully removing the suit and putting it into his work sack where no one would see. He helped with the rest of the deliveries without comment and Melissa, still disturbed by their earlier conversation, didn't ask.

He trudged home after work, the late spring gnats bunched in little fluttering clouds of gold and the smell of warm tar made the evening seem peaceful, almost normal, as if it were a day borrowed from Before, hung out for one last time. For a few blocks anyway. But then the quiet seeped back in as people reached home, shut their doors, left Henry walking alone down the road. He could have gone to Margie's. But they'd all been saving their tokens. He didn't want to visit the others, they'd just ask questions. So Henry went home instead. Turned the television on while he unpacked the bio-hazard suits and made dinner, just to have another voice around. It was the music again. The music and all the dead people. Henry ignored it for a while, busy with his plan, moving around the house. At last the adrenaline wore off, though, and he sat in a chair watching the faces cycle by in a slow moving blur. There had been a few broadcasts from inside the hospital, but they had been short, mostly allowing people to see that their friends and family were okay and hadn't become sick. Now that most people were out, there were occasional movies and short announcements. Almost all of the rest of the time, the dj played the photos and the music. Henry wondered when the guy running things slept. *Must be on a loop or something*, he thought and tried to concentrate on where he could find a body. He'd thought of asking Vincent if he had any funeral services coming up, but he knew there was no way to ask politely or that wouldn't make Vincent suspicious. Phil would know about them first anyway. No, the only way to do this was to make something that could pass for a body. He pulled out the map of the town that he'd been given on his arrival. Amos had laughed when he'd asked about a butcher. Meat just didn't exist anymore. Not unless you were truly wealthy. Hadn't there been something on the news about that? Henry tried to think. No, it wasn't the news. It had been Rickey. Just a day or two ago. Henry hadn't been paying much attention though, he'd been too busy, lost in his plots. He decided to pay his friend a visit.

Rickey was sitting in a creaky porch swing in his front yard, the sharp red star of his cigarette all that was visible in the dark. Henry sat down next to him. "So that house you were telling me about, the one where you had to shut off the electric, tell me that again."

"Tell you what again?"

"I don't know exactly, was it something about meat? I don't remember."

"Jesus, Henry, when you tune out, you miss *everything* don't you?"

"Sorry. Just tell me the whole thing again, I'm paying attention this time."

Rickey flicked his ash into the damp grass. "A few days ago, another electric worker and me were sent to go kill the power at this rich guy's house. We're not just talking has a few extra cans and a suit kind of rich here, Henry. This guy was *rich*. He had a security system, a lab in the basement, nice furniture, liquor. Stuff I didn't know you could get anywhere anymore. I think it was a bank before or something. Anyway, this guy had a stroke about a week ago and he was taken for medical care. But all that electricity costs a lot of man hours. And we've had to make up a lot of work with the hospital running extra hard and people in and out of quarantine. We just don't have enough warm bodies to keep things running at that rate. We've been going house to house all month shutting off anything left on in the empty places, you know, refrigerators, clocks, porch lights, those sorts of things. But this guy's house was something else. Lit up like Christmas even in the middle of the day. Guess the docs think he isn't going to recover, because they had us go in and shut everything off, right at the breaker. So we get to this place and I asked my buddy, 'what makes this guy so special' and he turns and stares at me like I'm from another planet. 'This is the guy that made the Cure,' he said. There were a couple of soldiers at the door guarding the place. Probably don't want anyone breaking in while this guy is gone. So one of them leads my buddy to the breaker in the house and the other soldier takes me down to the basement, where the lab is. Whole separate setup. We had to spend a lot more time down there, had to make sure all the equipment was shut off and safe so it wouldn't blow anything out when they started the electric up again. You don't see this kind of equipment anymore. I don't know if most people would have seen it Before either. Made me nervous just being there. So, you know me, I asked the soldier if he wanted a cigarette, just to take the edge off. He said sure, that he had to prop open the back door anyway, because he wasn't sure if it would lock when the power was out and we couldn't go out the main door because the elevator wouldn't be working. A fucking *elevator* to get to his lab, Henry. You believe that shit?"

Henry shook his head, but Rickey couldn't see him in the dark anyway. "So we're both smoking a cigarette and I'm starting to work on the equipment and this soldier starts shooting the shit with me. Nothing big, you know, normal stuff like how he got here, where I was from. And as we're working down there, I start smelling this odor. And my stomach started rumbling. It was real gradual. Like smelling someone way down the street start up a barbecue. It grew and grew. Finally, I asked the soldier about it. He grimaced. 'It's meat. These rich guys are the only ones that can afford it.'

'Hmm,' I said, 'it just smells weird. Not spoiled or anything, just– weird.'

The soldier took a peek outside the lab door and then came back and leaned over the lab table where I was disconnecting the gas line. 'Well, you didn't hear it from me, but there've been some rumors flying in the past few weeks about this guy. One of the guards at the court told me the prosecutor showed up to question Dr. Carton for the trial and found him down here in the lab with the walk in freezer door open. Hanging in the freezer was a corpse.'

'So,' I said, 'he's a scientist right? He probably needs bodies to test stuff on.'

The soldier shrugged. 'Sure, that could be it, but the guard said the prosecutor saw that there were chunks taken out of the legs of the dead guy before Dr. Carton shut the door. And that reporter? The pretty anchor who's in quarantine? She said she was in there earlier and there was a chunk of meat thawing in the sink, and she swore she saw a part of a tattoo on one part.'

'No way,' I said, 'that's got to be made up.'

The soldier looked around. 'Want to check it out for yourself?' he asked.

'Hell no,' I said, 'it ain't hardly lunchtime yet.' And we laughed and went on with our work. Thing is, Henry, I'm sure he was right. It was like as soon as he said it, I recognized the smell. It was like I'd been craving it this whole time and didn't know it. I've had nightmares for days because of it. Why would anyone do that?"

"Maybe he was Infected and just never got over it," said Henry.

"No dumbass, how could he make the Cure if he was Infected?"

They sat in silence for a few minutes. "You think they cleaned out that freezer?" Henry asked.

"I don't know. I doubt it. I think we were the last ones in there. Probably waiting for this Carton guy to kick the bucket then they'll go in and clean it out. Don't envy whoever has that job."

"Did the lab door lock when you closed it?"

"I didn't check."

"You still really fast at picking locks?"

Rickey sat up. "What are you talking about Henry?"

"You want Phil to suffer for what he did as badly as I do. More maybe. I can make it happen. But you have to help."

"What are you going to steal?"

"Nothing anyone will miss. Are you going to help me or not?"

Rickey got up from the swing. "Let me get my tools," he said.

Henry sat back and swung lazily back and forth, an unseen smile spreading over his face in the dark.

FORTY-ONE

The large house was a crisp, tailored shadow against the street lights. Henry and Rickey tried not to stumble into the back door to the lab. There were no soldiers standing guard now, the house was just an empty box, another thick tombstone in the almost desolate City. Rickey fumbled with his tools, scraping the metal door and setting Henry's teeth on edge. They had no light, batteries were too expensive, but Rickey said he could get the lights working in the lab and there were no windows for anyone to see them inside. The blanket around Henry's shoulders made him sweat in the warm spring night, but he knew he'd miss it later. There was no help for it. He had to have something to cover it with. Even in an empty city, Henry didn't want to risk being seen carrying a body over half the dark streets. Rickey gave the door a gentle shove and it clicked open.

"Wait here," he hissed, "and keep the door propped so I can see a little bit."

Henry pressed the door open farther to give Rickey as much light as he could. The lights flickered on within seconds and Henry slid inside, carefully closing the door behind him so no one would see. The smell hit him almost immediately.

"Pah! How could you say this was gradual? My eyes are watering."

Rickey was holding his shirt over his face. "The freezer was turned on then. It's been almost a week, those things warm up pretty quick. Is this even going to work?"

Henry nodded. "It's fine, it'll just be more convincing this way."

Rickey stood in front of the shining silver freezer door. He hesitated. "Hard to believe we smelled worse than this just a few weeks ago."

"Don't remind me. I can't tell you how grateful I am that this isn't making me hungry though. I was scared."

"You and me both, brother. I was really scared I was going to relapse or something too. I think I can definitely say I'm Cured now. You ready?"

"Wait, let me take a few deep breaths. It's going to be even worse when we open the door." They both forced themselves to breathe deeply and then hold it. Henry nodded and Rickey swung the heavy door open. There were four shelves on either side of the door, each holding a heavy plastic bag. There was another on a rolling cart in the middle of the warm and stagnant freezer.

"Oh God, there's more than one," said Henry.

"Maybe he doesn't like grocery shopping," said Rickey, trying to smile, but his face had gone very pale and his voice shook. "Who were they Henry?"

"I don't know. Someone's baby once though."

"Maybe we shouldn't do this. Maybe we should let them rest."

"This isn't any better Rickey. And however they got here, at least I'm going to give one of them a decent burial. They're going to do one last good thing first though. They're going to help me stop the devil." He rolled the silver cart out of the freezer and closed the door gently on the other faceless bags.

"At least we won't have to carry it on our backs," Henry said.

"Where are we bringing it? And what are we going to do with the cart afterward?"

"We're bringing it to the All-Work Station. Melissa parked the delivery truck there."

"Oh no. No. She'll kill us."

"I've already talked to her about it." Henry walked over to the wall and picked up a nicely bleached lab coat that hung near the door. "Take this and–" he looked around until he found a plastic face guard and a surgical mask. "These too. You're going to play doctor in the morning. Come on, we'll talk about it on the way. Let's get out of here." He pushed the cart toward the door.

"Henry, what about the cart– someone will know where we got it."

"You and Melissa can drop it at my house. Let them find it. After tomorrow I won't be going back there." He rolled the cart through the door and waited for Rickey to kill the lights.

The cart rattled on the broken pavement of the City roads and Henry kept looking nervously around. But they avoided the residential areas and it was almost midnight by the time they reached the truck. No one was around to see them. They rolled the cart up the truck's ramp and closed the rear door. Henry piled the bio-hazard suits and Rickey's disguise in a far corner. Rickey found the interior light.

"Jesus, Henry, it's moving," he said and slid backwards, hitting the side of the truck with a dull thump. Henry looked over at the opaque white bag. It wiggled and bulged.

"This is going to be bad," Henry said.

"What is it?"

"Maggots."

"No, it was sealed, in a freezer."

"A warm bag in a warm freezer, Rickey."

"It's not right," said Rickey jabbing a finger toward the squirming bag, "They shouldn't get to eat you if you're in plastic. That's why you get buried. To keep you safe from those things." Rickey gagged. *What difference does it make?* Wondered Henry. *It would have gotten eaten either way. What does it matter whose belly it's in?*

"Maybe you should go have a cigarette while I do this."

"You're really going to open that thing?"

"I have to. This won't work if I don't."

Rickey stumbled out of the truck and closed the door behind him. Henry took a deep breath. He rolled the cart sideways so that it touched the truck wall and then unfolded the blanket onto the floor beside it. He unzipped the bag. A gray mass of pulsing, curling mouths had covered it up to it's chest. Only a few had made it up to the face. Henry had prepared himself to be revolted, to shove the thing quickly onto the blanket and fling the body bag with it's seething, frothing mass of maggots away. But when he looked at the face, he could only feel a terrible sorrow. He almost recognized it. Neither male or female, just a face. But wrecked, broken long before Dr. Carton found it. Scarred and thin and stretched. A great blank with no identity. Like the woman in the snow from so long ago. Someone's baby once. Undoubtedly Infected. Henry blinked away the blur in his eyes. He wasn't sure if he was crying for the corpse, for missing the Cure and the world after that terrible madness had lifted, or if he were crying for himself for living long enough to wake up Cured. "I'm sorry," he said, "but we still have work to do. He gently rolled the bag onto the blanket and pulled the plastic away. He rolled the body with its legion of companions into the blanket and tied it shut with old, dirty pieces of rope. The corpse started leaking through the blanket almost immediately. It stained the cloth as he lifted it carefully onto the cart. Henry looked at the spreading dampness. *Good,* he thought, *it's scarier that way.* He pulled out on of the bio-hazard suits and spread it out against the wall of the truck. He turned it so the back faced him and made a thin slice down the back of one pant leg, not large enough to open until Phil put his leg in. Then he carefully folded it again and replaced it in its plastic bag. He did the same to the other suit, not knowing which one Phil would pick. He turned off the interior light and closed the truck door. He stuffed the body bag into the space between the spare tire and the truck undercarriage and then walked home with Rickey without speaking, saving his energy for a shower and climbing into bed.

FORTY-TWO

"Remember, I'll meet you at the farmhouse in two weeks," said Henry, helping Rickey with the surgical mask.

"I don't know if I can do this," mumbled Rickey behind the cloth mask.

"What? Go to the farmhouse? The others will be with you. Of course, I'll understand if everyone decides to stay here. Either way, I'll be there. And either way, you won't need to worry about Phil any more."

"No. I mean, I don't know if I can do *this*. Right now. What if he remembers me? He hurt us, Henry. All of us. I don't want him to know I'm alive still. I don't even want to see him again. Not ever."

Henry put a hand on Rickey's shoulder. "He's not going to recognize you. I promise. He's not in control any more. He can't hurt any of us. I won't let him. Trust me, this is the last time you'll ever see him."

Rickey took a shaky breath. "Okay. You better get into the station. I'll take the truck around the corner for now."

Henry nodded and started walking toward work. He turned around, "Hey Rickey! What did the zombie say to the prostitute?"

"What?"

"You can keep the tip."

"Ha ha. It was supposed to be a *cannibal* joke idiot. A zombie joke just ruins the whole flow–" Rickey yelled after Henry. Henry chuckled and waved to him before smothering his cheerful mood and heading for the All-Work Station. The work bell sounded and the place cleared out.

"Sorry Henry, can you wait again?" asked Stephanie, "I'll be so glad when this whole thing is over. I can't believe that guy is late *again*. I just talked to him about it."

Henry smiled. "Don't worry, Steph, I'll handle it."

"Thanks. See you in a little bit. Amos wants us to start bringing seedlings up from the greenhouses for planting. Can you believe how fast the spring is flying by?"

He shook his head and smiled and Stephanie led the

stragglers out of the station. He felt bad, not telling her. He'd thought about it, but she was young. Still optimistic. Still in love with the City. He didn't want to destroy her happiness and security. Someday she'd realize she deserved more from the place she dedicated her life to. He hoped she'd understand why so many had left.

Henry paced the bare concrete. He hated waiting. He walked out to the office waiting for Phil or the delivery truck. He saw Phil sauntering down the road, content and lazy. Henry heard the delivery truck coming around the corner. *Perfect timing,* he thought with relief. But the truck was going too fast and bearing down on Phil who was still oblivious. Henry glanced at Rickey through the windshield. *He's going to hit him,* Henry realized. For a bare second he thought about letting it happen. But that was too easy. Too fast. He opened the door and the flash of the glass caught Rickey's eye. He slammed on the brakes and squealed to a stop just in front of the station a few feet from where Phil was crossing the street. *Good,* thought Henry, *now play it up Rickey.*

He watched Rickey's mask suck in over his bony nose as he took a deep breath. Then Rickey got out of the truck and walked over to Henry. "Is the grave digger here?" he asked in a loud voice. Henry watched as Phil noticed and began to pick up speed.

"Uh, yeah, that's him coming down the road now."

Rickey waited until Phil reached them. "Got a job for you. Governor says double pay."

Phil's grin stretched wider. "What kind of job?"

Rickey glanced over at Henry. "It's got to stay secret. I'll pay both of you, you'll need two anyway."

Phil ran a hand over his scarred jaw. "Secret, huh? Yeah, I think Henry and I can handle that, right Henry?" He elbowed Henry.

"Why secret?" Henry asked, squinting at Rickey.

"Cause it's one of the people from the trial. Died of Plague last night. Governor doesn't want to cause a panic."

"The Plague?" said Henry, "No way. I'm not getting near anyone infected."

"The guy's dead Henry, how contagious can he be?" said Phil. Henry could practically see him counting the tokens he could make.

"Uh, actually, he's really contagious. You can't get anything on you. I've got bio-hazard suits for you."

Phil slid a step back. He shrugged. "Eh, what's the difference, I was immune last time."

"So was this guy," said Rickey in a low voice.

Henry glanced at Phil who was a little paler now. "We'll do it," said Henry, "but not for double. We want triple tokens and– and Phil, what else do we want?"

Phil's grin returned. "We want a bottle of whiskey a piece. Not that homemade shit either. I know the hospital's got some stashed away."

"Fine, fine, just take care of it. And keep your mouths shut," said Rickey, jabbing a gloved finger at both of them. "The keys are in the truck and the bio-hazard suits are in the front seat. We'll expect the truck to be returned to the hospital this afternoon. No joyriding. Just do your job and get back, understand?"

Phil mock saluted and Henry nodded. *Good job,* he thought, wishing he could tell Rickey. They walked over to the truck while Rickey walked toward the hospital and out of sight. Phil tossed Henry the bagged suit and started pulling his own on.

"You're a shrewd one," he said, glancing over at Henry, "I wouldn't have thought to ask for more."

"Yeah, well if we're going to risk our lives, we might as well make it worthwhile."

"You really think it's that dangerous?"

Henry shrugged. "That guy looked pretty damn rattled, didn't you think? Just be careful and don't tear your suit and we'll be drinking toasts in no time." He slid the cloth mask over his nose and mouth and pulled the plastic hood onto his head. "We should probably get into the truck pretty quick. We don't want anyone seeing us this way, they'll start asking questions."

"Right," said Phil, "I'll drive, we got to get the shovels

and pick axe first anyway. And I know a quiet spot where no one will stroll by to see us."

Henry slid into the passenger seat of the truck. It was only a short drive to Phil's house and the cemetery and Henry was silent during it. Phil chattered away though, already spending the tokens he'd get from the job. They stopped and he jumped out, returning with a pile of dirty tools. He shoved them roughly into Henry's lap and Henry wondered why he'd bothered to cut the bio-hazard suits in the first place. Phil drove the truck down the weedy gravel lane to a far shady corner. He parked the truck so that they would be hidden behind it. Henry got out and dropped the tools next to the plot Phil indicated. Then he picked up a shovel and struck it into the ground.

"Whoa there, where's the fire? You got to do this a certain way. Otherwise it's ragged," said Phil pulling a few boards from the tool pile. He made a square on the grassy turf and began at one end, carefully squaring the edges of the hole. "You start at the other side. Just take up the grass first. Then it'll be easier to dig. Henry just wanted it done, but he knew he had to make it look as real as possible. It didn't take long to peel up the grass and they managed not to fling too much dirt on each other. Henry was sweating heavily in the plastic suit by the time they were chest deep. "That's good," announced Phil.

"What? I thought these were supposed to be six feet."

"You try climbing out a six foot hole and see how you like it. I say this is good enough. This is always how deep they go. Haven't heard any clients complain yet." Phil roared with laughter. "Go on, go get the body," he said when he'd recovered. Henry pushed himself out of the hole and headed for the truck. He pulled up his face mask and opened the door. The silver cart shone and flickered in the mid-morning sun. It's burden was a dark shadow. The stains had spread until Henry could no longer see the pattern that had been on the blanket. He rolled it to the side of the grave.

"They couldn't even be bothered to bag it, huh?" said Phil shaking his head. "Okay, put the body on the ground and get that cart out of the way."

Henry began gently lowering the body to the dirt. "C'mon Henry, I don't want to be here all day. He ain't gonna feel nothin' just get him down there." Phil rubbed a dirty glove across the plastic covering forehead. Henry tried to keep his face from betraying his loathing for the man, but then remembered his expression was mostly hidden by the mask and relaxed.

"All right, lower his feet down to me and we'll swing him into bed and cover him up then go get a cold beer." He reached up for the body.

"You sure? You don't want to get out and lower him down together? He could fall on you."

"Nah, just do it. There's enough space down here."

Henry shrugged and yanked the loosely bundled blanket upward as he did so, testing whether it was going to slide or not. He lay the body's shoulders on the soil and then turned its feet toward Phil who grabbed the bottom of the blanket. Henry held his breath and lifted the head of the corpse again. He twisted his fingers into the sagging fabric and let the body underneath slide. "Phil–" he called out, once he was sure it was too late.

"It's sliding Phil, slow down!" There was a pattering, as if a sudden cloudburst had opened over the grave. It took Henry a second to realize it was the maggots raining out of the blanket.

"Shi–" cried Phil and then there was a squelching thud, as if he'd stuck his boot to the ankle in mud. Henry was still holding the bloody blanket. Henry leaned over the open pit to look. Phil was struggling to push the body from his chest and stand up at the same time. His plastic suit was covered in dark fluid, some even soaking his face mask.

"Jeez, Phil, you okay?" asked Henry in a nervous voice, "I'm real sorry, I was just trying to do what you said."

Phil glared up at him, finally shoving the disintegrating body to the side. "Just get me out of here," he growled. *Here we go*, thought Henry, extending his hand partway toward Phil's. He let a look of slow shock peel over his thin face and pulled his hand back. "What is it now?" asked Phil.

Henry's hand shook as he pointed to Phil's leg. "Your suit. Your suit is ripped." Phil tried to twist himself to see, bracing himself with one arm on the grave wall.

"It's just a little hole. Quick, pull me up and I'll clean it really good. There's still time."

Henry shook his head. "You're infected. I have to call the hospital."

Phil started to hoist himself out of the grave. "Don't be ridic–" he started to say. Henry took his shovel and pushed Phil back into the grave with the blade. "You must be itching for a beating, boy," snarled Phil.

"Sorry, I can't let you out. You need to go to the hospital." Part of Henry hoped Phil would try to fight back, right then. Even though he knew Phil would probably win. But Phil leaned back and squinted up at Henry. He couldn't see because of the mask, but Henry thought he might even have been smiling.

"We going to sit here all morning then, till someone comes to find us? Got news for you Henry. Nobody gives a shit where you or I are. We could sit here until the next doomsday and nobody'd come. So what say you let me out, I'll go take a quick shower and we'll go grab those beers together? We'll forget about the whole thing. It's just a tiny hole. There's no way anything even got in there."

Henry held the shovel out like a baseball bat. He shook his head again. "I didn't think I was infected either, when it happened. I can't let you go. I'm just going to call my friend Vincent. He's just over at the church, he'll hear me." Henry jerked his head in the direction of the church. Phil glanced over at the church. "Vincent!" Henry yelled, knowing the priest had taken the kids on a trip to the Barrier that day, "Vincent, come here, I need help–"

"Okay, okay, shutup!" hissed Phil, "I'll make you a deal. What do you want to keep this quiet?"

Henry wanted to laugh in disbelief. Instead he said in a low, shocked voice, "If I don't take you to the hospital, you could infect everyone– my friends, me, the whole City. And you want me to let you wander around like I don't know? In return for what? Money? Booze? Drugs? No thanks. I know what you are about to turn into. I can't let that happen again. Throw me the keys."

"Okay. I'll leave. You don't have to worry about the City. I'll hole up in my old camp for a month. I'll be fine, you'll see when I come back healthy as an ox. Just give me until tonight to get out of town."

"I don't trust you. Throw me the keys," Henry said grimly and held the blade of the shovel next to Phil's plastic covered neck.

"They're in my pocket. Inside the suit."

"So?"

Phil hesitated and swiped at his sweaty forehead with the back of a bloody glove. It left a smear on the plastic. "I'm not infected Henry! If I take off the suit to get the keys then I might get infected from that. If I'm not infected you'll be killing me." He shifted onto one leg, trying to keep the one with the tear out of the muck and maggots. "Please, Henry. Give a fellow a break, can't you?" said Phil when Henry didn't respond. And Henry knew Phil was scared. Deep down scared. Scared was good. Scared was obedient.

"How can I trust you to keep your word?" asked Henry.

Phil's eyes darted around as if searching for a solution. He stared at the truck behind Henry. "Take me there."

"Huh?"

"Take me to my old camp. Drive me there. The truck's three quarters full on gas, it'll get us there and you back. You can take me there, see for yourself that I'm gone, and then come back. It'll only take a few hours, but it'll take me weeks to walk back. It did the first time. No one will ever know about this and if I'm infected I won't make it back to hurt anyone. If I'm not, no harm, I'll just say I went to find a friend or something and things'll go on just as they was." Phil talked fast, as if Henry was trying to interrupt him. Henry was pleased. He'd thought he would have to be the one to bring up

- 278 -

the Lodge first as an alternative. Phil was practically offering himself up to Henry. He stood up and lifted the shovel away from Phil.

"Okay, here's how this is going to work," he said, "You're going to get out of the pit and take off your suit. Then you're going to hand me the keys. After that, we're going to bury this poor guy properly. Then you're going to get in the back of the truck so that you can't infect anyone on our way out and so I don't have to figure out how to explain you to the Barrier guards. You try anything funny and not only will I beat you with this shovel, I'll call Vincent and whoever else is in the area to come catch you. Sorry, but you're infected. There's no getting out of this. Do this nice and easy and we'll try your way. If not–"

"No problem, Henry. You'll see, nice and easy. I just want to get out of here, I don't want to make anyone sick." Phil climbed slowly out of the grave. Henry could see his hands shaking as he slowly stripped off the plastic bio-hazard suit.

"Drop it into the grave. We can't have it lying around with all that bacteria on it," said Henry grimly. Phil dropped it over the corpse and brushed away some stray maggots that had, indeed made it into his pant leg, wincing as each one fell away. "Now the keys."

Phil reached in his pocket and slowly placed the silver truck key into Henry's gloved hand. "See, no problem. We'll do it your way." Henry nodded toward the other shovel and they worked in silence, burying the unknown man, like so many thousands before him, just another casualty of the Plague. Henry wondered for a moment whether there really were more to come, but brushed it off. He knew there had been no indications that a new infection had taken hold. *Don't buy into your own con, Henry,* he thought. It was long past midday when they were finished and the sun felt more like late June than early May. Henry was swimming in his own sweat. He told Phil to get into the truck and locked the door behind him. He stripped off the bio-hazard suit and carefully taped the slit he had made in his own suit's leg so that it was invisible. No good risking discovery now. He took a deep breath in the light breeze and got into the truck. He drove it down the lane to the church and picked up the backpack of supplies he'd left there this morning. He wished he could say goodbye to Vincent, explain things. But he knew it would only make things worse. He'd see him when all this was over. He banged the side of the truck before he got back in.

"How do we get to your camp?" he yelled.

"Just get us past the Barrier," came the answer, "Then I'll show you."

Henry shook his head. Phil was getting sneaky again. He'd have to scare him back into obedience when they stopped. He realized that once they were outside the City, he'd have no more hold over Phil. He was going to have to outsmart him or at least convince Phil that Henry could be just as dangerous as him. Henry got back into the truck. *What's worse is that all he has to do back there is scheme and plan. By the time we stop he could be plotting anything,* he thought. Henry was a little scared too.

FORTY-THREE

Henry rolled to a stop in front of the Barrier's big gate. A guard squinted at him and then walked over. Henry felt his skin bunch and prickle as the guard tapped on the driver side window. He rolled it down and forced a smile.

"Why are you taking a delivery truck out of the City?"

"Oh, we got a call from the looting team—"

"Looting team? You mean the scavengers? The scav team?"

"Yeah, sorry, the scav team."

"You must be new. The City doesn't loot. We don't steal things from other people. We scavenge for things that nobody else is using."

"Right, sorry, still getting used to everything," said Henry, blushing, "anyway, we got a call that they've got something too big and need an extra truck."

"Why didn't they just call one of theirs?"

Henry shrugged. "Guess with what happened at the trial they left shorthanded because of the quarantine, they gotta make do like everyone else."

The guard nodded. "Yeah, we're all short people. You know what they found? Anything good?"

"They didn't say. Or at least, my boss didn't tell *me*. Just the delivery guy."

"All right, be careful. Reports are that *real* looters have been spotted in the area and a vehicle with gas is a prime target. Did your boss issue you a weapon?"

Henry shook his head and struggled to suppress a smile. *This is too easy,* he thought, *something has to go wrong.* "No, we're just the postmen," he said.

"You better come inside then."

Henry parked the truck next to the gate and hoped Phil would keep his mouth shut. He walked into the low brick building. The guard led him to a large caged in area that was filled with neatly polished guns, riot gear, and survival gear.

"This guy's got to go meet the scav team," said the guard to the old man sitting inside the cage, "Delivery's

- 281 -

sending him out for something, but they didn't give him a gun. Thought with the recent news he ought to take one."

The old man gave Henry a sharp look. "Did you verify that? Seems suspicious that Delivery would send someone."

The guard rolled his eyes. "Everyone's short staffed right now. Still, if it'll make you feel better, I'll check." The old man handed the guard an old cracked phone. The guard put it on speaker and dialed, each number sending a painful jolt of adrenaline racing up Henry's back. It rang and Henry held his breath as his heart sank down into his lower guts. *It's over,* he thought, but then Melissa's voice came floating out of the phone toward him.

"Delivery, Melissa speaking."

"Hey, this is Gruber over at the Barrier. Did you send a– what's your name again?"

"Henry."

"Did you send a Henry out to the scav teams with a truck to pick up surplus?"

"Um– Yeah," came Melissa's voice and Henry began breathing again, "is he there now?"

"Yep, but he's got no weapon. We're going to issue him one, rather than send him back there."

"Sounds good. Listen, you tell him to get that truck back here in one piece, okay? No one– I mean no surplus is worth getting hurt for."

"I hear you sister. We'll outfit him real well, he and the truck will be back with the goods before you know it."

The guard hung up. "Sound's like she might be a little sweet on you," he said with a grin and Henry blushed, humiliated and knowing exactly what Melissa had really meant. He was glad she had been quick enough to lie. He wasn't sure if any of the others would have pulled that off so smoothly. The old man cleared his throat.

"You ever fire a gun before?" he asked. Henry shook his head. "I see," grumbled the old man and hopped down off his stool. He rummaged around in the cage for a moment. He came back with a long green pack. "I'm not giving you a real gun," said the old man with a challenging glare at the guard, "you'll just end up shooting yourself or getting it taken from you along with the truck." He opened the pack. "I put everything you need in here. If you run into one or two baddies, you got your stun gun here. You have to move fast and have a plan, it's only going to knock someone down for a few seconds. It's got three shots so be careful." He pulled it out and Henry was surprised to see how closely it resembled a rifle. The old man showed him the charges and demonstrated how it worked. "I also put a knife in there too, cause you can always use a good knife, even when you aren't in trouble. If you get in real trouble, there are two cans of tear gas. Start em, throw em out of the truck and keep moving. Even if you got to run somebody over. When you get to the scav team, you come back with them. Even if that means keeping the truck out longer. Delivery will be okay. The scav team can protect you. Got it?" he handed Henry the pack.

"Got it," said Henry.

"I still think it's stupid to send an inexperienced driver out there," mumbled the old man. He pointed to a ledger for Henry to sign the weapons out.

"Henry's going to be fine. Aren't you?" asked the guard.

Henry grinned. "Sure, I'll be careful, don't worry."

The old man shook his head and went back into the rear of the cage. Henry followed the guard back to the truck. Phil was still quiet and Henry was somewhat relieved. He got back into the truck, waved to the guard and rolled out of the gate, back into the decaying world.

Henry pulled over just past the top of the first large hill, where he and the others had stopped to look down at the City for the first time. He pulled the truck keys from the ignition, peeking around him as he did. The old man knew what he was talking about. Henry wasn't going to risk being held up. He reluctantly got back into his bio-hazard suit, it stuck and skidded over his skin where sweat had clung. He thought about just leaving Phil in the back, not stopping, heading straight for the Lodge. He'd found it with Melissa on an old road map. But he didn't want Phil to realize who he was just yet. If he found out too early, Henry would never find out what he'd done to Marnie. He pulled the face mask up over his nose and got the stun gun out of the pack. He had no idea if it would be effective, but he hoped Phil would believe that it was. He slid the knife up his sleeve just in case. He looked back down at the City, it's Barrier a great spine of concrete curling in on itself. It was too bad. The whole thing. Waking up was bad, remembering was awful. The only way Henry could look with comfort, was forward. And the future just didn't look that good in the City. He'd be safe, sure. But he'd have to live with being cheated and knocked down, with trudging through thankless job after thankless job, of never improving. Even his kids, if he ever had them, couldn't hope to improve. They'd have the same trudging, cheated, second-hand life. And that was too bad for Henry to live with. He turned toward the truck doors. Out here he'd be in danger, constantly at risk of having it all taken from him, from his friends, under threat from other people and the natural world itself. But out here, there were no limits. He was no better and no worse than anybody else, no matter what he'd been. And out here, the things you did caught up with you. The way they were catching Phil now. The way they would someday catch up with Henry too.

He unlocked the truck door and opened them, his muscles tensed and ready to leap backward if Phil came flying at him. But the big man was stretched out on the truck bed, his arms underneath his head as a pillow, snoring in the dark.

"Wake up," Henry snarled. Now that he was alone with Phil, he wanted to keep him on edge, wanted him to be in constant panic of infection, like he had been. The fact that he was sleeping during their escape enraged Henry. Phil sat up and rubbed his eyes.

"Are we out?" he yawned.

"You said you'd tell me where this camp was."

"Oh yeah," Phil stood up and began moving toward the truck doors. Henry held up the stun gun.

"You can stay right there."

"Woah, relax. I have to see where we are to know

where we have to go."

Henry tossed a small notebook and a pencil onto the truck bed. "We're at the top of the hill in front of the gate. Just draw me a map. I don't want to risk getting infected."

Phil held up his hands and gave Henry a smarmy grin. "Okay, okay, don't get your panties in a bunch. I'm not gonna hurt you. We're a team, you and me, remember?" He sat down and began drawing in the notepad. Henry watched him, the thick plastic of his suit itching him and the pressure of a breeze on his back, taunting him, unable to cool him through the suit.

"Damn," said Phil, looking up from the notepad after a minute, "it was pussy wasn't it?"

"What?"

"I pegged you for a Nancy, but you're a pussy man ain't you?"

"What the hell are you talking about?"

"When I told you we could make a deal in the graveyard. You said I had nothing you want. But I bet if I offered you pussy you would have changed your mind, right?"

"No," said Henry, his lips tightening in disgust behind his mask.

Phil laughed and nodded. "Yeah you would have. That's why you been asking if I had a woman. Not that it matters," he continued, turning back to the notepad, "It's not like I got any on tap, if you know what I mean. Not since that little bitch and her zombie army."

Henry bit the side of his cheek. He waited a second for his breathing to slow and then said as casually as he could, "Yeah, you never finished telling me what happened to your camp."

Phil shrugged, still looking at the notepad. "Everyone died. What more is there to tell?"

"You caught the kid that did it?"

Phil looked up suddenly and stared at him. "Yeah," he said at last, "caught her myself when she was trying to run." He rubbed the thick scar on his jaw with one hand and tossed

Henry the notepad with the other. He suddenly grinned, more like a wild animal baring its teeth or a dog gone bad than any true humor. "But why you asking about her, Henry? You like em young, yeah? She *was* too. Little thing, not more'n thirteen or so. Nobody left to look out for her, teach her the way a lady ought to act. That's why she did what she did. So her uncle Phil taught her–"

"Shut up!" snapped Henry, "I don't want to hear any more about what you did to that little girl." He started to shut the truck doors, but Phil's thick hand slid out and stopped him. He leaned his face into the crack.

"I don't believe you. I think you want to hear every last, little detail. But that can wait until our next rest stop." He released the door and Henry slammed it closed and locked it. He opened the driver side door and threw everything in. Then he stripped off the plastic suit and paced for a few minutes in the warm afternoon air. He didn't know if he could stand knowing Phil was back there sleeping or imagining Marnie or just breathing for the hours it would take to get to the Lodge. He didn't know if he'd even be able to get there before dark. The thought of sleeping with him in the truck made him feel even sicker. He paced back and forth next to the truck, retreading the conversation too, in his head. He got in the truck, still undecided. Maybe he should kill Phil right there. Take the truck back to the City and pretend nothing happened. Maybe he should just run away. Leave Phil to die in the hot dark of the metal truck without food, without water, the way Phil had left him for eight years. Henry thought of the shed. The filthy, plastic entombed shed. His eyes slid over to the notepad. Instead of the small map Henry had expected, a few words were scrawled across the page, the letters so dark that Henry was surprised the pencil hadn't broken. It said, "You think I'm stupid. But I know who you are, Henry. I've known all this time."

Henry found the keys and started the engine. The dark maw of the empty shed filled all the unoccupied space in his mind.

FORTY-FOUR

The road flashed by for over an hour before Henry calmed down enough to actually pay attention to it. Phil was silent in the back, but Henry knew he must be plotting. He had to know now that Henry planned to kill him. The next time Henry opened those doors, Phil was going to try to fight back. Phil was bigger and stronger. Healthier. Henry was in real trouble, and he knew it. *So be it,* he thought, the better, saner part of him rising for a moment, *if he kills me, I won't have to live with what I'm about to do. Maybe it's better that way.*

But deep down he knew that there was no going back. Even if Phil did kill him, Henry's heart would still be full of murder. It was too late. It had been too late the minute Vincent had told him that Phil was alive. *Why couldn't he have let me go look for her?* He thought, *I would have found an empty camp. It would have been done.* He'd expected to find out that Marnie was dead. Even in the confusion and rage of the Plague he had understood what it meant for her when she released him. Even if she had escaped, her existence in the past several months must have been one of suffering, starvation, loneliness. But Phil made it sound even worse. Henry remembered the way she'd woken him the night Phil had shown up. How terrified she'd been to see that face leering into her window. Neither of them had known what he could do back then. The fear must have been so much worse when he caught her in the aftermath of the camp battle. Try as he might, Henry couldn't picture her as the courageous, defiant thirteen year old that she'd been the last time he saw her. He could only see the five-year-old's face shining out of the dark, holding her light up bear. He didn't want to know how she died. *He might be lying,* whispered his interior voice, *he knows who you are. He must know what you want, too. He can say anything he wants about Marnie, he knows you can't tell what the truth is. He may never have found her.* But Henry knew the scar on his jaw didn't get there on its own. Still, he hoped there was more to the story. That Marnie fought back or found a way to escape. The thought calmed him.

He realized the sun was beginning to set, he'd have to turn the lights on or stop soon. Melissa's map had been simple and the roads had been easy, large ones that hadn't decayed too badly. But now the roads began to peter out, get narrower, choked with new forest growth or just crumbling away under the tires after years of frost and rain. Henry turned off the highway and onto the back roads and began to see the remains of homes and farms. It was easy to pretend on the highway. There were never any signs of life on the big road, it could cut through whole cities without any of them being visible. Even the shoddy state of the broken tar didn't bother Henry so much. But now he could see the world rotting away around him and it was a shock he'd been unprepared for. He'd been with the others last time, they'd seen empty houses and caved in, ransacked stores, but they'd been together. Each of them had been warm, living proof to the others that the world was not completely dead. Henry had no friends this time. And he had only seen a few last time, little glimpses, like seeing where a disaster hit. The City had been like a return to normalcy after a storm. The truck moved much faster, much farther than a starved man on a rusty bike. It sank in that there was no City waiting at the other end of this. That there was no end of it. It started like a slow drip that built up. It was easy to ignore at first. The buildings that had slumped or fallen over were not very common. It'd only been eight years and most of the houses still had roofs that didn't leak too badly. A few had burnt, probably early on, when there was still electricity but no more fire department. A few had windows like broken teeth, jagged and hanging from their frames, if they had been looted. But most of the buildings were intact. It was the little bits of wrongness that added up in Henry's head. The little cues that screamed "empty" to anyone that could see. The color had faded, gone gray, like a permanent fog sat on the structures as the paint wore down and puffed into chalk or slid down the surface with each passing rain. They looked washed out, like old photographs that had sat too long in the sunshine, while the world around them took on extra greens and golds in the evening light. Downed trees lay over cracked driveways, shattered in storms and long naked of leaves, already crumbling into red sawdust. The humps of mailboxes just poked through the long grass that choked front yards or had open mouths filled with nests, themselves long abandoned. Nothing moved. Nothing struggled. Humanity just got swallowed up by the creeping, relentless trees and grass and rain. Henry yearned to see a freshly mowed lawn. Or smell grass cuttings warm and sweet in the last light of day. The sun was almost completely gone when the truck rolled into the town where Wyatt's store had stood so long ago. The light was just a pale smudge on the tips of the trees and Henry had to decide what he was going to do. He parked in the lot in front of the store. The asphalt was thickly covered in last year's leaves, they piled up in drifts against the building, clinging to the roof like rotten icicles. He waited to see if the noise of the truck would bring anybody, but the only thing that happened was that Phil banged on the wall of the truck after a minute or two and shouted, "We there yet? I have to piss like a racehorse." Henry ignored him but took the stun gun and the keys, just in case. He slid the knife into his pocket before he got out of the truck. He turned the headlights on so they shone inside the broken glass of the store's front door, ignoring the truck's warning buzzer.

He pushed the door open by the metal frame and stepped through. He wasn't sure why he had stopped here, except that he needed some time to think. The headlights didn't reach very far, but Henry knew the store had been empty for years the moment he stepped inside. There was a steady drip as an old leak worked it's way through the plaster ceiling and the leaves had blown in, covering the floor and a few of the shelves. The air smelled like wet dirt as the drywall melted away and molded. No one had been here for years. Henry ran his hand along the dusty counter. It was still cluttered with keychains and phone chargers, the kind of useless things that had made up life. There was something glimmering in the headlights next to the register. Henry picked it up. It was a new collar, a choke chain, just like the one he'd had. He wondered if this was where Phil had gotten them. This one must have been dropped, left behind, forgotten, just for him. He heard Wyatt's voice in his head, an echo of the last sane conversation he'd had before he became truly ill.

"Maybe everyone will wake up sane in a week or two. Then there'll be a reckoning, I guess. There'll be a reckoning for everyone."

Henry's hand closed around the sharp metal. He wasn't sure how much Phil knew or guessed, but Henry intended to let his plan play out as far as it would go. A shadow flickered in the headlight and Henry whirled around. There was nothing there. Henry had decided. There was no reason to stay and chance running into someone or something that wanted what he had. Or *who* he had. He had no way of knowing whether Phil was telling the truth about the death of all his men. He got back into the truck and started it up again, which brought a fresh round of banging from Phil.

Henry pulled off road next to Phil's ruined snowmobile. It had been pushed into the edge of the woods at some point, its edges rusted and it's skis pulled off, the handle bars barely sticking out of the old crumbling ditch. But Henry knew right where it was. He got out of the truck and took the keys and his large backpack with him. Phil shouted to be let out, but Henry ignored him, heading off into the woods to relieve himself and pick up a few bundles of sticks from the edge of the woods. He was taking a risk, not going all the way to the Lodge. But he didn't want to be surprised in the dark. He had no idea what to expect and it scared the hell out of him. He'd make a fire here and Phil could come out if he behaved or piss his pants in the truck if he didn't. It was all the same to Henry. *How liberating it is knowing Phil is going to die,* thought Henry as he walked back toward the dark road, *to know I don't have to worry if he doesn't eat or soils himself or injures himself. This must be how he felt about me for years. Every day expecting me to die, it not mattering much every day that I woke up alive. Until the last one.* It was a quick thought, gone almost before Henry realized he had thought it. But the shame in him was immediate and strong.

He fought it, trying to feel the justice in it rather than his own coldness. But he kept imagining Vincent with him, exhorting him to be a good man. *The world doesn't need good men any more. The age of the good man is over. The reign of the strong man has returned,* he thought. But it was no use. Vincent's words came back to him still: "You think I'm the weak one, that I'm vulnerable, naïve. Maybe silly and stupid. But I'm no fool Henry. It takes a strong man to strike his enemies down, to deliver justice to the wicked. But it takes a stronger man to stay his hand. To trust judgement to someone wiser and to show mercy to the people who seem to deserve it least."

There was a rustle in the brush and Henry leapt back onto the road and flipped the headlights on. Nothing came out. Still, he felt better with the lights on, even at the risk of attracting attention so he built the fire in their glow. He pulled a few packets of food that were wrapped in old corn husks out of his pack and began cooking them. The smell made Phil bang on the door again. The shame in Henry's heart stung him. He grabbed the stun gun and slid the plastic bio-hazard suit back on with a sigh. He walked around to the truck doors. "I'm letting you out to eat. I've got the gun. Don't try anything stupid or you'll be sorry."

Henry knew he sounded like an idiot, but he wasn't sure what else to say. He unlocked the door and dropped the key down the front of his suit. He held the gun up with one hand and turned the door handle with the other, quickly backing away as the door swung open. Phil was crouched in the front, obviously ready to leap, but Henry had the gun up in time and Phil changed his mind, giving Henry a nasty grin.

"You didn't read my note," said Phil in a mock hurt tone.

"I did."

"Then why the bio-hazard suit?"

"It doesn't change anything." Henry saw Phil's smile falter as a flicker of fear passed over him, and Henry knew Phil still believed he might be infected. "You getting out or what?"

Phil nodded and slowly climbed down from the truck,

his legs stiff and unsteady from the long ride. He stumbled when his foot hit the tar sooner than he expected. Henry saw and didn't waste the opportunity. "Careful," he said, "it feels like walking on a moving boat, doesn't it? It's going to get worse you know. Soon it won't just be your feet. Soon your hands won't do what you wanted them too. And then your tongue won't say the words that you tell it to. But it's all right. Soon you won't care anyway. That's what you believe, right? You'll just be another mindless attack animal. No better than a dog."

Phil sneered back at him. "I just tripped. Could happen to anyone."

"That's what I thought in the beginning too. That's what we all thought. Just a trip. Just a klutzy day. Just a dizzy spell. Just a bad argument. Until there weren't any normal times left, until the shambling, violent, hungry days were every day."

"C'mon Henry, this is all a bluff. I'm sorry you're angry about what happened, but we didn't know you were going to get better. And it made life a hell of a lot easier to have you around the way we did. You lived. I lived. You've had your little play at revenge. Let's cut the shit and tell me what it is you want."

"This is better than any revenge I could think up," said Henry, "and that body sure didn't seem like a bluff to me. I just took the opportunity as I saw it. See, I don't have to do anything except let you live. The rest is going to happen on its own. But I can't let you infect anybody else. I'll kill you if I have to, but I prefer to watch you suffer. The way you watched me suffer. The hell of it is, you won't even get to experience the worst part."

"What's that?" said Phil, squinting at him in the dim light from the fire.

"The worst part wasn't what you put us through. As terrible as you were, the collars, the pens, the starvation, the helpless people you threw in for us to kill, it pales in comparison. The worst part was waking up. But you don't have to worry about that. You'll never be cured. But it makes this whole thing kind of lose its sizzle."

Henry pointed toward the fire and Phil moved toward it, sitting on the warm tar nearby. "I can see why you had to think up worse and worse things as time went on," Henry continued, "it would have been so boring to be just routinely evil for so many years."

"See, Henry, that's what I don't get. You seem to be a fair man. You didn't try to kill me as soon as you got to town. You're friends with an Immune. Even talked to me like a reasonable person. Why is it you think I'm so evil? How am I worse than everyone else that survived? Hell, I think I'm better, I kept you all alive. It was a big risk, keeping you alive. And it was hard to do, feeding all those mouths. Not just yours but all the people at the camp. I worked hard to give everyone a decent life. I fought off other gangs, made the hard choices that no one else wanted to make, got us through eight years without starving to death. I had to keep you in those pens to keep you from hurting other people. And I had to keep you chained up to keep you from hurting yourself. I *saved* you Henry. All of you. Sure, it started for Dave's sake, but he wouldn't have made it a year without me. You'd be dead now if not for me. We're both just survivors of a terrible event. There's nobody guilty here." Phil turned toward the campfire and dragged the corn husks out of the coals with a stick. He began picking at the food. Henry nodded.

"You might have convinced me. Once. But that was before I knew about Elizabeth. And about what your men did to the people in the toothless pen. And what you did to Dave. And what you've implied you did to Marnie. I don't know how you can justify any of those things. Elizabeth least of all, because if she'd been allowed to finish giving us the Cure, we might now be allies and all the other terrible things you've done may not have happened. Maybe you were a good man once or even just an average man. Maybe you could have stayed that way if you let Elizabeth live. Maybe you even thought you could be a good man again if nobody knew about what you'd done. But I know. I can see the monster you really are."

"You don't understand how it was. You didn't live in constant terror. You didn't have to worry about feeding anyone or controlling anyone or protecting anything. *You weren't human any more.* You were just a fucking family pet, Henry. You were never supposed to wake up. You were never supposed to remember. I did what I had to do to stay alive. To keep your friends alive. The red light district– I guess what you call the 'toothless pen' was an outlet for my men. It was a way to control them. So they didn't get violent with normal women."

"How is that better?"

"You weren't real. You were animals. You didn't feel."

"I'm real. I felt, even then. Even animals deserve better. And we weren't animals. At worst we were insane. Vulnerable."

"You were going to die anyway. What did it matter what happened before?" Henry felt a cold wave of disgust slap him in the chest as Phil spoke out loud the very thing he'd been thinking just moments before. It left a bad taste behind. It made Henry not want to go through with it. Deep down he didn't really think he'd ever be as evil as Phil, but there it was, in the open, like a perfect still pond, the same thought engulfing each.

"And Dave was a victim of his own cowardice," continued Phil around a mouthful of food, "he wouldn't do what the group needed him to do to survive. He was dead weight. We had to get rid of all the useless people or we would have starved."

"And Elizabeth?" asked Henry, already sure he didn't want to hear any more.

Phil held out the other corn husk. "You going to eat?"

Henry tapped his face mask. "Not what you've touched or breathed on."

Phil shrugged and opened the second packet of food. "Our camp was fragile. Our lives were fragile. Everything we did was based on the idea that people like you were trying to kill and eat us. That you were incurable. That you were either evil or incapable of restraining your urges. It was you or us. I

- 294 -

told Elizabeth to wait. I told her to let me explain things to everyone, to give me time to let them come around to a new idea of what you were. But she didn't want to wait. The whole thing would have fallen apart. It would have been chaos. We would have fought with you or there would have been suicides or people would have fled. We needed everyone working together in their proper places if we were going to survive. Elizabeth upset that. I did what needed doing to protect us all."

"It's time to get back in the truck," Henry snapped.

"You aren't going to ask me about the girl?"

"I don't want to hear what you have to say. You'd just lie anyway."

"But isn't that why I'm still alive? Isn't that why we're out here?"

"We're out here because this is where you suggested. You're still alive because I want to see you turn. I don't want to hear any more about the girl."

Phil spat into the fire. "Suit yourself. But I gotta take a leak before I get in the truck." He started walking toward the woods.

"Hey!" yelled Henry, "Stop right there."

Phil turned around. "I told you, I need to piss."

"You can do it right there."

"I can't with you watching."

"Then hold it."

Phil sighed and turned his back on Henry, undoing his belt buckle.

"Uh-uh, turn around. I want to be able to see your hands."

"Should I put them on my head? Maybe you can hold it for me while I go. Or you just curious how you measure up?"

Henry's arms were getting tired of holding up the gun and his patience was completely exhausted. "Either go now, the way I said, or get back in the truck and hold it. Or wet yourself. I really don't care."

Phil hesitated and then grinned. He urinated into the

fire causing an acrid plume of steam. The meager bundle of sticks Henry had built it with collapsed into a pile of dull coals. He was surprised by the sudden dimming of the light. Phil was quick, lunging at him before Henry even realized he'd finished. He pulled the trigger and Phil fell immediately onto the tar. Henry dropped the stun gun and leaned forward, sliding his knife out of his plastic sleeve and putting it under the large scar on Phil's jaw line. He waited for Phil to stop convulsing.

"You ready to get in the truck now?"

Phil started laughing, still lying on the ground. "It's not even a real gun? You think you can keep me from killing you by holding me hostage with a thirty second shock?"

The fire began to recover and Henry could see the humor in Phil's face fade as Henry spoke. "You keep misunderstanding our position Phil. I don't need anything from you. I don't need to control your actions or direct where you go. *You* chose to come out here, not me. All I have to do is make sure you don't infect anyone else. Including me. I only need the stun gun to slow you down."

Phil's adam's apple retracted and bobbed back under the flat of Henry's knife. "Am I really infected Henry? What's going to happen to me?"

Henry shrugged. "What does it matter? You're already dead. Get back in the truck."

Phil got up slowly. "You're bluffing," he said with a slow smile.

Henry didn't say anything, just prodded Phil toward the truck doors with the butt of his knife. He bent down and picked up the gun as Phil sauntered back to the truck, his momentary doubt forgotten or buried. "You got a blanket or something?" he asked.

"Nope," said Henry, "it's a warm night. You won't freeze. Be thankful you aren't chained to a post outside without clothes."

"You saving that one for tomorrow night Henry?"

Henry shut the truck door and leaned against it while he fished out the keys and locked it. He didn't feel like talking any more. He walked over to the smoldering fire as he stripped his bio-hazard suit off again. He threw another handful of sticks on it, more for the light than the heat and pulled another packet of food from his bag. He half dozed between bites, too tired even to get back into the truck. He sat up confused, a little while later. The fire was barely glowing cinders and Henry was sure he'd heard a rustle in the bushes across the road from him. He gathered everything up and threw it into the truck bed. Except the mostly uneaten packet of food in his hand.

"I don't know who is there," he said loudly, "but we don't have to fight. And you don't have to hide. There's plenty. It's okay if you're scared. I understand. We're leaving in the morning, we won't bother you. I'll leave this here, just in case." He placed the food next to the coals and climbed back into the truck's cab. *You're crazy Henry. Talking to yourself*, he thought. But he locked the doors before he fell asleep, just in case.

FORTY-FIVE

The morning was clear and warm, almost cruelly beautiful. Henry stalled, repacking his bag, putting a fresh charge into the stun gun, sweeping away the cold ashes from the fire. The food that he had left was gone and he thought about looking for who or whatever had crept so close while he slept, but Phil began banging on the side of the truck again and Henry knew it was time to face the place he'd dreaded for so long. He started the truck and double checked his tear gas cannisters and rolled down the last mile and a half toward the Lodge.

It wasn't the rescue mission he'd envisioned a few months earlier. He wasn't the same man who'd envisioned it. He shouldn't be doing this alone. Henry was disappointed to see the log fence was still there, it's gate standing open, but not hanging off kilter or splintered or torn away. He tried to remind himself that it had only been a few months as he pulled into the driveway.

He'd expected it to be a ruin. Burned or torn down or rotting away. The soil salted and empty. The camp was the same as the last time he'd seen it, even the footpaths worn into the yard hadn't been shrunken by new grass yet. He parked the truck and got out. The only thing that had changed was the overwhelming silence. Henry walked to the large clump of prefabricated sheds where the Immunes had lived. Some of the doors were open and in a few Henry could see a few bones scattered across the dirt floors. But scavenging animals had taken most of them away. The little huts were still filled with old belongings, some tumbled and broken, but most neatly put away. As if everyone just got up and walked away. *It isn't fair,* thought Henry, *that this place of misery can exist still, completely untouched, when all the people have vanished. The place should die with the people.* He wondered which had been Dave and Marnie's, but he didn't go looking for it. He didn't want to see what had survived them. He wandered toward the front pens, where his friends had been.

The gate was closed and Henry glanced around,

wondering if there were people still living at the lodge, maybe watching him wander through. He didn't see anyone and decided it was too late to worry about that now. He unlatched the wooden gate and it swung open. His breath snagged in his chest as he caught sight of the line of posts sunk at the center of lonely dirt circles. The chain leashes still dangled from some. Others were anchored to the earth by bones. Henry walked up to one of the bodies, it's neck still inside the shining metal collar. Henry didn't know who it was. Just another Infected stranger unlucky enough to wander into Phil's domain. It's arms were stretched as far as they could reach. Marnie had let them all go. Someone else had put these people back. Then walked away and let them starve. It wasn't hard for Henry to imagine how it had felt. Pacing that circle day after day, straining to reach anything that moved, that collar suffocatingly tight for a while, then looser and sagging as time went on. Eventually even the insane rage of the Plague would have lost to hunger. Eventually they must have spent the days lying down, reaching toward the gate but unable to struggle against the chains any longer. Henry crouched on his haunches and sobbed with his hands over his face as if the image were in front of him instead of playing a constant dragging loop in his head. They escaped. Henry could understand them being killed in self defense. He knew that if he looked hard enough in the little huts he'd find jumble of bones, tiny battlefields where people had fought and died and were crumbling away to dust. But these had escaped and someone had recaptured them instead of killing them. Someone had taken the time to not only trap them in the pen, but chained them back to their posts. Without food, without water, without the opportunity to end it for themselves. Henry looked out of the gate to where the brown delivery truck sat glinting in the warm sun. Only one person had been left alive to do it. Only one person had walked away from the camp knowing there were still people trapped here.

Henry stood up and left the pen, gently shutting the gate behind him to keep scavenging animals out. He was going to burn the camp down when he was done. Make it burn until the whole place was a gray smudge of grief being swallowed by the forest. But first Phil was going to understand what he'd done here. Henry walked to the back of the lodge where the old shed and his own dirt circle orbited a tall splintering post. He wondered what good it would do to revisit the place where he had suffered so much, but he was drawn to it anyway. Haunted by an older self. Compelled to touch the dirt circle that had been the circumference of his entire world for so long. He ran his fingers down the length of the cool chain, hearing again the soft clinking as it moved. He could still see his own bare footprints where they had frozen and then baked into the mud. He had intended to put Phil here, at the end. To let him see the world as Henry had seen it, to bake in the sun without water or food as Henry had. But after returning, Henry didn't know if he could go through with it. He didn't know if he could calmly chain another man, even one who had done the things he knew that Phil had. He didn't know if he could sit here day after day and watch him go mad first with fear and then thirst and finally die. Henry sat in the dirt and leaned his back against the warm post and looked up at the lodge beyond the fence palings. He could hear the metallic ringing of Phil banging on the truck. It was no use pretending that he didn't know what he was there for. He knew Phil deserved what was coming, probably more than what Henry had planned. He tried to muster up all the old anger and hurt he had felt since waking up, but returning to this place had been a mistake. All he felt was sorrow. He turned his head. The old woodshed was there, its tin door still closed, the dark seeping out of the bottom cracks. There was no point to putting it off any longer. It was time to do what he had promised himself and the others he would do.

The shed was still lined with plastic and Henry could still see flecks of dark matter that the hose hadn't reached. It was sweltering inside and he was surprised at the lack of smell, but then, it had been six years since he had been kept inside. No windows, no light, no air. Henry backed away from it and left the door propped open. He returned to the truck and struggled with the plastic suit for what he hoped was the last time. He used his right sleeve to conceal the choke collar and a leash restraint he'd picked up from the pens. He unlocked the back doors and leveled the stun gun as they shot open and Phil threw his weight out toward Henry. Henry took a quick step back, allowing Phil to fall into the dirt in front of him.

"You ought to be more careful now," he said, "Your body won't do quite what you tell it to any more. You'll overestimate distance or put your foot in the wrong spot and down you go. It gets worse and worse."

Phil glared up at him. "I'm not sick."

"You ready to cooperate?"

Phil slowly stood up and dusted himself down. He started walking toward the lodge. "Nope. Not that way," Henry said.

"Fuck you. What are you going to do about it? Hit me with your useless shock gun? I'll just beat the shit out of you when I get back up."

"Try it and see," said Henry, his voice cool, his mind calm now that things were in motion. He let the choke chain and leash slither down his sleeve and into his palm where Phil couldn't see. Phil sneered and turned back toward the lodge. Henry shot and Phil fell shuddering back into the dust. Henry leapt onto his back in a perverse replay of the night he had escaped. He wrapped the collar around Phil's neck and snapped it closed while Phil was still twitching. Then Henry stood up and began dragging Phil behind him toward the back pens. Phil scrabbled to get his fingers between the chain and his throat. Henry let up to give him a breath, but as soon as Phil's fingers touched the collar's clasp, he took off again, Phil gasping and turning purple behind him. Henry let up again as they rounded the corner for a few breaths and dragged him the remaining distance to the open door of the shed. Henry lifted the gun again and unclipped the leash but left the collar. He waited until Phil's breath evened out.

"Get in."

Phil rolled his head to the side, looking at the dim interior of the shed. "No way," he said, his voice harsh and ragged.

"If you want to do this the hard way, we can."

Phil turned to look at him. "You're really going to do this? Put me in there, wait for me to die? Are you enjoying this?"

"I could chain you to a post instead. Bind your hands and keep you on a leash. I would enjoy that more. I thought this was marginally kinder for both of us. You'll be free to move around inside the shed, able to relieve yourself when you wish, for as long as you're sane enough. Be able to change positions, be out of the elements. All things I was denied. And I won't have to look at you or wear this suit until you die. I thought it was a fair trade, but again, I'd much rather chain you outside, like a bad dog waiting to snap."

Phil slowly stood up, the shock and near suffocation had taken a toll on him. He stooped to enter the small shed. Henry shut the door behind it and slid the bolt home. He shucked the plastic suit and hung it on the door of the shed. He walked away toward the big house, not sure if he was going to return and need it again or not.

FORTY-SIX

The lodge had changed during the years Henry had
been ill. It had been expanded and winterized, the well had
been fitted with a hand pump and most of the modern
appliances had disappeared. Still, nothing had been done to
make the place sustainable in the long term. There was no
garden, no work rooms and Henry had seen no hand tools of
any kind except for a hammer and saw that must have been
used to improve the lodge. These people weren't creators.
They didn't produce anything. They lived off the lives of
others, either scavenging goods from abandoned homes or
raiding nearby camps and taking what and who they wanted.
There was always more, so what they had they didn't care for.
The inside of the lodge was not the spare, clean place Henry
remembered. There were piles of trash in the corners and thick
dust lay over almost everything. There had been struggles
inside the house, leaving scratch marks and broken furniture,
but most of the mess had been there for a long time. Empty
liquor bottles rolled over the kitchen floor as Henry opened
the back door to enter. He started to pick them up and stack
them neatly on the counter but then realized what he was
doing. *What's the point? It's going to burn in a few days
anyway,* he thought. He waded through a few inches of trash
to get to the living room, not sure what he was there for. He
didn't know if the living room had been converted into some
kind of camp clinic that nobody ever cleaned or if it had been
the scene of a very bloody battle the night of his escape. The
once gleaming wood floor was dark and chalky with dried
blood and the only furniture were some overturned cots
blocking the front door. Henry wondered if this was where
Marnie had hidden with the people who couldn't defend
themselves. A breeze blew the tattered curtains from the front
window. He walked up to them and looked out of the missing
pane at the bright summer day. He remembered stapling
plastic over it from the other side, trying not to hear the news
bleeding through the walls from the television as he did. There
was a green wire hanging down from the upper sill. Henry

reached out, careful not to touch the jagged glass and gently pulled on it. The wire fell into his hand, one chili pepper light still hanging from it, the rest of the strand long gone. Henry walked farther into the house, its addition becoming a warren of bedrooms made of warping plywood. They were dark without windows, just simple boxes with a dirty mattress in each. Whether they had been used by Phil's men or as hospital beds or for more twisted purposes, Henry wasn't sure and didn't try to determine.

Light came from the very back cube and Henry walked toward it, curious. It was even smaller than the others, but it had a small square of wood cut out from the back wall. Plastic sheeting, probably from the very same roll Henry had used, was stapled over the hole to make a crude window. The little box was tidy, unlike the others. It didn't have a mattress, just a few thin blankets carefully spread over the splintery plywood. There was a short stack of books in one corner and a dingy piece of red velveteen hung from a nail on the wall alongside a tiny whisk broom that had evidently been used in the room since it lacked the grunge all the other rooms were covered in. Henry sat down in the hallway and took off his shoes. It felt wrong, somehow, to bring in the dirt that had been kept out for so long. He walked up to the piece of velveteen in his socks and picked it up. It was an old Christmas stocking, the kind that used to come prefilled from the drug store. Henry placed it gently back and turned to the window. He was surprised to see that it looked out into his pen. With the gate open he could see his old post clearly. He didn't need any more clues to know whose room this had been, but his foot brushed against something soft and lumpy beneath the edge of one of the blankets. He leaned over and pulled the blanket back. It's stuffing had clumped and fallen into it's lower paws and the battery for its light had long ago died or corroded, but Henry recognized Marnie's bear as soon as he saw it. He sat down on the pile of blankets and closed the flimsy plywood door to shut out everything else. The saggy bear sat on his stomach staring its disappointed one-eyed stare at him as he lay back on the dusty blankets. Henry tore a small strip of frayed blanket and tied it around the bear's forehead, covering it's missing eye.

He thought back to the first night he'd seen the bear, when it was almost new. In the car with Marnie. If only he'd said no when Dave asked him to come with them. If only he'd hidden in his apartment instead. And then the bear had been a flashlight for him and the girl the night the power went out. He could still feel her small fingers in his palm as they'd walked down the hall together, away from the scary face in her window. This was all his fault. This whole place, everything that had happened here. Phil would have died in that shed if he hadn't brought him back inside. He could have died on the living room couch a few days later if Henry hadn't gone to get medicine. He could have been kicked out and died in the snow down the road somewhere if Henry had warned Dave and Elizabeth about the woman he found strangled near the snowmobile. Henry curled around the bear, rubbing a shirt sleeve over its dead light. Everything came from Henry's decision that night. They'd been safe and he invited the devil in. *All my fault,* his brain kept repeating, his breath thrumming against the lump in his throat like wind in a wire. *What am I going to do? I can never lessen it. I can never make it right.* He fell asleep, worn out with guilt and grief.

He dreamed that Vincent stood in the doorway of the small room. "I can never make it right," said Henry.

"Neither can Phil. You think its easy to avoid conflict, to let those who have wronged you go free. I suffered here too," said Vincent, gazing out the plastic window toward the empty pens. "It's hard to let go. It takes a strong person to forgive."

"You know what he did."

"Yes, as well as you."

"You want me to let him go? Let him live out his life? Die old in his bed, maybe surrounded by people that love him, though he doesn't deserve it?"

Vincent smiled. "None of us *deserve* to be loved Henry. That's why we can't just take it, it has to be given. If Phil can become the kind of man who someone can love, if he can become a good man, who are we to stop it? Don't you want the chance to become a better man too? Isn't that what all of this has been about?"

Henry woke up to find he had been weeping in his sleep. The sun was shining directly into the room and Henry's skin was damp with sweat. He wiped his face and opened the door. He pulled his shoes on and took Marnie's bear out to the truck. He looked around him at the tortured mess the once peaceful place used to be. He'd already decided to let Phil go, but he couldn't let the place stand. It had to be struck from the earth. He backed the truck up to the road. He got out and locked the truck. He tied the chili pepper light to the key ring and buried the keys in leaves on the side of the road, just in case Phil didn't feel like leaving peacefully. He started going through the sheds, gathering paper and old bottles of alcohol, kerosene lanterns and the tiny propane tanks from camping stoves. After the first week in the City, the weather had been dry and clear. Henry hoped it had been the same here. He pushed piles of leaves into the central hut and soaked them in alcohol and kerosene. He lit it and watched it begin to roar and expand, catching on the shed's thin walls and consuming everything that had been left behind. Then he went back to the woodshed to talk to Phil. He banged on the tin door. There was no answer. Henry unbolted the door.

"Phil?" he said. He could hear the crackle of the fire several hundred yards behind him, but that was all. He swung open the door, holding out his knife.

"I've had a long time to think Henry," Phil's voice floated out of the dark mouth of the shed, but Henry couldn't see him. "You remember how we first met? It was right here."

"I remember," Henry muttered, the words tasted bitter on the roof of his mouth.

"Thing is, Henry, I can't decide if you're the kind of man who would actually infect me with something. I think you're bluffing. What was the plan? To make me think I was turning and then– well, what? Kill me? Torture me?" Phil appeared in the doorway, his eyes glittering as they adjusted to the afternoon light, his grin like a dog's, there in shape, but not on purpose. "See, the guy that dragged me out of this shed and patched me up, he wouldn't torture anyone. Not even after all these years. And the guy that was chained to that post over there, he wouldn't risk getting infected again. Not for the sweetest revenge in the world. I think you're bluffing." He didn't wait for Henry to respond, he just sprang and twisted the knife out of Henry's hand.

Henry fell onto the hard ground and lost his breath as Phil knelt on his chest and slid the choke chain around his neck. "See, I don't need a fucking stun gun," he said, twisting the collar into Henry's throat. Henry knew this was it. Whatever intentions he may have had, whatever regrets might pass through his mind later, none of it mattered now. He shoved upward with his feet and twisted, trying to throw Phil off, but Phil was heavier and already in control. Henry collapsed again, no better positioned than before. His sight began to gray out at the edges as Phil squeezed the collar even tighter. Henry knew he was going to lose. He was no match for the man hovering above him. He decided to use his last breath as Wyatt had. To let everything go, to be free of it all at last.

"I was going to let you go," he croaked.

"What?" said Phil, without loosening his grip.

"I– forgive– you," gasped Henry. Phil punched him, shattering his nose with a violent burst of warm blood and Henry lost consciousness.

FORTY-SEVEN

When Henry opened his eyes, He was standing, tied upright to his old post, his collar clipped to it's old chain and his hands bound behind him to the pole with an old belt and a thick, spiny rope. The flames had spread from the sheds to the front pens now and onto the porch of the lodge. He thought he could make out a man's figure in the smoke several yards from him but his eyes were already swelling closed. The heat of the blood on his face made him nauseous. He struggled for a few seconds, trying to slip his hands out of the belt, but they too, were swelling and he was unable to feel them after a few moments. He knew he was going to die. Maybe he'd known the whole time. Maybe that's what he'd come back to do. Part of him worried about his friends, now that Phil was free, but he didn't regret letting him go. This place would soon be gone, and Henry with it. All the misery of it swept away and only living in Phil's conscience. His friends would go on, safely hidden at the farmhouse, start a better life. A free life. Outside the City, outside the guilt that history tried to pile on a person. Brand new.

The smoky figure became larger as it grew nearer. It was Phil. He broke through the cloud of ash and Henry saw him running across the camp toward him. He reached Henry. "Where are the keys?"

"What keys?"

"The truck keys, where are the damn truck keys?"

Henry started laughing. "Your legs work," he said.

"Your's won't if you don't tell me where the keys are," growled Phil.

Henry's throat was laced with fire from the choke chain and the smoke, but he didn't stop laughing. "I'm about to die, Phil. What does it matter what happens before?"

Phil's hand flashed up and twisted the collar again. Henry's laughter was cut off. "I'll make it matter. I'll make these the longest, most hideous seconds of your miserable dog life," Phil hissed.

Henry's eyes rolled back in his head and he saw a

flicker of a shadow behind Phil. The chain released and he sucked in a ragged breath. The world's sound came back in slow chunks. "Told you–" started a girl's voice, "ever came back, I'd–" Henry blinked and heard a sigh and then a thud. He looked down and Phil was bleeding on his feet, lying there, his breath bubbling away in dark gurgles of blood pouring from his throat. He looked at the girl who was wiping a long knife clean on Phil's shirt. She was young, fourteen maybe. Too skinny. Far too skinny. She looked up at Henry, her eyes squinting at him as the smoke rolled over them both.

"Why didn't you kill him? I only waited this long because I thought you were going to." she said.

Henry felt tears start rolling down his face. "It wouldn't change anything. I thought it would. I was wrong. He told me you were dead. I wanted to come back and find you, he said you died, he killed you. So I was going to kill him. But you'd still be dead. And I'd still be here and nothing would have changed but me."

The girl stood up and Henry ached to see how baggy her father's old clothes sat on her small frame. "What are you talking about? Who are you?"

"Marnie, don't you recognize me? It's Henry. I know I'm bloody and my hair is cut, but it's me, all the same. I came back, like I promised your mom I would. Like I promised *you*. I came back to take care of you, because you took care of me."

Marnie shook her head and moved around behind the post. She unclipped the collar from the chain and took it off his neck. "No Henry is dead. I sent him away with the others. He starved or got shot or fell in a well."

Henry shook his head. "No, we made it. We have friends, I'll take you–" He felt something cold snake between the skin of his wrists and the rope.

"No, I don't go with strangers. Not men anyway. And don't follow me, or you'll get what he got." She finished cutting through the rope and the belt and kicked Phil's body.

"Marnie, wait– can you drive a truck?"

"If you were Henry you'd know I was too young when

everything happened."

Henry held out a hand toward her to stop her and she flinched. "That's okay," he said quickly, "There's a pile of leaves near the truck on the road. A little pile in the ditch. There's a dusty red chili pepper sitting on top. Don't you remember hanging those party lights with me? You said the chili peppers were your favorite."

Marnie frowned. "Why would you come back here for me? You aren't my father. Henry barely knew me. He was just a family friend. He wouldn't come back to this terrible place for me."

"I would. I did. You're the only person I know from Before. You're all that's left. Come with me."

The knife glittered a wild gold, reflecting the fire as she pointed it at him. "I told you. I don't go anywhere with strange men."

"I understand. I won't force you to go. Just find the keys. You have to look really close, Marnie or you'll miss it. If you pick up the chili pepper you'll find the keys. In the truck is a bag. It's got food, lots of food," he glanced at her bony arms and legs again, "if you won't come with me, just take it. There's a map inside too, a map to a farmhouse. With friends. Lots of friends and lots of food. You'd never have to be hungry again–"

"What do I have to give you?" Marnie asked in a low voice.

"Give me? Nothing. I came back to help you Marnie. Won't you come with me?"

Marnie shook her head.

"Okay, okay, that's all right. Just take the bag. And if you want to, you can come to the farm when you're ready. We'll be there. The doors will be open whenever you want."

"You better not follow me," she said.

Henry shook his head. "I just want to help," he croaked.

Marnie looked toward the road, it was masked in smoke now, the lodge becoming engulfed. "I'm glad you burned this place down. I was too scared to do it," she said, and then tensed. "There's someone coming, a man."

Henry took a few stumbling steps past her and pushed her gently behind him, trying to look larger than he felt. He could see a figure running toward them now. He recognized the silver hair and the eye patch. He turned around. "It's a friend, Marnie. It's Vincent, he was here–" but Marnie had disappeared. Henry tripped over Phil's body as he took a few steps toward the dark forest to see if he could find her. He caught himself on the wooden post that had been the axis of his world for so long. And then Vincent was helping him stand straight up again.

"Easy, it's okay," said Vincent. He held Henry up, leading him toward the road.

"I was going to let him go, Vincent. I did let him go–"

"I take it he didn't go peacefully."

"Marnie was here. Marnie saved me."

"Henry," Vincent said gently and turned to face Henry in the dark smoke, "Marnie is dead. Everyone here is dead. Remember? It's all done. You don't have to think about this part of your life any more."

"She's not Vincent– she's here somewhere, we need to find her, she so thin, I don't think she's eating."

Vincent shook his head and pulled Henry toward the road and out of the smoke.

"Why did you come?" Henry asked as they reached the front gate.

"I told you that I would. I told you if you came back that I would come with you. I just wish I'd been here sooner."

"You were."

"What?"

"You were here. Before the fire. You convinced me to let him go. You made me be a good man, despite myself."

"I was down in the village an hour ago, Henry, I saw the smoke and ran as fast as I could. I wasn't here. You made that decision yourself. If you are a good man, it's because it's who you chose to be, not because of me."

They reached the truck and Henry grinned. "What?" asked Vincent.

Henry pointed to the keys that were still swinging in the ignition. His bag and stun gun were gone. The torn teddy bear looked at him with it's one eye. "She *is* here. She made it."

"She took your supplies," Vincent said with a dry smile.

"That's okay," said Henry, "I brought them for her anyway. I have to find her."

"Not like this, you don't."

"We can't just leave her." Henry struggled with Vincent but the fight with Phil had left him weak and exhausted.

"She doesn't want to be found. She took your bag. She's got a map. When she wants to find us, she will." Vincent helped him into the passenger seat and then walked around and got into the cab. He started up the truck. "You kept your promise, Henry. You did everything you could. The rest is up to her," he said.

Henry looked over at him, his eyes still stinging from the smoke. "Nothing's changed though. Marnie's still all alone. The world's still an empty, cold, messy place. There are still people just like Phil out there, doing their thing, day after day. Nothing's better." His voice trailed off into a hoarse whisper as he swiped at his face.

"The world's been the same since it was spun into being. Cold and messy and all. Marnie might be on her own right now, but she knows she's not alone anymore. That's something that's better. *You're* better, Henry. That's all that has to change for everything else to change too." Vincent smiled and shifted into gear. The truck rolled down the broken tar, the ash of the camp breaking up and swirling away around them until the land in front of them stretched green and bright through the windshield. "C'mon. We've got work to do before the others arrive," said Vincent as they picked up speed.

EPILOGUE

Two Months Later

"Where's Henry?" asked Rickey, slinging another heavy rock into the bucket. Amos shook his head and hacked away at another dirt clod.

"Out looking again. Same place he is every morning."

"We need him here," scowled Stephanie, standing upright to stretch, "We still have half an acre to plant and the wall is only partway built. The City troops could roll up here any day. I don't think we should be relying on old associations alone to protect us."

Rickey spit into his furrow. "What are they going to do? We worked for what we took, we paid for it fair and square."

Amos laughed. "We also took a nice chunk out of their workforce. They aren't going to let that go so easy. If we don't get those defenses up, the City's going to make us a colony. We'll be paying taxes before we know it and right back under the same rules as before."

"I don't know," said Molly, nesting a seedling in the warm soil, "Melissa got the crank radio working last night and it seems like that disease they thought they contained isn't so contained after all. They aren't saying how far it's spread yet, but I don't think we need to worry about soldiers on our doorstep for a while."

Rickey whistled low and long. "We'll have to worry about refugees though," he said with a glance toward Amos.

"Let's go find Henry," Amos stood up straight and handed the hoe to Stephanie, "We'll be back soon. In the meantime, make sure that the others get those seedlings in. We can't do anything if we don't eat."

Amos and Rickey headed toward the road, passing large clusters of tents around the barn. There were shouts and hammering and the air was sweet with sawdust as they wove their way through the little settlement of log cabins that were quickly spreading over the north field toward the woods.

Rickey waved to a few of the men who were sanding logs or packing mud in the chinks. Amos kept his eyes on the road for Henry, no less friendly for it though. They met him near the edge of the next farm, his head low, his shoulders curled around him. Amos exchanged a glance with Rickey.

"Henry," called Amos, "we got news about the City. We have to have a meeting."

Henry looked up. "No luck today?" asked Rickey. Henry shook his head.

"She'll come tomorrow," he said, twirling the plastic chili pepper on his wrist, "There are lots of places to stop between the lodge and here. She's got time. It's only early summer."

Amos shot another glance at Rickey.

"What's the news?" Henry asked.

"Maybe we should have Vincent–" Rickey began.

Amos shook his head. "No, this has gone on long enough. Henry, the Plague is back. It wasn't stopped in the City. People there have got it."

"That's too bad," said Henry, beginning to walk back toward the farmhouse, "but what's it to us?"

"There are going to be people looking for a safe place. We weren't exactly secret about where we were going. We're the largest settlement outside the City. They aren't even going to know they're infected. We have to keep the people who are already here safe."

"What do you want to do?"

"We have to get the wall up. Fast. And we have to stop letting people in."

"You want to turn people away?"

"Do we have a choice?"

"We can't just send them out *there*. There's nothing out there. What if we make a hospital or a quarantine?"

"How are we going to feed them? How are we going to put a shelter up for them when we don't have enough homes for our own?"

"What are we going to do when some of them turn?" broke in Rickey. They had reached the break in the low rock wall that would be the gate to their home.

"What do Melissa and Vincent say?" asked Henry.

"We haven't asked yet," said Rickey.

Henry nodded and headed for the barn where Vincent would be teaching the settlement's children how to recognize poisonous plants. He waited for the lesson to end and caught Vincent as he was cleaning up. "Did you hear about the Plague?" he asked the priest.

"Yes, Melissa told me this morning."

"Are you in favor of closing our gates too?"

"What choice do we have? If we don't protect the people that are already here, there will be no safe place for anyone."

"Marnie is out there somewhere."

Vincent put a hand on Henry's shoulder. "And you did what you said that you would for her. You went back as you promised her mother you'd do. You offered her shelter and help as you promised you would do. And you didn't follow her as you promised not to do. You've made other promises, Henry. To the people here. To your friends. These people trust you to do what's right for them."

"Isn't there some other way?"

"I believe there is," a strange, high voice interrupted. Vincent looked up and Henry turned around. A bulky figure in a strange burlap cowl stood at the end of the barn, the morning light filled with dust motes around him like a halo.

"I'm sorry," said Henry, "I don't believe we've met. I'm Henry. Who are you?"

"The savior," the figure replied. Vincent stepped forward, side by side with Henry.

"What is it you want?" asked Henry.

"To give you another way," said the figure.

"And what way is that?" asked Vincent. Henry could feel the priest's muscles tensing next to him, his hand closing over the shovel that leaned against a nearby barn beam.

"Why, Brother Vincent, Transubstantiation of course." The figure's cowl fell and Vincent gasped and dropped the shovel.

In the world of The Cured:

After the Cure

http://www.amazon.com/dp/B00ER
VTFCM/

Thank you to all my generous beta readers April, Michael, Lora, Siobhan, Tim and my Dad. You have made this book immeasurably better than it was and I couldn't have done it without each of your opinions and guidance!

I owe my cover to the gorgeous and haunting photography of Pamela Little from Little Pictures of Maine, whose huge, beautiful gallery and store can be found at http://ltlpicsme.smugmug.com/ which always makes me homesick in the best way possible.

And, as always, thank you to my husband, Tim, for countless things, but in this case, unwavering support, honest opinions, and great sense of humor—even when mine is broken.

CPSIA information can be obtained
at www.ICGtesting.com
Printed in the USA
LVOW13s0958240117

521984LV00018B/566/P